www.kidsatrandomhouse.co.uk

JOHN STEPHENS

THE EMERALD ATLAS

The Books of Beginning

DOUBLEDAY

THE EMERALD ATLAS
A DOUBLEDAY BOOK
Hardback: 978 0 857 53018 9
Trade paperback: 978 0 857 53019 6

Published in Great Britain by Doubleday,
an imprint of Random House Children's Books
A Random House Group Company

This edition published 2011

1 3 5 7 9 10 8 6 4 2

Copyright © John Stephens, 2011
Jacket illustrated by Jeff Nentrup © 2011
Illustrated figures by Blacksheep © 2011
Logo design by James Fraser

The Random House Group Limited supports The Forest Stewardship Council (FSC),
the leading international forest certification organisation. All our titles that are printed
on Greenpeace approved FSC certified paper carry the FSC logo. Our paper procurement
policy can be found at www.**randomhouse**.co.uk/environment.

Mixed Sources
Product group from well-managed
forests and other controlled sources
www.fsc.org Cert no. TT-COC-2139
© 1996 Forest Stewardship Council
FSC

RANDOM HOUSE CHILDREN'S BOOKS
61–63 Uxbridge Road, London W5 5SA

www.**kidsatrandomhouse**.co.uk
www.**emeraldatlas**.com

Addresses for companies within The Random House Group Limited can be found at:
www.**randomhouse**.co.uk/offices.htm

THE RANDOM HOUSE GROUP Limited Reg. No. 954009

A CIP catalogue record for this book is available from the British Library.

Printed and bound in Great Britain by Clays Ltd, St Ives plc

For my parents

Contents

PROLOGUE

The girl was shaken awake. Her mother was leaning over her.

"Kate"—her voice was low and urgent—"listen very closely. I need you to do something for me. I need you to keep your brother and sister safe. Do you understand? I need you to keep Michael and Emma safe."

"What . . ."

"There isn't time to explain. Promise me you'll look after them."

"But—"

"Oh, Kate, please! Just promise me!"

"I . . . I promise."

It was Christmas Eve. Snow had been falling all day. As the oldest, Kate had been allowed to stay up later than her brother and sister. That meant that long after the voices of the carolers had faded away, she'd sat with her parents beside the fire, sipping hot chocolate as they exchanged presents—the children would receive theirs in the morning—and feeling very adult for her four years. Her mother gave her father a small, thick book, very worn and old, that seemed to please him greatly, and he in turn gave her a locket on a gold chain. Inside the locket was a tiny picture of the children—Kate, two-year-old Michael, and baby Emma. Then, finally, it was up to bed, and Kate lay there in the darkness, warm and happy under her blankets, wondering how she would ever fall asleep, and it seemed the very next moment she was being shaken awake.

The door to her room was open and, in the light from the hall, she watched as her mother reached back and unclasped the locket. She bent forward and slid her hands underneath Kate, fastening it around her neck. The girl felt the soft brush of her mother's hair, smelled the gingerbread she'd been cooking that afternoon, and then something wet struck her cheek and she realized her mother was crying.

"Remember your father and I love you very much. And we will all be together again. I promise."

The girl's heart was hammering in her chest, and she had opened her mouth to ask what was happening when a man appeared in the doorway. The light was behind him, so Kate couldn't see his face, but he was tall and thin and wearing a long overcoat and what looked like a very rumpled hat.

"It's time," he said.

His voice and that image—the tall man silhouetted in the doorway—would haunt Kate for years, as it was the last time she saw her mother, the last time her family was together. Then the man said something Kate couldn't hear, and it was as if a heavy curtain was drawn around her mind, obliterating the man in the doorway, the light, her mother, everything.

The woman gathered up the sleeping child, wrapping the blankets around her, and followed the man down the stairs, past the living room where the fire still burned, and out into the cold and darkness.

Had she been awake, the girl would've seen her father standing in the snow beside an old black car, her brother and infant sister swaddled in blankets and asleep in his arms. The tall man opened the back door, and the children's father laid his charges on the seat; then he turned, took Kate from the woman, and laid her beside her brother and sister. The tall man closed the door with a soft thunk.

"You're sure?" the woman said. "You're sure this is the only way?"

The tall man had moved into the glow of a streetlamp and was clearly visible for the first time. To a casual passerby, his appearance would not have inspired much confidence. His overcoat was patched in spots and frayed at the cuffs, he wore an old tweed suit that was missing a button, his white shirt was stained with ink and tobacco, and his tie—this was perhaps the strangest of all—was knotted not once but twice, as if he'd forgotten whether he'd tied it and, rather than glancing down to check, had simply tied it again for good measure. His white hair poked out from beneath his hat, and his eyebrows rose from his forehead like great snowy horns, curling over a pair of bent and patched tortoiseshell glasses. All in all, he looked like someone who had gotten dressed in the midst of a whirlwind and, thinking he still looked too presentable, had thrown himself down a flight of stairs.

It was when you looked in his eyes that everything changed.

Reflecting no light save their own, they shone brightly in the snow-muffled night, and there was in them a look of such uncommon energy and kindness and understanding that you forgot entirely about the tobacco and ink stains on his shirt and the patches on his glasses and that his tie was knotted twice over. You looked in them and knew that you were in the presence of true wisdom.

"My friends, we have always known this day would come."

"But what changed?" the children's father demanded. "There's been nothing since Cambridge Falls! That was five years ago! Something must've happened!"

The old man sighed. "Earlier this evening, I went to see Devon McClay."

"He's not . . . he can't be . . ."

"I'm afraid so. And while it is impossible to know what he told them before he died, we must assume the worst. We must assume he told them about the children."

For a long moment, no one spoke. The woman had begun crying freely.

"I told Kate we'd all be together again. I lied to her."

"Darling—"

"He won't stop till he finds them! They'll never be safe!"

"You're right," the old man said quietly. "He will never stop."

Whatever "he" they were referring to seemed to require no explanation.

"But there is a way. The one we have always known. The children must be allowed to grow up. To fulfill their destiny—" He stopped himself.

The man and woman turned. At the end of the block, three dark figures, in long black overcoats, stood watching them. The street became very still; even the snowflakes seemed to hover in midair.

"They are here," the old man said. "They will follow the children. You must disappear. I will find you."

Before the couple could respond, the old man had opened the door and slid across to the wheel. The three figures were moving forward. The man and woman backed toward the house as the engine woke with a rumbling cough. For a moment, the wheels spun uselessly in the snow; then something caught, and the car skidded away. The figures were running now, passing the man and woman without so much as turning their heads, focused solely on the car that was slipping and sliding down the snowy street.

The white-haired man drove with both hands tight on the wheel. Luckily, it was late, and with the snow and it being Christmas Eve, there was no traffic to slow him down. But as fast as the man drove, the dark figures drew closer. They ran with an eerie, silent grace; every stride covered a dozen yards, the black wings of their overcoats billowing out behind them. Rounding a corner, the car bounced off a parked van, and two of the figures leapt into the air, grabbing on to the town houses that lined the street. The man glanced in the mirror and saw his pursuers scrambling along the faces of the houses like gargoyles that had broken free.

His eyes showed no surprise, but he pressed the accelerator to the floor.

The car shot across a square, barreling past a midnight crowd emerging from a church. He had driven into the old part of the city, and the car was bumping along cobblestone streets. In the backseat, the children slept on. One of the figures launched itself off the side of a brownstone, landing atop the car with a shuddering crash. A moment later, a pale hand punched down through the roof and began peeling away the metal shell. A second attacker seized the back of the car and dug its heels into the street, tearing grooves through the century-old stones.

"A little further," the man murmured, "just a little further."

They entered a park, white with snow and utterly empty, the car skating across the frozen ground. Just ahead, he could see the dark swath of the river. And then everything seemed to happen at once: the old man gunned the engine, the last figure attached itself to the door, the roof was ripped open so the night air poured in; perhaps the only thing that didn't change was the children, who slept through it all, oblivious. Then the car flew off a small rise and was launched out over the river.

It never struck the water. At the last possible moment, it simply vanished, leaving behind three dark shapes that splashed, thrashing, into the river.

A second later and two hundred miles to the north, the car, without a mark on it, pulled up in front of a large gray stone building. Its arrival had clearly been expected, for a short woman in dark robes came sweeping down the steps to meet it.

Together, she and the old man gathered up the children and carried them inside. They climbed to the top floor, then proceeded down a long corridor decorated with garlands and tinsel. They passed room after room of sleeping children. They turned in at the last doorway. The room was empty save for two beds and a crib.

The nun—the short woman's name was Sister Agatha—carried the boy and infant girl. She laid the boy in a bed and his young sister in the crib. Neither stirred. The old man placed Kate in the other bed. He drew the quilt up around her chin.

"Poor dears," Sister Agatha said.

"Yes. And so much depends on them."

"You believe they'll be safe here?"

"As safe as they can be. He will hunt for them. That is certain. But the only people alive who know that they are here are you and I."

"What am I to call them? They'll need a new surname."

"How about"—the old man thought for a moment—"P."

"Just P?"

"Just P."

"What about the oldest girl? She'll remember her real name."

"I will see she doesn't."

"Hard to believe it's really happening, hard to believe . . ." She looked up at her companion. "Will you stay for a while? I lit a fire downstairs, and I still have some of the monks' ale. It is Christmas, after all."

"Very tempting. Unfortunately, I must check on the children's parents."

Sighing, "Ah me, so it really has begun . . . ," the woman passed into the hall.

The old man followed her to the door, then paused to look back at the sleeping children. He raised his hand as if in blessing, murmured, "Till we meet again," and walked out.

The three children slept on, unaware of the new world that awaited them when they awoke.

CHAPTER ONE
Mrs. Lovestock's Hat

The hat in question was owned by Mrs. Constance Lovestock. Mrs. Lovestock was a woman of some years, even greater means, and no children. She was not a woman who did things by half measures. Take her position on swans. She thought them the most beautiful, graceful creatures in the world.

"So graceful," she said, "so elegant."

When one approached her large and sumptuous house on the outskirts of Baltimore, one saw shrubbery cut to look like swans. Statues of swans taking flight. Fountains where a mother swan spat water at baby swans. A birdbath in the shape of a swan where lesser birds could have the honor of bathing. And, of course, actual swans gliding across the ponds that encircled the house, and sometimes waddling, not as gracefully as one might have hoped, past ground-floor windows.

"I do nothing," Mrs. Lovestock was proud of saying, "by half measure."

And so it was one night near the beginning of December, while sitting before the fire with her husband, Mr. Lovestock—who took a vacation by himself every summer supposedly to collect beetles, but actually to hunt swans at a private reserve in Florida, blasting them at near-point-blank range with a mad grin on his face—so it was that Mrs. Lovestock sat up on the swan-shaped couch where she had been knitting and announced, "Gerald, I am going to adopt some children."

Mr. Lovestock took the pipe from his mouth and made a thoughtful sound. He had heard clearly enough what she said. Not "a child." Rather "some children." But long years had taught him the futility of direct confrontation with his wife. He decided it wisest to give up some ground with a combination of ignorance and flattery.

"Why, my dear, that is a fabulous idea. You'd make a wonderful mother. Yes, let's do adopt a child."

Mrs. Lovestock tutted sharply. "Don't toy with me, Gerald. I have no intention of adopting just one child. It'd hardly be worth the effort. I think I shall begin with three." Then she stood, indicating the discussion was over, and strode out of the room.

Mr. Lovestock sighed, replacing the pipe in the corner of his mouth and wondering if there was a place he could go in the summer to hunt children.

Probably not, he thought, and went back to his paper.

• • •

"This is your last chance."

Kate sat across the desk from Miss Crumley. They were in her office in the north tower of the Edgar Allan Poe Home for Hopeless and Incorrigible Orphans. The building had been an armory in centuries past, and in the winter, the wind blew through the walls, rattling the windows and freezing the water in the toilets. Miss Crumley's office was the only room that was heated. Kate hoped whatever she had to say would take a long time.

"I'm not joking, young lady." Miss Crumley was a short, lumpish woman with a mound of purplish hair, and as she spoke, she unwrapped a piece of candy from a bowl on her desk. The candy was off-limits to children. On their arrival at the Home, as Miss Crumley was explaining the list of dos and don'ts (mostly don'ts), Michael had helped himself to a peppermint. He'd had to take cold showers for a week afterward. "She hadn't said not to eat them," he complained. "How was I supposed to know?"

Miss Crumley popped the candy in her mouth. "After this, I'm done. Finished. If you and your brother and sister don't make yourselves as agreeable as possible so that this lady adopts you, well . . ." She sucked hard on her candy, searching for a suitably terrifying threat. ". . . Well, I just won't be responsible for what happens."

"Who is she?" Kate asked.

"Who is she?!" Miss Crumley repeated, her eyes widening in disbelief.

"I mean, what's she like?"

"Who is she? What's she like?" Miss Crumley sucked

violently, her outrage rising. "This woman—" She stopped. Kate waited. But no words came. Instead, Miss Crumley's face turned bright red. She made a gagging sound.

For the briefest of seconds—well, perhaps more like three seconds—Kate considered watching Miss Crumley choke. Then she jumped up, ran around, and pounded her on the back.

A gooey greenish lump flew out of Miss Crumley's mouth and landed on the desk. She turned to Kate, breathing hard, her face still red. Kate knew better than to expect a thank-you.

"She is"—Miss Crumley gasped—"a woman interested in adopting three children. Preferably a family. That is all you need know! Who is she! The nerve! Go find your brother and sister. Have them washed and in their best clothes. The lady will be here in an hour. And if either one of them does anything, so help me . . ." She picked up the candy and popped it back in her mouth. ". . . Well, I just won't be responsible."

As Kate descended the narrow spiral stairs from Miss Crumley's office, the air grew colder, and she drew her thin sweater more tightly around herself. Adults seeing Kate for the first time always took note of what a remarkably pretty girl she was, with her dark blond hair and large hazel eyes. But if they looked closer, they saw the furrow of concentration that had taken up residence on her brow, the way her fingernails were bitten to the quick, the weary tension in her limbs, and rather than saying, "Oh, what a pretty girl," they would cluck and murmur, "The poor thing." For to look at Kate, pretty as she was, was to see someone who lived in constant anticipation of life's next blow.

Leaving the side door of the orphanage, Kate saw a group of children gathered around a skeletal tree at the edge of the yard. A small girl with thin legs and short, chestnut-colored hair was throwing rocks at a boy in the branches, yelling at him to come down and fight.

Kate pushed through the crowd of laughing, jeering children as Emma picked up another stone.

"What're you doing?"

Emma turned. There were red circles on her cheeks, and her dark eyes were bright.

"He ripped my book! I was just sitting there reading and he grabbed my book and ripped it! I swear, I didn't do anything! And now he won't even come down and fight!"

"It's not true," cried the boy in the tree. "She's crazy!"

"Shut up!" Emma yelled, and threw the rock. The boy ducked behind the tree as it bounced off the trunk.

Emma was small for eleven. All knees and elbows. But every child in the orphanage respected and feared her temper. When cornered or aroused, she would fight like a devil. Kicking and scratching and biting. Kate sometimes wondered whether her sister would have been as fierce if they'd never been separated from their parents. Emma was the only one who had no memory of their mother and father. Even Michael had hazy recollections of being cared for and loved. As far as Emma was concerned, this was the only life she had ever known, and it had one rule: When you stopped fighting, you were finished. Unfortunately, there were always a few older boys who went out of their way to rile her, relishing the way Emma worked herself into a fury. Their favorite target, not surprisingly, was the children's single-letter surname. Since Kate was the oldest, at fourteen, it was usually her job to calm her sister down.

"We have to find Michael," Kate said. "There's a woman coming to see us."

A hush fell over the children. There had not been a prospective parent at the Edgar Allan Poe Home for Hopeless and Incorrigible Orphans in months.

"I don't care," Emma said. "I'm not going."

"She'd have to be a loon to want you," called the boy in the tree.

Emma seized a rock and winged it. The boy wasn't quick enough, and it caught him on the elbow.

"Oww!"

"Emma"—Kate took her sister's arm—"Miss Crumley says this is our last chance."

Emma pulled herself free. She stooped and picked up another rock. But it was clear the fight had gone out of her, and Kate waited quietly as Emma tossed the rock from hand to hand, then threw it weakly against the tree.

"Fine."

"Do you know where Michael is?"

Emma nodded. Kate took her hand, and the children parted so they could pass.

The girls found Michael in the woods above the orphanage, exploring a cave he'd discovered the week before. He was pretending it was the mouth of an old dwarf tunnel. All his life, Michael had been obsessed with stories of magical creatures. Wizards who battled dragons. Knights who fought off maiden-hungry goblins. Clever farmhands outwitting trolls. He read everything he could get his hands on. But he was particularly fond of stories about dwarves.

"They have a long and noble history. And they're very industrious. Not always combing their hair and mooning about with mirrors the way elves do. Dwarves work."

Michael had a very low opinion of elves.

The source of this passion was a book titled *The Dwarf Omnibus*, written by one G. G. Greenleaf. Waking up that first morning of their new lives, parentless, in a strange room, Kate had discovered the book tucked into Michael's blankets. She'd immediately recognized it as their mother's Christmas present to their father. Over the years, Michael had read the book dozens of times. It was, Kate knew, his way of staying connected to a father he barely remembered. So she tried, and tried to convince Emma, to be understanding when Michael would launch into one of his impromptu lectures. But it wasn't always easy.

The air in the cave was damp and mossy, but the ceiling was high enough that Kate and Emma could walk upright. Michael was a dozen feet from the entrance, kneeling beside a flashlight. He was just this side of scrawny, and he had the same chestnut hair and dark eyes as his younger sister, though his were hidden behind a pair of wire-rimmed spectacles. People often mistook them for twins, which irritated Michael no end. "I'm a year older," Michael would say. "I think it's pretty obvious."

There was a flash, then a whirring, and Michael's battered

Polaroid camera spat out a picture. He had found the camera in a junk store in downtown Baltimore a few weeks earlier, along with a dozen packs of film that the owner had more or less given him, and ever since, he had been using it for his exploring game, constantly reminding Kate and Emma how important it was to document your discoveries.

"Here." Michael showed his sisters a rock he'd just photographed. "What do you think that is?"

Emma groaned. "A rock."

"What is it?" Kate asked, willing to go along.

"An old dwarf ax head," Michael said. "There's water damage, obviously. These are hardly ideal conditions for preservation."

"That's funny," Emma said. " 'Cause it looks just like a rock."

"All right, enough," Kate said, for she could see Michael was about to get upset. She told him about the woman coming to see them.

"You go," he said. "I've got work here."

Most orphans longed to be adopted. They dreamed of a rich, kind couple whisking them away to a life of comfort and love. Kate and her brother and sister did not. For that matter, they refused to be referred to as orphans.

"Our parents are alive," Kate would say, or Emma would say, or Michael. "And one day they're coming back for us."

Of course, they had nothing to support this belief. They had been left at St. Mary's Orphanage on the banks of the Charles River in Boston one snowy Christmas Eve ten years earlier, and since that time they had not heard the faintest whisper from their parents or any other relation. They couldn't even say what the *P* of their last name stood for. But still, they continued to believe, deep in their hearts, that their parents would one day reappear. This was due entirely to the fact that Kate had never stopped reminding Michael and Emma of their mother's promise, on that last night, that they would all be together again as a family. It made the thought of being claimed by some stranger totally unacceptable. Unfortunately, this time, there were other considerations.

"Miss Crumley says this is our last chance."

Michael sighed and let the rock fall from his hand. Then he picked up his flashlight and followed his sisters out of the cave.

In the past ten years, the children had been in no fewer than twelve different orphanages. Their shortest stay had been two weeks. Their longest by far had been at their first home, St. Mary's. Nearly three years. But then St. Mary's had burned down—along with the Mother Superior, a kind woman named Sister Agatha, who took a special interest in the children but who had a bad habit of smoking in bed. Leaving St. Mary's was the start of a journey that took them from orphanage to orphanage to orphanage. Just as the children would get settled in one place, they would have to move again. Finally, they stopped expecting to stay anywhere more than a few months, stopped trying to make friends. They learned to count only on each other.

The reason behind all this moving about was that the children were, in adoption-speak, "difficult to place." To adopt one, a family had to adopt all three. But a family willing to adopt three children in a single stroke was a rare thing, and the Miss Crumleys of the world were not long on patience.

Kate understood that if this lady didn't take them, Miss Crumley would cite it as proof that she had tried her best but the children were hopeless, and they'd be shuffled off to the next orphanage. Her hope was that if she and her brother and sister were well behaved, then even if the interview was a failure, Miss Crumley would think twice about sending them away. Not that the children had any great love for their present home. The water was brown. The beds hard. The food made your stomach ache if you ate too much, but if you ate too little, your stomach ached anyway. No, the problem was that as the years had gone by, each new orphanage had been worse than the last. In fact, when they'd arrived at the Edgar Allan Poe Home for Hopeless and Incorrigible Orphans six months earlier, Kate had thought, This is it, we've reached the bottom. But now she wondered, What if there's someplace even worse?

She didn't want to find out.

Half an hour later, washed and dressed in their best clothes (which was not saying a great deal), the children knocked at the door of Miss Crumley's office.

"Come in."

Kate led Emma by the hand. Michael followed close behind. She had counseled them, "Just smile and don't say a lot. Who knows? Maybe she'll be great. Then we can just stay with her till Mom and Dad come back."

But when Kate saw the large woman wrapped in a coat composed entirely of white feathers, holding a purse in the shape of a swan and wearing a hat from which a swan's head curved upward like a question mark, she knew it was hopeless.

"I suppose these are the foundlings," Mrs. Lovestock said, stepping forward to loom over the children. "Their last name is P, you say?"

"Yes, Mrs. Lovestock," Miss Crumley tittered. She only came up to the giant woman's waist. "They're three of our best. Oh, I do love them so. But painful as it would be to part with them, I could force myself to. Knowing they'd be going to such a wonderful home."

"Hmp." Mrs. Lovestock bent to inspect them, causing the swan's head to dip forward with an air of curiosity.

Kate glanced over and saw Emma and Michael staring wide-eyed at the bird.

"I should warn you now," Mrs. Lovestock said, "I don't go in for any childish higgledy-piggledy. I won't have running, shouting, yelling, loud laughter, dirty hands or feet, rude comments about the bank. . . ." Each time she ticked off something she wouldn't tolerate, the swan's head nodded as if in agreement. ". . . I also don't care for excessive talking, rubbing of the hands, or full pockets. I despise children with full pockets."

"Oh, these children have never had a thing in their pockets, I can assure you, Mrs. Lovestock," said Miss Crumley. "Not a thing."

"In addition, I expect—"

"What's that on your head?" Emma interrupted.

"Excuse me?" The woman looked startled.

"That thing on your head. What's that supposed to be?"

"Emma . . . ," Kate warned.

"I know what it is," Michael said.

"Do not."

"Do too."

"So what is it?" Emma demanded.

Mrs. Lovestock turned on the quivering orphanage director. "Miss Crumley, what in the world is going on here?"

"Nothing, Mrs. Lovestock, nothing at all. I assure you—"

"It's a snake," Michael said.

Mrs. Lovestock looked as if someone had slapped her.

"That's not a snake," Emma said.

"It is too." Michael was studying the woman's hat. "It's a cobra."

"But it's all white."

"She probably painted it." He addressed Mrs. Lovestock. "Is that what you did? Did you paint it?"

"Michael! Emma!" Kate hissed. "Be quiet!"

"I was just asking if she painted—"

"Shhh!"

For what felt like a very long time, there was just the whisper of the radiator and the sound of Miss Crumley nervously clasping and unclasping her hands.

"Never in my life . . . ," Mrs. Lovestock finally began.

"My dear Mrs. Lovestock," Miss Crumley twitched.

Kate knew she had to say something. If they were to have any hope of not being sent away, she needed to smooth things over. But then the woman said the thing.

"I understand one can expect only so much from orphans—"

"We're not orphans," Kate interrupted.

"Excuse me?"

"Orphans are kids whose parents are dead," Michael said. "Ours aren't."

"They're coming back for us," Emma added.

"Pay them no mind, Mrs. Lovestock. Pay them no mind. It's just idle orphan chatter." Miss Crumley held up the bowl of sweets. "Candy?"

Mrs. Lovestock ignored her.

"It's true," Emma insisted. "They're coming back. Honest."

"Listen to me." Mrs. Lovestock leaned forward. "I am an understanding woman. You may ask anyone. But one thing I will not tolerate is fantasy. This is an orphanage. You are orphans. If your parents had wanted you, they would not have left you on the street like last week's garbage without so much as a civilized name! P indeed! You should be thankful someone such as myself is willing to excuse your atrocious lack of manners—and your complete ignorance of the most beautiful waterfowl in the world—and take you into my home. Now, what do you have to say for yourselves?"

Kate saw Miss Crumley glaring at her around the woman's waist. She knew if she didn't apologize to the Swan Lady, Miss Crumley would almost certainly send them somewhere that would make the Edgar Allan Poe Home for Hopeless and Incorrigible Orphans look like a fancy vacation resort. But what was the alternative? Going to live with this woman who insisted that their parents had thrown them away like trash and had no intention of ever returning? She squeezed her sister's hand.

"You know," she said, "it does look like a snake."

CHAPTER TWO
Miss Crumley's Revenge

The train jerked, waking Kate. She'd fallen asleep against the window, and her forehead was cold. After stopping in New York at midmorning, the train had continued north along the Hudson, past Hyde Park and Albany and a dozen other smaller towns that clung to the water's edge, and now, as she looked out, she saw that ice had crept in along the sides of the river, and they were traveling through a landscape of rolling, snowy hills, marked here and there with farmhouses. They had left Baltimore early that morning. Miss Crumley had taken them to the station herself.

"Well, I hope you're better behaved at your next home." The children stood on the platform, each holding a bag that contained their clothes and a few possessions.

Kate had known Miss Crumley wouldn't pass up the chance for a final scolding.

"I told the head of your new orphanage—Dr. Pym, I think his name was, yes, Dr. Stanislaus Pym—that you would all probably grow up to be criminals and murderers, and he said that was exactly the type he was looking for. Ha! I can only imagine what's in store for you three."

It had been two weeks since the disastrous interview with Mrs. Lovestock. Miss Crumley had immediately contacted every orphanage she knew, searching for any place that would have the children. Only days earlier, Kate had been outside her office and heard her pleading into the phone, "I understand you're an animal shelter. But really, these children don't need much." Then the call had come that an orphanage was willing to take them.

"Where is it we're going?" Kate asked.

"Cambridge Falls. It's up near the border apparently. Never been there myself."

"Is it supposed to be nice?"

"Is it nice?" Miss Crumley chuckled as if this was the best joke she had heard in a very long time. "Oh, I should say not. Oh no, not a bit. Now, here're your tickets for the train. You take it to Westport. Then go to the pier just past the main docks. There'll be a boat to carry you across the lake. Dr. Pym said someone will meet you at the other side. Off you go. I wash my hands of you."

The children climbed aboard, found an empty compartment, and settled in. They could see Miss Crumley on the platform, watching them.

"Look at her," Emma said. "She's staying to make sure we

really leave. I'd love to get at her just once." She balled her hands into fists.

"Anyone want a piece of candy?"

The girls stared in amazement. Michael was holding a plastic bag bursting with candy. He shrugged. "I snuck into her office last night."

On the platform, Miss Crumley watched with satisfaction as the train heaved into motion. But walking back to the orphanage, she was troubled by the memory of the youngest hooligan, Emma, sticking out her tongue as the train pulled away. Miss Crumley could swear the girl had been eating a piece of licorice. But that was ridiculous. Where would such a child get licorice?

When they'd stopped in Albany, Kate had jumped off and used the little bit of money she had to buy cheese sandwiches, which the children ate as they were carried north and the landscape outside became more and more hilly. Their lunch dispatched, Michael and Emma went off to explore the train while Kate settled back and let her eyes drift closed. She was asleep almost instantly.

Kate had a dream in which she was standing before a large stone house. It was massive, dark, and threatening, and she very much did not want to enter. But then suddenly she was inside it and descending a dimly lit stairwell. At the bottom of the stairs, she pushed through a door into a study. On the surface it looked normal enough, a desk, chairs, fireplace, bookcases. But every time she turned around, the surroundings changed. The walls slid back. The books reshuffled themselves. The chairs switched places. And then it gripped her—an awful, heart-stopping fear. There was danger here. Terrible danger for herself and her brother and sister.

That was when the train jerked and she woke, her head against the cold glass of the window. She felt a sharp need to see Michael and Emma, and she got up and hurried forward.

Kate was the only one who had real memories of their mother and father; Michael's memories, which he sometimes embroidered, were little more than vague impressions. Kate could clearly recall a beautiful woman with a soft voice and a tall man with chestnut hair. She had memories of the house they lived in, of her bedroom, a Christmas. . . . She could see her father sitting on her bed, reading a story, but she couldn't remember what it was. Over the years, she had spent countless hours trying to recover more pieces of that other life; invariably, when a memory did come to her, it was unexpected. A phrase, a smell, the color of the sky would trigger something, and Kate would suddenly remember her mother cooking dinner, walking down the street while holding her father's hand—some fragment from that time when they all used to be a family. But her clearest memory, the one that was always with her, was from the night she, Michael, and Emma were sent away. Kate could still feel her mother's hair against her cheek, her mother's hands fastening the locket around her neck, and hear her voice whispering that she loved her as she made Kate promise to take care of her brother and sister.

And Kate had kept that promise. She'd looked out for her

brother and sister, year after year, orphanage after orphanage, so one day, when their parents did return, she could say, "See? I did it. They're safe."

She found Michael and Emma in the dining car, sitting at the counter devouring donuts and hot chocolate, which the waitress had given them for free.

"I've thought of a new one," Michael said, his face painted with a glazed-donut clown smile. "Pugwillow."

"Pugwillow," Kate repeated. "Is that a name?"

"No," Emma said. "He just made it up."

"So?" Michael said. "It still could be a name."

One of the children's principal activities over the past decade had been to speculate about what the *P* of their last name stood for. They had come up with thousands of possibilities: Peters, Paulson, Plainview, Puget, Pickett, Plukowsky, Paine, Pone, Platte, Pike, Pabst, Packard, Padamadan, Paddison, Paez, Paganelli, Page, Penguin (Emma's longtime favorite), Pasquale, Pullman, Pershing, Peet, Pickford, Pickles, and on and on and on. The hope was that hearing the right name would jog Kate's memory, and she would suddenly exclaim, "Yes, that's it! That's our name!" and they could use it as a clue to find their parents. But that had never happened.

Kate shook her head. "Sorry, Michael."

"It's okay. It's probably not a real name anyway."

The waitress came and refilled the hot chocolates, and Kate asked what she could tell them about Cambridge Falls. The woman said she had never heard of the town.

"It probably doesn't even exist," Emma said when the waitress had moved off. "I bet you Miss Crumley was just trying to get rid of us. She's hoping we'll get robbed or murdered or something."

"It's very unlikely all three of us would get murdered," Michael said, slurping down his hot chocolate. "Maybe one of us, though."

"Okay, you can get murdered," Emma said.

"No, you can get murdered."

"No, you—"

"No, you—"

They began giggling, Emma saying how a murderer seeing Michael simply wouldn't be able to help himself, he'd just have to murder him, he might even murder him twice, and Michael replying how there was probably a whole bunch of murderers waiting for Emma to get off the train and how they'd have a lottery to see who got to do it. . . . Kate just let them go.

The locket her mother had given her had the image of a rose engraved on the outside. Kate had acquired the habit of rubbing the metal case between her thumb and forefinger when she was troubled, and, over the years, the rose had been worn nearly away. Kate had tried without success to break the habit, and she rubbed the locket now as she wondered where it was that Miss Crumley was sending them.

Westport was a small town perched on the shores of Lake Champlain. Garlands snaked up lampposts, and lights were strung over streets in preparation for Christmas. The children had no problem finding the docks, or the pier. But finding a person who had heard of Cambridge Falls was a different matter.

"What Falls?" barked a grizzle-faced, squint-eyed man whose age looked to be somewhere between fifty and a hundred and ten.

"Cambridge Falls," Kate said. "It's across the lake."

"Not this lake. I'd know. Sailed it all my life."

"I told you," Emma grumbled. "Crummy Miss Crumley's trying to get rid of us."

"Come on," Kate said. "It's almost time for the boat."

"Yeah. The boat to nowhere."

The pier was long and narrow and had many broken and rotted slats; it stretched out past the shelf of ice and into open water, and the children walked to the end and huddled there, pulling their coats tight and leaning together like penguins against the bitter wind blowing in across the lake.

Kate was watching the sun. They had been traveling all day, and soon it would be dark and colder still. Despite what Emma said about Miss Crumley sending them on a wild-goose chase—and the fact that no one seemed to have heard of Cambridge Falls—Kate still believed there would be a boat. Miss Crumley's meanness was the cruelty of pinches and hair-pulling and constant daily reminders of one's worthlessness. Sending three children out into the middle of winter to be abandoned was beyond the scope of that petty woman. Or at least, that's what Kate told herself.

"Look," Michael said.

A thick wall of fog was rolling in over the surface of the lake.

"It's coming kind of fast."

By the time he'd finished speaking, it was upon them. The children had been sitting on their bags; now they stood, staring into the grayness. Pearls of moisture collected on their coats. Everything was silent and still.

"This is weird," Emma said.

"Shhh," Michael hissed.

"Don't shhh me! You—"

"No, listen."

It was the sound of an engine.

The boat materialized out of the fog, coming directly toward them. As it got close, whoever was steering reversed, then killed the engine so that the craft coasted in silently. It was a small, wide boat, the black paint on its wood hull chipped and peeling. There was only one man aboard. He deftly looped a rope over a pylon.

"You three for Cambridge Falls?"

The man had a thick black beard and eyes set so deep in his head as to be invisible.

"I said, you three for Cambridge Falls?"

"Yes," Kate said. "I mean . . . we are."

"Come aboard, then. Time is pressing."

Afterward, the children disagreed about how long they were on the boat. Michael said half an hour, Emma was sure it was only five minutes, and Kate thought an hour at least. Maybe two. It was as if the fog played tricks not just with their vision but with their sense of time. All they knew for sure was that at a certain point, a dark shoreline rose from the fog, and, as they got closer, they could make out a dock and the waiting figure of a man.

The boat master threw the man a rope. Kate saw that he was old and had a neat white beard, a neat if ancient brown suit, neat little hands; even his bald little skull seemed to have shed its hair to further the impression of neatness. He wasted no time welcoming the children. He took Michael's and Emma's bags, said, "This way, then," and hobbled off down the dock with a practiced limp.

Michael and Emma clambered out; Kate was about to follow when she felt a hand on her shoulder. It was the boat master.

"You be careful in that place. You watch out for your brother and sister."

Before she could ask what he'd meant, he'd untied the boat and was shoving off, forcing her to jump onto the dock.

"Hurry now!" came the voice through the fog.

"Come on!" Emma called. "You gotta see this!"

Kate didn't move. She stood there watching the boat melt into the grayness, fighting the urge to call it back, gather her brother and sister, return to Baltimore, and tell Miss Crumley they would live with the Swan Lady.

She was seized by the arm.

"We must hurry," the old man said. "There isn't much time."

And he took her bag and hustled her down the dock to where Michael and Emma were sitting in the back of a horse-drawn cart, both of them wearing enormous grins.

"Look." Emma pointed. "A horse."

The old man helped Kate haul herself in beside her brother and sister, then leapt nimbly into the driver's seat and snapped the reins, and with a jerk that made the children grab hold of the sides, they were off. Almost immediately, the road cut upward, and as they climbed through the thinning fog, the air once again became crisp and cold.

They'd only been traveling for a few minutes when Michael cried out in surprise.

Kate turned, and had Michael and Emma not been beside her and seeing the same thing, she would've thought she was imagining it. Rising up in front of them were the craggy peaks of a great mountain range. But how was that possible? From Westport, they had seen only rounded foothills, far off in the distance; these were real mountains, massive, stone-toothed, looming.

Kate leaned forward, which was difficult given the pitch and how the cart was bouncing on the rutted dirt road. "Sir—"

"Name's Abraham, miss. Not necessary to call me 'sir.' "

"Well—"

"You're wondering why you didn't see the mountains from Westport."

"Yes, si—Abraham."

"Light off the lake can be funny in the afternoon. Plays tricks on the eyes. Sit back now. We've an hour to go, and we'll be hard-pressed to make it before nightfall."

"What happens at nightfall?" Michael asked.

"Wolves."

"Wolves?"

"Night falls. Wolves come out. Sit back now."

Emma muttered, "I hate Miss Crumley."

The higher they climbed, the more desolate and bleak the landscape became. Unlike the countryside around Westport, there were few trees here. The land was rocky, barren, wasted-looking.

Finally, when the sun had slipped behind the mountains and the sky above was streaked with red and Kate was sure she saw wolves lurking in every shadow, the road looped over a saddle between two peaks, the old man called out, "Cambridge Falls, dead ahead," and there, stretching away from them, was a crooked, sloping valley with a river running down its center like a vein from the mountains above. The town was nestled on the river's near bank, and the road took them down a lane of shops and houses. More homes, separated by snaking and crumbling stone walls, dotted the hillside. But for all that, most of the windows were dark, smoke came from only a dozen chimneys, and the few people they passed hurried by with their heads down.

"What's wrong with this place?" Emma murmured.

Abraham snapped the reins sharply, forcing the horse into a trot. Both road and town ended at the wide gray-green river, and the old man turned the cart along the riverbank, following a set of fresh wheel tracks in the snow.

"Where're the orphanage?" Michael asked.

"Across the river."

"And what's Dr. Pym like?"

Abraham didn't answer right away. Then he said, "Different."

"Different how?"

"Just different. Anyway, he's not around much. Miss Sallow and meself do most everything."

"How many children live here?" Emma asked.

"Including you three?"

"Yeah."

"Three."

"Three? What kind of orphanage only has three kids?"

This was a valid question and deserved an answer, but they were at that moment traveling along the edge of a gorge some hundred feet above the river—the banks had been growing steadily steeper since they'd left the town—and just as Emma asked her question, the cart slid on the icy track, skidding right up to the lip of the chasm.

"Do we have to go so fast?" Kate asked as the children tightened their grips on the sides of the cart.

"Look up," Abraham said.

The red had faded from the sky, leaving behind a bruised blue-black. Night was only moments away.

The old man turned onto a narrow bridge. As the horse's hooves clattered across the icy stones, the children peered down to the river rushing through the gorge below. Then they were across and Abraham was urging the horse up a winding path.

"Almost there!"

Kate had an awful feeling in her stomach. There was something wrong with this place. Something beyond the lack of people or trees or life.

"Is that it?" Emma exclaimed.

They'd rounded a hill, and there before them was the largest house the children had ever seen. It was made of black stone, the whole thing bent and crooked, its uneven rooftop spiked with chimneys. There were turrets at the corners and high, dark windows. Only a few lights burned on the ground floor. It seemed to Kate that the house squatted on the hillside like a great dark beast.

Abraham cracked the reins again and whooped.

Just then they heard the howl of a wolf. Others took up the cry. But the howls were far off, and the cart was even then pulling up to the house—the same house, Kate was sure, that she had seen in her dream.

CHAPTER THREE
The King and Queens of France

"Still asleep, are we? The King and Queens of France need their beauty rest, is that it? Lounge all day while others work. That's the way it's done in Gay Paree?"

Kate opened her eyes. Miss Sallow, the old crab-backed housekeeper and cook, was whipping open the curtains, letting in the morning. Emma groaned softly. Michael pulled the covers over his head.

They'd been put in a bedroom on the fourth floor. Through the windows, Kate could see the village of Cambridge Falls across the river. The old woman yanked the blankets off Michael on her way out.

"Breakfast in five minutes, Yer Majesties."

Since they'd arrived the night before, Miss Sallow had accused the children of acting as if they were "the King and Queens of France" a good twenty times. Where she'd gotten the idea they thought so highly of themselves was a mystery. They were barely inside the front door when she'd scuttled up, scolding them for being late.

"Took our time getting here, didn't we? Perhaps the young ladies and gentleman were expecting a carriage with four prancing horses, is that it? Chocolates and cake to eat on the ride?" She wore an old red sweater with holes in the elbows and men's work shoes with no socks. Her gray hair was covered by a knitted cap. Without waiting for them to speak, she'd grabbed Kate's and Emma's bags.

"I've made dinner. I doubt it will be up to the gourmet standards of the King and Queens of France, but it will have to do. Chop off my head if you don't like it; I'm past caring. This way, Your Highnesses."

They ate at a wooden table in the kitchen. Miss Sallow shuffled around, banging pots and pans and muttering about various character flaws the children shared with the French royal family. But even so, Miss Sallow served them the best meal they'd had in years. Roast chicken, potatoes, a very small amount of green beans, warm rice pudding. If the price for eating like this was being called the King and Queens of France, then Kate, Michael, and Emma were happy to pay it.

When they had eaten all they possibly could, Miss Sallow yelled, "Abraham!" and a few moments later, the old man limped into the kitchen.

"So they've had their dinner, then," he said, looking at the clean plates and the glazed, sated expressions on the children's faces.

"Oh, you're a sharp one, Abraham," the old woman said. "Nothing gets by you now, does it?"

"I was just making an observation, Miss Sallow."

"And thank the heavens for that, for where would the rest of us be without the benefit of your keen insights? Now, do you think you could show Their Royal Highnesses to their chamber or do you have more enlightening observations you need to impart?"

"This way, young 'uns," Abraham said.

He led them up four different staircases and along dark, crooked corridors. The light in his gas lamp wobbled as he limped. Emma leaned heavily on Kate, and Michael, already half asleep, walked into two different tables, one lamp, and a stuffed bear. Once in their bedroom, Abraham built up a fire large enough to burn through the night.

"Now you listen to me," he warned, "and don't be wandering about these halls at night. They'll twist you about so you can't find your own nose and you have to cry for Miss Sallow to come get you, and then, young 'uns, you'll have wished you'd stayed lost."

He started out, then paused and came back.

"I almost forgot. I brought you this."

He took an old black-and-white photograph out of his pocket and handed it to Kate. It showed a wide lake and, in the distance, the chimney-peaked roofs of houses rising above the trees. She passed it to Michael, who, without opening his eyes, slid it between the pages of his notebook.

"I took that near fifteen years ago. Remember the gorge we drove along? Used to be there was a dam on it; plugged up the river and made a lake stretching from the big house here to the village."

"A dam?" Michael yawned. "Why'd the town need a dam?"

"Boring," Emma mumbled, and rolled toward the window.

Abraham went on, undeterred: "Why, so's to build a canal to the lower valley. Cambridge Falls made its bones in mining, pulling ore out a' them mountains. That's all done with now, but time was, this was a different place—a decent place. Men had work. Folks were neighborly. There was trees covering the hillsides. Children—" He stopped himself.

"What about the children?" Kate asked.

And suddenly, despite her fatigue, it occurred to her that while passing through the village, they had not seen a single child.

Abraham waved his hand as if brushing the question aside. "Nothing. It's late and me old brain's muddled. That photo's just to know your new home wasn't always the benighted and bedeviled place it is today. Now good night, and no wandering about."

Then he was gone, shuffling out the door before she could press him further. Left alone, Michael and Emma were asleep immediately, but Kate lay awake long into the night, watching the firelight on the ceiling and wondering what secret Abraham was keeping. The dread she'd felt when she first saw the house had wrapped itself like cold metal around her heart.

Eventually, the journey, the large meal, the warmth of the fire all overcame her, and she fell into an uneasy sleep.

The children got lost trying to find the kitchen. They ended up in a room on the second floor that had at one time been either a picture gallery or an indoor tennis court. They were hungry and frustrated.

"Dwarves have an excellent sense of direction," Michael said. "They never get lost."

"I wish you were a dwarf," Emma said.

Michael agreed that would be nice.

"Do either of you smell bacon?" Kate asked.

Following the smell, ten minutes later the children stumbled into the kitchen, where Miss Sallow pronounced herself honored that the Emperor and Empresses (the children had somehow been promoted) saw fit to grace her with their presence and said that next time they were late, she would give their food to the dogs.

"We need to learn our way around," Michael said as he tucked into a thick stack of pancakes. Kate and Emma agreed, and, after breakfast, they went back to their room and Michael dug in his bag till he found two flashlights, his camera, paper and pencils for making maps, a small knife, a compass, and gum.

"All right, I guess it's obvious I should be the expedition leader."

"Hardly. Kate should be leader. She's oldest."

"But I have the most experience in exploring."

Emma snorted. "You mean poking around in the dirt, saying,

'Oh, lookit this rock! Let's pretend it belonged to a dwarf! I want to marry it!' "

Kate said it was fine if Michael was leader, and Michael said Emma could carry the compass, which was all she wanted anyway.

Over the next several hours, they discovered a music room with an ancient, out-of-tune piano. A ballroom with cobwebbed chandeliers slumped on the floor. An empty indoor pool. A two-story library with a sliding ladder that came crashing down when Emma tried to ride it. A game room with a billiards table that had families of mice living in the pockets, and bedroom after bedroom after bedroom.

Michael dutifully recorded each new discovery in his notebook.

They made it to the kitchen in time for lunch, and Miss Sallow served them turkey sandwiches with mango chutney and—apparently in honor of their visit—French-fried potatoes. After lunch, the children decided to go see the waterfall, it being, after all, what the town was named for. And so, their bellies full, they left the house and walked across the narrow bridge and through the snow along the edge of the gorge. Soon, they heard rumbling, and as they came over a small rise, the ground ended suddenly in a sharp cliff. The children found themselves looking out across a wide basin. In the distance, they could see the blue-gray expanse of Lake Champlain with the dark knot of Westport hugging its shores. And there, directly below them, the river shot out of the gorge and plunged hundreds of feet down the face of the cliff. It was dizzying, standing there amid the thundering of the water, the spray blowing back cold and wet on their faces.

Emma held on to the back of Michael's coat as he leaned forward and took a picture looking down the flume of water.

For a long time, the children lay on their stomachs in the snow, watching the river tumble down the cliff. Kate could feel the snow melting into her coat, but she was content not to move. The sense of lurking danger she'd felt that first moment of arrival had not gone away. She had so many questions. What had happened to this place? What had killed the trees? Made the people so unfriendly? Why hadn't they seen the mountains from Westport? Where was the mysterious Dr. Pym? And why—this troubled her most of all—were there no children anywhere?

"Well, team"—Michael stood and brushed the snow off his coat—"we'd better be getting back." Since becoming leader, he had taken to referring to Kate and Emma as his team. "There're still a few rooms I want to get to before dinner. And I heard Miss Sallow mention something about beef potpie."

Returning to the house, they discovered a room filled only with clocks, another that had no ceiling, and another that had no floor. And then they discovered the room with the beds.

It was on the ground floor at the southwestern end. There were at least sixty old metal bed frames, all ordered in rows. "It's a dormitory," Michael said. "Like in a real orphanage." But when they opened the curtains, the children found iron bars on the windows. They didn't stay in the room long.

It was close to dinnertime when they descended a flight of stairs and pushed through a half-rotted door into the wine cellar. The air was cold and musty. The beams of their flashlights played across row after row of empty racks.

Michael found a narrow corridor at the back of the cellar and followed it to where it ended in a brick wall. He'd just turned away when Emma and Kate came around the corner.

"What'd you find?" Emma asked.

"Nothing."

"Where's that go?"

"Where's what go?"

"Are you blind? That."

Michael turned. Where moments before had been a solid brick wall, there was now a door. He felt the breath go out of him and his heart begin to pound against his chest.

"What's wrong?" Kate asked.

"Nothing, just"—he struggled to keep his voice steady—"that door wasn't there a second ago."

"What?"

"He's kidding," Emma said. "It's part of his exploring, pretending-dwarves-are-real, boring-everyone-to-death game, re-member?"

"Is that true?" Kate said. "You're just playing?"

Michael opened his mouth to tell her no, he was telling the truth; then he saw the look in her eyes and knew if he said that, she would make them leave. And what was he saying? That the door had appeared out of nowhere? That was impossible. Obvi-ously, he had missed it somehow.

Only he hadn't. He knew that. . . .

"Michael?"

"Yes. I was kidding around." And he smiled to show that everything was okay.

"Told you he was being weird," Emma said. "Look how he's smiling."

The door opened easily and revealed a narrow flight of stairs going down. Michael went first, counting each step aloud. Twenty, twenty-one, twenty-two . . . forty-three, forty-four, forty-five . . . fifty . . . sixty . . . seventy. At the eighty-second step, they came to another door.

Michael stopped and faced his sisters.

"I have a confession. I lied. The door wasn't there."

"What—"

"I'm sorry. Leaders should never lie to their team. I just really wanted to find out what was down here."

Kate shook her head angrily. "We have to go—now."

Emma groaned. "He's just playing that game again. Tell her."

"Come on, both of you!"

"Kate—" Michael went up a step so he was close to her. "Please."

Afterward, Kate would sometimes think about this moment— out of all the moments—and wonder what might have happened if she hadn't given in, if she hadn't looked at Michael and seen his eagerness, his excitement, the desperate plea in his eyes. . . .

"Fine," she sighed, telling herself that in the dimly lit cellar he simply hadn't seen the door, that there was no need to over- react. "Five minutes."

Instantly, Michael had his hand on the knob. The door opened to darkness.

They moved forward in two groups, Kate and Emma to one

side, Michael to the other, their flashlights revealing a lab or study of some kind. The ceiling was curved, giving the space a cave-like feel, and it was either very large, very small, or sort of normal-sized. Each time they turned around, the walls seemed to have shifted. There were books and papers everywhere, piled on the floor, on tables, stacked on shelves. There were cabinets crammed with various-sized bottles and long brass instruments with dials and screws. Kate found a globe, but as she turned it, the countries seemed to change, assuming shapes she didn't recognize.

Had the lamps been lit or the fire burning, Kate might have recognized the room sooner. As it was, she simply stumbled about in the darkness, counting the seconds till they could leave.

"Look at this," Emma said. She was standing in front of a row of jars, pointing to one in particular. Kate leaned in close. A tiny lizard with long claws hung suspended in amber liquid. Folded onto the lizard's back was a pair of papery wings.

Across the room, Michael raised his camera. Just as he snapped the picture, he heard Kate behind him, saying something that sounded like "Oh no."

His camera spat out the photo, and Michael waved it dry, blinking to erase the spots from his vision. He'd taken a picture of an old book he'd found on the desk. It was bound in green leather, and all the pages were blank.

Kate hurried up, dragging a protesting Emma.

"We have to get out of here."

"Look." He used one hand to flip through the book. "All the pages are empty. Like it's been wiped clean."

"Michael, we shouldn't be here. I'm not kidding."

His photo was dry, so Michael slipped it into his notebook. As he did so, he found the photo Abraham had given them the night before showing the lake with the village in the distance.

"Are you listening to me?" Kate asked. "We shouldn't be here."

"Let go!" Emma was struggling in Kate's grasp.

"You said five minutes. Anyway, it's just someone's study. This is probably an old photo album. See?"

As Michael reached down with Abraham's photo, Kate took hold of his arm. She was saying something. Something about a dream she'd had. But the instant Abraham's photo touched the blank page, the floor disappeared beneath their feet.

CHAPTER FOUR

The Countess of Cambridge Falls

"This is—oh boy—I mean, we must've—"

"Michael, are you okay?"

"—there's no other—I mean, it happened, right, we—"

"Michael—"

"—oh boy—"

"Michael!"

"What?"

"Are you okay?"

"Am I—I mean, yes, I'm fine."

"Emma?"

"I'm okay. I think."

They were on the shores of a large, smooth lake. In the distance, chimneys and the peaked roofs of houses rose above the pine trees. It was a cloudless summer day. Kate could smell the flowers blooming.

"What . . . happened?" Emma asked. "Where are we?"

"I can answer that." Michael's face was flushed with excitement, his words tumbling all over themselves. "We're in Abraham's picture! Well, not in the actual picture itself; that would be ridiculous"—he allowed himself a quick chuckle—"we've been transported to the time and place the photo was taken."

Emma stared at him. "Huh?"

"Don't you see? It's magic! It has to be!"

"There's no such thing!"

"Really? Then how'd we get here?"

Emma looked about and, seeing no clear way to argue, wisely changed the subject. "So where are we, then?"

"Cambridge Falls, of course!"

"Ha! There's a big giant lake out there! And trees and stuff! Cambridge Falls looks like the moon!" She was pleased to prove him wrong about something.

"I mean before! The way it used to look! You didn't see the picture! This is it exactly! I put it in the book, and now we're here! Wait—the book! Where—"

The book, its cover now deep emerald in the sun, lay on the ground a foot or so away. Michael snatched it up and quickly flipped through the pages.

"The picture's gone! But it really did bring us here!" Grinning hugely, Michael slid the book into his bag and gave it a pat. "It's real. It's all real."

Kate had stepped away and was half staring at an enormous

boat floating far out in the middle of the lake. Being responsible for her brother and sister had made her very literal-minded. She'd never indulged in the games of fantasy Michael played. But he was right: he had put the photo in the book and now they were here. Only what did that really mean? That the book was magic? That they had traveled through time? How was that possible?

"Bless me. . . ."

Kate spun around. A small man stood a few paces off, holding a camera. He wore a brown suit, was completely bald, and had a neat white beard. His mouth hung open in astonishment.

"It's Abraham," Michael said. "That makes sense. He'd have to be here to take the picture. It's him, but younger."

"Still bald," Emma said.

Kate took a deep breath. She had to pull herself together. But just then a scream echoed out from the woods, a scream unlike any the children had ever heard before. It passed through them like an icy wind, rippling the water on the lake.

Abraham groaned, "Oh no . . ."

A figure emerged from the trees, running toward them through the high grass. It was dressed in dark rags, and some kind of mask covered its face. As it came closer, Kate saw that the creature ran with an odd, herky-jerky lope, as if with each stride it had to throw its legs forward.

"Run," Abraham hissed. "You must run!"

"What is it?" Kate asked.

"Just run! Run!"

But Michael was fumbling with his camera and Emma had

already snatched up a rock, and Kate knew it was too late. The creature pulled out a long, curved sword and screamed again. This time was much worse; Kate felt her legs tremble and her heart crumple in her chest as if all the blood, all the life, were being squeezed out of her.

The creature knocked Abraham to the ground.

Shaking, Kate stepped forward to put herself between this thing and her brother and sister.

"Stop!"

Amazingly, it did. Coming to a halt right in front of her. It was not breathing hard, despite having run all the way from the trees. In fact, Kate wasn't sure it was breathing at all. Up close, the creature's clothes were discernible as the tattered remains of an ancient uniform. There was a faded insignia on its chest. The metal of its sword was tarnished and chipped. But what truly drew her attention was the creature's skin. It was a muddy, greenish color and covered here and there with bits of dirt, small sticks, and even patches of moss. As Kate watched, a thick pink worm slithered out from beneath the creature's ribs.

She forced herself to look at its face. It wasn't wearing a mask. Rather, strips of black cloth were wrapped around its head so that only its eyes were visible. The eyes were yellow, with thin vertical pupils like a cat's. The creature smelled like something that had been buried in a swamp for centuries and then dug up.

It raised its sword and pointed back the way it had come.

"You'd better go," Abraham said. "It'll make you anyway."

Stepping around Kate, the creature seized Michael and

practically threw him toward the trees. It turned on Emma, but Kate moved again into its path.

"Stop, okay, stop! We're going!"

"Get my camera!" Michael called.

Kate stooped, retrieved the camera, and draped it around her neck. Emma was still clutching the rock she hadn't thrown, so Kate took her free hand and together they joined Michael, the three of them walking toward the line of evergreens, with the thing, whatever it was, trudging behind.

The forest the children were driven through held little relation to the Cambridge Falls they knew. The trees were tall and thick, ferns blanketed the ground, the air was filled with birdcalls. Everything around them was rich and alive.

". . . And I bet you Dr. Pym's a wizard," Michael whispered excitedly. "That had to be his room, don't you think? I wonder what else he's got in there."

Kate had now accepted that what had happened to them was magic. The truth was, it explained a great deal, not just the book Michael had found, but how, for instance, an entire mountain range could have been hidden from view. So fine, magic was real. Right now, she was more concerned with how they were going to get out of here.

"Where do you think he's taking us?" Emma asked.

"He's probably going to execute us," Michael said, pushing up his glasses. The day was warm and humid, and they had all three begun to sweat.

"As long as he executes you first, Mr. It's-Just-a-Photo-Album. 'Cause I'm definitely gonna watch that." She turned to their captor. "Where're you taking us, stinker?"

"Don't talk to it," Kate said.

"I'm not afraid."

"I know you're not," Kate said, though in fact she knew the opposite to be true. "But don't anyway."

After ten minutes of being forced along with grunts and shoves, the children came overtop a short rise, the woods opened, and Michael stopped in his tracks.

"Look!"

He was pointing toward the river. At first, Kate didn't understand what she was seeing. It was as if the water had gotten halfway down the gorge, gone under the narrow stone bridge, and suddenly stopped, a quarter mile shy of the falls. Only there were no falls! No river shooting down to tumble over the cliff! Kate looked back along the dry groove of the chasm to where the blue strip of water halted. She noticed what looked like a wide wooden wall built across the gorge, and it hit her: Abraham's dam!

She glanced toward the town, to the shimmering lake in the distance, and saw the same large boat from before, floating on the glassy surface. In the other Cambridge Falls, the one they'd left, there was no dam, no lake, and hardly any trees. What had happened to change everything? Was their ragged captor to blame?

"In *The Dwarf Omnibus*," Michael was saying, "G. G. Greenleaf writes about dwarves being master dam builders. Not like elves. All they ever want to build are beauty parlors."

Emma groaned and said that she and Kate didn't want to hear about dwarves. "We're gonna die soon enough; don't torture us."

The creature emerged from the trees behind them and began waving its sword.

"Come on," Kate said.

As the children picked their way down the hill, Kate's hand went to her mother's locket. It was up to her to get them out of here, up to her to protect them. After all, she had promised.

"Are those . . . ," Emma said.

"Yes," Kate said.

"And—"

"Yes."

"What're they doing with them?"

"I don't know."

The creature had brought them down out of the woods to a clearing beside the dam. Up close, it was indeed like a huge wooden wall—perhaps twenty-five feet thick—and the whole thing was bowed, curving in a gentle C from one side of the chasm to the other. The front faced a long stretch of still water. The back—nothing, a void.

But none of them, not Kate, not Emma, not even Michael, were looking at the dam.

The reason was simple.

They had found the children of Cambridge Falls.

In the center of the clearing, forty or fifty boys and girls were massed into a tight knot. Kate guessed the youngest was about six, while the oldest looked to be near Michael's age. There was no shouting, no pushing, no running about; none of the behavior Kate knew was normal when children were gathered together. Fifty children, give or take, stood in one place, perfectly still and quiet.

And around them paced nine of the black-garbed, moldering creatures.

There was a harsh bark, and the children's captor drove them forward.

"Emma," Kate whispered, "we need to ask these kids questions. So don't do anything, okay?"

"What're you talking about?"

"She means don't start a fight," Michael said.

"Fine," Emma grumbled.

The creature forced them into the back of the pack. Kate was relieved that most of the children seemed to be looking at the woods across the gorge and didn't notice their arrival. One boy, however, was staring directly at them. He had a round face, a mop of wildly curly red hair, and very large front teeth.

"What're you looking at, you—" Emma began.

"Emma."

Emma closed her mouth.

"You ain't from around here," the boy said.

He kept his voice low, and the look on his face was one Kate recognized. She'd seen it on children who after years in orphanages had decided no one was ever going to adopt them. The boy had no hope.

"My name's Kate," she said, speaking in the same near-whisper as the boy. "This is my brother and sister, Michael and Emma. What's your name?"

"Stephen McClattery. Where're you from?"

"The future," Michael said. "Probably about fifteen years. Plus or minus."

"Michael's our leader," Emma said brightly. "So if we all die, it's his fault."

The boy looked confused.

"That thing found us in the woods and made us come here," Kate said. "What are they?"

"You mean the Screechers?" Stephen McClattery said. A small girl had come up to stand beside him. "We call 'em that 'cause of how they yell. You heard 'em yell?"

"I hear 'em when I'm sleeping," the little girl said.

Kate looked at her. She was younger than Emma and had pig-tails and glasses with lenses that made her eyes look huge. She was clutching a very worn doll that was missing half its hair.

"Is this your sister?"

Stephen McClattery shook his head. "This is Annie. She used to live a house over back in the village."

The little girl nodded vigorously to show that this was in fact true.

"Where do you live now?" Kate asked, though she already knew the answer.

"The big house," Stephen said.

Kate glanced at her brother and sister. It was clear they were all picturing the large room with bars on the windows and row upon row of beds.

"You're orphans?" Emma asked. "All you kids?"

"No," Stephen said. "We got parents."

"Then why don't you live with them?" Michael asked.

Stephen McClattery shrugged. "She won't let us."

Kate felt a shiver of dread; surely here was the answer behind the missing children. But before Kate could ask who "she" was, one of the children cried out, and the mob surged forward. The children were jumping, screaming, climbing over top of each other, their fear of the creatures seemingly forgotten. Stephen McClattery and the girl had disappeared into the crowd.

"What is it?" Emma asked. "What's over there?"

Kate strained to peer over the heads of the children. Across the gorge, figures were streaming out of the woods. She realized why the children were yelling.

"It's their mothers."

The figures on the other side were all women. They were waving, calling the children by name.

Kate looked around. The Screechers—that was what the boy had called them—were at the front of the mob, pushing the children back. This was their chance to escape. But where would they go? They were still trapped in the past.

Then it came to her.

"Michael! Do you still have the picture?"

"No, it disappeared when I put it in—"

"Not the one Abraham gave us. The other! The one you took with your camera! When we were in the room! Tell me you have it!"

Michael's eyes went wide as he realized what she meant.

Putting Abraham's photo in the book had brought them here. So maybe the picture he had taken in the underground study would get them back.

"Yeah! Yeah, I got it right here!"

But even as Michael reached into his bag, there was a new sound.

Arruuuggga—arruuuggga!

It was coming from the trees behind them, and Kate saw the children and their mothers fall silent and look toward the noise. For a few seconds, nothing happened. Then she heard the unmistakable chugging of an engine, and a shiny black motorbike emerged from the forest, its thick, knobby tires chewing through the dirt. The driver was a very small, very odd-looking man. His chin was long and thin, the top of his skull narrowed almost to a point, and yet the middle of his face was wide and flat. It was as if someone had seized his chin and the dome of his head and pulled. He had pale stringy hair and was dressed in a dark pin-striped suit and an old-fashioned bow tie. He wore a pair of bug-eyed goggles. He hit the horn.

Arruuuggga!

The motorcycle had a sidecar. But Kate couldn't make out the features of the passenger. Whoever it was had on an old driving duster, a leather helmet, and the same bug-eyed goggles as the driver.

Arruuuggga!

The motorcycle bumped and chugged in a circle around the children and came to a stop at the edge of the dam. Kate noticed that the Screechers had not moved. They seemed to be waiting.

The driver shut off the engine and ran around to his passenger, who had already stepped clear of the sidecar. The figure removed its duster, goggles, and helmet and dropped them on the little man. Standing before them was a girl of sixteen or seventeen. She had flawless white skin and golden hair that fell to her shoulders in perfect ringlets. She wore a frilly white dress that seemed to Kate old-fashioned, and her arms were bare and slender. She wore no jewelry. She didn't need any. She was the most radiantly beautiful creature Kate had ever seen. She seemed almost to exude life. Spotting a yellow flower at her feet, the girl let out a cry of delight, plucked it, then turned and skipped to the dam.

"Who is she?" Michael asked.

"That's her," Stephen McClattery said quietly. "That's the Countess."

"I don't like her," Emma said. "She looks stuck-up."

The girl, or young woman (however one chooses to classify a girl of sixteen or seventeen), reached the dam and started up a set of stairs. Till now, Kate had been too focused on the children to take in just how massive the dam truly was. Rising six or seven feet above the lip of the gorge, it formed a sort of wide, curved bridge to the other side. Kate watched as the Countess, arriving at the top, danced across till she came to the center; there she stopped, poised over the heart of the gorge, backed by nothing but sky and the tree-covered walls of the valley.

She turned from the shawled mothers to the children and gave a little hop of excitement. "Oh, look! You all came! I'm so happy to see everyone!"

"She doesn't seem that bad," Michael whispered.

"Oh, shut up," Emma hissed.

The girl's voice was gay, and she had, Kate noticed, a slight accent.

"Now, I'm sure you're all wondering why I asked you here. Well, you may thank my secretary, Mr. Cavendish." She gestured toward the little man, who was attempting to plaster down his greasy hair. "Oh, isn't he just the most darling thing! Well, he reminded me that today marks the second anniversary of my arrival in Cambridge Falls. *C'est incroyable, n'est-ce pas?* Two whole years we've been together! How perfectly wonderful!"

If anyone else thought it was wonderful, they kept it to themselves.

"And yet, Mr. Cavendish also reminded me that your men seem no closer to finding what I asked them to find than they were the day I arrived. Boo." She stuck out her lower lip in a pout.

"She has a nice way about her, don't you think?" Michael said.

This time Kate told him to shut up.

The Countess continued: "But do not despair, *mes amis*! Your little Countess thought and thought till her head hurt, and I've found where I went wrong! Yes, I blame no one but myself! You see, I told your men, 'Find me what I want and I will go away. You'll be reunited with your families. All shall be as it was.' *Quelle imbécile!* How could I have been so dull-witted?! I ask your men to find something, and the reward for finding it is that you will be deprived of my company?! Is it any wonder no progress has been made?! You don't want to let me go! You love me too much! I don't blame you, of course. But it simply won't do. So, difficult as it is, we must make you try to love me less."

She waved her hand, and suddenly, one of the black-garbed, decaying creatures was striding toward the children. It reached into the mass of small bodies, and a second later, little Annie was tucked under its arm, being carried toward the dam. A cry went up from the children and the mothers. The creature stepped up beside the Countess and, holding the girl by the scruff of her jacket, dangled her over the edge of the dam.

Annie's scream pierced Kate's ears. Her legs kicked in the empty air. A woman on the other side of the gorge fell to her knees.

"What's he doing?!" Emma cried, gripping Kate's arm so hard it hurt. "He can't—he can't—"

The Countess put her hands to her ears and danced around in a circle, crying comically, "Too much noise! I can't hear myself think!"

Finally, the cries subsided till there was only the sound of Annie's whimpering.

The Countess smiled sympathetically. "I know! It's terrible! But what am I to do? It's been two years; that is right, isn't it, Mr. Cavendish? It has been two years?"

The Secretary nodded his oddly shaped head.

"And believe me, *mes anges*, I do not enjoy playing the grump! But I must cure you of your excessive love of me!" The Countess picked up the doll that Annie had dropped and smoothed its patchy hair. "So, the word has already been sent to your men. They'll find me what I'm looking for, or beginning this

Sunday—I do hate Sundays, they're so dull—beginning this Sunday, your town will lose a child each week I have to wait."

With a giggle, she tossed the doll off the dam. As it tumbled into the void, cries rose on both sides of the gorge. Kate could feel terror race through the children. Then something brushed past her shoulder. She looked up and, seeing a torn, faded uniform, at first thought it was one of the Screechers. But something was different. The figure moved smoothly, without any of the creatures' jerkiness. And it was enormous. Taller than any of the Screechers and two or three times as wide. If he'd been a man, he'd have been the largest man Kate had ever seen. As he passed, he glanced down. His eyes were a deep granite gray. Then he was gone, moving through the crowd of children, making directly for the beautiful creature on the dam.

"Who is that?" Emma asked. "He's not a Screecher. You see his eyes?"

Up on the dam, the Countess nodded her golden head, and the Screecher pulled Annie back from the edge and tossed her toward the stairs. Sobbing, the girl scrambled to her feet and ran to join the other children.

"Well, this has been a delightful visit. You all look very well indeed! I like to see you taking care of yourselves. However, I must—"

"She's seen him!" Emma said.

"Seen who?" As the man had passed, Michael had been busy cleaning his glasses, rubbing at the lenses as if he could somehow erase what he'd just witnessed. "What're you talking about?"

The Countess was staring at the large man who was just then

emerging from the mass of children. Kate saw her whisper something to the Screecher beside her, and the thing opened its mouth, and once again they heard the scream.

Michael and Emma put their hands over their ears, but it did no good. The other children reacted as if struck, many falling to their knees. Gasping, Kate watched as three of the creatures pulled their rusting, jagged swords and closed on the man. In an instant, the man was holding his own sword. The mob of children fell back. Emma was knocked over. Kate and Michael pulled her to her feet, stumbling backward so they weren't trampled. Above the cries of the children, they could hear grunting and the clanging of swords, and then, one by one, the horrible screams were cut short.

When they had pulled themselves free from the throng, Kate saw the three Screechers lying on the ground. They seemed to be melting into the dirt with a horrible hissing sound. The man was breathing heavily. His head scarf had been ripped away. He had long dark hair and a scar down the side of his face.

"He killed 'em!" Stephen McClattery gasped. "He killed those Screechers! No one's ever done that!"

Six more Screechers charged toward the man.

Atop the dam, the Countess was holding up the flower she'd plucked, gazing over it like a girl watching her dance partner across the room. Kate saw that Cavendish, her driver with the football-shaped head, was trying his best to hide behind the motorbike.

"He can't fight six of them," Michael said. "It's too many."

Apparently, the large man had reached the same conclusion.

As the creatures moved to attack, he turned toward the dam and reared back.

"Die, witch!"

But before he could throw his sword, the Countess blew on the flower. Kate saw a golden swirl sweep toward the man and envelop him. Reared back, muscles tense, he became absolutely still. A Screecher kicked him in the chest, and the man toppled over, landing in the dirt and sending up a cloud of dust, still without changing position. The Countess gave a small laugh and skipped in place.

"Did you see that?" Michael said. "Did you see what she did?"

"She's a witch," Emma said. "Someone should push her off that dam. Or burn her. That's what you do with witches."

Kate knew they had to get away. It didn't matter who saw them. And she was about to tell Michael to get out the book when the beautiful young woman turned and looked directly at them.

Kate felt as if she'd been stabbed.

The Countess extended her arm, her finger aimed at Kate's heart. Her voice was a shriek. "Stop them!"

"Michael," Kate hissed, "the book! Now!"

"Someone will see—"

"It doesn't matter!" And she reached into his bag and yanked the book out herself. The dark shapes were running toward them. One of them screamed. Then another. And another. Kate had the awful feeling of being held underwater, unable to get air. She couldn't breathe.

"Where's—where's the picture?"

Michael didn't move. Kate could see the creatures' screams had frozen him in place. Then Emma slapped him.

"What—what'd you do that for?"

"The picture!"

Michael glanced at the dark figures closing in, throwing children out of the way. The Countess screamed again, "Stop those children!" He fumbled in his pockets, pulled out the picture, and immediately dropped it.

Kate fell to her knees, opening the book in her lap.

"Emma—grab my arm!"

Hands trembling, she reached for the picture, but Michael had put his foot on it.

"Where is it?" he said. "I can't see it!"

"You're standing on it! Move!"

The Screechers were getting closer. Their cries stronger than ever. She had to focus, focus. . . .

Then, for a moment, silence. It seemed the creatures had to breathe after all. Kate felt the air return to her lungs, her heart pump blood through her body. She pushed Michael out of the way and grabbed the picture. It was covered with dirt and creased from his shoe. Out of the corner of her eye, she saw Stephen McClattery tossed aside.

"Hurry!" Emma yelled.

"Hold on to me!" Kate said.

As two dark shapes closed in, Kate placed the photo on the blank page. She felt a tug in her stomach, and the ground disappeared beneath them.

Kate blinked. Everything was dark. The air felt cool. She

blinked a few more times, and then, as her eyes adjusted, relief swept through her. They were in the underground room in the mansion. She was kneeling on the floor with the book in her lap. Across the room, she could see the three of them, Michael and Emma and herself, their bodies outlined by the flashlights.

And then, suddenly, they were gone.

Kate felt herself being released. As if some force had been holding her in place.

"Kate." Emma's voice was beside her. Kate became aware of how fiercely her sister was gripping her arm. "Kate, where's Michael?"

Kate looked to where Michael had been standing. Where Michael should be standing. Their brother was not there.

CHAPTER FIVE
Dr. Stanislaus Pym

At dinner, they told Miss Sallow that Michael wasn't feeling well and had gone to bed. They themselves barely touched their food, and barely heard the old woman as she grumbled about her cooking not being up to the standards of Versailles and no doubt they'd be leading her to the guillotine first thing in the morning. Abraham had already built up the fire when they got to their room, and the girls climbed into the bed they shared and held each other.

"It's going to be okay," Kate told Emma. "We're going to get him back."

Sometime during the night, Kate sensed that Emma had fallen asleep. But she lay awake, her mind turning over what had happened. Had one of those Screechers yanked him away at the last moment? Or, even worse, had she put the photo in the book before Michael could touch her? Had he reached for her only to have her vanish before his eyes? She kept imagining Michael grabbing at the air where she and Emma had been just a second before and the terror that must've swept through him when he felt the cold grip of the Screechers. Lying there in the dark, Emma breathing deeply beside her, Kate whispered, over and over, "It's all my fault, it's all my fault." Her mother had asked her to do one thing. Keep her brother and sister safe. And she hadn't done it. What would she say to her? How would she explain it? Her only hope was the book hidden under their mattress. They would use it. They would get another old photo and they would go back in time and bring Michael home.

The sky outside the window had just begun to lighten when Kate shook Emma awake.

"Get dressed," she said. "We're going to see Abraham."

Abraham lived in an apartment at the top of the north tower, and they stood outside his door, knocking for more than a minute, but no one answered. In the kitchen, they found Miss Sallow rattling pans on the stove.

"Abraham's gone to Westport," Miss Sallow said, slapping a pair of sausages on Kate's plate. "Picking up Dr. Pym."

"What?"

"I'm sorry I don't speak French, Your Highness, but if you can understand plain English, I'll say again, he's gone to Westport to pick up Dr. Pym. Left early this morning. Should be back anytime."

"Kate," Emma whispered, "remember what Michael said? The book's gotta belong to this doctor guy. You think he really is a wizard or—"

"Where's your brother?" Miss Sallow demanded.

"In bed," Kate said. "He's still not feeling well."

"Hmp. Imagine he's on a hunger strike from the slop I'm serving. Well, you can carry up food to him anyways. Let him throw it down the stairs if he likes."

She went off to get a tray from the pantry.

As soon as she was gone, Emma leaned over the table and hissed, "Dr. What's-His-Name's gonna know we took the book! He'll turn us into toads or something! We gotta—"

She cut herself off as there were uneven footsteps approaching from the hall. A second later, Abraham limped into the kitchen, still dressed for the cold. "Good morning, young 'uns, good morning." He crossed to the kettle, rubbing his hands together. "It's cold as the grave out there today. Said as much to the Doctor, I did, as we were coming across the lake. 'You've hit it there, Abraham,' says he. 'It is as cold as the grave.' Ah, we had a lovely chat, the Doctor and me."

"Abraham?"

"Yes, miss?" He had poured himself tea and was dropping lump after lump of sugar into his mug.

"We have a favor to ask. We need another—"

"Are you not finished yet? Too bad!" Miss Sallow had shuffled into the kitchen, and she snatched up Kate's and Emma's plates and dumped them in the sink. "Into the library, Your Highnesses. Saw the Doctor in the hallway. He wants you now, he does."

"Us?" Kate said. "But—why?"

"And how should I know? Maybe he wants your autographs. Well, what're you waiting for? Trumpeters and heralds to announce you? Go! And, you"—she threw an onion at Abraham—"stop stealing my sugar!"

"Two lumps is all I took, Miss Sallow."

"Two lumps? I'll give you two lumps! And two more! And there's two more!"

Miss Sallow chased Abraham around the table, whacking him with a wooden spoon.

Kate sighed. "Come on."

Kate and Emma paused at the door to the library.

"Remember," Kate whispered, "we don't know anything about him. He could just be an ordinary man who runs an orphanage."

"An orphanage with only three kids in a weird old house filled with magic stuff. Yeah, right."

Kate had to admit her sister had a point, but just then a voice called out, "Come in, come in. Don't stand there whispering."

Not seeing they had much choice, Kate took Emma's hand and opened the door.

They had been in the library the day before, when Emma had broken the sliding ladder, and so were familiar with the room. There were two full stories of books and, facing the door, a wall of narrow, iron-framed windows that looked out over the ruined stables. To their left was a small fireplace and four extremely worn leather chairs. A white-haired man in a tweed suit was kneeling with his back to them, attempting to light a fire. A traveling cloak, a walking stick, and a battered old satchel had been dropped on one of the chairs.

"Sit down, sit down," his voice echoed up the chimney. "I'll be with you in a minute."

Kate and Emma each took a chair. Kate wondered if the man had any idea what he was doing. Sticks and newspaper were piled up willy-nilly in the fireplace, along with a few rocks, an old soda can, and some used tea bags. He kept lighting matches, but nothing seemed to happen.

"Hang this," the man said. Kate heard him mutter something under his breath, and all of a sudden a cheerful fire sprang up in the grate. "Yes, that's the ticket!"

Emma elbowed Kate in the ribs and pointed as if to say, "See!"

The man stood and turned toward them, dusting off his hands. He was clearly very old, but his movements were easy, with none of the usual creakiness of age. He had thick, horn-like eyebrows that matched his snowy hair, and his eyeglasses were bent and sat slightly askew on his face, as if he'd recently been in an accident. His suit looked as if it had been in the same accident and maybe a few others to boot. "It's a lost art, building a fire. Not everyone can do it. Now allow me to introduce myself. I am Dr. Stanislaus Pym." He bowed very low.

Kate and Emma stared. The man seemed like someone's harmless, slightly dotty old uncle. Still, Kate thought, there was something strangely familiar about him. Like she'd seen him somewhere before. But that was impossible. . . .

Dr. Pym was looking down at them with one eyebrow cocked expectantly.

"Oh—" Kate fumbled, "I'm, um, Kate. This is my sister, Emma."

"And you have a last name?"

"No. I mean—yes. Kind of. It's P. The letter. That's all we know."

"Ah yes, I remember that now. From your files. And you have a brother, I believe. Where might he be?"

"Michael's not feeling well," Kate said.

Dr. Pym looked at her, and Kate's image of him as a charming, slightly bumbling old man vanished. It felt like his eyes saw right through her. Then, just as quickly, he was smiling again. "A pity. Well, let me know if there's something I can do. I have certain talents other than starting fires. So"—he sat down across from them—"let's have it, then. Your life story. Now take your time. One thing I hate is when someone rushes through a story. We have a nice fire. Miss Sallow can bring us tea. We can take as long as we need."

He pulled a pipe from his pocket, held a match to the bowl, puffed a few times, then exhaled a large cloud of bluish-green smoke. The smoke didn't rise so much as expand, wrapping its arms around Kate and Emma and pulling them in. "Begin anytime," he said amiably.

For a moment, Kate didn't speak. She was remembering how, after their interview with the Swan Lady, she'd overheard Miss Crumley on the phone, threatening, pleading, offering bribes, searching for someone, anyone, who would take Kate and her siblings. Out of nowhere, this man had come forward. Why? What did he want? That he had brought them here for a reason, she had no doubt. So what was it?

"Is there a problem, my dear?"

Kate reminded herself that what mattered now was saving Michael. She took a deep breath; the Doctor's pipe tobacco tasted faintly of almonds.

"We were left at St. Mary's Orphanage on Christmas Eve ten years ago. . . ." She was planning to hit a few of the major points, then apologize and say they had to go check on their brother. But a strange thing happened. Before she was even aware of doing it, she heard herself, with Emma chiming in, telling the Doctor every detail of their lives, how kind Sister Agatha had been to them, but how she always smoked in bed and one night she sent herself and the rest of St. Mary's up in flames, and how their next orphanage was run by a very fat man who stole all the good food for his fat family and many nights they only had a bit of old bread and a little watery soup for dinner, and on and on, she and Emma both talking, telling about all the different orphanages they'd lived in, the children they'd met, how they'd refused to let themselves be called orphans because they knew their parents were coming back one day. She was dimly aware of Miss Sallow entering and setting down tea and toast and jam and then sometime later taking away the empty plates. She and Emma kept on talking, telling things they'd never told anyone: Kate's memories of their parents, their dreams about the house they would all live in when their family was back together. Emma talked for a long time about the dog she was going to have; he was going to be black with white markings and his name would be Mr. Smith and he wouldn't do tricks because that was demeaning, all of which was news to Kate. At some point, Miss Sallow entered again, this time with a tray of sandwiches, and they were telling about Miss Crumley and the disaster with the lady in the swan hat, about the train ride north, how thick the fog had been on the lake, and how Abraham had been waiting for them with a horse-drawn cart, which was the first time they'd been in a horse-drawn cart, and suddenly Kate was aware that Dr. Pym was talking.

"My, what a journey you've had! And here the day has slipped half away, tut-tut. Well, as enjoyable as this was, I won't keep you longer. No doubt you have more important things to do than entertain an old man."

Kate felt as if she was coming out of a dream. She looked at the empty plate where the sandwiches had been. Had they eaten them? She couldn't remember. The fire was still crackling away in the grate, but outside, the sun had passed the windows. How long had they been here?

"We'll talk more later. But I would like to give you a word of warning." He leaned forward in his chair. "There are places in this world that are different from all others. Almost like separate countries. A forest here, an island there, part of a city—"

"A mountain range," Kate said.

"Yes," Dr. Pym said. "Sometimes a whole mountain range. Cambridge Falls and all that surrounds it is such a place. Now, the town itself is quite safe. But do not go deeper into the mountains.

There are dangers there you cannot possibly imagine. One day I will explain all of this more fully, but for now, do we understand each other?"

He looked at Kate, and once again, she felt that he could see right through her. She nodded, and he sat back, smiling his grandfatherly smile. "Excellent. By the way, I asked Miss Sallow to do something special for dinner tomorrow. Goose, perhaps. It is Christmas Eve, after all."

"What?!" chorused Kate and Emma.

"Why, yes. Hadn't you realized?" Then, as if a thought had occurred to him, he murmured, "Oh, of course. It was Christmas Eve you were left at your first orphanage, wasn't it? So tomorrow will be"—he appeared to be doing the math in his head—"the ten-year anniversary of your parents' disappearance."

Kate was dumbstruck. Was tomorrow really Christmas Eve? How had she not known that? It was almost as if while they were talking to the Doctor, it wasn't just hours that had passed, but days.

Dr. Pym stood up. "Perhaps by tomorrow, your brother will be fully recovered and I'll have the pleasure of meeting him." He guided the girls, both of whom still felt fuzzy-headed, to the door. "Tell me, are you possibly on your way to see Abraham?"

Kate didn't question how he might know this. She just nodded thickly.

"Ask him to show you the last picture he ever took. I think you might find it interesting."

And with that, he ushered them out and closed the door.

. . .

As soon as Kate and Emma were out of the library, their heads cleared.

"What happened?" Emma said. "It was like my brain got all mooshy."

"Me too."

"You figure he did some magic on us? I said stuff I never told anyone. You think it's all right?"

Kate could hear the worry in Emma's voice. She probed her own feelings. She knew the normal reaction to having shared too much of one's heart. You felt shame and regret and wished you could take it back. But the truth was, she felt as if she had been allowed to put down something she'd been carrying for so long that its weight had become part of her. And climbing up the spiral stairway to Abraham's tower, she felt oddly light. She was aware of the coldness of the air drafting through the walls. The song of a distant bird. The creak of the stairs beneath her and Emma's feet. And though the task in front of them was daunting—for she had no real idea how she and her eleven-year-old sister were going to rescue Michael from the witch and her demon soldiers—she felt a hundred times better than she had that morning.

"Yes," she said. "I think it's okay."

"Me too," Emma said. And Kate saw she was smiling.

They pounded on Abraham's door for a full two minutes, but again, no one answered.

"He's really starting to make me angry," Emma said.

Downstairs, they found Miss Sallow scrubbing the floor of the main hall.

"I've sent the old coot to get the Doctor's Christmas goose. He'll probably have to go back down to Westport. He'll be here by nightfall."

"But we need to talk to him now," Emma said.

"Oh, do you, Your Highness? Well, perhaps in the future we should arrange our schedules with your personal secretary. But until that blessed day"—she stuck a mop in Emma's hands and pushed a bucket and brush into Kate's—"you two can make yourselves useful."

She hustled them to the large formal dining room, where, she said, Dr. Pym wanted to have Christmas Eve dinner. It was an enormous, wood-paneled room with a long oak table in the center. Above the table hung two wrought-iron candelabras between which spiderwebs were strung like tinsel. There was a stone fireplace so huge Kate and Emma could've fit their entire bed inside it. At present, a family of foxes lived there. Two stone dragons held up the mantel, and they, like everything else, were covered with a thick coating of dust and grime.

"Dr. Pym says not to disturb the foxes, but the rest I want clean as Sunday morning at your Paris Louvre."

"This is stupid," Emma said when Miss Sallow had left. "We have to help Michael."

"I know," Kate said. "But we can't do anything till we get a picture from Abraham."

Emma grumbled something unintelligible, but she bent over

and started to mop the floor. Kate wet her brush and went to work scrubbing one of the dragons. As they worked, two small foxes watched them from the depths of the fireplace.

When dinnertime rolled around, Abraham still wasn't back, and Kate and Emma ate alone in the kitchen. They told Miss Sallow they'd bring a plate of food to Michael. Climbing the stairs, they felt none of the lightness that had followed the interview with Dr. Pym. They were bone-tired and desperate with worry.

It was their second night trying to sleep while staring at Michael's empty bed. The children had never been apart this long. Tomorrow, Kate told herself, tomorrow we'll get him back.

In the middle of the night, she awoke with a gasp. She realized she hadn't checked to see if the book was still there. She got out of bed and reached under the mattress. She felt about, her heart tight in her chest. Then her hand touched the leather binding. She pulled the book out slowly.

The moon was up, and a silvery light fell across the bed, giving the book's emerald cover an otherworldly shimmer. She opened to a page in the middle. It was blank. She ran her fingers over the parchment; the paper was dry and rippled with age. She turned over one stiff, creaking leaf. Blank. Another page; also blank. And another. And another. All blank. Then, just as she was about to close the book, something happened.

Her fingers were resting on the page she had open, and it was as if an image was suddenly projected in her mind. She saw a village on the banks of a river. There was a tower. There were women doing laundry. And the picture wasn't still. She could see the water moving, the wind rustling the branches of a tree. She thought she heard the far-off clanging of a bell.

"What're you doing?" Emma groaned.

Kate shut the book. She slid it back under the mattress.

"Nothing," she said, climbing under the covers. "Go back to sleep."

CHAPTER SIX
The Black Page

Miss Sallow put them to work first thing the next morning, and between finishing tasks for the housekeeper and avoiding Dr. Pym, it wasn't until midafternoon that Kate and Emma were sitting beside Abraham's fire, drinking cider and listening to him gripe about how far he'd had to go to find a goose.

"Not that I'm complaining. I like a fat goose as much as the next man, but sending an old fella like me wandering over half the country on a day cold as yesterday? Cold as the grave it was. As two graves! More cider?"

Abraham's room in the tower was completely round, with windows facing out in every direction. But the room's most notable feature, apart from its perfect circularity, was the fact that every available bit of wall was covered with a photograph. And the pictures didn't stop there. There were piles on the floor, piles stacked under chairs, loose piles sliding off tables. There were hundreds, thousands of photos, all of them yellow and faded with age.

"Used to be," Abraham said when they'd entered and were gazing about in amazement, "I had a great passion for photography. Perhaps because I was born with this bad leg and couldn't work the mines. But times change. I haven't taken a photograph in years."

He leaned forward, topping off their mugs with cider.

"You're sure nothing's amiss? You two seem a bit off. Hope you haven't caught what your brother has."

"We're fine."

Unspoken between Kate and Emma was the fact that it was Christmas Eve and ten years to the day since their parents had disappeared. As they were getting dressed that morning, Emma had suddenly and without explanation hugged Kate. They'd stood there in the center of their room and held each other for almost a minute, wordlessly.

"So you met the Doctor. 'E's not from Cambridge Falls, you know. Just showed up one day and bought this old place, oh, more'n ten years ago. Took on me and old Sallow."

"Abraham . . ." Kate and Emma had decided to be up front; they needed answers, and the old caretaker was their best, and safest, hope of getting them. "Do you, um, do you remember us? From before. One day beside the lake. Did we just sort of . . . appear?"

Kate knew if she'd asked this question two days earlier, Abraham would have had no idea what she was talking about. But since then, she and Emma and Michael had gone back in time. The past was different now. That meant Abraham's memory should also be different. And in fact, even before she'd finished asking the question, the old man was smiling.

"Remember you? Three young 'uns just—pop—appearing out a' nowhere? A person doesn't go forgetting a thing like that. When I saw you lot get off the boat day before yesterday, I said to myself, Abraham, old boy, them's the same that stepped out a' thin air near fifteen year ago, and look at 'em, not a day older. But I'm glad you finally fessed up; I feared I was getting soft." Abraham leaned closer. "I take it you've pieced it together, then? The truth about Cambridge Falls?"

Kate shook her head. "That's why we're here."

"Oh, you're having me on! Two children who go skipping about through time, and I'm to believe you've not realized the very nature of the place you live?"

"We thought . . . I mean, we suspected there was something strange. . . ."

"Strange, oh yes. That'd be putting it mildly."

"And Dr. Pym . . . is he . . ."

"Is he what, miss?"

"Is he a . . ." Kate couldn't bring herself to say the word.

Luckily, Emma's patience had reached its limit. "Is he a wizard?!"

"Shhhhhhh!" Abraham scooched his chair even closer, gesturing them to lower their voices. "Let's not be announcing it in

Westport!" Then he winked, grinning. "But you've hit it there. The man's a wizard, true as life."

Kate set her cider on the floor. She no longer trusted her hands.

"And how did the two of you find out? Did he do a spell, perhaps?"

"He sort of made a fire appear," Emma said.

Abraham nodded knowingly. "Yes, a brilliant man, the Doctor, but he couldn't start a fire to save his own life. Tell me, are you witches, then?" A look of worry crossed his face. " 'Cause if you are, I'll just say I've never been anything but friendly toward you, and don't reckon being changed into a goat or growing an extra bottom—"

"We're not witches," Kate assured him.

"Yeah," Emma said. "We always thought magic was just some stupid thing Michael talked about."

"Is that so?" Abraham rubbed his beard. "You didn't know magic was real?"

"It's not unusual," Kate said. "Most people don't think magic is real."

"Not even Michael," Emma added. "And he's pretty weird."

"Then how in heaven's name did you come—"

"We'll tell you everything," Kate said. "But you have to tell us about Cambridge Falls. The truth."

He looked at them for a long moment, then sighed. "Very well. I suppose the cat's out of the bag. But I'll be needing my smoke." And he took out his pipe, tamped the bowl with his thumb, and lit it with a stick from the fire. "Now, the first thing you must know is that the magic world used to be entwined with our own. Like this." Abraham threaded his knobby fingers together. "Was that way for thousands a' years. Till people—normal people, I'm talking about—started spreading out and multiplying, putting up towns and cities. Finally, the magical types saw that humankind was unstoppable. So they began carving out territories and made 'em invisible to human eyes and impossible to enter unless you knew the way. Whole chunks just vanished off the map. This went on a century or more. Then, last day a' December, 1899, what was left a' the magical world up and disappeared. Whoosh!"

"But," Kate interrupted, "that's not that long ago! People would remember!"

"This is deep magic we're talking about, girl. People was made to forget. Forget about the missing islands and forests. Forget such a thing as magic ever existed. Whole history of the world was rewritten. Only thing was, here and there a human town got dragged along. Cambridge Falls was one a' those. Me, Miss Sallow, folks in the village, we've lived next door to magic folk all our lives. Even had dealings with them in better times. But we're as human as you. Not like them you'd find out there." He gestured with his pipe out the window. "There's things in them mountains you wouldn't believe."

The old man leaned forward.

"Now it's your turn, my dears. If you're not witches, how'd you show up that day fifteen years ago?"

The girls glanced at each other. Their fear was if they told him about the book, he might say it belonged to Dr. Pym and make them give it back. And if that happened, how would they ever save Michael?

"We lied," Emma said. "We are witches. We just wanted to see what you knew. Congratulations. You passed."

Kate thought that this was a stunningly bad lie, but Abraham was nodding as if he'd suspected something of the sort all along.

Fair enough, she thought.

"Abraham," Kate said, "we need some old photos. From when . . . she was here."

Despite the merry little fire, a chill seemed to settle on the room.

Abraham lowered his voice. "You mean the Countess, do you? And what would you be wanting with her? Dark times those were. Better forgotten."

"Please, we really need them."

"And if you don't give 'em to us, we'll turn you into a toad." Emma squinted at Abraham and wiggled a finger. The old man immediately jumped up and scampered to a chest against the wall, whipping it open and beginning to tear through the contents.

Kate looked at Emma reproachfully.

Emma shrugged. "He's getting them."

Abraham returned with a thick leather folder stuffed with photographs.

"She made me her official photographer, you know. Vain creature she was. Always going on about how it was my duty to record her beauty for posterity." He snorted and handed the folder to Kate. "You can have 'em. I'm well rid of the lot."

Kate glanced inside. There were hundreds of photos. Surely, they could find one that would take them back to whenever or wherever Michael was.

"Abraham, who was the Countess? Is she the reason Cambridge Falls is the way it is?"

Abraham looked like he didn't want to answer, but Emma narrowed her eyes, and he held up his hands in surrender. "Fine, I'll tell you what I know. But who she was, where she came from, I've truly no idea. She just appeared in Cambridge Falls with fifty a' them ghouls. Screechers, the children called 'em. I remember one took you three away that day beside the lake, so you know what terrible, cursed creatures they are." A log hissed and cracked, and Abraham paused to stir the fire with the poker. When he continued, his voice had grown quieter.

"It was summer. Beautiful day. Not a cloud in sight. Most of the men were in the mines. That's two hours' walk into the mountains. So it was just the women and children in the village. And me, thanks to this leg of mine." One hand absently rubbed his bad leg. "I was in my cousin's house and heard this scream. A sound like nothing I'd ever heard before. Robbed the breath right out a' me. I ran outside, and one of them monsters was chasing a boy down the street. Picked 'im up and carried 'im off 'fore I could say a word. I followed 'em to the square. Couldn't believe what I saw. Children everywhere. And them Screechers. They 'ad their swords out and were pushing the mothers back, cutting 'em off from their little ones. And that's when I saw that golden hair a' hers, shining there among all them black shapes. She said something, and those monsters drove the children in front of 'em like sheep, down to the gorge and across the bridge. I followed along with the women, who were all wailing and screaming, and . . ."

Abraham stopped speaking. He was looking at Kate.

"You feeling okay, miss?"

"Your face is all white," Emma said.

"I—I'm fine," Kate stammered. "Please go on."

But she wasn't fine. She was thinking of the children, how scared they must've been, how she had left Michael with those monsters. . . .

"Please. I'm fine."

Abraham nodded and took a drink of cider.

"Well, old Mr. Langford was living in the big house then. A tiny thumb of a man, he was. And a right rich little bugger too. His family'd run the mines since forever. And he's standing there on the front steps when she comes up with them monsters a' hers and all them crying children. He starts asking what she thinks she's doing, private property and et cetera and so on and does she know who he is, when she gives this little giggle and Lord if one a' them creatures didn't cut Mr. Langford right in half. What a sight. One minute the fella was standing there telling her to clear off. Next minute there was two pieces of him. Course, truth be told, no one much liked Mr. Langford, stuck-up little plug he was, but still, terrible way to go. His mouth was still moving when the top part fell off the bottom."

Kate and Emma sat completely still, hardly daring to breathe. Abraham stirred the fire again; he was deep in the past. "We'd sent runners to the mines. But it was nightfall before the men were back. We got torches, as many weapons as we could lay our hands on, and crossed the bridge." Abraham laughed humorlessly. "What were we thinking? We weren't fighters. And here she was a dark witch with a horde of demon warriors. Utterly hopeless." Abraham shook his head. "She came down the front steps to meet us. Three of them Screechers with her. But she didn't have to do no more than hold up her little hand like this"—Abraham raised one palm—"and everyone stopped. She said in that high, sweet voice a' hers, 'I have your children inside; there's a blade at each of their throats. They'll be dead before you reach the door.' Oh, the silence was awful. Not a soul moved. I remember the two halves of Mr. Langford's body still lying there on the steps, and she looking out at us, so beautiful and terrible in the torchlight. Then she told us there was something in the mountains she wanted. Said if we found it for her, she'd give us back our children."

"What'd you do?" Emma asked breathlessly.

"What do you think we did, child? The men went into the mountains with a gang a' them monsters to guard 'em. The women went back to the village, and she stayed in the house with the children."

For a full minute, no one spoke. The only sound was the hissing and crackling of the fire. Kate realized she had been gripping the folder so tightly that her hands had locked in place. She opened them slowly, flexing her fingers.

"And no one ever tried to fight?" Emma asked finally.

"A few did. A man would just get too fed up, missing his wife or little ones, and go crazy."

"What happened to them?"

"She had a boat. Used it like a floatin' prison for anyone who disobeyed. At night, you could hear the cries coming across the lake." Abraham shuddered. "Rumor was she did things to people there. Awful things."

Kate remembered how, when they'd gone back into the past, she'd seen the large boat floating far out on the lake. That had to be the one he was talking about.

"What was she looking for?"

"She never said exactly. But there was talk."

"What kind of talk?"

Abraham's voice had fallen to a whisper. "People said it was a book of some kind. A great book of magic that'd been buried in the mountains long ago. Imagine"—his voice lowered even further, and Kate and Emma had to strain to hear—"imagine something so fearsome and terrible it had to be buried away from the sight of men."

Kate glanced at Emma. Her sister's dark eyes had grown very wide. They were thinking the same thing. Was the book the Countess wanted their book? But they had found it in the house. It couldn't be the same one.

"What happened in the end?" Emma asked.

Abraham shook his head. "No, I've said all I'll say. Turn me into a newt. Some things are better left alone."

"Please," Kate said, "we have to know what happened to the

children." And she said the thing that had been trembling inside her. "She has our brother."

"What?"

"He's not sick. We left him there. In the past . . . I left him."

"Oh Lord . . ." Abraham drew a mottled hand over his face. "Yes, I remember now. I've blocked out so much a' those days, but I do remember your brother." He shook his head. "No, I can't tell you. Don't ask me to. I'm sorry. You must go to Dr. Pym. He's the only one who can help. I'm sorry—"

He started to get up, but Kate grabbed his sleeve.

"At least show us the last picture you ever took? Please?"

The old man blinked several times, clearly surprised at the request. Then he hobbled to a desk, unlocked a drawer, and removed a single old photograph. With shaking hands, he passed it over.

The photo was dark and blurry. It seemed to show a group of women running along the edge of the gorge. Many of the figures held torches. But as poor an image as it was, both Kate and Emma could sense the women's alarm and fear.

A door slammed. They looked up and saw that Abraham had climbed the spiral staircase to his bedroom and shut the door.

"Come on," Kate said. She slid the photo in her pocket, and they left the tower.

They went down to the kitchen, as it was nearly evening and they hadn't eaten since breakfast. Miss Sallow had the goose roasting in the oven and was too busy with dinner to upbraid them for missing lunch. They grabbed bread, cheese, and salami and escaped upstairs.

Abraham had been right about one thing: the Countess was vain. They had to wade through dozens of shots of the Countess in evening gowns. The Countess wearing jewels. The Countess boating. The Countess playing badminton with her strange-looking secretary. Usually, she was glancing coyly at the camera, as if caught by surprise. Yet somehow, it always favored her left profile.

"Look at this one." Emma was on the floor, surrounded by photos and holding up a picture of the Countess looking coquettish under a lace parasol. "I told you she was stuck-up." She tossed it onto a growing pile in the corner.

Kate was sorting through pictures on the bed, and whenever she came upon a photo of a Screecher, she quickly slid it to the bottom of the stack. Over the past two days, she'd been keeping at bay the thought of what Michael might be going through. It had been necessary if she was to function. But now that she'd heard Abraham's story and seen pictures of these creatures with their frayed black clothes and long, jagged swords, fear for her brother was flooding her heart. She came to a picture of a particularly gruesome-looking Screecher and found herself pushing the entire stack away, overcome with worry.

Emma made a noise and threw another photo in the corner.

The book was resting beside Kate's knee, and, for a moment, she let her fingers drift over the emerald cover. She thought about her vision of the night before. Had she just imagined it? She opened the book and pressed her fingers to a blank page. The effect was immediate. As clearly as if she was there, she saw the village on the banks of the river. But it had grown. There were stone streets, a wall. A market. She saw men and women, all milling about. She could hear the press of voices.

She turned another page and touched her fingers to the parchment. She saw a vast army marching along a road, the dust rising from their sandals. She heard their spears and shields clanking together, the rhythmic pounding of a drum. Behind them, in the distance, Kate glimpsed the village on the river, burning. She gasped and flipped a few more pages. The army vanished. She saw a fleet of ships at sea. They rocked on the waves, their sails snapping in the wind. She could hear the shouts of sailors, the whip crack of ropes, could feel their wooden holds bursting with the treasures of distant lands. She turned more pages. She saw people fleeing as a black dragon and a red dragon battled in the air above a town, belching flame. They tangled together and fell, crushing buildings, spreading fire. Another page. A knight in armor advanced into a cave as a monster with long, scaly arms slithered out of the gloom, hissing. She turned a handful of pages and saw a hot-air balloon rising in the sky as women in long dresses and men in white straw hats applauded. Another page. She saw a city filled with old-fashioned motorcars. She turned to a place deep into the book. She waited. Nothing happened. She stared at the blank parchment. At its very center, a small black dot appeared. As Kate watched, it began to spread, like an ink stain. Suddenly, the entire page was black. And then, she saw with horror, the blackness begin to spread up her fingers.

"Kate!"

Emma was looking down at her. Kate realized she was lying on her back.

"What happened?"

"You screamed."

"What're you talking about? I didn't scream."

"Uh, yeah, you did," Emma said. "And you kind of fainted too."

She helped her to sit up. Kate stole a glance at the book. The page was blank again.

"What happened?" Emma said.

"Nothing." Kate reached over and shut the book.

"Uh-huh, well, look what I found." Emma handed her a photograph.

A cry caught in Kate's throat. There, in faded black and white, staring up at her from the past, was Michael. He was alone, a corner of the house visible in the background. And he was holding a handwritten sign that read HELP ME.

Someone tried the door.

"What's this? Who's locked this door?!"

It was Miss Sallow.

"Hurry," Kate hissed. They quickly cleared an area on the bed, and Kate pulled the book toward her. "Make sure you're touching me."

"Worried someone's gonna sneak in and make off with the crown jewels of France, is that it? Unlock this door!"

Kate picked up the photo of Michael and opened the book. Once again, the pages were blank. Her heart began to beat faster.

She knew she had to do it now, quickly, before she lost courage. She reached down with the photo.

"Wait!" Emma had grabbed her arm.

"What're you doing? We have to—"

"We need a picture to get back."

Kate's heart stopped. She had almost sent them into the past with no way of returning home. Emma grabbed Michael's camera, aimed it at Kate, and snapped a picture. The machine spat it out a moment later.

"Are the royal ears deaf, is that it? The goose is cooked, and Dr. Pym's sent me to fetch Your Highnesses. Including the Dauphin, whether he's feeling better or not. So *ouvre la porte* or I'll be letting myself in!"

"Just a second!" Kate called, trying to sound relaxed. "We'll be out in a second!"

Emma blew on the photo and put it in her pocket. "Okay," she said, taking hold of Kate's arm.

They could hear Miss Sallow muttering on the other side of the door, sorting through the keys on her belt.

Kate paused, holding the photo over the blank page. She felt it again, the darkness creeping up out of the book, threatening to engulf her.

"What's wrong?" Emma asked.

Taking a breath, Kate focused her mind on Michael and placed the photo on the page.

CHAPTER SEVEN
Guests of the Countess

"I'm so sorry," Kate said, for the sixth or seventh time. "I'm so sorry. . . ."

The moment they had appeared, Kate and Emma had run at Michael, nearly knocking him down with their hug. They asked if he was okay, how long had he been held prisoner, if the Countess had hurt him. Emma said she would go murder that witch right now; Michael only had to say the word.

It was early evening. They were about twenty yards from the house, at the edge of a thick grove of pine trees whose intertwined branches rose into the darkening sky.

"I'm fine," Michael was saying. "I've only been here a few days. Guys, I can't breathe."

He managed to extricate himself from their embrace, but

Kate continued to hold his arms with a fervor that suggested she would never let him go ever again. Her eyes shone with tears. "We didn't mean to leave you. I thought you were touching me. I would never—"

"Look," Michael said as he straightened his glasses, "we don't have time for that right now. I mean, of course I forgive you and everything. But we have to get out of here. They may already be looking for me. Let me have the book."

Kate hesitated just for a second—why, she couldn't have said—then she handed it over.

"Excuse me?"

Kate turned. Abraham was behind them, fiddling nervously with his camera. She hadn't even noticed him till now. "So, I'm fine with the appearing out of thin air and whatnot, seems to be what you lot do, but if it's all the same, I'm just going to slip off, then, right? Right, I'll just—" And before anyone could speak, he hobbled away through the trees.

Kate turned back and saw that Michael hadn't even looked up. He was busy paging through the book. A question rose in her mind.

"How'd you get away from the Screechers? Weren't they keeping you with the other kids?"

"And how'd you find Abraham again?" Emma asked. "Was he just hanging around?"

Michael snapped the book shut.

"You have to trust me. Whatever happens, everything's going to be okay."

"What're you talking about?" Kate said. "We need to get out of here." And she was about to tell Emma to get out the photo she'd taken in the bedroom when someone giggled.

The sound was like cold water trickling down her spine.

The Countess's secretary stepped out from behind a tree. He was wearing the same pin-striped jacket he'd worn that day at the dam; only now, up close, Kate could see the tears and grease stains. He was smiling, his teeth gray and narrow. A tiny yellow bird was perched on his shoulder.

"Oh yes, good, good, good." His voice had a high, almost hysterical quality. He rubbed his hands together gleefully. "The Countess will be so happy, so happy."

"I told you they'd come back for me," Michael said.

Kate thought she must be hallucinating. This wasn't possible. Michael would never betray them. And she was still telling herself that as two black-clad Screechers emerged from the shadows.

Approaching the front of the house, the Secretary yelled at the Screecher standing guard to open the door. But the dark figure ignored him, and the man had to open it himself, grumbling as he did about lack of respect and how the Countess would most certainly hear of it.

He led them down a twisting series of corridors. Several times Michael looked about to speak to his sisters, but each time Emma glared at him until he turned back around. Michael's glasses were bent, and he had a red welt on his cheek. The second after the Screechers appeared, Emma had flown at him, knocking him to the ground. She whaled away with both fists, calling him a traitor and a rat and yelling that he wasn't her brother anymore. Her attack caused him to drop the book, and Kate and the Secretary dove for it at the same time. A tug-of-war ensued. It ended when one of the Screechers dealt Kate a vicious backhand blow. Lying on the ground, her ears ringing, she watched the other Screecher pull Emma kicking and screaming off Michael.

Kate's head still throbbed. But even so, she couldn't help noticing the difference in the mansion. Windows and mirrors were clean. Candles gleamed off polished wood floors. None of the furniture was torn or broken or serving as the home for a family of animals. The Countess might be evil, but she could teach Miss Sallow a thing or two about housekeeping.

Kate took her sister's hand. Emma's face was a frozen, tear-stained mask.

"It's not Michael," she whispered. "It's that witch. She put him under some spell. It's not Michael. Remember that; it's not him."

Emma nodded, but the tears continued to roll down her cheeks.

The Secretary stopped at a set of double doors in a dim hallway. Kate knew they were outside the ballroom. She could picture the cobwebbed chandeliers slumped on the floor, the half-collapsed balcony, the broken windows.

"You stay here," he ordered the Screechers, their yellow eyes glowing in the shadows.

Cavendish leaned in close. He wasn't much taller than Kate, and his breath stank of onions. He was the single most repulsive person she'd ever met.

"You take my advice, little birdies, and not make the Countess angry. You don't want to go to the boat, do you? Little birdies don't like the boat." He smiled his gray-toothed smile.

"You need to brush your teeth," Emma said. "For like a year."

Cavendish closed his lips and scowled. Jerking his head for them to follow, he pushed through the double doors.

It was like stepping into a dream. Kate and Emma blinked a few times, dazzled by the light, and then blinked again, hardly believing what they were seeing. A hundred couples moved about the floor, turning and spinning as a thirty-piece orchestra played a waltz. Kate could see the conductor, his arms waving, glancing back at the dancers like a proud parent. Some men wore tuxedos, with long tails that flew out when they twirled their partners. Others were in uniforms with red and blue sashes, their chests shining with golden medals. The women were dressed in gowns embroidered with rubies, pearls, and emeralds. And everywhere Kate saw diamonds on bare necks, refracting the light from the thousands of candles that burned in the chandeliers. A servant in green livery and high white stockings passed by carrying a tray of champagne to the older men and women who stood along the walls.

"Little birdies wait here," Cavendish hissed. "The Countess will come when she likes."

And then Kate saw her, the golden hair shining at the dead center of the dancers. Her skin was pure white, her gown the color of blood, and the diamonds covering her throat and chest shone as if they alone gave light to the room. Her partner was an athletic, uniformed young man who had the most impressive brown whiskers Kate had ever seen. The Countess said something, and the young man stepped back and bowed. She gave a tiny curtsy in return and, holding up the hem of her dress, skipped through the couples to where the children stood beside the eagerly squirming Cavendish.

The Countess's face was flushed from the warmth and exercise, and her eyes sparkled with life. They were a deep, almost violet blue, and the moment they landed on her, Kate felt as if she were the luckiest person in the world.

"You're here! My beautiful Katrina!" The Countess took Kate's hands and, before she could react, kissed her cheeks. Behind her, couples whirled about in unison, creating a dizzying backdrop. "And how lucky you arrived in time for the ball. The *crème* of St. Petersburg is here. Even the Tsar is supposed to turn up later, though of course he won't, the dullard. Now tell me, my dear"—she moved closer to Kate, whispering—"what do you think of the gentleman I was dancing with?"

The young man in question had moved off the dance floor to join two other men in uniform. He stood ramrod straight, one hand tucked in his belt and the other stroking his whiskers.

"That's Captain Alexei Markov of the Third Hussars," the Countess said in a conspiratorially low voice. "He is a bit too proud of his whiskers, but he's a handsome beast for all that. We'll have an affair shortly, though it won't end well." She frowned theatrically. "Alexei will insist on bragging about it at his club, and I'll have no choice but to slaughter him and his entire family."

Kate smiled, and as she did, she saw Emma staring at her in

horror. It was like being slapped awake. She yanked her hand away from the Countess, her heart pounding.

If the Countess had noticed Kate pulling her hand free, she said nothing. She was pointing with her fan to a very old man with white muttonchops who was asleep in a chair. The old man sported such an enormous collection of medals that he was listing to one side. Kate half expected the weight to drag him crashing to the floor.

"Behold my beloved husband," the Countess said, speaking over the orchestra. "Isn't he too revolting for words? And do you know that when I married him at sixteen, I was hailed as the greatest beauty in Russia? Shall we take a turn about the room?" She started away, and Cavendish, still clutching the book to his chest, gave Kate and Emma a shove to follow.

"I admit," the Countess said, moving through the crowd, nodding to people on either side, "there were those who insisted on praising Natasha Petrovski and her curdled-milk complexion and watery cow eyes. That was before, of course, she had that awful accident with the pitcher of acid. Poor dear, I heard she died in a Hungarian asylum. Mad as a hatter and raving on and on about a witch." The Countess giggled, covering her mouth with her fan and giving Kate an aren't-I-bad look. "But what was I saying? Oh yes, my husband. When I married the Count, everyone said he had no more than six months to live. I don't need to tell you I didn't plan on allowing him even that long. But wasn't it just like the old mule to creak on for nearly a year? Honestly, he must have survived a half dozen of my attempts to poison him. Never marry a finicky eater, my dears. Nothing but trouble."

None of the guests appeared to notice the children. As the girls or Michael, or the Secretary for that matter, approached, the immaculately dressed people simply moved out of the way without ever looking at them directly.

The Countess gave a bright little laugh. "Finally, I went to a hag and bought a potion of bees' root, amber paste, and willow's breath. No need for him to swallow a thing. He just breathed it in as he slept and come morning was as dead as a peasant in winter, leaving me sole mistress of the largest estate in the Tsar's realm." She turned to them, her face glowing at the memory, and curtsied low. "The Countess Tatiana Serena Alexandra Ruskin, at your service."

Kate and Emma stared at the bowed, blond head. Michael leaned forward and whispered, "It's polite to—" but Emma elbowed him in the ribs. Kate was thinking of the day they'd first seen the Countess at the dam, how she'd seemed almost too radiant, too beautiful, too full of life. Now Kate understood: it wasn't real. The Countess wasn't sixteen or seventeen. In fact, if she was who she said she was, if she'd been alive when there were still tsars in Russia, she could be a hundred. Or more. Magic was keeping her young. No wonder she sometimes seemed like she was playing the part of a teenager.

The Countess rose with a soft rustle of silk and gazed out over the dancers.

"Yes," she said with philosophical weariness, "this was my world. I had wealth, position, beauty. Simpleton that I was, I thought I had actually achieved something. But I was still to learn the true meaning of power." She clapped her lace-gloved hands, and it all disappeared, the men in uniforms and tuxedos, the women in gowns, the orchestra, the green-liveried servants, the light from the chandeliers, all gone. The children were suddenly alone with the Countess and her rat-toothed secretary in the large, silent room. Only a few candles flickered along the walls.

"Now," she said with a smile, "shall we go out onto the verandah? I'd like to take the air. And I believe you have something for me."

The Countess made Kate and Emma wait with the Secretary while Michael helped her on with a black silk wrap. Kate watched the Secretary for any sign his attention was wandering, anything that would give her a chance to seize the book. She'd already whispered to Emma to be ready with the photograph.

But mostly, she wished her hands would stop trembling. She'd balled them into fists and, when that didn't work, shoved them in her pockets so Emma wouldn't see. She didn't want her sister to know how terrified and truly hopeless she was.

The Secretary muttered something to the tiny bird on his shoulder and hugged the book even closer.

Suddenly, Kate felt Emma's hand in her pocket, prying her fingers apart, sliding her small hand into hers. She looked over and saw her sister's face turned upward, her dark eyes full of trust and love.

In a voice only Kate could hear, Emma said, "It's gonna be okay."

Kate thought her heart might burst. She'd always known her sister was strong, but she was still three years younger, and at this moment, when everything seemed so bleak, for Emma to be the one offering her strength . . .

"Come along," the Countess said, sweeping past them toward the door.

She led them to a stone patio off the back of the house. The night was warm, the air heavy and sweet with the smell of blooming flowers. Glass dragons of every color were strung overhead, candle flames dancing in their open mouths. A porcelain jug stood on a table at the center of the patio and, beside the jug, a crystal carafe filled with dark liquid.

"Please," the Countess said, gesturing to the chairs. "I do love sitting outside on a summer's evening. Perhaps it's my Russian blood reminding me that winter is never far off. Do you care for lemonade? I promise it isn't poisoned."

Without waiting for an answer, the Secretary began pouring, slopping a fair amount onto the table.

Scared and worried as she was, Kate couldn't help thinking how familiar everything seemed. The house, the stables. This was the place where they lived. And yet they were such a long, long way from home. She stole another glance at the book under the Secretary's arm. Somehow they had to get it back.

Suddenly, the night was rent by a scream. Kate felt Emma's hand grip hers more tightly. The scream was far off, from somewhere deep in the woods. But there was no mistaking the source.

The Countess was pouring herself a glass of whatever was in the carafe. It was a deep ruby color and oddly thick.

"Now and then women from the town attempt to reach the house. No doubt wanting to see their brats. You'd think they'd learn. They have no hope of getting past my guards." The Countess swirled the liquid around her tiny glass. "They are amazing creatures, the *morum cadi*. They never grow tired. They know neither pain nor fear nor compassion. They are possessed solely by a hatred for every living thing." She lifted the glass to her lips and drained it off.

"What did you call them?" Kate asked, cursing the tremor she heard in her voice.

"*Morum cadi*, the deathless warriors," the Countess said. "Though I admit Screecher is a fitting name. They were men, hundreds of years ago. But they traded their souls for power and eternal life. Which they were granted, of a sort."

"They're not so bad," Emma said. "Mostly smelly is all."

The Countess smiled indulgently. "Aren't you a brave little liar?" She poured herself another glass. "They say the scream of a *morum cadi* is the cry of a soul being torn asunder, over and over, for eternity. One is awful enough, but a thousand together on a battlefield? I've watched whole armies turn and flee." She raised the red liquid to her lips. "It really is quite a sight."

Kate imagined someone's mother running through the forest, her legs growing heavy, the screams drawing closer.

"Ow," Emma said.

Kate was crushing her sister's hand. She loosened her grip, whispered, "Sorry."

"Such devotion," the Countess cooed, "but I see the truth." She reached across the table and placed a finger on the base of Kate's throat. "Abandoned by those dearest in the world. The wound hangs over you like a shadow. But I could make it go away. It would be so easy. . . ."

She withdrew her hand; a wispy gray tendril clung to her fingertip. She seemed to be drawing it out of the center of Kate's chest. As it pulled free, Kate gasped.

"What did you . . ."

"What have I done? My sweet little Kat, I've set you free! Oh, the weight you've had to bear! Can't you feel how it's worn you down, little by little, every day of your life? But it's gone now, all the pain and hurt, all the fear; I've taken it away. Imagine living that way always."

She was right, Kate thought. It was as if she could breathe for the first time in years.

"Say the word, and you'll never feel it again."

The tendril drifted in the air, still clinging to her fingertip. Kate thought back to her mother leaning down, telling her to watch over her brother and sister, and though the memory was there, the feeling of her mother's love, of that last kiss, was gone.

"Give it back."

"Are you sure, *mon ange*? There's a great deal of pain here."

"Give it back." If holding on to that one moment meant a lifetime of pain, Kate would take it.

The Countess shrugged and touched her chest. Kate felt the weight settle on her like a shroud.

"Well, shall we take a look at what you've brought me?"

The Secretary had been hovering a few feet away, both arms wrapped greedily around the book. Now he scurried forward and placed it in the Countess's outstretched hands. She let out a small gasp as her fingers touched the emerald cover.

She was clearly trying to control herself, but still her fingers trembled as she opened it and turned the pages. After a minute, and with obvious effort, she set the book aside.

Kate heard her whisper, "Finally."

The Countess looked at the children, her eyes glowing brighter than ever. "*Alors, mes enfants*, would you like to know what it is you found?"

The Countess began by saying that to understand where the book came from, the children first had to imagine an age long past when the worlds of magic and men were one, back before the magical world had begun to pull away and humankind had been made to forget—

"Yeah," Emma interrupted rudely. "We know all that."

"Well," the Countess continued, her voice still soft and sweet, "the center of the magical world, the seat of the highest learning and power, was Alexandria. Or Rhakotis, as it was then known, where the great desert met the sea. The city was ruled by a council of wizards who traced their line back to the dim beginnings of the world. Their knowledge was ancient, primordial. Passed down from master to student for thousands of years. But powerful as they were, they saw their time was ending, that the age of humans was approaching, and they feared the day they would be forgotten.

"You see"—and here the Countess smiled at Kate and Emma—"though wizards, they were also men. And like men throughout time, they could not imagine a world where they would cease to matter. So what did they do, these wise, foolish men? They wrote their secrets down, those things said at the birth of the universe, the words spoken aeons ago, in the darkness and the silence, to call everything into being, all so that they, through their knowledge, would endure."

The Countess laughed, but it was not the bright, gay laugh from before. The sound was hard, scornful. "Their ancestors had understood. Some things are too powerful to be controlled by any one person. For this reason, the knowledge had always been divided among the council, with none knowing exactly what the others possessed. In this way, there was safety. When it was proposed that the secrets be collected, there were voices that argued against it. Who said such power, gathered together in one place, was too dangerous, that perhaps it should be lost. But other voices won out, and thus the great magics were committed to simple paper.

"They were not complete ignoramuses, to be sure. They built in protections. You've seen yourself that the leaves are blank. It would take a lifetime of magical study to read and understand a single page. In addition, they established an order of guardians whose sole mission it was to protect the Books."

"You mean," Kate said, "there's more than one?"

"Yes. The wizards created three great books, which they named the Books of Beginning. And they buried them in a secret vault far below the city."

"So what happened?" Emma asked petulantly, as if she didn't care, though Kate could see she was hanging on every word.

The Countess shrugged. "What happens to every great civilization. Convinced they were the most enlightened society on earth, they grew decadent and soft. The council of magicians fought among themselves and fell apart. They had been right, you see: the age of magic was waning. Finally, the city was overrun by Alexander, the first great human warlord. He burned it to the ground. And when the ashes were sifted, the Books had disappeared.

"Everything now becomes conjecture. Some believe Alexander took the Books with him, that they remained in his possession till his death, when they were stolen by his chief magician. Others believe that the order of guardians created by the wizards spirited the Books away before the siege, splitting them up and hiding them in the far corners of the earth. Others think that in the confusion of the city's fall, the Books were stolen by those who had no conception of their importance, and they were passed from hand to hand through the ages. If someone did chance upon their nature, they made use of the Books' power in the crudest, simplest way, as you three did when you traveled back through time. Of course, there were always rumors that this or that book had come to light, but none were ever proven. As far as I know, no one can honestly claim to have seen one of the Books of Beginning since Alexander marched into Rhakotis more than two thousand years ago. That is, until now."

She laid her hand lightly on the cover of the book.

For a few moments, no one spoke. Kate wanted badly to say, "And so what?" It didn't matter to her that the book was written by a bunch of wizards a long time ago. She just needed it to get her brother and sister home.

Then Michael said, "So now will you do it?"

Kate looked at him. He seemed to have grown paler as they sat there, and he was visibly sweating. His glasses kept slipping down his nose.

"I mean, you've got it now, right? So you'll do what you promised?" His voice was pleading.

"What's he talking about?" Emma demanded.

"It's very simple, my dear," the Countess said. "I wished you and your sister to return with the book. So I made your brother an offer. In return, he agreed to lure you here and turn you over to me."

Emma snorted. "You think we're gonna believe that? You got him under some spell is all."

"I'm afraid not. Your brother helped me of his own free will."

The Countess said this as if she were stating no more than plain fact. Kate felt a stab of ice at her heart.

Emma seemed to sense it as well for she pushed back, harder than ever. "No, that's not true! Michael'd never do that! Not to us! Would you, Michael?"

She looked at him, imploring. But Michael just stared down at the table.

"Tell them, Michael," the Countess said, her voice low but firm. "Tell your sisters."

Kate held her breath. No, she thought, please. Let him be under a spell.

Very quietly, Michael said, "It's true."

"No!" Emma grabbed him by the shoulder and began to shake him roughly. "No! You're under some spell! I know it! You gotta be! You wouldn't do that to us!"

"Don't be too harsh with him, my dear," the Countess said. "I looked into his heart and saw the thing he desired most. He couldn't resist."

Emma was crying. Large tears tumbled down her cheeks.

"Shut up! You're lying! There's nothing you could give him that'd make him betray us! He's our brother! You don't know anything! You're just an evil witch is all! You—"

"Emma—" Kate said.

"No!" Emma cried. "He'd never—he—" She broke off, burying her head in Kate's shoulder, sobbing. "He's our brother. He'd never . . . he'd never . . ."

"The poor thing," the Countess cooed. "She's actually quite fragile, isn't she?"

Kate glared at her. Her fear had vanished. Her whole body was suddenly consumed with a white-hot rage. She wanted to leap over the table and scream at the Countess, tell her how year after year, orphanage after orphanage, with nothing, not even a bed to call her own, Emma had never given up. She'd always fought. Because she knew, wherever they went, her brother and sister would be there. They were her family, the one sure thing in her life. And now the Countess had taken that away.

Kate tasted salt and realized she was crying too. She wiped her tears and looked at the beautiful, violet-eyed creature across the table and made a silent promise that if she ever got the chance, she would kill her for what she'd done.

"Tell them what I offered you," the Countess said.

Michael was crying and his voice hiccuped when he spoke. "She said she'd . . . find them."

"What're you talking about?!" Emma whirled on him, still crying, but furious now. "Huh?!" She started hitting him. Michael didn't fight back or defend himself. "Find some stupid dwarf?! I hate you!"

But Kate suddenly understood. "She promised she'd find Mom and Dad."

Emma stopped, one hand still balled into a fist. She was stunned, wild-eyed.

"Why," Kate pleaded, "why would you—"

"Because"—Michael looked up, his face a mess of tears, his nose running freely—"what if they're not coming back?"

And that was it. The thing none of them had ever said. Even the air seemed to sense it and grow still. Then Kate imagined herself shouting at Michael, telling him he was wrong: she was the one their mother had promised, not him; she knew. She saw Emma staring at her with huge eyes, begging her to say something. But Michael—who for a moment had looked as shocked as his sisters—was already barreling on.

"You say they are, but what if they're not? It's been ten years! She can find them! She promised she would!" He turned to the Countess, tears still streaming down his face. "Do it. You've got the book now. You said you'd do it when you had the book. Find our mom and dad. Please. Do it."

The Countess reached out and caressed Michael's hair. "My sweet boy, I wish I could. But you see, I don't have the book."

She nodded to where it lay on the table.

"What—what's happening to it?" Kate said.

The edges were becoming fuzzy and indistinct. It was as if the book was slightly out of focus.

"A funny thing about the universe, my dear Kat: it respects individuality. A person or object may truly exist only once in a given moment. Multiple versions are verboten. That day you left Michael at the dam and returned to your time, there must have been a second or two when you saw yourselves. Do you remember how it felt?"

Kate did. There in the underground room, watching herself and Emma and Michael, she'd felt a huge force pressing down on her. Then, the moment their other selves disappeared, it lifted.

"Now, magic can bend those rules," the Countess said, "especially magic as powerful as contained in the book. For a brief period, two copies can be made to exist at once. But sooner or later, the universe asserts itself. Ever since you arrived here, the other copy of this book, the one that already exists in this time, has been exerting its dominance."

The book was growing more and more faint. Kate felt panic rising in her.

"Do something!"

"I wish I could. Regrettably, even I can't change the laws of nature. Though I am grateful. I was about to give up. Two years I've been in this backwater, seemingly no closer to attaining my goal. But the fact that you found the book in this house, that tells me I am close. Take a good look now."

Then, before their eyes, the book faded away and vanished.

There was a cracking in the sky, and a cold wind blew across the patio. A storm was coming in.

"But"—Kate couldn't stop herself—"how will we get home?"

"My dear," the Countess said, her eyes shining in the candle-light, "you are home."

CHAPTER EIGHT
Wolves

Two Screechers appeared and yanked Kate, Emma, and Michael out of their chairs as a wall of rain swept toward the house. Kate could hear Michael protesting, shouting pleas to the Countess.

They were dragged along candlelit hallways, the Secretary scrambling to keep up. Emma clawed at the hand gripping her arm, yelling at the creature to let go. The Screecher responded by throwing her over his shoulder, but Emma just continued to pound, albeit futilely, at its back. Kate knew there was only one place they could be heading.

They stopped at a set of double doors, and the Secretary pulled out a ring of keys.

"Wait—" Kate began, but the doors opened and they were thrown inside. The lock snapped into place behind them, and

Kate heard the Secretary's high-pitched giggle fading away down the hall.

The room was silent and utterly, completely dark. Outside, rain hammered on the roof.

Suddenly, there was a scrambling, a scuffling, someone grunting in pain. Emma had found Michael and thrown herself on him.

"Emma, stop it!" With difficulty, Kate pulled her sister away, getting an elbow in the cheek in the process.

"I hate you!" Emma yelled. "I wish you were dead! You're not my brother!"

"No!" Kate put her face against her sister's. Emma's cheek was wet with tears. "Don't ever say that! You hear me? Don't ever say that!"

Emma let herself go limp and Kate held her as she sobbed. Michael was sniffling on the floor. Kate knew she should go to him and comfort him, tell him she understood why he'd done it, but she couldn't bring herself to, not yet.

There was a thud a few feet away. Emma stopped crying. None of them moved. They stared into the dark, listening.

"Where are we?" Emma whispered.

In answer, the night sky ignited, and for a flickering instant, white light flashed across the room. Kate stifled a cry. Fifty children were standing there, staring at them. Kate could see the rows of beds, the shadows from the barred windows stretching across the floor. Then thunder shook the house, and once again, there was darkness.

A voice said, "Who's got the light?"

A scratch, the flare of a match, and then a lamp glowed at the back of the room.

"Give it here," the voice said, and the small globe of light passed from hand to hand, illuminating one pale face after another, till it stopped at the speaker.

"You," Emma said.

Stephen McClattery stepped toward them, bringing the lamp near their faces. He studied them for a long moment, then said, "Hold 'em."

A flowing mass of children swarmed around them.

"Wait!" Kate cried as her arms were pinned at her sides. "What're you doing?"

"He's with the Countess." Stephen pointed at Michael. "We seen him."

"So what?" Emma said, kicking at the children trying to hold her. "We're not!"

"He's your brother, ain't he? You're probably all in it together."

Kate saw that most of the children were young, no more than six or seven, their faces half savage with fear and excitement.

"He's a traitor," Stephen said. "He's helping her."

"No!" Kate said. "He made a mistake! That's all!"

"Still makes him a traitor. Quiet now. We gotta talk."

Turning away from Kate, he began whispering to four or five boys and girls, all about his age. Kate had been in enough orphanages to see children this way before. Left alone, they formed their own laws. Their own societies. The secret, she knew, was not to show fear. Show fear, and they'd tear you apart.

Stephen McClattery turned back around.

"We decided. We're gonna hang him."

"What?!"

Stephen nodded seriously. "That's what you do with traitors. I read it in a book."

Apparently, that was good enough for the other children. They started chanting, "Hang 'im! Hang 'im!"

"Somebody get a rope!" Stephen McClattery said.

"We ain't got no rope!" a voice called out.

"You could tear up some sheets," Emma said. "Then tie 'em all together!"

"Emma!"

Emma looked at Kate and shrugged, unconcerned.

"Thanks," Stephen McClattery said. "You three, tear them sheets."

Three boys stripped the sheets off a couple of beds and began trying to rip them into strips.

"You can't hang him!" Kate was still being held by half a dozen hands, and to talk to Stephen, she had to yell across the room. She was trying not to panic. She knew it would only feed their tempers. The mob had taken the children over. "He made a mistake! Everyone makes mistakes!"

"What about this?" A girl ran forward with a velvet rope she'd pulled off one of the curtains.

"Yeah, that'll work," Stephen said, and with surprising deftness, he quickly fashioned it into a noose. "Bring 'im here! And you three stop messin' with them sheets!"

Michael was carried forward so that he and Stephen stood in the middle of the crowd of children.

"Hey, wait . . ." Emma was starting to look nervous.

"You been found guilty fair and square of being a traitor," Stephen said. "You got any last words?"

Michael was crying. He mumbled something under his breath.

"What's that?"

Michael raised his head and looked at Kate and Emma. "I said . . . I'm sorry."

Michael's tears glistened in the lamplight, and it seemed to Kate that he was hardly aware of the other children or what was about to happen, or if he was aware, then he didn't care. All that mattered to him was that his sisters understood.

"Well, that's fine," Stephen McClattery said, "but rules is rules." When it came to executions, the boy was clearly all business. "You're a traitor and we gotta hang you." He looped the noose over Michael's head, and the cry went up a second time, "Hang 'im! Hang 'im!" The mob began to drag Michael away. Kate knew now that she'd have to fight. She'd have to fight Stephen McClattery and beat him. If she did that, the other children would fall in line. She was about to launch herself at him when a voice spoke—it was a voice she recognized.

"For the love of all that's— Nobody's getting hanged."

Stephen swung the lamp around, and Abraham limped into

the light. Behind him, Kate saw a sort of a door in the wall where none had been before.

"Clear off, you hooligans," he said, pushing through the children till he could take the noose from around Michael's neck. The children holding Kate and Emma melted away. "Hanging. That's what you're up to now, is it?" He cuffed Stephen lightly on the back of the head. "Where's your sense, boy?"

"He's a traitor," Stephen said. "They're probably all traitors."

"These two ain't. I promise you that." He gestured to Kate and Emma. "I saw 'em nabbed by the Screechers."

"Well, he is. We can't just let 'im go."

Abraham took the lamp and held it up to Michael's tear-stained face.

"That he is. But listen to me, all of you." Despite the muffling of the rain, Abraham kept his voice low. "These are bad times. Everyone's done things that want forgiving. But we start turning on each other, and she's won. What matters is we hold together. That's all we got in the end. Each other. Remember that."

No one spoke for a few moments. Kate saw Emma bend down and pick up something from the floor. Michael's glasses. They'd been knocked off in the scuffle. Emma turned them over in her hands, then silently held them out.

"Thanks," Michael said, choking a little.

The other children seemed to have forgotten Kate and her siblings. They were pressing around Abraham.

"What'd you bring us?"

"What you got, Abraham?"

Kate was amazed at how quickly the hysteria had left the

children. She had seen it happen before, with other groups of children, but never quite so suddenly.

"Everyone settle down," Abraham said. "I want to see Annie first."

A murmur passed through the crowd, and the little girl with pigtails who'd been dangled off the edge of the dam moved to the front. Abraham knelt down. He pulled a handmade doll out of his jacket. "I made this myself. I'd be happy if you'd take it."

The little girl accepted the doll and hugged it to her breast, not uttering a word.

Abraham produced a stack of letters. "Now, let's be quiet as I hand these out. Stephen and the others will help you young 'uns read 'em."

A reverent silence fell across the room. One by one, as Abraham whispered the names on the letters, the children stepped up, received the envelopes, and carried them back to their beds.

When he'd finished, Abraham came over to where Kate stood with Michael and Emma. "The witch don't know about the secret passageways in the house, so I try and sneak in least once a week. Bring food. Letters from their parents. I'm sorry about earlier, you girls getting nabbed and whatnot. I was just told to take a photo a' the boy holding that 'help me' sign. Didn't know it was some sort a' trap. Anyway, I saw them monsters drag you off and I figured you'd end up here. Seems I arrived in the nick a' time."

"Thank you," Kate said. "I don't know what would've happened."

He waved his hand dismissively. "They're good children. Just been scared for too long is all. They wouldn't a' really hung your brother . . . most likely. Now, you three best be coming with me. The Countess has something in mind for you, and I tremble thinking what it might be."

"But if you can just come and go," Emma asked, "why don't they all escape?"

Abraham gave a dry laugh. "That's where she's smart, the witch. Keeps everyone separate, children, mothers, fathers. Has them monsters a' hers guarding 'em all. These young 'uns know if they try and escape, their mothers and fathers will be put on the boat. Tortured. Worse, even."

Stephen stepped up and whispered something in Abraham's ear. He nodded.

"I need to check on one that's been sick. Then we go."

He followed Stephen to a bed a few yards away. Kate felt someone tug her hand. Annie was standing there, clutching her new doll. The little girl raised her arms. Kate understood at once. Most of the children here were younger than Emma. Besides that day at the dam, they probably hadn't seen their mothers in years. That made her the next closest thing. Kate picked the girl up, and Annie wrapped her thin arms around her neck.

"Kate," Emma said.

She turned. Twenty small children had gathered around. They were staring at Kate and Annie with eyes of deep longing. Kate felt her heart throb with pain and wished she could comfort them all.

Abraham approached with Stephen. "All right, then. Time to go. There's no telling when she'll send one of them ghouls to check on you."

Kate lowered Annie to the floor.

"You leavin' us?" Annie asked.

Without thinking, Kate said, "I'll come back; I promise."

"She don't mean it," Stephen McClattery said.

"Yes, she does!" Michael had spoken hotly, and everyone looked at him in surprise. "When my sister says something, she means it. She came for me, didn't she?" He looked at Kate and Emma. "If she says she'll come back, she will."

"That's right," Emma said. "And if any of you try and hang my brother again, you're gonna have to hang me first!" She nodded fiercely at Michael, and Kate saw it was forgiven.

"Quickly now," Abraham said, and he stepped into the passageway. Kate followed Emma and Michael through. She looked back at the ghostly faces of Annie and Stephen and the other children. Then Abraham closed the door with a soft click, and all was dark.

"Hold here a moment," Abraham whispered. And they heard him move off down the passage.

The air was musty and stale, and their shoulders pressed against each other in the tight space. Kate felt Michael shudder, and when he spoke, his voice was raw.

"I thought . . . I could do something myself. You've always taken care of us, Kate. I just thought, for once, I could . . ."

"It's okay."

"And I know Mom and Dad are coming back. I shouldn't have—"

"It's okay. Really."

"Yeah," Emma said. "Just don't be so stupid again."

And there, in the darkness, they sought each other's hands.

Abraham returned, bringing the smell of rain and mud on his clothes.

"It's clear. Now we can't risk a light, so the going'll be slow. The rain's a help, but be quiet as you can. All our lives depend on it."

He set off, Emma behind him, Michael following, and Kate bringing up the rear.

The passageway was only a couple of feet wide, and Abraham would whisper back warnings to duck or step over a board or about holes to avoid. Now and then slivers of light penetrated the walls. But for the most part, Kate could only just discern the dim outline of Michael's head. Abraham guided them, left, right, up a few stairs, down a couple. After ten minutes of winding through the maze-like corridors, he paused. It had grown lighter, and they could make out each other's features. Abraham put a finger to his lips, warning them to be even quieter.

It was a good thing he did, for when they turned the corner, the Countess was waiting for them. She was not in the passage-way itself. Rather, she was in one of the mansion's many sitting rooms, staring through an oval window that was set into the wall that separated her room from the passage. Emma couldn't help but emit a small gasp, and Abraham immediately clamped a hand over her mouth. But it was too late; the witch had noticed them.

Or had she? Seconds passed, and the Countess simply stood there, inches from the glass, calmly turning her head this way and that. Then Kate remembered: she'd been in that room. There was a mirror on the wall. Exactly where the Countess stood. And as Kate watched, the Countess touched a hand to her hair and, still giving no sign of having seen the children, turned and stepped away.

Abraham motioned the children to come along, and they were about to follow when someone in the Countess's room began talking.

"And what will milady do now, if her poor servant may inquire?" The gray-toothed Secretary was hunched at a drinks cart, pouring ice-cold vodka into a glass, the yellow bird perched atop his shoulder.

Across the room, the Countess reclined in a comfortable chair, her dainty feet resting on a stool.

"I will make a full report. I should have done so when the children appeared the first time."

"Yes, yes, of course, an indubitably intelligent course of action." Scraping low, the man handed her the glass.

The two-way mirror was on the wall directly opposite where the Countess was seated; this meant the children, clustered in the passageway, had a clear view of all that transpired. It was thrilling to be so close, the more so since Kate couldn't quite believe they were invisible. Each time the Countess's gaze drifted over the wall, Kate had to fight the urge to run. She was thankful for the enveloping thrum of the rain, certain that otherwise the Countess and her secretary would hear her heart hammering against her chest.

"What is it, you sniveling little rodent?" the Countess snapped. "I know you're thinking something."

Twisting his fingers, the man Cavendish bowed quickly three or four times. "Just . . . no, impossible, not my place to venture, no—"

"Your place is to do what I tell you, you gnat. Now, what is transpiring in that putrid brain of yours?"

Alone with her secretary, the Countess apparently felt no need to be charming or to act the part of the airy, gold-speckled teenager. She looked the same, certainly, but her manner, her voice, everything about her now spoke of power, malice, and a greedy, jackal-like hunger.

Cavendish sucked in his head like a turtle. He spoke in moist little gasps. "Yes, milady, and forgive my imbecility, I was just inquiring of myself what exactly the Countess would report? That she had one of the Books of Beginning and lost it?"

"That was beyond my power to control. You know that."

"Undeniable, yes, certainly undeniable, the Countess is innocent. And fortunately"—he corkscrewed two of his fingers and gave a ghoulish, insincere smile—"fortunately, our master is known for his understanding nature."

Their master? Kate was stunned. There was someone else?

Someone maybe worse than the Countess? How was that even possible? She looked over and saw Emma shake her head and mouth the word "great."

"You think I should not tell him," the Countess said slowly.

Cavendish took an eager step forward. "The missing book must be close, milady. You said so yourself earlier—very beautifully, one might add. And a person, even a person as dull as myself, can't help but conjecture how much better it would be to say, 'I have your prize, Master.' Not, 'I had it, then lost it. Oops!'"

Sipping her vodka, the Countess rested her head against the leather back of her chair. "You have a point, worm. Very well. I will wait."

The man bowed even lower, as if being called "worm" was the highest compliment. But he continued to study her from the tops of his small eyes.

"How is it," she said quietly, "that after all these thousands of years, three unremarkable children should just stumble on one of the Books of Beginning?"

"Chance, perhaps? Simple hazard?"

The Countess laughed scornfully. "There is no such thing as chance where magic is concerned. Those children are important somehow. In a way I do not fully understand."

Back in the passageway, Abraham plucked at Kate's sleeve, signaling they had to leave. But Kate shook her head. She and Michael and Emma were being discussed. She wanted to hear what was said.

The Countess finished her drink and held out the glass for Cavendish to refill. "And you've searched the cellar completely?

This chamber the boy spoke of, the underground study where they found the book, there's no trace of it?"

"None, milady. And no evidence of enchantments hiding such a space. This chamber, if the child was telling the truth, must have been created in the future. Does milady still believe the old man is behind this?"

"Of course," the Countess sneered, "who else could it be?" She tapped her fingernails against the glass, suddenly gleeful. "Imagine, once I bring our master the book, I shall be raised up higher than any other. I will rule at his side."

Cavendish dropped the carafe with a clatter onto the cart. The Countess looked up sharply. "Careful, toad!"

"Yes, yes, Countess. A million thousand pardons." He fiddled with the bottles pointlessly, knocking them against each other.

"You truly are a moron, you know that? When you have something to say, say it. Instead of blundering about like a drunken parlor maid."

The man turned. He was pulling on his fingers with such force that Kate thought he might yank them free of his hands. "It is just, milady, I worry for you, yes, I worry for you, I do."

She laughed. "For me? And why should you worry for me, you walking collection of dirt?"

He shuffled close to her chair, still twisting and wrenching his fingers, seemingly unable to look her in the face. "The Countess is so beautiful and so strong, and our master, terrible and awesome as he is, has been known to be . . . unpredictable."

The room became very still. The Countess stared at the sweating, twitchy man.

"You think he will deny me my reward?"

"No, no," he said, glancing up quickly. "I would never say that. Never. But . . ." He put his fingers in his mouth and bit them viciously.

"What would you have me do? Speak."

"It's just . . ." He inched closer. His voice was like the hiss of a snake. "The Countess is already so powerful that I wonder, once she has the book, who then would be more powerful? The Countess or—"

The Countess's hand shot out and seized the man by his stringy hair. The bird took off from his shoulder in alarm.

"Are you suggesting, you miserable creature, that once I am in possession of the book, I betray our sworn master and turn its power to my own purposes?"

"Milady, no! Never! You misunderstand—"

"Do I?" She gave his hair a terrific yank.

"Please, Mistress! I beg you! I never—never—"

She smiled then, beautiful and deadly. "Calm yourself, Mr. Cavendish. I know you only mean to protect me. And in any case"—she smoothed the man's greasy hair—"I do not yet possess the book, do I?"

In the damp and dark of the passageway, Kate felt a chill as she watched the man and woman look at each other and something pass between them.

Abraham pulled her sleeve again. Insistent. She nodded. Every moment they lingered was dangerous. She'd just started to turn when the Countess said:

"Did you notice the oldest one, the girl? The book has marked her."

Kate froze.

"I wonder," the Countess murmured, "is it possible. . . . No, it can't be. . . ."

The Secretary grinned horribly. "I know what milady is thinking. Impossible, and yet if it were true . . . Perhaps the Countess wishes to examine the child again? Before I entered, I took the liberty of dispatching one of the *morum cadi* to retrieve her. She should be here any moment."

Emma and Michael looked at Kate, their eyes wide with panic. They had to go—now. But before any of them could move, a scream ripped through the walls of the house.

They ran, no longer making any attempt at being quiet. They heard the shrill, raised voice of the Secretary, the far-off uproar in the children's room, the cries of the Screechers.

Very quickly, they reached what looked like a dead end. They could hear more Screechers outside, circling the house. Abraham was breathing heavily.

"I'll go first. You three wait till you hear me draw 'em off. Then run for the trees. Keep going as far and as fast as you can. Find someplace to hide tonight. Come morning, head south along the river. Watch the sky. Folks say the witch uses birds as spies. A day's walk and you'll reach the lake. Any boat should take you to Westport. I'm sorry I can't help more."

"You've done so much," Kate said. "Thank you."

"Tell me this," Abraham said, "is it true you're from the future?"

"Yes."

"And you're here to set things right?"

"What? No, we—we just came to get Michael."

"You promised them kids you'd come back."

"And I will. But I don't know how to help them."

For a moment, Abraham just stared at her. "Maybe not," he said finally. "But you heard the Countess. There's no such thing as chance when it comes to magic. Things happen for a reason. Including you being here. Now, enough talk."

Kate and Emma both hugged him. Michael hung back, still too ashamed, but Abraham put his hand on the boy's shoulder.

"You made a mistake, but you're a good lad, and your sisters here love you."

Michael nodded, swallowing thickly. Abraham grasped a handle protruding from the wall. Kate could just discern the outline of the door.

"Remember, run and don't look back." And he opened the door, letting in a blast of air and rain, and was gone.

Darkness again. They waited, listening to the cries outside.

Emma fidgeted. "So who do you think this master guy is?"

"I've got a few theories," Michael said.

"Like what?"

Michael paused, straightening his glasses. "I'm not quite ready to share them."

Emma gave an annoyed huff, but it was obvious she wasn't really annoyed, that she was glad things were back to how they used to be, with Michael driving her crazy. "I bet you that old man the Countess was talking about was Dr. Pym, though. You haven't seen him, Michael. He really is a wizard."

"Really?! Did he do any magic?"

"Well, me and Kate went to see him and he made a fire just like appear, didn't he, Kate? And I think he's got a magic pipe."

"What kind of pipe?"

"How should I know? The magic kind, dummy."

"I meant, the kind you smoke or the kind you blow into?"

"Duh, the kind you smoke. Does being in the past make everyone stupid?"

Kate kept her ear near the door so she could listen to the sounds outside. But it was hard to concentrate. Her mind kept going back to what the Countess had said.

Did you notice the oldest one, the girl? The book has marked her.

She thought about what had happened in the bedroom, when she and Emma had been looking through photos, how she'd put her hand on the page and then watched as blackness spread across the parchment and up into her fingers. What had it done to her?

"Kate . . ." Michael touched her arm. "I think Abraham's led them away."

There were shouts and commotion from the other side of the house.

Kate took hold of the handle. "I'll go first. Just keep running. No matter what."

After the Screecher sent by the Secretary failed to find Kate and her siblings, pandemonium erupted in the dormitory. Children ran about, shouting, jumping on one another's beds; a few of the younger ones began crying. Chaos reigned for several minutes. Then the door opened, and the Countess walked in. All became very still.

She waved her hand. Instantly, candles were burning along the walls. She smiled, and the children felt themselves pulled toward her.

"Where are they?" Her voice was comforting, sweet.

No one answered.

"I'm not going to hurt them. Goodness! I want to help them! They're in great danger. Please. Tell me where they went."

There was something so gentle in the way she spoke. The children would tell her everything, about Abraham, about the secret passages, about Kate and Michael and Emma. She was their friend.

"Where're who?"

The Countess looked at the boy who'd spoken. Stephen's jaw was set tight and his arms were crossed. She bent close, letting her perfume drift over him.

"The three who were brought here. Two girls and a boy. Oh, you're just being silly!" She brushed his hair back playfully. "I know you know who I mean."

"They ain't . . . they ain't here."

"Yes, my love, that much I put together myself! Now, where did they go?"

Stephen stared into the beautiful eyes. His fingers gripped his arms. He was fighting hard against the pull. She was the enemy.

Like Abraham said. He had to show the others how to resist her. He forced a shrug.

"Dunno. Just disappeared."

One of the children stifled a laugh. The Countess looked up, her eyes flashing.

"They disappeared?"

"Uh-huh. Like magic or something."

"Yeah," another child said. "And there was a bang!"

"And smoke," said a third. "With lightning!"

"Yeah! We had to jump out a' the way!"

"I see." She'd lost them. Somehow they'd found their strength in this boy.

The Secretary rushed in, panting and soaked, his hair webbed against his skull.

"Did you find them?" the Countess snapped.

He shook his head. "Just that crippled fool of a photographer. The lout was drunk again."

The Countess said: "Release the wolves."

The children gasped. Even the Secretary looked surprised.

"Milady"—he giggled breathlessly—"forgive me, those beasts are not easy to control. They've been starved. Wisely, of course. Makes for more eager hunters. But what's to stop them from tearing the children limb from limb?"

"I suppose that's a chance we'll have to take, isn't it?" She paused at the door and gestured toward Stephen. "Oh, and have that one taken to the boat."

◆ ◆ ◆

"I hate this!" Emma cried as she landed face-first in another puddle. "I hate stupid rain!"

Leaving the house, they'd sprinted the short distance to the
trees without seeing a single Screecher, but since then, the going
had been slow. The storm had turned the forest floor into a
swamp, and their feet kept slipping into puddles or sliding off
rain-slick leaves.

Michael had fallen once, and they'd wasted precious minutes
searching for his glasses. Emma had been particularly annoyed
after she'd reached her hand into a mucky, nasty, wormy hole and
the missing glasses turned out to be hanging from Michael's ear.

All three were soaking wet, extremely muddy, and tired.

As she and Michael helped Emma to her feet, Kate wondered
how far they had to go tonight. Where would be safe?

Things seemed truly dismal.

Then they heard the howl.

It wasn't a Screecher. But it came from the direction of the
house. In seconds, there was a chorus of savage cries. Just as
quickly, they died off.

Kate said, "They're coming."

The children ran like they'd never run before, ignoring the
heaviness in their legs, the pain in their sides. Soon, Emma had
pulled away. She disappeared through a tangle of bushes. As Kate
ducked under a branch, she heard her sister shriek. A second
later, she and Michael had pushed through the bushes, and Kate
saw for herself.

"No!"

They were on the edge of a cliff, looking out over a dark valley lit up by lightning flashes. It was hundreds of feet to the bottom and nothing but sheer rock walls in either direction. Kate cursed herself, remembering their first day in the orphanage and how they had gone to the waterfall and savored the dizzy, excited rush of watching the river plunge over the cliff. She should've realized where they were heading.

Another series of howls from the forest. Whatever was making that noise was getting closer.

"What're we gonna do?!" Emma cried.

"There!" Twenty yards away, a narrow path twisted down the face of the cliff. Kate had no idea if it went all the way down, but it was their only hope.

"Come on!"

The path was steep and slippery, never more than a couple feet wide and usually much less. It zigzagged back and forth, and the children clung to each other as their shoes slid in the mud and gusts of wind tried to pull them into the void. They descended thirty feet, fifty, seventy-five, the rain lashing their faces.

Bringing up the rear, Kate kept glancing over the side, hoping the valley floor would come into view. If only they could get to the bottom, they would have a chance. They could find a cave to hide in or—

"Kate!"

Emma had stopped and was pointing up the cliff. Kate looked upward as lightning forked across the sky, illuminating the outline of an enormous wolf poised at the top. The creature let loose a howl that echoed over the valley.

"Run!" she screamed.

Any caution that remained was cast away. They raced along the path, their feet miraculously finding the bits of firm earth amid the mud. Thirty more feet—fifty. Kate spared a glance skyward. A half dozen of the creatures were tearing down the path at breakneck speed, headlong and reckless. As Kate watched, the pack collided at a corner, there was a yelp, and one dark body dislodged from the mass.

"Get back!"

She grabbed Emma, and the two of them and Michael flattened themselves against the rock as the flailing, snarling creature fell past, inches away.

"Okay," she panted, her heart pounding in her throat, "we're okay."

"No," Michael said.

"Yes, we just have to hurry."

"No! Look!"

Kate peered around Emma to see where he was pointing, and her legs almost gave out. The path continued a few yards, then disappeared into space. Literally just stopped. She felt herself wanting to give up. To sit down and have it be done. But another, stronger voice spoke inside her and said it wasn't going to end this way. She wouldn't allow it. Squinting through the rain and darkness, she saw that the path did in fact continue, but twelve feet further on. She quickly weighed their options. The valley floor was finally visible, but it was still a hundred feet straight down. Retreat was hopeless. The wolves were on the path and getting closer with every second. There was no other choice.

"We have to jump!"

"Are you crazy?!" Michael yelled.

"It's the only way!"

Just then a wolf let out a long, heart-shuddering howl.

"Right," Michael said, and he turned, took three steps, and leapt into the darkness.

Kate and Emma held their breath as he hung in the air. Luckily, the other part of the path was lower, and he landed with a couple feet to spare, falling forward onto his hands and knees.

Then the lip of the path gave way.

Kate started to scream, but Michael was already scrambling to safety. Not wasting another moment, she turned to Emma. "You'll have to jump farther. You can do it."

"I know." Emma's eyes had a fierce, determined gleam. She crouched and took off running, kicking back flecks of mud as she threw herself into the air. Michael stood at the edge of the path, ready to catch her if she was short.

Emma landed on top of him.

Kate heard the thud of impact and Michael's "Oomph!" as they fell in a tangle. She couldn't help but be impressed. Unfortunately, the impact had caused another two feet of the path to crumble into space.

At the top of her vision, Kate sensed movement and without looking she dropped to the ground. A body passed over her, jaws snapping at the air where she'd been. There was a frenzied yelping as the wolf plunged over the side, unable to stop itself. Kate stood in time to see it disappearing into the darkness below. Looking up, she saw that the rest of the pack wasn't far behind. There was no time to wait.

She ran the few steps and leapt. But as she jumped, her foot slipped in the mud, and the moment she was airborne, she knew she wasn't going to make it. She stretched out her arms, but she could see Emma and Michael falling past her, screaming her name as they reached out their hands. It was just too far. But then, miraculously, an enormous gust of wind swept up the face of the cliff and pushed her forward. Her chest slammed into the path. The breath was knocked out of her. She scrabbled for a grip in the mud, but she was sliding backward, falling.

Then two pairs of hands were pulling her to safety.

A moment later, all three children were on their knees in the mud, holding each other, shaking with relief. Even with the rain and the wind, Kate would happily have stayed like that all night. But she knew they still weren't safe. The leap that had almost killed her would be nothing to a wolf. She pulled away and looked back up the cliff. The pack was rounding the last corner, close enough for the children to hear their harsh animal panting.

"If only I had a sword!" Michael said.

Kate seriously doubted that would've done much good, but now wasn't the time to argue. "Help me."

She started jumping up and down at the edge of the path. The ground was soft and unsupported and the rain had weakened it even further. Twice Kate slipped as earth fell away, but both times her brother and sister pulled her back. In seconds, the children had widened the gap from fifteen feet to eighteen to twenty until by the time the first wolf launched itself into the air, there was a twenty-five-foot chasm.

And perhaps it was fear, or exhaustion, or the knowledge that if the wolf did reach them, then further flight was pretty much pointless, but the children didn't run. They just stood there, rain-soaked and mud-splattered, watching the great beast fly toward them.

It's not enough, Kate thought. He's gonna make it.

The wolf crashed into the end of the path. The children fell back instinctively, but the animal didn't attack. Kate saw it hadn't actually made the jump. The lower half of its body was thrashing in the air as it clawed at the loose rocks and mud, its huge jaws snapping furiously. Then the creature lurched forward, heaving itself upward, its hind legs finding purchase. And just as the cry to run rose in Kate's throat, four feet of earth gave way, taking the wolf with it.

Kate exhaled, unaware till then that she'd been holding her breath. She squinted through the rain at the three remaining wolves. They were crowded at the end of the path, a growling, quivering mass. She could feel their hunger, but she knew they wouldn't chance the leap.

"What's a' matter, you big chickens!" Emma yelled. "Come and get us!"

The wolves spun about and raced up the path, disappearing into the darkness.

"Look at that!" Emma said, turning to Michael and Kate in triumph. "They're giving up."

"Unlikely," Michael said. "They're probably looking for another way down."

"Come on," Kate said.

It was only another sixty feet to the bottom, and they reached it quickly. The bodies of the wolves who'd fallen lay broken on the rocks. Kate looked up the cliff, but she couldn't see the rest of the pack.

She heard Emma saying that she bet Miss Crumley had planned all this, and Michael replying that he very much doubted that, and Emma saying something about Michael's head being shaped like a turnip.

She shut them out and tried to think. It was raining harder than ever. They were all exhausted. She had no idea how long it would take the wolves to find another way down; the question was, should they keep running, or did they immediately start looking for a place to hide?

"Kate . . ."

"Let me think."

"Kate." Emma tugged on her arm. Kate turned.

Thirty yards away, a dark shape was moving over the tops of the boulders.

"Run!"

They broke for the trees. A growl erupted behind them. They struggled up a small rise. Every second, Kate expected to feel the weight of the animal on her back. Keep going, she told herself, just keep going.

Glancing over her shoulder, she emerged from the trees to a clearing at the top of the hill and slammed into Michael and Emma, almost knocking them down.

"Don't stop! We—"

The words died in her throat. A wolf was crouched in front of them.

For a long moment, no one moved. The creature's gray fur was matted with rain; its mouth hung open, teeth bared in a hideous grin, as a low growl emanated from its gut. Emma and Michael were frozen. It was up to her to do something. What if she ran right at it? The beast wouldn't be expecting that. It might give her brother and sister time to get away. The fact that she wouldn't survive didn't faze her in the least. Readying herself, Kate saw another wolf step out of the rain, its head low, its eyes fixed and murderous. Then a sound at her back told her the first wolf had closed the circle. And she finally understood: there was nothing she could do. They were going to die here.

"Kate—" Emma said, her voice shaking.

"Hold hands," Kate said. They did, standing back to back in a circle. "Now close your eyes," Kate commanded. "Do it!"

Michael and Emma obeyed, but Kate kept her eyes wide open, watching the wolves circle. This was her responsibility. Her failure. She wouldn't spare herself seeing it through.

She locked eyes with the largest wolf, letting it know she wasn't afraid. She no longer felt the rain whipping at her face, the fatigue in her body. Her mother flashed through her mind. I'm sorry, Kate thought, I did everything I could.

The animal crouched low, gathering itself.

Kate squeezed Emma's and Michael's hands and whispered, "I love you," as the wolf launched itself into the air.

The animal's teeth never reached her.

There was the sound of fast, heavy footsteps, of something swinging through the rain. The wolf saw it coming and tried to change directions but was already committed. The object, a long gray blur, was in Kate's vision for an instant, then it struck the wolf in the head, close and loud enough for Kate to hear the creature's skull shatter.

Then a man was beside them. He was huge, a giant. His long dark hair obscured his face, and thick chains hung from either wrist. With fierce growls, the two remaining wolves threw themselves at the man. He caught one in midair and broke the creature's neck with a dull crack. The second fastened itself on the man's arm, sinking its fangs deep into his flesh. He wrenched the creature away and threw it as a normal person might a cat. It struck a boulder and fell to the ground, dazed. The man took two long strides, put his boot on the animal's neck, and stepped down. There was a thick crunch. The wolf lay still.

He walked back to the children. Michael and Emma had opened their eyes and were staring up at the man with wonder. He loomed over them, his face hidden in shadow, but even so, Kate recognized him. He was the man who'd attacked the Countess that day at the dam.

He said: "Come with me."

CHAPTER NINE
Gabriel

It went like this: Kate would pick out a tree or boulder and she'd tell herself, That far, I'll just go that far, and while she walked, she wouldn't allow herself to think about how wet and heavy her clothes were, how they chafed against her skin with every step, how the muscles in her legs had been replaced with so much un-responsive mud; she would only think, That far, I'll make it that far. Then, when she reached whatever rock or tree she'd picked out, she'd look forward, past the giant man, through the rain and the darkness, to single out another tree or rock, and do it all again.

She glanced at Michael. He had entered a state of numb, mindless plodding. His head had drooped to his chest, and water was sluicing off his nose as he put one wobbly foot in front of the other. But even so, he was doing better than Emma. She had actually fallen asleep while walking. The third time it happened—after she'd tripped and woken herself up with a "Huh? Who did that?"—the giant man had turned and scooped her into his arms. Kate had expected protests. Emma never let adults coddle her. But her sister had just curled up and gone to sleep.

That left Kate, exhausted as she was, to try and pay attention to where the man was leading them. She'd asked, of course, but the giant had merely grunted for Kate to be quiet, and she'd had to satisfy herself with what she could glean from their surroundings, which, considering the rain and the dark and the fact that one tree or rock looked pretty much like every other tree or rock, was not much. And so they marched on, along crooked, muddy, tree-choked paths, clambering over boulders, jumping across impromptu streams, steadily climbing and steadily climbing, till Kate decided that "wet" and "tired" were just different words for pain and she forgot about picking trees or rocks to mark her progress and just lowered her head and let herself be guided by the thud of the man's footsteps and the clinking of the chains that hung from his wrists.

And then suddenly, they stopped.

Kate raised her eyes. She saw the outline of a small cabin tucked into the hillside. The man pushed open the door and stepped inside, and Kate and Michael stumbled in after.

The air in the cabin was cold and musty. Clearly, no one had been there in a long while. But for the first time in what felt like forever, it was not raining on the children. They stood in almost total darkness, listening to the man move about. There was the rasp of a match, and he lit a lantern that hung from the center of the ceiling. Without a word, he turned and busied himself at the fireplace, giving Kate and Michael a chance to inspect their surroundings. There was a wide bed with a bearskin blanket on which Emma was already fast asleep, the stone fireplace where the man was piling up kindling, an old wooden table with stools and benches; the walls were covered with snowshoes, fishing rods, ice axes, bows and arrows, knives, a long spear, while from the ceiling hung a collection of traps, along with pots and pans of various shapes and sizes. The cabin was small, certainly, but well cared for, and everything one might need was close at hand. Soon, a bright, warm blaze had filled the room, and when Kate looked to Michael, she saw he'd climbed onto the bed beside Emma and was snoring lightly.

The man stepped up.

"Hang your clothes by the fire. And keep the curtains closed. The bed is yours."

Then he was gone.

With effort, Kate got her brother and sister to stand and take off their sopping wet shoes and clothes. Not bothering to open their eyes, Emma and Michael dropped everything in a puddle on the floor, pulled on the dry, knee-length shirts the man had laid out, then staggered back to bed and crawled under the covers. Kate placed their shoes on the hearth; the clothes she wrung out in a bucket, then draped over a rope she'd found and strung before the fire. She felt herself in some country past fatigue, as if she would never need sleep again, but pulling on the last dry shirt, she climbed into bed anyway, just to be next to her brother and sister. Where had the man gone? And who was he? Certainly, he was no friend of the Countess, but could they trust him? He was obviously extremely dangerous. She lay there, her thumb and forefinger making tiny worried circles on her mother's locket. She felt the heaviness of the bearskin blanket and how warm and dry the sheets were against her skin. The rain overhead sounded very far away. She resolved to stay awake till the man returned.

Her eyes snapped open. How long had she been asleep? It was still night, still raining. But the man was back. He was sitting on the stone hearth, sawing at the metal cuffs that bonded his wrists as the firelight played over the long scar running down his face. Now was the time to ask him who he was. Why he'd tried to kill the Countess. But Kate just lay there, listening to her brother and sister breathing, listening to the rain on the roof, the soft crackling of the fire, the steady back-and-forth of the saw cutting through metal. She was so tired. She would just close her eyes for a minute. Then she would talk to him.

Kate fell into a series of troubled dreams. In the last, she saw an underground city. It rose up in the hollowed-out heart of a great mountain, and the buildings were like none Kate had ever seen. They looked to have been sculpted straight out of the rock, as if the city had not been built so much as excavated. The effect was massive, brutal, and strangely beautiful. Suddenly, the ground began to shake and split apart. Buildings crumbled. Fires erupted. Then the earth seemed to swallow the city whole.

Kate woke, breathing hard, covered in sweat. The fire had

gone out. Daylight filtered through the curtains. The chains that had been attached to the man's wrists lay curled beside the hearth. She was alone. Emma's and Michael's clothes were gone from the line. She felt her own. They were dry. She dressed quickly and went outside.

It was a shock, stepping into the bright sunlight, and she blinked several times, shielding her eyes. The cabin was perched on the side of a mountain and looked out across the valley. It was a beautiful, cloudless morning. The air felt cool and clean. In fact, were it not for the evidence all around her—the still-muddy ground, the rain glistening on the treetops below, her torn and filthy clothes, the dried blood on her hands—she could almost believe that the night and everything that had happened—the storm, the wolves, the sudden appearance of the man—had been no more than a dream.

"Morning!"

Michael was sitting on a rock a few yards away, his notebook balanced on his knee. "Just bringing my journal up to date. Be done in a second."

Kate glanced around and saw neither Emma nor the man.

"Michael—"

"Just a second."

Kate closed her eyes and pressed her fingertips to her temples. She needed to think. Were they still going to Westport? If so, where were they now? How far had they walked during the night? The man could tell them. But where was he? And where was Emma? Kate was about to tell Michael to finish his journal later when her dream, which had faded on waking, suddenly returned—not in the way dreams usually returned, with vague, disjointed flashes, but exactly, vividly, so she was watching it all again, the underground city, the earth opening up—

"Kate?!"

Michael was shaking her. She blinked and realized she was lying on the ground. Had she fainted again?

"What happened? You—"

"I'm fine."

The Countess's words were ringing in her ears: *Did you notice the oldest one. . . . The book has marked her.* She was very clearly not fine. But she saw how Michael was staring at her and managed a smile.

"Just . . . stood up too fast. Where's Emma?"

"I don't know," he said, still watching her closely. "She was gone when I got up."

When Emma woke, it was just getting to be dawn. A dim gray light had crept into the cabin. Kate and Michael were still asleep. The man was stomping out the fire, black fossils of logs crumbling as ash billowed around his foot. His arm was bandaged where the wolf had bitten him. She watched as he pulled on a shirt, took a knife, bow, and small quiver from the wall, and—throwing a glance in her direction—left without a word.

Immediately, Emma got up, dressed, and hurried outside. A heavy morning mist hung over the valley, and she was in time to see the man's large form disappearing into the gray. She padded silently after him.

Why she was following the man, Emma couldn't have said. As a rule, she didn't find adults very interesting. In her experience, they were either to be put up with or openly disobeyed. Abraham was all right, she guessed, and Dr. Pym had been interesting, being a wizard and all. But until this man had appeared, there'd never been an adult she'd actually felt drawn to.

Emma ducked behind a boulder as the man stopped. He seemed to be listening to something in the fog.

A memory was coming back to her. It was from a few years earlier. A rich old man had paid for all the kids in their orphanage to be taken to the zoo. Emma had figured the guy was dying and trying to do something nice so he'd get into heaven. Whatever the reason, that trip to the zoo was easily the greatest day of her life. There were pandas and jaguars and long-necked giraffes and spotted monkeys that whooped and chattered as they fell through the trees; crocodiles from the Nile that people used to worship; snow leopards from the Himalaya; emerald-green snakes that could swallow a man whole. Everywhere you turned, there was more to see. But the animal that caught her attention, the one that held her in quiet rapt amazement, was a lion. He was enormous, twice the size of any of the other lions. His fur was a heavy, brownish gold, his face scarred from many battles, and his eyes the deepest, darkest black Emma had ever seen. Clinging to the outer bars of the cage, she had sensed the power and intelligence in him, and further, beneath the stillness, a pure animal violence waiting to erupt.

Something about this man reminded her of the lion.

She watched as he left the path and melted down into the

mist. She waited a moment, then followed. The earth was wet and slippery, and as she braced herself against trees, cascades of raindrops showered onto her head and shoulders. She entered a glade and paused. The man was nowhere to be seen.

As she pondered which direction to go, there was movement, and a stag stepped out of the trees. It was tall and strong, with great swept-up antlers. Hidden by branches, Emma held her breath, awed by the beauty of the animal. It stretched out its neck and nibbled at a bush.

She wished Kate and Michael were here. Kate especially. Michael would probably have ruined it by saying something stupid about dwarves.

The stag suddenly raised up, its whole body taut. It turned to bolt, but just then the man flew out of the mist and landed on the deer's back, driving it to earth. His knife flashed, and in a second the animal's throat was slit.

Emma gasped, stunned by the speed and ferocity of the act. She watched as the man knelt and placed a hand on the animal's head. She could see his lips moving, whispering. Then he looked up; his eyes met hers.

She knew he meant her to approach.

Her legs shaking, Emma walked over. Steam was rising from the cut in the animal's neck, and the smell of blood was strong in the air. She wasn't scared. Too much had happened in the last few days for her to be scared now. But there was something so naked about the scene, about the man and the stag and the kill in the hushed wood; it made her heart tremble.

She stopped beside the body. The man's eyes had not left her.

"Do not be frightened."

Emma wanted to tell him she wasn't. But she found she couldn't speak.

The man's large hand still rested on the deer's head. "The wolves last night were evil. I felt no regret in killing them." His voice was low and strong. "But to kill a creature such as this is a sacred thing. It must only be done when there is true necessity. And you must ask pardon of the spirit."

He looked at her for understanding, and Emma nodded, reminded again of the deep, dark eyes of the lion.

The man cut into the stag's abdomen and began to clean it. He was expert, and did it quickly and without waste. Emma felt queasy watching him remove its organs and place them in a lined leather bag, but she didn't turn away. She told herself if Michael were here, he would be throwing up nonstop, and that made her feel better.

"Last night, with the wolves, you were scared?"

Emma considered lying, but then said, "Yes."

"You did not show it." Emma thought she heard his approval, and warmth exploded in her chest.

The man said, "You are not from Cambridge Falls."

It wasn't a question, but he expected her to respond.

"No. We're from . . . well, we're kind of from, you know, the future." She was feeling easier now. "See, we found this magic book, and if you put a photo in it, you go to wherever the photo was taken, right? And that's what we did, we put the photo in the book, and so, we're here."

The man had stopped what he was doing and was staring at

her. In a flash, Emma knew two things. The first was why she'd followed him. It was because the night before, as he'd carried her through the rain, she'd felt safer than she had in her entire life. The second thing she knew was that suddenly—the way he was looking at her, the blood on his hands, the knife, the two of them alone in the woods—she did not feel safe at all.

"Sorry," she said quietly. "I could've told that better."

She fought the urge to run. She forced herself to stand there, staring into his eyes across the still-warm body of the stag. The moment passed. Nodding slowly, the man wiped the blade of his knife on the animal's hide, then replaced it in its sheath.

"My name is Gabriel."

"I'm Emma."

He stood, lifting the deer onto his shoulder. "Let us return. Your brother and sister will be awake. We have much to talk about."

The first thing Kate saw was the man coming around the bend of the path with a body over his shoulder.

Oh no, she thought.

Then Emma appeared, trotting beside him. She smiled and waved.

As the man went to hang up the stag in a shed attached to the cabin, Emma excitedly told Kate and Michael everything that had happened, that the man's name was Gabriel, about him killing the stag, how if Michael had been there, he would've thrown up—

"Hey!"

"Sorry," Emma said. "But you would've."

"You shouldn't have gone off," Kate said. "It's dangerous."

Emma nodded and tried her best to look remorseful.

"What did you tell him about us?"

"Oh, you know . . . that we were from the future and . . . about the book."

Kate noticed Emma shifting about nervously.

"What is it?"

"Nothing. Just when I told him about the book. He acted kinda weird."

"Weird how?"

"Oh, you know." Emma kicked at the mud and shrugged. "Like he was thinking about killing me or something."

"What?!"

Just then the man returned and called them to breakfast.

They ate at the wooden table in the cabin. The man, or Gabriel, since that was how Emma at least had begun to think of him, had changed his shirt and washed the blood from his hands in the stream that ran behind the cabin. He told them they couldn't risk a fire during the day. The Screechers would be abroad in the valley, searching for them, and would see the smoke. For breakfast, they would have to make do with bread and honey and the berries he and Emma had picked on their way back to the cabin.

Kate and Emma hadn't had a full meal since breakfast the morning they'd gone into the past, and Michael's meals with the

Countess, while lavish, had been magical concoctions where you gorged yourself, then felt ravenous ten minutes later. But still, it was only when the man had laid the food on the table that the children realized how hungry they were. Within moments, they were cramming huge, honey-globbed chunks of bread into their mouths, followed by handfuls of berries that exploded between their teeth. At one point, Gabriel brought over a pitcher of milk, which he poured into four cups. Michael reached for his, slurped half of it in a single gulp, then turned and sprayed it across the cabin.

The man looked unconcerned. "Goat's milk," he said. "Sour if you're not used to it. Drink; it's good for you." And to Michael's dismay, the man refilled his cup.

Emma swallowed a large mouthful and did her best not to wince. "It's great," she said, forcing a smile. "I love it."

Though she ate as greedily as her brother and sister, Kate kept one eye on their host. He was sitting across from them, taking up an entire side of the table, and seemed very intent on his meal. Finally, the man licked the last dabs of honey from his fingers, drank off his milk, and, running the back of his hand across his mouth, sighed.

"Now," he said, "tell me everything."

Normally, Kate would've resisted such a command, her natural impulse being to reveal as little about herself and her siblings as possible. But as the man turned his gaze upon her, Kate felt what Emma had felt earlier, that something about him demanded the truth.

So, once again, she told their story: how their parents had

disappeared, how the three of them had been moved from orphanage to orphanage, how they'd finally been sent here, to Cambridge Falls.

"And the Cambridge Falls of your time," the man said, "what is it like?"

Kate described a bleak wasteland where the trees had vanished and the people were frightened and unfriendly. She said how there was no dam stopping up the river and the water ran down the gorge and plunged over the cliffs. She said the only animals were the wolves that prowled the night. She said there were no children.

"What of the witch?" The man's voice was even, but they could see the hatred in his dark eyes. "Is she still there?"

Kate shook her head. The first they'd learned of the Countess, or her Screechers, was when they'd found the book and traveled into the past.

"Tell me about this book."

With Emma and Michael now starting to chime in, she told about exploring the house, about the door in the wine cellar that led to the underground room, about Michael coming upon the book.

"We thought maybe it was Dr. Pym's study or something," Emma said.

"Dr. Pym?"

"Yeah. He runs the orphanage. Supposedly he's a wizard. Though all we've seen him do is start a fire."

"Your Dr. Pym," Gabriel said, "he is an old man with great white eyebrows?"

"Yeah!" Emma exclaimed. "You know him?"

The man ignored her question. "Finish your story."

So Kate told about going into the past, about watching him try to assassinate the Countess, how Michael was left behind, how she and Emma got another photo from Abraham so they could rescue him.

"Then we went back into the past—"

"You left something out."

"No, I didn't."

"You're lying."

"She's not," Emma said. "I was there. That's what happened."

"Then there is something she hasn't told you."

Kate saw Emma look at her, confused, questioning. She had wanted to skip this part; it scared her to think about it and she didn't want to share that fear with Michael and Emma. But the man was giving her no choice. So, her heart racing, Kate told about putting her hand on the blank page of the book, about the visions she'd seen, about the blackness that had seeped into her fingers.

Afterward, Emma and Michael stared at her, their mouths literally hanging open.

"You saw dragons?!" Michael gasped. "Fighting?!"

"What do you think that black stuff was?" Emma asked. "Maybe it was ink, huh? Like magic ink? And why didn't you tell us?"

Kate started to explain. She didn't understand what it meant. She didn't want them to worry—

But the man interrupted and told her to continue. He was looking at her more closely than ever.

Kate felt Michael tense as she arrived at their capture by the Secretary and his own betrayal, and though for his sake she glossed over it as best she could, once again the man pounced.

"You helped the witch to lure and trap your sisters?"

Kate saw Michael open his mouth. She could see the arguments forming on his lips, the explanations why at that time turning over his sisters had been a reasonable course of action. Then he sighed and looked down at the table.

". . . Yes."

A sound, almost like a growl, escaped from the man.

"We've forgiven him," Kate said quickly.

She went on, telling how the Countess had taken the book only to have it disappear in front of their eyes, how she'd locked them in with the other children, how Abraham had smuggled them out through secret passages. She told about running through the forest and hearing the howl of the first wolf.

And there she stopped. He knew the rest.

The man picked up a crust of bread and dunked it in the honey jar.

Kate felt drained. Telling the story had been difficult. She looked across at the man. He was chewing, pondering what he'd heard. Her gaze traveled to his scar. It started an inch from his left eye and curved crookedly down to his jaw. It gave his face a terrifying aspect. But even so, it occurred to Kate that he was broodingly handsome. Her face flushed hot, and she stared into her lap.

What was wrong with her? Here they were, trapped in the past, pursued by who knew how many of those awful Screechers; what was she doing thinking about how good-looking this man was?

"So, will you tell us your story, then?" Emma asked. "Please?"

Kate and Michael gaped.

"What?" Emma said.

"You said 'please,' " Michael said.

"So?"

"You never say 'please.' "

"Yes, I do."

"No," Kate said, "you don't."

"I didn't think she knew what it meant," Michael said.

"Oh, shut up," Emma muttered.

"Very well," the man said, the rumble of his voice silencing them. "You have told the truth. You deserve the same in return. What is it you wish to know?"

Kate thought their first priority should be finding out who this man really was.

"What's your name?"

"Gabriel Kitigna Tessouat."

Michael giggled. "Really?"

Gabriel looked at him.

"Because it's a very nice name," Michael added quickly.

Kate asked if the man was from Cambridge Falls.

He shook his head. "For centuries, there were two human communities in these mountains. Cambridge Falls. And my people. The way it is handed down, one day a magician came to our village. He told us how, in every land, the magical world was withdrawing. He said the rest of the world would no longer be able to see us. They would forget we had ever existed. We and the people of Cambridge Falls were given a choice. Resettlement, somewhere out in the normal world, or we could stay in our mountains and be hidden for all time. We both chose the latter."

He paused to refill his milk, and Emma leaned over, whispering to Kate and Michael, "I bet that magician was Dr. Pym, huh? That's how he knew about him having white hair and all."

Kate shushed her. She was thinking how something about the man had hinted of another, older world. Now she understood why. She asked how he'd come to be there that day at the dam.

Gabriel said that he periodically came to Cambridge Falls to spy on the Countess. He'd seen the witch and her secretary leave the mansion and, curious, he had killed a Screecher, dressed in its clothes, and followed them to the dam. Once there, he saw the Countess dangling a child off the edge. Before he knew what was happening, he was striding toward her with his sword raised to strike.

"And then she cast that spell on you," Emma said. "Otherwise, you'd have killed her for sure. I know it."

"When I awoke, I was in a cell," the man said. His face grew dark remembering. "There was no light, and at first I did not know where I was; then I felt everything move and heard the lapping of water."

"The boat!" Emma cried. "Abraham told us about it! He said

it's a prison where they torture people. Do experiments on 'em and stuff!"

"It is not a prison," said Gabriel. "It is a cage. For a monster."

It seemed to grow very still in the cabin.

"The first thing I did was to call out and see if I was alone. No one answered. But I thought I heard something below. The stench in that place, so thick with death!" He closed his eyes, as if waiting for the smell to clear. After a few seconds, he went on. "The floor was an iron grid, and I could see that a large cage ran below all the cells on my level. I called again. Again, no answer. I became very quiet. Then I heard it, deep in the blackness: raspy breathing, the clicking of claws, and a faint whispering voice, promising itself, 'Soon . . . soon . . .' And I knew then what the creature below me knew. I was not a prisoner. I was food."

If it had been quiet before, it was nothing compared to when the man finished speaking.

Finally, Emma said, almost hopefully, "Maybe it was a Screecher."

"No. This was something else."

"But why would the Countess keep it on a boat, whatever it was? Why not keep it under the mansion?" Kate asked.

The man shrugged.

"I bet it's hydrophobic," said Michael.

Kate asked him to explain. Michael coughed and pushed his glasses up his nose. Emma groaned. That was the signal he was going to tell them something really boring he'd read in a book.

"In stories, it's not uncommon for witches and evil wizards

to keep a monster around. Kind of like a weapon of last resort. Of course, dwarves never did that sort of thing. They were too honorable—"

"Michael—"

"Right, well, the thing about having a monster around, whether it's a werewolf or a dragon or a mud troll or whatever, lots of times it ends up attacking its master. So people build in all these protections and safeguards. I was thinking if this monster is afraid of water—that's what 'hydrophobic' means—"

"That's what 'hydrophobic' means," mimicked Emma under her breath.

Michael ignored her. "The Countess could control it by keeping it on the boat. Then if she needs it, she just has it brought ashore."

Gabriel nodded. "You are probably right."

"Really?" Emma said, unable to hide her annoyance. "Are you sure?"

"But how did you escape?" Kate asked.

"The cage has not been built that can hold me."

He said it as if no further explanation was necessary. And looking at him, Kate agreed.

"So are you gonna try and kill the Countess again?" Emma asked. "We can help. We'd love to kill her!"

"No," he said. "I will return to my village. I must tell them what you have said. The things that will happen to our forests. And our wisewoman must be consulted about this book the witch desires. She will know what it is."

"What's a wisewoman?" Emma asked.

"It's a woman that does magic," Michael said.

"I wasn't asking you," Emma growled.

"He is right," Gabriel said.

Emma glared at Michael.

Kate was quiet. An idea had come to her. She held it carefully in her mind, afraid it might slip away. Now she spoke:

"Take us with you."

The man shook his head. "I will have to move quickly, and the path I will take is dangerous. You will be safer here. With the stag I killed, there is food enough. The stream behind the cabin is safe to drink. Wait till night to light a fire. As soon as I can, I will send someone to look after you."

"But—" Kate said.

"We—" Emma said.

"No!" And he slammed his huge hand flat on the table, rattling the plates and cups and ending the discussion. He stood and took a brass telescope from the wall, saying that there was a ridge above the cabin from which he could see the entire valley. He would make sure there were no Screechers nearby. Then he must leave.

The moment the door shut, Emma turned to Michael.

"It's your fault he won't take us."

"What?"

"He hates know-it-alls. He told me this morning after he killed that deer. He said, 'I really hate know-it-alls.' "

"Right, I'm sure he said that."

"Quiet!" Kate hissed. "We have to make him take us. He said this wisewoman will know about the book. Maybe she even knows where it is. We've gotta find it before the Countess does. That's the only way we're ever going to get home." Kate paused. She'd just had a horrible thought. "Emma, you still have the photo, right? The one to get us back?"

For several stomach-churning moments, they watched Emma dig in her pockets.

Finally, she pulled out the photo. It was creased down the center and bent at one corner, and a bit of pink gum was stuck to the back, but there was Kate, sitting in their bedroom, looking out at them from the future.

The children released a silent, collective sigh.

"Emma," Kate said gently, "maybe I should hold on to it."

"Yes, please," Michael muttered.

"Fine." Emma pulled off the gum and handed her sister the photo. Smoothing it out as much as possible, Kate tucked it into the inner pocket of her jacket.

"Returning to the matter at hand," Michael said, "how're we gonna get him to take us?"

As it turned out, this particular problem solved itself, for just then they heard pounding footsteps, the door slammed open, and Gabriel rushed in and said, "We're leaving. Now."

Before the children could even begin to wonder what had changed his mind, the cry of a Screecher echoed up the valley.

"Twenty of them," Gabriel said as he took down a long, canvas-wrapped object that had been tucked among the rafters. "They will be here in three minutes."

"What're we going to do?" Michael asked. "How're we going to get out?"

"We'll fight our way out," Emma said, her voice full of passionate anger. "Won't we, Gabriel?"

But he had gone to the fireplace, and now he put his hand against a stone and pushed. Very slowly, with a rough rock-on-rock scraping, the entire hearth swiveled, exposing a dark passage leading straight back into the mountain.

"This way," he said.

CHAPTER TEN
The Maze

Once in the passageway, the man ordered Kate, Michael, and Emma to stay exactly where they were. Then he pushed the hearth back into place with a dull *thrudd*. The children stood there in the darkness, breathing stale air, listening to Gabriel move about. He struck a match and used it to light two battered gas lanterns that had been hanging on the wall. He gave one to Kate.

"Where are we?" she asked.

With the shadows from the lamp playing over his scar, Gabriel looked more fearsome than ever.

"We are in the place where you are quiet and do as I say. Come."

He turned and headed down the passage.

They arrived at a set of jagged stairs, at the bottom of which was an iron door with a series of bolts and locks. Gabriel opened it, ushered the children through, and then closed and locked the door behind them. They were now in a different tunnel. It was wide and had rough-looking walls. Two iron rails ran down the center of the floor.

After they'd been walking for perhaps fifteen minutes, Kate ventured again, "So really, where are we?"

For a moment, she thought the man simply wasn't going to answer. Then he said, "One of the old mining tunnels used by the town. It will lead us through the mountain to the valley where my village lies."

They kept on, Gabriel and Emma in front (the tunnel was wide enough to walk two abreast) and Kate and Michael following. Back in the cabin, when she'd told her brother and sister her plan for getting them home, Kate had tried to sound confident. But in her heart, she suspected that even if Gabriel's wisewoman could tell them something useful, the chances of the three of them finding the book before the Countess and all her Screechers were slim indeed.

As they walked, Gabriel surprised Kate by beginning to speak. He told them about the mountains, how they were full of deep, old magic and as such had to be respected. He said that the men of Cambridge Falls had always known there were places one did not dig, things one did not dare disturb. Such as the *hannudin*— hope killers, they were called—half-alive ghouls who came up behind you in the darkness and whispered that all the worst thoughts you ever had were true: your friends were disloyal, your wife did not love you, your children would grow to hate your name. Men would blow out their lamps and sit down in the darkness to be found months or years later, having starved to death on the spot. There were the *salmac-tar*, an ancient race, little more than beasts, who had supposedly given birth to goblins ages ago and lived down deep below the roots of the mountains. They had no eyes but huge, bat-like ears, and they moved around making clicking noises, listening to the sounds echo off the rock walls, their razor-sharp teeth and claws able to cut through iron and bone.

"But even such creatures," Gabriel said, "are part of the balance. It was different when the witch came; everything changed."

He fell silent, and for a while there was only the crunch of their footsteps along the gravel floor. Kate found herself thinking about the twenty *morum cadi* the man had seen in the valley. She imagined them tearing apart the cabin, finding the secret door behind the hearth, then pouring one after another into the tunnel, their yellow eyes scouring the darkness. . . .

She knew this kind of thinking wasn't helpful, but she couldn't stop herself. What finally brought her back was Gabriel; he was speaking again, describing something as a pair of invisible hands reaching into your chest and crushing your heart and lungs. He was describing, Kate realized, the shriek of a Screecher.

"But it is an illusion," he said. "The pain comes entirely from your mind."

"What?!" The suddenness of her anger surprised her. "You're saying we imagined it?! That all those kids at the dam imagined it?!"

"I did not say that," the man corrected. "The scream creates panic and fear in your mind. So great is the fear that your body begins to shut down. That is the pain you feel. It is real, but it comes from your mind."

"So how do you stop it?" Michael asked.

"By killing Screechers," Emma said. "Obviously."

"Accept the scream has no physical power to hurt you," Gabriel explained. "Then learn to manage your fear. That is the only way." He added, "Besides killing them."

Kate thought of telling the man that it was probably a lot easier to "manage your fear" when you were a sword-wielding, wolf-killing giant, but Michael was already scribbling in his journal, murmuring, "Manage . . . fear," and she let it go. Instead, she asked the question that had been troubling her since the night before:

"Do you know if there's someone else? Besides the Countess. We heard her say something about her master."

"That's right," Michael said. "She and the Secretary, they both said it. I have it in my notes."

Gabriel shook his head. "I have not heard of any master. We will ask the wisewoman. It is possible she—"

He stopped and turned, staring back down the passage. Everything about him was alert and tingling. Kate peered into the darkness, but the tunnel was as silent and still as a tomb.

"Maybe it's one of those goblin-bat things," Michael whispered.

"Quiet." Gabriel handed his lantern to Emma and unwrapped the length of canvas. It was not, as Kate had suspected, a sword. What appeared was more like an extremely large machete. The blade was slender near the handle, then expanded as it lengthened so that the end was very wide indeed. It was made of some dark metal, and the edge gleamed in the lamplight.

Gabriel took a step forward.

Still, nothing moved.

Kate opened her mouth to ask what he thought he'd heard. Just as she did, the Screecher materialized out of the darkness. It made no sound at all but charged toward them, sword raised, yellow eyes glowing. Later, Kate would reflect that this was what had been most terrifying, for as awful as their screams were, at least they gave you time to run. Now, already, it was too late. She could only stand there and await the blow.

There was a loud, reverberating clang as Gabriel's blade met the other's, and the creature's sword shattered. A moment later, the two halves of its body lay on the floor, hissing, an evil-smelling smoke rising from its corpse. Kate looked at Gabriel. His blade was smoking as well. He had sliced clean through the Screecher, sword, body, and all.

He said, "Run."

They obeyed, running as they never had before. Through winding corridors, up stairs, down stairs, around blind corners, Gabriel always urging them faster and faster. The tunnel kept splitting, but he seemed to know where he was going, "Left . . . right . . . that passage there, go!" It wasn't long before they heard the first scream. More soon joined it, the inhuman shrieking billowing down the narrow tunnels. Kate felt weakness sweep through her, and she almost stumbled. She glanced at Michael and Emma and saw they were struggling as well. She tried telling herself the pain was only in her mind, that the screams couldn't hurt her, but it made no difference. She still felt as if she was running uphill with a stone upon her back.

And all the time, the screaming drew closer.

They emerged suddenly from one of the tunnels and found themselves at the edge of a huge underground chasm. They could see neither the ceiling nor the bottom—nor even the other side. A rope bridge extended out into the darkness and disappeared. The shrieking in the tunnels was louder than ever. The horde would be on them in moments.

"Go," Gabriel commanded. "I will hold them as long as I can. Follow the tunnel at the other end of the bridge. You will come to a chamber. Take the second passage to the left. Keep going. Always choosing the second left. Once outside, you'll find a trail that leads to my village. Stray at all, and you will be lost forever. Go now. I will catch up."

"But—" Emma protested.

"Go! There's no time!"

"Come on!" Kate seized Emma's hand and pulled her onto the bridge. Michael was already running ahead. The bridge swung beneath them as their feet pounded on the wooden slats. Halfway across, Kate felt an icy draft rise up out of the darkness. The air had a cold, ancient dampness that made her skin crawl.

"Look!" Emma yelled.

Kate turned. Two Screechers had emerged from the tunnel behind them. As they charged, Gabriel moved forward to meet them. Blades flashed and rang. Gabriel ducked a blow, grabbed one of the creatures, and hurled it into the abyss. Its scream was swallowed by the blackness.

"Come on!" Kate cried, pulling at her sister's hand. They ran the last twenty yards to where Michael was waiting. It was now too dark to see Gabriel on the other side. But more Screechers were apparently pouring out of the tunnel, as there were more cries and the clang of metal against metal was constant and furious. A deadly battle was taking place in utter darkness.

"We can't leave him!" Emma cried, her eyes wild with desperation. "We have to do something!"

"There's nothing we can do!" Kate said. "And he told us to go on, remember?"

"The entrance is right here!" Michael called.

Half dragging Emma, Kate led them down the passageway. Soon, the sounds of the battle had faded, and after a minute of hard running, they came to the chamber Gabriel had told them about. It was a large, circular, high-ceilinged room, with six identical doorways.

"We shouldn't have left him!" Emma had pulled free from Kate, and there were tears of frustration and shame in her eyes. "He helped us, and we ran away like a bunch of cowards!"

"We didn't have a choice!"

"That's the doorway we want." Michael pointed. "Second on the left."

"Can we at least wait?" Emma pleaded. "Just for a second to see if he comes. Please, Kate. Just for a second."

Kate looked at the tears running down her sister's cheeks. She knew she should say no. They needed to put as much space between themselves and the Screechers as possible. She sighed. "Just for a second."

Watching Emma turn and stare down the dark passageway, Kate envied her. Emma lived at the furthest reaches of her feelings. She loved and she hated and she didn't constantly question the thousand possible consequences of every action. Kate knew if she let her, she'd be back in an instant to help Gabriel, even if it meant certain death.

Michael came up and coughed discreetly.

"You need to get better about saying no."

"Okay, Michael."

"I'm just saying because—"

Kate gave him a look, and he evidently got the message because he stepped away, murmuring something about the craftsmanship in the room being of a different level than the rest of the mine and he was going to examine this cornering over here. . . .

Kate decided they would wait another thirty seconds. Then she would make Emma come away, even if she had to drag her. Her gaze happened down one of the dark passages to her right.

The vision came without warning.

She saw a room lit with candles. Two figures sat at a wooden table. One was a man with long ginger hair, dressed in a dark cloak. The other was in shadow. A package wrapped in linen sat on the table between them. Kate knew it was the book.

From a long way off, Kate heard Michael telling Emma it really was time to go.

Kate took a step closer to the doorway, and the vision became stronger. She could hear that a deal was being struck. The shadowy figure was agreeing that he and his people would hide and protect the book.

In a voice like granite, he said, "We will build a vault."

Before she knew what she was doing, Kate shouted, "Follow me!" and sprinted down the passage.

A voice in her head screamed in protest. She was disobeying Gabriel's warning! They would all be lost forever! She had to stop, go back. . . .

But a stronger voice was saying that the book was out there, calling to her. And if she hesitated, if she paused to explain her vision to Michael and Emma, she would lose the connection, lose the book. . . .

So she ran, and from behind she heard shouts to stop, to wait, and then the sound of running feet.

She came to another room, identical to the first and with six more doors. She waited till the footsteps and cries of "Kate! Stop!" had almost reached her before plunging into another passage. Somehow she knew exactly where to go. She ran for five minutes, ten, fifteen, through a dozen identical rooms with identical doorways, each time pausing long enough for the footsteps behind her to almost catch up before diving through another door, trusting that her brother and sister could follow the glow of her lantern.

As she ran, she continued to have visions. She watched the vault taking shape deep below the mountain; she watched the ginger-haired man, the book open before him, moving his fingers over the blank pages so that words and images would appear and fade; she watched, finally, as he stepped into the finished vault and placed the book on a pedestal in the center. . . .

Kate stopped. Her chest was heaving. The passage had ended

abruptly in a rock wall. This wasn't right. She must've taken a wrong turn somewhere. But how was that possible?

A hand seized her arm. Michael was bent over, gasping.

"Michael! This is it! I can—"

Michael shook his head. ". . . Emma . . ."

"Emma? What do you—"

"I thought she was following, but she . . . I had to . . . either go back . . . but you wouldn't stop. . . ." He lowered his head, still trying to get his breath.

There was no other light coming down the tunnel. No sound of footsteps.

"She must've gone," Michael panted, "to . . . help Gabriel."

All thoughts of the book were swept from Kate's mind.

"We have to go back."

"How? It's . . . a maze! Didn't you see?! Every room's the same! That's why Gabriel warned us! We'll never find our way back!"

"We have to! We—"

"Kate!"

She turned. A line of black had appeared in the middle of the wall. The rock was splitting open. A wind swept through, and the flame in her lantern fluttered and went out.

A voice like iron spoke in the darkness:

"Hold them."

CHAPTER ELEVEN
The Prisoner in Cell 47

Gabriel stood with his back to the swinging bridge, his chest heaving, the haft of his falchion slippery with sweat. He had half a dozen cuts on his arms and a deep slash in his side. The swords of the *morum cadi* were poisoned. Any one of his wounds had the power to kill him. But Gabriel wasn't thinking about that.

He had destroyed six of the monsters already: four he'd cleaved through, two he'd thrown into the void at his back. But there were still more than a dozen clustered around him in a half circle, swords raised, yellow eyes glowing, their breath, or whatever they had that passed for breath, rasping through the cloth that covered their rotting skulls. They had only to advance, and they would overwhelm him.

So why had they stopped attacking?

The answer revealed itself as a torch that emerged from the tunnel and bobbed toward the back of the throng. The Screechers moved aside to allow the Secretary to step through. The short man was breathing hard and mopping his brow with a lacy lavender handkerchief.

"My, my," he gasped, "all this running about. Must be a better way."

He waved his handkerchief at the Screechers.

"My companions keeping you entertained, hmm? So, introductions first, yes? Griddley Cavendish, at your service." He bowed and smiled his awful smile. "And you are, my dear sir?"

Gabriel gauged his chances of reaching the man with a lunge. He thought he could make it, but in doing so, he would leave himself open to the Screechers.

"Come, come," Cavendish said, his voice slippery and coaxing, "clearly you are a person of substance. Escaped the boat. Able to kill Screechers and wolves at will. Not to mention the clever little passage behind your fireplace. I confess, I almost missed it. Almost, but . . . the Countess, so intelligent, yes, fortunately, some time ago, condescended to enlighten my ignorance with a few simple spells, such as those that reveal secret doors and panels. Such radiance and foresight. Little wonder children love her. So, your name, sir?"

"Come closer, and I'll tell you," Gabriel said.

The Secretary giggled and punched his leg a couple times as if he found this very amusing, all the while shaking his head vigorously. "A sense of humor to boot! Well, well, thank you for the invitation, but we do in fact see what you're thinking, yes? That long, sharp thing there, hmm? Yes?" He jabbed a crooked finger at Gabriel's blade and then, for some reason, touched the side of his nose.

Gabriel was beginning to think the man was insane.

"Very well, no names. How about you simply tell us where the children are? Otherwise, I shall have to have my decaying friends here chop you into more manageable bits."

Gabriel's face betrayed nothing. But his mind was racing. The Countess wanted these children badly, so badly she had dispatched her secretary and twenty Screechers. That was nearly the entire guard from the town. Was it just their connection to the book or was there something else? Were the children important in some way? He sensed he had made a terrible mistake in leaving them.

"Sent them across the bridge, I imagine. Hmm? Into the maze? Dangerous, don't you think? So easy to get lost?"

The Secretary took one careful step closer.

"Perhaps we make a deal. These children mean nothing to you. You found them in the woods. Came to their aid. Understandable. Pursued by those terrible wolves. Anyone would've done the same. Help us find them. Do this," he wheezed, straining to maintain his grin, "and the Countess will give you whatever you desire. Wealth. Power. She can be very generous."

The Secretary had recklessly taken another step forward. A single stroke and his head would fly from his shoulders. But Gabriel knew he would only have time for one blow before the Screechers were on him. What would happen to the children then?

"Tell the witch . . ."

"Yes?" The man Cavendish leaned forward eagerly.

"I am coming for her."

He spun around and, with one swipe of his sword, severed the ties holding the bridge. Instantly, it fell into the void, and Gabriel leapt, leaving behind the furious cries of the Secretary.

He reached out with his free hand, straining into the darkness. But there was nothing. Just cold black air. Then he was falling. He had failed everyone. The children would be on their own. His people—

His hand smacked against a board. It slipped off, but Gabriel seized the next one just as the bridge snapped taut, and then he was swinging forward. He struck the rock wall with shuddering force. He hung there for a second, getting back his breath. He saw the wavering torchlight high up the other side of the chasm. The Secretary's hollow-sounding voice was screaming curses at him.

Suddenly, purely on instinct, he lifted his knees just as a sword smashed into the planks where his feet had been. In the darkness below, Gabriel saw the yellow eyes of a Screecher. It must have leapt after him and seized one of the ropes trailing from the bridge.

Sheathing his weapon, Gabriel began to climb. He had no hope of fighting the Screecher while hanging on the bridge. He needed to get to the top.

"Gabriel!"

He looked up. Forty yards above, illuminated in the glow of a lantern, the pale face of the younger girl, Emma, was peering over the cliff.

His regret at sending on the children was instantly replaced by annoyance. He opened his mouth to scold her, but just then the Screecher's sword struck again, the tip nicking the heel of his boot. He began to climb more quickly. He didn't notice Emma's face disappear behind the edge of the cliff.

His feet were too large to fit in the narrow gaps between the slats, so he had to pull himself up hand over hand. Every slat he passed, he ripped away the board to make it more difficult for the Screecher. But he could hear the creature climbing upward all the same.

"Gabriel!"

He didn't look up.

"Gabriel!"

Her voice was strained, insistent.

"Gabriel!"

He chanced a look, intending to tell her in very clear terms that any conversation would have to wait. She was standing at the edge of the cliff, struggling to hold a rock several times larger than her head. Seeing him look up, Emma let go of her burden. Gabriel swung himself out to the left. The rock plummeted past, missing him by inches, and caught the Screecher full in the face, connecting with a crunching *thuck* and knocking the creature off the bridge.

Gabriel watched its body disappear into the void, then turned his gaze back to Emma.

The girl waved at him, smiling. "It's okay! I got him!"

Children, he thought.

He quickly ascended the rest of the way and pulled himself

over the edge. The girl was holding the lantern, her eyes bright with excitement. Gabriel looked around, still breathing heavily.

"Where are your brother and sister?"

"I left them."

"I told you to go on. You should not have come back."

The girl's smile vanished; she looked hurt.

"Stop there!" The Secretary's thin voice carried across the chasm. "In the name of the Countess!"

"Come," Gabriel said, "we have to move." He started off, but the girl turned her back on him and crossed her arms.

"I saved your life. I think you could at least say thank you."

Gabriel was tempted to pick her up and carry her. Any moment, the Secretary and his *morum cadi* would begin looking for another way across the chasm. Yet, in spite of himself, he found he was smiling.

"You are right," he said. "I am in your debt."

Emma glanced at him, as if to make sure he was serious. Then she nodded. "You're welcome. But you're not in my debt or anything. It makes us even is all. Now, I think we should probably get going."

"A good idea," Gabriel said, as if he himself had not just suggested the same thing.

"What're you smiling at?" Emma demanded.

"Nothing."

"Uh-huh, well, let's—"

There was a swishing through the air, then a soft *thunk*, and Emma gasped and staggered back. Gabriel caught her before she fell. Twelve inches of black arrow protruded from her back. Another two feet stuck out of her stomach.

"Gabriel . . ." Her eyes were huge and terrified.

Seizing the lantern, Gabriel gathered the small girl in his arms as quickly and carefully as he could. The Secretary was screaming on the other side of the chasm. It sounded as if he were admonishing the creatures.

"Shhh," he said gently as Emma whimpered in pain, "I have you now," and he carried her off into the passageway.

Their hands and feet were tied. Hoods were drawn and knotted over their heads. Everything had taken place in utter darkness so that Kate still had no idea who their captors were. But now torches were being lit. She couldn't see them (it was an unusually thick hood), but she could feel the heat and hear the flames. Then she was picked up and slung across a shoulder, and they were moving, marching.

"Michael," she called out, "are you there?"

"I'm here!" He sounded a few feet behind her. "I'm okay."

"Quiet!" barked a gruff voice.

An hour passed. Maybe more. It was impossible to tell in such darkness. Kate's ribs rubbed painfully against her captor's shoulder, and she shifted about to relieve the pressure. She had quickly given up on trying to keep track of where they were heading. All she knew was that every step was taking them farther and farther from Emma and the hope of ever being reunited. She had to bite her lip to keep from crying. She didn't want Michael to hear her and despair.

Finally, the gruff voice called for a halt.

Kate was set on a stone floor. Her hood was unknotted and

removed. She blinked, unable to focus in the sudden glare of the torches. Michael was beside her, having his hood removed as well.

"Michael," she whispered, "are you okay?"

"Yeah. My ribs hurt, but . . ."

His mouth fell open. As Kate watched, his eyes expanded to an unnatural, almost alarming size.

"Duh . . . ," he bubbled. "Duh . . ."

"Michael? What is it? What's wrong?"

"Dwa . . ."

Kate turned and, her eyes having adjusted, saw a dozen short, stocky, bearded men gathered about them in the tunnel. For the most part, the bearded men were paying little or no attention to the children. Some had taken out food. A few were in conversation or sharpening weapons. Many had pulled out long, thin pipes and were starting to light them. All of them, Kate noticed, had short swords and fearsome-looking axes stuck in their metal belts.

"They're . . . dwarves," Michael gasped, finally managing to form the words.

They were indeed dwarves, with beards and axes and armor, exactly as Michael had always described them. Kate didn't know why she was surprised to find out that dwarves actually existed. From the moment she and Michael and Emma had discovered that magic was real, it should've been logical that dwarves might be real as well. Her only defense was that it had been a very busy couple days.

"I always knew," Michael murmured. "I mean, I didn't

know, I just . . . hoped." He stared about dreamily, repeating, ". . . Dwarves . . ."

One of the troop stepped away from the others. He was stocky (though they were all stocky to some degree) and had a weathered face and a long reddish beard that was braided into neat plaits. He knelt before the children, setting his helmet on the floor with a light clank, and cleared his throat. "Now then"—it was his voice that had been giving orders—"let's have it."

Kate was confused. "Have what, sir?"

"Your story," he said, pulling off his mace gloves. "How you came to be knocking about our territory. Trespassing the like."

At the word "trespassing," there was general harrumphing among the dwarves.

"We weren't trespassing," Kate said. "We—"

"You're a dwarf!" Michael blurted out.

The red-bearded dwarf glanced at Michael. He took in the boy's wide, goofy grin and dazed expression and apparently decided to ignore this rather obvious remark. He turned back to Kate. "Oh, you weren't, were you? So you had permission? Let's see it, then. You have a letter of passage, I assume."

"Well, no, we don't—"

"No letter of passage."

"No."

"No visa? Transit papers? No magical golden ring given your ancestors centuries ago by a dwarfish king granting you rights of access to all dwarfish lands?"

"Um . . . no."

"Then that, my girl, means you was trespassing!"

This second, more forceful "trespassing" was followed by even more harrumphing from the others.

"Now," the dwarf said with an air of satisfaction, "as we've settled that you're a pair of lowly trespassers—"

"You're dwarves!" Michael exclaimed. "All of you!"

The red-bearded dwarf cocked an eyebrow and nodded at Michael. "He simple or something?"

"No," Kate said. "He's fine. He . . ." She hesitated saying that Michael just really liked dwarves. She had a feeling this red-bearded dwarf might find it condescending. He seemed a little prickly. "He's . . . never met a dwarf before."

"Well," the dwarf said, smoothing down his beard, "then it's a great day for him, ain't it? So, what business did you have, trespassing in our lands?"

There were echoes of "Aye, aye, what business indeed, ye trespassers!"

"We weren't trespassing!" Kate protested. "We were lost!"

"You hear that, boys?" the dwarf called over his shoulder. "It's the old 'we were lost' story! A couple of lost little lambs we got here!"

The dwarves roared with laughter.

The red-bearded dwarf shook his head. "Oh, you'll have to do better than that, my girl, much better indeed. The last fellow who was so-called lost found his way well enough. 'At's right! Found his way to the edge of my ax!"

At this, the dwarf leapt up, whipped his ax from his belt, and swung it in a wide arc just above the children's heads, so close that

184

Kate and Michael both felt the wash of air as the blade passed over them. Kate had no idea what her and Michael's faces looked like following this, but it was enough to send the dwarves off into more peals of knee-slapping laughter.

It occurred to Kate that this was not at all the behavior she would've expected from dwarves.

"Stop laughing!" she demanded. "It's not funny." Which of course just made them laugh the more. "There were Screechers after us!"

Silence. The red-bearded dwarf, his face serious, leaned in close.

"Screechers, you say? In dwarfish land?"

Kate nodded.

"Let's have this cock-'n'-bull story, then. But be quick, and try not to tell too many lies."

"It's not a lie," Kate said, aware even as she said it that she was planning on a few strategic omissions. She told him that they'd been prisoners of the Countess and had managed to escape. She said that as they were fleeing, they'd stumbled into an old mining tunnel. A band of Screechers had come after them, chasing them across the rope bridge and into the maze (that was the term Michael had used and it seemed to fit). In the maze, they'd been separated from their little sister. Kate did not mention Gabriel or the book or that they were from the future.

"Your sister," said the dwarf. "So there's another a' you."

"Yes. She's the youngest. You have to let us go find her!"

"Well, your story's full of lies and omissions; that much is apparent. But I can't argue that a child shouldn't be wandering out there alone, even a low-down criminal trespassing child. Better off in our dungeons. No doubt the *salmac-tar* have gotten her by now."

"The *salmac-tar*," Kate said, remembering the creatures Gabriel had told them about, the ones with no eyes and large, bat-like ears, the ones with claws that could slice through bone. "I thought . . . they lived deeper down."

"They've been growing bold of late. Pushing up into our territory. That's why we've been out on patrol." The dwarf's face seemed to cloud over. "It's her fault. The witch's. Disgraceful it is, the whole miserable . . ." He trailed off, muttering a string of unintelligible words, of which Kate could only pick out "king" and "witch" and "misbegotten."

"My lord"—Michael was suddenly struggling to his knees—"I fear we have not properly introduced ourselves; my name is Michael P. This is my sister Katherine. We are alone and in great danger, and in the name of King Ingmar the Kind, we humbly throw ourselves on your mercy and beseech your help in this, our hour of need."

The dwarves all stopped and looked at him. Kate was equally amazed. And then, as one, the dwarves burst out laughing again.

"Did you hear him?" called the red-bearded dwarf to the others, who were really too busy laughing to hear much of anything. "In the name of King Ingmar the Kind?" he mimicked, shaking his head and appearing to wipe away a tear. "Aye, it's too good! It's too good!"

Michael looked confused and a little wounded.

"Now, now," said the red-bearded dwarf, placing a stubby

hand on his shoulder. "We're just having fun. What you said was very fairly spoken and in all the correct forms of address, if a bit out of the mode, perhaps. It was just a shock, it coming from a little human lad like yourself. So you know something about our history, then?"

"Ye-yes," Michael stammered. "Your history. Your traditions. I know what to bring when you go to a dwarf's house for dinner. I can tell you how dwarf inheritance law works. I've memorized the lyrics to seventeen different dwarf drinking songs. I know everything there is to know about dwarves."

"Do you now?" The dwarf brought his face close to Michael's. "Then tell me, lad, what's the one thing we value above all else?"

Kate was expecting Michael to say hard work or craftsmanship or devotion to duty or any of the qualities he was always going on about. But he said something she'd never once heard him mention. And when he spoke, his voice was very quiet.

"I can tell you that. It's the thing I like best about dwarves. The most important thing to you . . . is family."

Kate felt as if the floor had disappeared.

"The clan," he went on, "the family, is the basis of dwarf society. You look out for each other. Once someone's a part of your clan, they're in it for life. You never . . . you never leave him. Ever."

Kate could feel tears coming to her eyes. All these years, all Michael's talk about dwarves, and she finally understood. A family that would never leave you. Had her hands not been tied, she would've put her arms around him and told him that he had that family in her and Emma and he always would.

"You've struck the mark," the dwarf said. Kate could see the other dwarves nodding in the background. "But how do you know so much about us? You're a little on the short side, perhaps, but I don't see anything particularly dwarfish about you."

"Oh . . . if you look in my bag . . ." Michael wiggled about to bring his bag forward, and the dwarf reached in and pulled out a small, thick book that Kate recognized immediately.

"*The Dwarf Omnibus*, by G. G. Greenleaf!" exclaimed their red-bearded captor. "I remember this well enough. Old G.G. was quite the clever dwarf."

"Wait! You mean"—Michael was nearly beside himself— "G. G. Greenleaf was a dwarf?! My book was written by an actual dwarf?!"

"Was G. G. Greenleaf a dwarf? Listen to 'im! Course he was a dwarf! Why, this is every dwarf child's required reading! But how did a human lad like you come upon it?"

"It was my dad's. He left it to me. The only thing he left me." The tunnel had suddenly become very quiet. "Truth is, I don't really remember him. Not really. That book's all I know about him."

It was a long moment before the red-bearded dwarf spoke, and his voice was gentle. "Must've been an interesting man, your father. I'm beginning to think you're not a moron child after all. Last question, how do you feel about elves?"

Kate saw the dwarves all lean slightly forward, watching Michael.

"Well, to be honest," Michael said, "I think they're kind of . . . silly."

A great cry went up among the dwarves, and the red-bearded dwarf, followed by six or seven others, came forward and slapped him hard on the shoulder. " 'Silly' is exactly the word for them!" cried the red-bearded dwarf. "Little show ponies they are!" A few of the dwarves were now imitating elves, pretending to comb their hair or tease their eyebrows or batting their eyelashes and prancing about on their tiptoes.

Kate was beginning to think that as silly as elves might be, dwarves had to be even sillier.

"You're a good lad," said the dwarf. "My name is Robbie McLaur; I extend you my hand in friendship. Oh, your hands are tied, aren't they? Well . . . ," and he clapped Michael on the shoulder again.

"So," Kate said, "will you let us go, then?"

"Oh no, lass. I can't do that, I'm afraid. You see, the King has issued a decree. All trespassers are to be captured and thrown in the dungeon until he can interrogate them himself."

"But," Michael said, "we're not dangerous. And we're only trespassers because we got lost."

"True," said the dwarf Robbie McLaur. "Or perhaps not true. Now, you say you started at the swinging bridge and then went into the maze. Well, 'twas a maze indeed you came through. Built by the greatest dwarf architects centuries ago. Why, you could travel your whole life in there, ten lives, and never find your way out! But the two of you went in one end and came bang up against our secret door. Do you know what the chances a' that are? I wouldn't give a wooden galleon for the odds. And yet, you somehow managed it. How is that, then?"

Kate shrugged. "We just got lucky."

The dwarf shook a stubby finger. "No, girl. You're hiding something." Kate started to protest, but he held up his hand. "Now, I've no love for the witch and her Screechers and think all alliances with such creatures are a betrayal of the great dwarfish tradition—"

"Wait!" Kate broke in. "An alliance? You're working for the witch? How could—"

The red-bearded dwarf raised his ax and slammed down the hilt with such force that it cracked the stone floor. The children felt the impact through their legs, and the dwarves who'd been talking fell silent as the sound echoed away down the tunnel.

"I'll say this once," growled Robbie McLaur. "I. DO. NOT. WORK. FOR. THE. WITCH." His eyes were dark with anger, and for a moment Kate was terrified. But then, just as quickly, the fury seemed to leave him, and he looked off, sighing. "However . . . she and the King have . . . an understanding of sorts."

"He's letting her dig, isn't he?" Michael said. "For the . . . the thing she's looking for. He's letting her dig in your lands."

The dwarf nodded. "Aye."

"So you have to let us go!" Kate said. "You know it's wrong!"

The dwarf shook his head, lowering his voice so that only Kate and Michael could hear. "No, lass. For though I may not personally agree with the King's policies and even think him to be a drunk and disaster and the greatest tragedy to befall the dwarfish nation for a thousand years, his orders are his orders, and I will not be the dwarf that disobeys his king, no, I will not."

"But"—Kate was pleading now—"can't you at least send

some of your men to look for our sister! If those *salmac*-whatever things really are out there, she shouldn't be alone!"

"You're right enough there. But I can't send my soldiers on a rescue mission for some trespasser. What would happen if two or three of them ran into a horde of *salmac-tar*? It would be dwarf kebab for those monsters. Could never defend that to a board of review. I'm sorry, but your sister will have to take her chances."

Kate was furious. She could feel hot tears streaming down her face. "How can you say you care about family? You don't care about family at all!"

"Oh, but I do, lass. I care about my own."

Then he tucked the *Omnibus* into Michael's bag and, pulling on his mace gloves, nodded to two dwarves, who heaved the children onto their shoulders. The troop marched down the tunnel and around the corner into a large chamber, at the end of which were a pair of iron doors and two dwarves standing sentry. Craning her neck around the dwarf who was carrying her, Kate could see that the doors were inlaid with an intricate carving of a very good-looking dwarf with a flowing beard that sparkled in the torchlight. As they got closer, Kate could see the sparkling came from hundreds of perfect diamonds.

Without stopping, the red-bearded dwarf called out, "Captain Robbie McLaur returning with two captives for King Hamish," and the sentry dwarves rapped the butts of their spears on the ground, and the great doors swung open, and Kate saw another chamber and, at the far end of that, another set of iron doors swinging open and, past that, another chamber also with iron doors swinging open and, past that, another and another, all the doors swinging open (and all of them engraved with the same handsome, diamond-bearded dwarf). She and Michael were carried through chamber after chamber as the sentries stood at attention next to spears twice their size and saluted Captain Robbie McLaur. Each set of doors was shut and locked behind them, and when the troop passed through the final pair, Kate saw they had arrived at a great stone bridge fronted by twenty-foot statues of fierce, ax-wielding dwarves. The bridge arched over a huge chasm, and brilliant white light emanated from below, illuminating everything around them.

"Captain," Michael called, his voice coming out in huffs as he was bounced along, "where's that light coming from?"

"King Hamish's palace," said the dwarf. "The entire roof is inlaid with diamonds. His own addition and design, I'll have you know." He said this as if he did not fully approve of diamond-inlaid roofs. "You'll see it closer when he questions you. I imagine he'll get around to it in fifty or so years."

"What?!" Kate exclaimed.

"Dwarves live hundreds of years," Michael said. "They think about time differently than us."

"Great," Kate said. "That's just great."

At the other end of the bridge, they entered another tunnel and were carried down a steep stairway that seemed to go on and on and on, Kate feeling every step through the mail-clad shoulder of her captor, till finally they reached a stone corridor lit by torches fixed in the wall. The dwarves they passed here were not like the cheerful dwarves of Robbie McLaur's troop. They wore cloaks that covered their faces and they stared at the ground, and even Robbie McLaur's dwarves seemed to avoid contact with them.

"Jailer," she heard Robbie McLaur's voice, "I have two trespassing prisoners for the King."

"Cell 198 is free," replied the jailer. "The occupant died this morning. Or perhaps it was last week. We just noticed the smell."

"Hmm, the body is still in there, I suppose."

"Aye. But I can get it removed in the next few days. Till then, I doubt he'll trouble your prisoners much," the jailer said, cackling gleefully.

Kate glanced at Michael. When they were alone, she was going to tell him in no uncertain terms exactly what she thought of dwarves.

"And why not put them in cell 47?" Robbie McLaur suggested.

"There's already an occupant in cell 47. A highly dangerous occupant. Your captives look a little tender to me."

"No, it's cell 47 I want, Jailer. Yes, yes, that's the one for them. If this fellow tenderizes them a little, so much the better. It'll be that much easier when the interrogation comes."

"Of course, Captain. This way."

Kate heard a key turn in a lock, and then she and Michael were carried through a low doorway, passing Robbie McLaur, who was leaning over a table, signing an official-looking document.

"Captain, please!" Kate called. "We'll take cell 198! Please!" But Robbie McLaur didn't look up, and then they were through the door and it was shut behind them.

The jailer led them along a dank, torchlit corridor. Kate and

Michael could see iron doors on either side and hear pounding and scraping and growling from inside the cells. They went down a flight of steps, around a corner, down more steps, along an even narrower passage, and then stopped.

"Here," the jailer said. "Cell 47."

The two dwarves set Kate and Michael on the floor and cut the ropes tying their hands and feet. The jailer banged on the door with a club.

"You in there! Stay back and don't try anything! There's two that's coming in!"

The jailer waited, but there was only silence. He fit the key in the lock, then with a quick motion turned it, swung open the door, and hissed, "Now!" The two dwarves pushed Kate and Michael into the room and slammed the door shut behind them. Kate heard the key turn and the bolt shoot into place.

All was quiet and still and completely, utterly dark.

They had landed on a stone floor that was sparsely covered with straw. Kate reached out and found Michael's arm.

"Michael," she whispered, "are you okay?"

"Uh-huh. I think so."

Quietly as possible, the two of them got to their feet. Kate stared into the darkness. Something was in there with them. Something dangerous, the jailer had said. But what? Could it see them?

"What're we going to do?" Michael hissed, and Kate could hear the panic in his voice.

There was a noise across the room. It sounded like someone, or something, standing up.

"Don't come any closer!" Kate shouted. "I'm warning you! Stay where you are!"

But whatever it was came closer. They could hear slow footsteps moving over the straw. Kate and Michael retreated till their backs were pressed against the cold metal of the door.

"I said stop! Or I'll . . . I'll . . ."

Before Kate could think of a credible threat, the something spoke.

"Perhaps we just see what we're dealing with."

Kate froze. That voice . . . How did she know that voice?

A flame appeared in the darkness, and a man's shape separated itself from the shadows. At first, Kate thought he had a lantern. Then, as he came closer, she realized he was holding the naked flame cupped in his open palm. But that was not what caused her to gasp in surprise. It was the man's face.

"Well, well," said Dr. Stanislaus Pym, "what have we here?"

CHAPTER TWELVE
Breakfast for Dinner

The child weighed nothing. Gabriel gently laid her on the floor of the first chamber so that she rested on her side. Her shirt, front and back, was soaked with blood.

"Gabriel . . ."

"Close your eyes."

She did so, and Gabriel grasped the feathered end of the arrow. For perhaps the first time in his life, his hands trembled. He snapped the shaft with a sharp crack. Emma whimpered but kept her eyes closed. He did the same to the end of the arrow sticking out her back. This time a small shuddering cry escaped Emma's lips. Her hands were clenched together as in prayer, and tears welled from the corners of her eyes. Now only a few inches of the dark, bloodstained shaft stuck out from either side. He had decided to leave the fragment in her body. Its poison had already contaminated her, and the shaft at least served to stanch the bleeding. He gathered her up and turned down the second doorway to the left, moving as fast as he dared.

"Michael and Kate didn't come back," Emma said in a weak, trembling voice, half muffled against his chest. "I thought . . . I thought they'd come back for me."

"Don't speak. You need your strength."

Time, he knew, was their greatest enemy. He needed to get her out of the mountain and to his village as quickly as possible. Once there, Granny Peet, the tribal wisewoman, could treat her. But would Emma survive that long? Would he? The same poison that was on the arrow had been on the swords of the Screechers. Gabriel had half a dozen wounds on his arms and a large gash in his side; he could feel the poison, like ice in his blood, moving toward his heart.

And what of her brother and sister? Had they kept moving through the maze, simply assuming Emma was with them? Sooner or later, they would have realized the truth and turned back. But with each deserted chamber, each dark, empty tunnel, Gabriel knew the chances of meeting the other two children grew smaller. Had they gotten lost? Or had something found them? These tunnels were not empty of life.

Gabriel glanced down at Emma. Her eyes were closed and her breathing was fast and shallow. Droplets of sweat stood out on her face. She would not make it to the village. He paused in a chamber and set her down. He did not like stopping here, but he had no choice. He rolled up her shirt to expose the wound. The poison had spread. It was visible around the nub of arrow, a large black spider under her pale skin, stretching its dark legs.

He took out a small leather pouch and removed the contents: several different types of leaves, a gnarled root, a vial of yellowish liquid. He laid the pouch flat on the ground and crumpled the leaves into a small pile. They were dry and quickly turned to dust.

"What're you doing?"

Lying on the floor, Emma had opened her eyes.

"I must treat your wounds. The arrow was poisoned."

Gabriel took his knife and cut two thin slices off the root. These he chopped into small pieces and added to the crushed leaves. Then he removed the stopper from the vial and carefully released three yellow drops. The roots and leaves began to hiss and smoke. Gabriel took the handle of his knife and began kneading it all into a brownish mash.

"They're lost because of me, aren't they, Gabriel?" Her voice was almost a whisper. "I shouldn't have left them. They figured out I wasn't there, so they went back to look for me and got lost. That's what happened, isn't it? It's all my fault. You gotta find them, Gabriel. You gotta leave me and go find them."

"I will find them. If I have to return with every man and woman in the village." He dipped his finger in the brownish-yellow paste. It had a warm, peaty smell and stuck to his fingers. "But first I must take care of you."

"No—"

"Do not argue."

Gabriel began to apply the salve, and Emma sucked in her

breath to keep from crying out. Where it touched the edges of her wound, Gabriel's concoction bubbled and hissed. Emma thought it must be burning right through her skin.

After a moment, when she knew she could control her voice, she said, "I'm gonna die, aren't I?"

"This will slow the poison," he said, continuing to spread the salve.

"It's okay." He was applying the medicine to her back now. It was still burning, but the feeling seemed a long way off, like she had drifted away from her body. "I'm not scared. But when you find Michael and Kate, say I'm sorry, okay? For running off? And tell Michael it's okay what he did. I probably would've done the same. And say I love them. Make sure you say that most of all."

Gabriel wiped the last of the salve around the nub of arrow protruding from her back. He had done all he could. Her survival now depended on her own strength and how quickly he could get her to the village.

He took a moment to look at her, lying there in the light of the lantern. He had always been solitary. Even among his own tribe. But he felt connected to this child in a way he had never felt toward any living thing. He laid his large hand gently upon her head. Her eyes were closed. Despite his medicine, she was slipping away.

"You have a great heart." He brushed the hair back from her sweaty forehead. "You will not die today."

And then he heard it. *Click-click*. He looked toward one of the doorways. Though he saw nothing but darkness, he knew that sound. It was the tap of claws on stone.

He glanced at Emma; she was unconscious. A small blessing.

He stood, his legs shaking from the poison coursing through his body. He took the falchion off his back.

There was no hope of flight. The creature was too close.

He stood there, facing the doorway, waiting for it to emerge from the shadows.

"So I run an orphanage! Amazing! The turns one's life takes!"

Kate and Michael were sitting on piles of straw across from Dr. Pym. The flame, which Dr. Pym had placed on the stone floor of the cell and caused to grow into a cheerful little fire, crackled away between them.

"Well, to be honest," Michael said, "it's not much of an orphanage."

"Michael!"

"I'm just saying, what kind of orphanage only has three children?"

"He's quite right," Dr. Pym said. "It sounds as if I've made something of a hash of it. Or I will. In fifteen years or what have you."

When the old wizard had first emerged from the darkness, Kate's reaction had been bafflement. That it was actually Dr. Pym she had no doubt. She did not think she was having another vision. But what was the head of their orphanage doing locked in a dwarfish prison? She stayed as she was, her back pressed against the door. "Dr. Pym! What're you . . . doing here?"

Michael gaped. "He's Dr. Pym?! The Dr. Pym?!"

"Hello," the wizard said, smiling at them over the flame dancing in his palm.

Kate put her hand on the wall to steady herself. She was having the same feeling she'd had that day in the library, that she had met this man before. The image of him standing in shadow clawed at some memory deep inside her.

"You're really Dr. Pym?" Michael said.

"That I am. Who might you be?"

"Michael," Kate said. "Our brother. He wasn't there the day you met me and Emma." Kate was fighting to stay calm. She had to think clearly. Emma was in danger. They needed help if they were going to find her. But could they trust Dr. Pym? As the shock of seeing him had abated, her doubts about the wizard had come rushing back.

He was looking at her now. "And who are you, my dear?"

She managed to say, ". . . What?"

"I asked, 'Who are you?' Of course, I'm always happy to meet new people. But I gather you do know me."

"Yes! Don't you remember? We met . . ." The words died on her lips as Kate realized her mistake. She and Emma wouldn't meet with the wizard in the house in Cambridge Falls for another fifteen years. The man smiling down at them, wearing, she was certain, the same tweed suit he would wear a decade and a half in the future, had no idea who she was. She felt foolish and defeated. ". . . I mean, we're going to meet. . . . It's complicated."

"The reason you and I haven't met," Michael said helpfully, "is that I was already trapped in the past."

"I see," Dr. Pym said. Then he shook his head. "Actually no, I don't see at all. Here, you had better come in and explain everything."

He led them deeper into the cell, which was about the size of a comfortable living room, a comfortable living room, that is, made entirely of stone and iron with no windows and only old straw for furniture. Dr. Pym gathered the straw into two piles and told Kate and Michael to sit down. Then he slid the flame out of his palm, blew on it, and the fire sprang to life. Dr. Pym settled himself on a third heaped-together pile, folded up his long legs, and pulled a pipe from his inside jacket pocket.

"Now," he said as he began to pack the bowl, "start at the beginning."

"Wait—" Kate had made up her mind to ask him for help. What other choice did they have? Emma was lost. "We'll tell you everything, okay? But first—"

"Ah yes, introductions. Quite right. I'm Stanislaus Pym. But you knew that. Did I hear your name was Kate? Is that short for Katherine?"

"Yes, but—"

"Katherine what?"

"P! Katherine P. And this is Michael, again! But—"

"P? You mean like the letter? That's unusual."

"We don't know our real last names! Look, I said we'd tell you everything! But first you have to find our sister, Emma! She's probably in terrible danger!"

"She ran off to help Gabriel!" Michael said. "Even after Kate told her not to. She's always doing that kind of thing."

"Michael, not now."

"Sorry," Michael mumbled, ". . . but she is."

"So your sister is with Gabriel, then?"

"You know him?" Kate was taken aback.

"Oh yes," Dr. Pym said. "And if that is the case, you have nothing to worry about. Gabriel is one of the most capable individuals I have ever met."

"But we don't know for sure that she is with Gabriel! Can't you just do some spell—"

"Katherine, first off, magic doesn't work like that. You don't say 'hocus-pocus' and have someone simply pop out of the air. Well, sometimes you do, just not in this case. Secondly, rest assured, even as I am sitting here talking to you, I am already working to locate your sister."

"You are?" She was unable to keep the skepticism out of her voice.

"Oh, most definitely."

"But you're just . . . sitting there," Michael said. "Chewing your pipe."

"Yes." Dr. Pym smiled. "Quite amazing, isn't it? But now I insist you begin your story. I promise, everything you tell me that gives me a clearer picture of your sister will aid me in finding her."

Kate relented (again, what choice did she have?), and they began telling their story, though in a somewhat abbreviated form (Kate reasoning he'd just hear the whole thing again in fifteen years), but hitting all the major points: their parents' disappearance, moving from orphanage to orphanage, arriving in

Cambridge Falls and learning from Abraham that the head of the orphanage, Dr. Pym, was a wizard—

("My, this Abraham fellow is a bit of a gossip, isn't he?" Dr. Pym said.)

—finding the book in the underground room—

("Was that your study?" Michael asked.

Dr. Pym shrugged. "No idea. I don't own the house yet. Was it nice?"

"A little creepy," Michael said.

"Oh," Dr. Pym said, sounding disappointed. But then he waved his pipe for them to continue.)

—and they told about using the book to go into the past, seeing the Countess, Michael being trapped, Kate and Emma going back to rescue him—

("Very brave," Dr. Pym said approvingly. "Very noble.")

—about the book disappearing before their eyes, the children in the dormitory whom Kate had promised to help, their escape, the wolves, Gabriel, the chase through the tunnels, getting separated from Emma, and then their capture by Captain Robbie McLaur and his dwarves.

"My, my, my," Dr. Pym said. "What a time you've had. Little wonder you look so exhausted."

"Listen"—Kate's impatience was getting the best of her—"I understand you're a wizard, and probably know what you're doing, but maybe you need to try another spell or something because clearly Emma isn't here yet—"

"My dear, I am doing all I can," Dr. Pym said, peering down at her from under his snowy eyebrows. "But the truth is, my powers are somewhat depleted at the moment."

"What do you mean? You can do magic!"

"Correction—I can do some magic. This cell—"

"It's the iron, isn't it?" Michael exclaimed. "The dwarfish iron in the walls!"

"Ah," Dr. Pym said admiringly, "I see you know something about dwarves."

"I think dwarves are the most noble, most—"

"All right, Michael, we know. Dr. Pym, why's it matter if there's iron in the walls?"

"While not magicians themselves, dwarves are magical creatures. Everything they build is infused with magic. The greater the craft involved, the greater the object's magical properties. And dwarves have no peer when it comes to working in iron. So when they build a cell like this, the iron is wrought in a way that serves to dampen the powers of one such as myself."

Kate was about to say something she probably would've regretted—something along the lines of "Then what good are you?"—but at that moment the door opened, and four dwarves entered the cell. One carried a short-legged square table. The other three balanced trays packed high with steaming plates of food.

"Ah," Dr. Pym said, "dinner."

Except it wasn't. The dwarves were laying out stacks of butter-smeared pancakes, piles of fatty bacon, thick, cheesy meat-stuffed pies, jars of jam, marmalade, and honey, brackets of golden toast, steaming bowls of porridge, hunks of soft cheese, pyramids of plump jelly-filled donuts, and, finally, a jug of what had to be hot apple cider.

"Dwarves," Dr. Pym said, "are strong proponents of breakfast for dinner, and I must say I have grown to like the custom. Thank you, my friends."

The serving dwarves bowed low, their beards sweeping the floor as they backed out and closed the iron door.

"Come now, you two. I know you're worried about your sister, but you must keep your strength up. You're no use to anyone if you get run down. And I have some things to tell you that I think you will find very interesting indeed. So let's dig in, shall we, before it gets cold?"

And he leaned forward and cut himself a thick slice of ham, egg, and cheese pie. Michael glanced at Kate. She nodded, and they both took up positions around the table and went to work.

"Now let me start by asking you something." Dr. Pym was eating a jelly donut and trying, without much success, to keep it from dripping onto his suit. "Am I correct in assuming that you are yourselves looking for the book?"

"Yes," Kate said; she was sawing through a thick stack of blueberry pancakes. "It's the only way we're ever going to get home. Only we have no idea where the book is."

"Well—" The old wizard popped the last of the donut in his mouth, a large dollop of jelly landing unnoticed on his tie. "Then it is a good thing I do."

Kate and Michael both froze.

Then Kate said, "What?"

"It is a good thing I do know where it is." He'd begun sorting through a pile of cinnamon twists, searching for the longest and sugariest. "Ah, here we are." He pulled free one doughy, golden spiral and held it up for admiration.

He told them that the book was hidden beneath the Dead City.

And what was the Dead City?

The Dead City, Dr. Pym explained as he chomped panda-like down the stalk, was the ancient dwarf capital. It had been abandoned some five hundred years earlier after being devastated by an earthquake.

"Are you all right, my dear? The pancakes not agreeing with you?"

"I'm fine." Kate's voice was strained. She was recalling her dream from the night before, of the city inside the mountain, how the earth had split open to swallow it. Was that the same city? It had to be.

"Anyway"—Dr. Pym licked clean his fingers—"the book is locked in a vault beneath the ruins."

Kate felt a chill come over her. Why was she having these visions? Once again, she remembered the Countess saying that the book had marked her.

"Does the . . . does the Countess know?"

"Well, she clearly knows something. She's had the men of Cambridge Falls digging there for the past two years."

"Bhuhoduuknoballdis?" Michael asked (he had most of a banana pancake crammed into his mouth).

"A good question," Dr. Pym said. "Perhaps I should start farther back."

He brushed a shower of golden crumbs off his jacket, reached for a donut, and began. . . .

As the children already knew, there were once three great books of magic. The so-called Books of Beginning. Of the Books' various properties and powers, Dr. Pym did not think it necessary to delve into at present. Suffice it to say, twenty-five hundred years earlier, after the city of Rhakotis was sacked by the armies of Alexander the Great, two of the Books of Beginning did indeed vanish. However, the third was smuggled out of the city by a very clever, very attractive young wizard. (He mentioned the young wizard's handsomeness several times. It seemed to be a key point in the story.)

For years, this young wizard remained on the move, secreting the book from one hiding place to another. He knew there were many dark forces who craved the book's power and who would have used it to foul and destructive ends. Eventually, after perhaps a thousand years, the no-longer-quite-so-young wizard carried the book over the ocean, climbed into these mountains, and made a pact with the dwarf king to hide it.

Once again, Kate felt a shiver of recognition. This was the vision that had led her through the maze. Was the book giving her clues? Did it want her to find it?

"Are you going to eat that waffle?" Michael whispered. "Because it's chocolate chip—"

Kate pushed the waffle at him.

The dwarf king had his greatest masons build a vault deep

below the city, and there the book was placed. For another ten centuries, all was quiet. Then the earthquake struck, and it not only destroyed the city, it killed much of the population, including all who knew of the book's existence. So when the dwarves moved south to rebuild their capital, the book was left behind, forgotten under the ruins.

"Now, how I myself learned of the book's existence and location is not important—"

"How did you?" Michael asked. This was the kind of practical detail he couldn't resist.

"My boy, I said it is not important."

"I bet you found some old manuscript in a library. But it was pushed way in the back with all these other manuscripts, and for years and years nobody gave it a second glance, then you saw it and realized it was the young wizard's diary and—"

"No, that was not how it happened."

"Oh! I bet the trees told you, didn't they? The old oak trees. They were probably just small baby trees way back then, but they saw the young wizard carry the book into the mountains and you cast a spell to make them talk—"

"Don't be silly; no one can make trees talk. At least not oak trees. They're terribly dull."

"Then I bet—"

"You were the wizard!" Kate exclaimed.

"That's crazy," Michael said. "He'd have to be thousands—"

But he stopped himself, for Dr. Pym was smiling at Kate. "My dear, how did you know?"

Kate thought of telling the truth, that she'd suddenly realized that the ginger-haired man in her vision, the one who'd given the book to the dwarf king for safekeeping, was Dr. Pym—only much much much younger. But if she told him that, Dr. Pym would begin asking questions; he would want to know everything about her visions.

She shrugged. "Just a lucky guess."

Dr. Pym glanced at her but went on.

He told them how, in the beginning, he had made a practice of returning to the region every few years. But as time passed and the book lay undisturbed, particularly after the earthquake, when he was the only living soul who knew of the book's location, his visits became less frequent. His last trip was five or six years ago. It was then that he met Gabriel. And he discovered, to his alarm, that stories had grown of an object of great power buried in the mountains. It was as if those who lived here had begun to sense the book's presence. Dr. Pym knew that sooner or later, these rumors would reach the wrong ears. He began searching for a new hiding place.

He scoured the globe, rejecting an undersea cavern here, a mountain fortress there. He was in the Amazon, examining a system of caves, when the news reached him of the Countess's arrival. He returned immediately. By then, the Countess had been at her work for nearly two years. The men of Cambridge Falls, under the whips and blows of their guards, had dug a warren of tunnels beneath the Dead City. While they had not yet discovered the vault, Dr. Pym felt that day could not be far off. The book had to be moved immediately.

"What about the men?!" Kate cried. "Or the children?! Why not free them first?!"

"Katherine, your feelings do you credit. But the safety of the book had to take precedence. If it were to fall into the Countess's hands, many more lives would be in peril."

Kate set the scone she'd been eating back on the table. Her hands were trembling with anger. She told herself that given the choice, even if it meant that she and Michael and Emma would be trapped in the past forever, even if it only saved the life of one child and reunited just one family, she would let the Countess have the book.

The question, Dr. Pym continued, was how to retrieve the book. The Countess's soldiers had set up a prison camp in the Dead City. Avoiding their sentries would not be easy. But even more daunting was reaching the vault itself. The earthquake, all those years before, had completely sealed off the passage.

"But I bet there's a secret way, isn't there?" Michael said.

"What a bright lad you are," Dr. Pym beamed. "A good thing you're not working for the Countess; our collective goose would be cooked."

"Oh, I'd never work for her," Michael said stoutly, then he glanced at Kate and muttered, "I mean . . . never again."

Dr. Pym explained that when the vault was built, the dwarf king had a sort of back door constructed. It was intended for just such a calamity.

"Good old dwarves." Michael grinned. "Always one step ahead."

This secret entrance was accessed through a cavern far below the throne room. The walls of the cavern were covered with a rare kind of lichen that glows gold in the dark. Get to that cavern, and you could get to the vault.

"So how do you get to the cavern?" Kate asked.

"That, my dear, is precisely the problem. The earthquake jumbled everything about. Tunnels. Passages. Though I managed to infiltrate the Dead City, I could not find the correct entrance. My goodness! Have you tried one of these?" He held up a fat, custard-filled donut from which he had just taken a large bite.

"You got the last one," Michael said sullenly; he had been eyeing the donut for several minutes.

"Oh, my apologies." Dr. Pym tore it in two and handed over half; a somewhat messy operation, but Michael seemed to appreciate the gesture.

"So what'd you do?" Kate asked impatiently.

"Well, realizing I needed a guide, one who knew the tunnels below the Dead City and would recognize the cavern I described, I came to the only place to find such an individual—the dwarfish court. Everyone had enough to eat? Excellent. I think it's time for tea."

Dr. Pym took up the small iron kettle and poured out three cups of steaming amber liquid, cautioning them not to burn their tongues. He remarked that while frustrating in some respects, dwarfish iron did make for a truly first-rate kettle. Then he sat back, stuffed a wad of tobacco in his pipe, lit a match, sucked till it had begun to draw, and exhaled a long stream of almond-scented smoke.

"Now we have come to the second part of my tale. The story of Hamish." Dr. Pym took a delicate sip from his teacup. "Until recently, the dwarves in this region were ruled by a queen, a just, wise old lady and a great and dear friend of mine. During my last visit—again, this was about five years ago—she assured me that her younger son (she had two) would become king upon her death. Her younger son was everything a future king should be: good and true and all those other dull, necessary qualities. Her other son, the elder, was a thug. A creature of ungoverned passion and very poor hygiene. It was clear to all that he would be a disaster as king. But alas, shortly after my visit the Queen died without leaving a will. Or at least"—Dr. Pym looked significantly at the children—"a will was never found, and so Hamish became king instead of Robbie."

"Wait—you mean Captain Robbie?" Kate asked.

"Ah yes, you'd said you'd met the fine Captain Robbie. He and Hamish are brothers. Though as unlike as night and day, as"—he paused, searching for another comparison, then shrugged—"well, night and day pretty much says it.

"Now, Hamish had not been king long when the Countess and her *morum cadi* appeared at court. She flattered him with gifts and promises and begged permission to dig in the Dead City. She did not tell him what she was digging for. In fact, she claimed not to know herself. She said she was following a legend, a rumor. A story about some lost magical artifact. But she promised that when she found this mysterious object, she and Hamish would share it. In the end, he granted permission."

"Is he an idiot?" Kate asked.

"Oh, most certainly," Dr. Pym said. "But even so, it didn't take him long to realize he had been duped, that the Countess knew exactly what she was searching for and had absolutely no intention of sharing it. You may well ask, so why didn't Hamish simply retake the Dead City by force? After all, his forces far outnumbered those of the Countess. For now, I will only tell you that he had reason, good reason, to fear open confrontation. And so, he simply sat on his throne and stewed—quite literally, for the oaf refuses to bathe—and such was the state in which I found him.

"He was in the midst of one of his endless feasts. I think the buffoon actually believed I had come to congratulate him on his ascension to the throne. 'What've you brought me, Magician?' Those were his first words. I replied that far from bringing a gift, I required one.

" 'Oh, do you now?' he snorted. 'Is it bloomin' Magicians' Christmas? Why didn't anyone remind me, eh?'

"I said I needed a guide. That I intended to outflank the Countess and spirit away the object of her efforts. I had considered spinning some elaborate yarn to mask my plan, but I felt that Hamish's suspicions were so raw he would have sensed the ruse immediately. In any case, the effect of my words was instantaneous. Hamish pounced like a tiger—a dirty, foul-smelling, half-literate tiger.

" 'You know what she's after, then?!' he shouted.

" 'I do,' I replied.

"He demanded I tell him all I knew. I refused. He threatened me. Still, I refused. He became irate. He screamed. He spat. He threw plates. Overturned tables. He punched his minister of culture. It was a tantrum such as I have never seen, and all the while he was shouting that as this object was buried in dwarfish lands, it belonged to the dwarves, that is to say, to him, and no one else."

"He does have a point," Michael murmured.

"I told Hamish," Dr. Pym went on, "that the dwarves had merely been the custodians of the object. It did not belong to them.

" 'So you refuse to help me?!' he screamed. 'You think I can't hurt you, Magician?! Is that what you think, you scoundrel?! You great white-haired ninny!'

"I replied that I knew full well he could hurt me. But even so, I would not tell him what was buried beneath the Dead City. And that"—Dr. Pym spread his hands to encompass the walls of his cell—"was how I ended up here. All this happened four days ago."

The children were silent, holding their still-steaming cups of tea, thinking of all Dr. Pym had said.

Michael asked if Dr. Pym had a key to get into the vault.

The old wizard smiled. "Of a sort. Yes. But I have talked too long for one night. You are tired and must sleep. Something tells me tomorrow will require all your strength."

"But what about Emma?" Kate had listened to everything Dr. Pym had said, about the book's journey, the vault, Hamish. . . . She had been patient. But enough was enough. "You said you were looking for her! Where is she? Is she safe? Is she even alive? Can you tell us that?"

"She was in great danger," Dr. Pym said quietly. "But she is past that. She is now in Gabriel's village, being treated by their wisewoman. I assure you, my dear, your sister is quite safe."

For a moment, Kate and Michael were both too stunned to speak.

"Really?" Kate asked.

"Yes. Would you like to see for yourself?"

Kate nodded.

Dr. Pym smiled. "Very well."

And suddenly, it was as if Kate's entire body was filled with sand. Her arms and legs became impossibly heavy. Her eyelids drooped shut. Instinctively, she fought to stay awake. She felt Michael slump against her.

"But . . . ," she mumbled, "we . . ."

She was asleep before she hit the straw.

As she slept, she dreamed she was back in the maze, floating down one of the dark corridors. There was a light ahead, coming from a chamber. She moved toward it, out of the tunnel, and the scene that opened before her was worse than any nightmare. Emma lay unmoving on the ground. The lower half of her shirt was black with blood. Kate could see the dark nub of arrow sticking out of her back. Gabriel stood over her, his terrifying machete-like weapon grasped in both hands, its edge gleaming in the light from the lantern. And moving toward him across the floor of the chamber, the most horrible creature Kate had ever imagined.

Its skin was a translucent, gooey white and dotted with greenish sores. Its arms and legs were hideously long and thin, its back curved from generations of moving through low-ceilinged tunnels. Its claws tapped the floor as it advanced, and Kate saw the milky, sightless eyes and huge, bat-like ears. The *salmac-tar* made a gurgling hiss deep in its throat and threw itself at Gabriel, its long claws outstretched. Kate tried to scream, but no sound came out. Gabriel stepped forward, swinging his weapon over his head in a shining arc. Man and monster met in the center of the room, and Kate felt her chest tighten in fear, but then the monster's head was flying away from its body, rebounding against the far wall and rolling over, once, twice, three times, before coming to rest, facedown.

For a long moment, nothing moved. Even the headless body stood where it was, as if not yet realizing what had happened. Then, slowly, it dropped to its knees, toppled forward, and lay still. Gabriel wiped the blood off his blade, started to turn toward Emma, then stopped, listening.

Then Kate heard it too. *Click-click . . . click-click . . .*

The sound was coming from one of the dark doorways. Then another. And another. The clicking rose like the hum of insects, growing louder and thicker. Gabriel sheathed his blade, gathered Emma and the lamp, and ran.

Kate felt herself moving with him as he flew down the dark corridors. She could hear his breathing, smell his sweat. Behind him the clicking grew louder and louder. Emma never opened her eyes. Gabriel plunged from chamber to chamber, tunnel to tunnel. Looking back, Kate could see ghostly shapes in the darkness, scurrying toward them, climbing the walls, coming faster and faster.

Suddenly, they were no longer in the maze. They were running across a great empty cavern of natural rock, and Kate could see the white shapes pouring out of the mouth of the tunnel behind them, and Gabriel tripped and nearly fell and they would have been on him in an instant with their teeth and claws, but he caught himself and was splashing across a stream and stumbling down another short tunnel, and then they were outside, out of the tunnel, out of the mountain, and the night was cool against her face and the moon lit the darkness, and though it was a dream, she filled her lungs with gulps of clean, fresh air.

Gabriel paused and looked back. Though she could not see them, Kate could hear the fury of the creatures inside the mountain. For some reason, they seemed unable to come outside. Gabriel started down a trail along the ridge. Kate could see, in the valley below, a fluttering collection of fires she knew was Gabriel's village; Emma was safe.

Kate woke, smelling Dr. Pym's tobacco.

"Good morning," said the wizard. "You've slept nearly nine hours. I believe you both were exhausted."

Kate rubbed her eyes. The fire was crackling away. Michael was still passed out on the straw.

"I had the strangest dream."

"Did you now? I can't wait to hear all about it." Dr. Pym was smiling at her with the same kindly smile, his face wreathed in smoke. "You know, I've been studying you and your brother. You say you don't know your parents at all?"

"I have a few memories. But I don't know their names or anything. Why?"

Dr. Pym knocked his pipe against the stone floor, emptying the ashes, and replaced it in his pocket. "Oh, we can talk about it later. You'd best wake Michael. They will be here any moment."

"Who will?" Kate felt groggy, as if she was still half inside her dream. Had it even been a dream? It'd felt so real. And why was Dr. Pym asking about their parents?

There was the sound of a bolt being shot back; the door swung open, and Captain Robbie McLaur entered.

"Right, then, up and at 'em! The King wants to see you lot."

CHAPTER THIRTEEN
Hamish

Four dwarf guards, led by Captain Robbie McLaur, guided Dr. Pym and the children along a series of passages and stairways to the throne room of King Hamish.

"Not that it's any of my business, Wizard," Robbie McLaur said as they marched along the torchlit corridor, "but for the sake of these children, I'll warn you that my brother is not a dwarf to be trifled with."

"We appreciate your concern, Captain," said Dr. Pym. "But I think we can handle ourselves."

"Fair enough; it's your necks. Just don't like seeing children chopped into bits and pieces when it can be avoided. Old-fashioned, I guess."

Soon, they began to pass dwarves going the other way, carrying serving trays piled high with the greasy remains of a great feast. One trotted by with a dozen empty flagons rattling along a stick, and then, at an intersection, they had to stand aside as two dwarves rolled a wooden cask down the corridor, yelling, "The King demands more ale! More ale for the King!"

"Oh dear," Dr. Pym said, "I do hope he is not too drunk."

"I wouldn't bet money on it," Robbie McLaur muttered.

As they approached a set of enormous golden doors, the dwarf captain called out in a booming voice, "Captain Robbie McLaur escorting the prisoners requested by King Hamish!" and the two dwarves standing sentry pushed the doors open to admit them.

Kate reached for Michael's hand.

"Stay close."

Michael nodded, but said nothing. He was afraid if he spoke, his sister would hear how excited he was to be entering the throne room of a real dwarf king.

"And maybe don't grin so much," Kate suggested.

"Quiet!" Robbie McLaur barked, for they were just then stepping over the threshold. But he needn't have said anything; the hall itself silenced the children.

It was the largest room the children had ever seen. It stretched on and on and on. The ceiling was so high that the great stone columns supporting it seemed to rise up and disappear into darkness. But beyond the size and scale, it was the wealth on display. Diamonds embedded in the ceiling sparkled like stars in the night sky. Precious gems were laid into the floor like flagstones. Murals painted in gold and silver covered the walls, depicting dwarf victories over trolls, goblins, dragons, hordes of *salmac-tar*. Everything about the hall was designed to impress the visitor with the majesty of the dwarfish throne.

Kate and Michael stood in the doorway, staring.

Then Kate said, "It's a pigsty."

All around them were stacks of dirty plates, rotting scraps of food, half-empty flagons of ale, and unconscious, filthy dwarves. Exhausted servers hustled back and forth along the sides of the great hall, exchanging empty plates and flagons for full ones. Robbie McLaur let out a low growl of displeasure.

"King Hamish is known for his appetites," Dr. Pym whispered. "A feast might go on for days or weeks at a time."

"This isn't right," Michael said. "Dwarves shouldn't behave like this."

"Aye, lad," growled Robbie McLaur, "truer words were never spoke."

"Well, lookee lookee!" called a voice from the other end of the hall. "If it ain't the conjurer! And he's got brats with 'im too! Bring 'em 'ere! Bring 'em 'ere!"

The guards marched their group forward. The children took care to step over snoring dwarves and puddles of fetid ale.

"Very 'appy you could trouble yourself to visit us, Magician! Ha! You prat!"

Hamish sat at the center of a long table of greasy-faced dwarves. A few were still eating and drinking listlessly, but most were unconscious, either slumped forward onto the table or propped sideways against a neighbor. Hamish was the only one still going strong.

He was by far the largest dwarf the children had yet seen. Though only the height of a small man, he possessed enormous mass. Kate thought he looked like a giant, bearded warthog.

"Hope you've been comfortable down in the dungeons. We like to keep our guests happy, we do. Wouldn't want people speaking ill of us." He laughed unpleasantly and took a long slurp of ale, most of which ended up on his beard. Kate thought that his beard, which spread down his chest fan-wise, resembled nothing so much as a hairy blond apron. She could even see things stuck in it: bits of cheese and pie, a crust of bread, a drumstick, a fork. He was a sharp contrast to Captain Robbie McLaur, standing at attention beside them, with his neatly trimmed beard and spotless uniform.

As Hamish drained the last of his ale, a serving dwarf quietly removed an empty platter and began to hurry away.

"Oi!" Hamish yelled, hurling his goblet so it bounced off the dwarf's head. "I wasn't done with that, you!"

Amid bows and mumbled apologies, the dwarf returned the platter, and Hamish scooped up the last crumbs of whatever it was and crammed them into his mouth.

"There!" he mumbled, tossing the platter over his shoulder so it clanged loudly against the floor. "Now you can take it." Then he wiped his fingers on his beard—in the process dislodging several miniature sausages—and belched. The sound echoed the length of the hall and back and seemed to rouse the dwarves at the table, for they all suddenly sat up and began belching in unison, as if trying to cover for their king's lapse in manners. Soon the great hall reverberated with the echoing symphony of burping dwarves.

Brrrraaaappht—

Errrapphth—

Grrappphhaaaa—

Blllluuupppgggg—

Ugggrrraapphhhh—

"E-NOUGH!" shouted Hamish, bringing a fist down on the table. The dwarves instantly fell silent, and in a few seconds the last *eerrrppptt* had died away.

"Honestly," said Dr. Pym, "he does set a terrible example."

"Dr. Pym"—Kate tugged on the old man's sleeve—"what're we going to do?"

But the wizard only shushed her and kept looking at the King.

Suddenly, Hamish clapped his hands. At first, nothing happened; then, in the distance, the children heard a rhythmic thundering. It grew louder and louder, and all at once the great doors flew open and two lines of armored dwarves marched into the hall. They separated, stamping their mail-bound feet as they came down the line of columns, and in what seemed like mere moments, the hall was filled with hundreds of dwarves, their helmets gleaming, the edges of their axes razor-sharp and shining in the torchlight.

"Right, then, Magician"—Hamish loaded the word with as much contempt as he could muster—"I believe I'm ready to receive you proper-like. But 'fore we get started on the whole thingamabob, what're the names a' these brats a' yours who think they can just go walkin' in my land when and where they please? Eh? Tell me that."

"It wasn't on purpose," Kate began. "We—"

"Oi!" Hamish smacked the table. "Did I tell you to speak?! Huh? Did I say, 'I want to hear from one of the brats'? Did I say, 'I wish one a' them brats would pipe up'?" The dwarves around him shook their heads vigorously. "No! I said, 'Magician.' That's 'im!" He pointed a chicken wing at Dr. Pym. "So you, lassie, just keep your yapper shut. Bloody manners on this one."

"May I present," Dr. Pym said calmly, "Katherine and Michael. Surname P."

Kate managed sort of a half curtsy, but Michael just continued staring glassy-eyed at Hamish. He seemed to be in a state approaching shock.

"And as I believe Katherine was about to tell you, their presence in your lands was entirely due to chance. You see, they had fled from the Countess—" At the mention of the Countess, there was a great deal of ill-tempered harrumphing. "And in running away, they stumbled into your lands."

"A likely story," Hamish said. "Very neat and pretty."

"In fact, while in your maze, they became separated from their younger sister. If Your Majesty would give leave, they wish very much to be reunited with her."

"Youngest sister, you say? How old's she?"

"Eleven," Kate said. "Her name's Emma."

"Little Emma out there all alone. That's right terrible, that is. Brings a bloody tear to me eye. Don't it bring a tear to your eye?" Hamish smacked the dwarf on his right, who nodded and wiped at some gravy dribbling down his cheek.

"Well, then," said the King, "since you been so honest with

me, about how it was you come here and your business and all, I guess I got no choice but to let you go, maybe send out a party to escort you to your sister, then. How's that sound, hmm?"

Dr. Pym smiled genially. "That would be most kind, Your Highness."

"Specially since"—Hamish dug his paw into the middle of a pie, scooping out a hunk of meat and cheese—"these 'ere children are just innocent and all, and not after the same bleedin' magic book you and that witch're after, the one buried in some bloomin' secret vault under the Dead City and that by rights belongs to the dwarves! Ain't that so?"

Hamish stuffed the mass of pie into his mouth and smiled through it at Dr. Pym. Kate felt her legs suddenly lose all strength. They were in deep trouble.

"Your Highness—" Dr. Pym began.

"Shut yer yap, you!" Hamish jumped up and swept his arm across the table, sending platters and goblets crashing to the floor. His face was bright red and bits of food flew from his mouth as he jabbed a short, thick finger at Dr. Pym. "Don't go lying to me! Who the bloody 'ell you think you're dealing with, eh?! You think Hamish's some Simple Simon simple dwarf, that it? You think 'cause I'm a dwarf and my body's smaller that my brain's smaller than yours too, that it?! Think it's so easy to fool me?! You think I don't know every bloody word that's spoke in my own bloody dungeons! That there weren't bloody dwarf stenographers listening to your every snore and whisper?! That I don't have a bloody complete and spell-corrected transcript of every prisoner's midnight bloomin' murmurings delivered every morning?" He reached under his beard, presumably into his shirt, and pulled out a sheaf of parchment, which he threw across the table. "And you come here and try to lie to me! To me! To take treasure that belongs to the dwarves! Bloody Books of bloody Beginning. I think not! I think not indeed!"

Dr. Pym kept his voice calm. "No, Your Highness, the book does not belong to the dwarves. They were merely guarding it."

"It's buried beneath a dwarf city! In a vault built by dwarves! It belongs to the dwarves! Period! Full stop! End of the bloody story!"

Dr. Pym looked at the children and smiled. "Don't worry."

"Don't worry?" Kate hissed back. "How are we not supposed to worry?"

"Well," Dr. Pym said, "maybe worry just a little bit."

Hamish was still ranting. "I'll teach you to trifle with a dwarf, my good conjurer."

"My King—"

Hamish waved his hand. "Nah nah nah, don't you go 'my king-ing' me; we're too late in the day for that." Hamish stood and began pacing back and forth, running his hand down his beard and talking half to himself. "Now 'ere's what's gonna happen. We slip in quiet-like to this back door, find Mr. Magic Book all on 'is lonesome— What's that? Why, yes, we will 'elp ourselves— book goes in the bag, we sneak out all rickey-tick, and the witch never has to know it was us that took it. She just finds the vault and thinks, Oh, 'ello, empty vault, what?"

"Yes, but as you no doubt read in your transcript, I cannot remember how—"

"The bleedin' golden cavern; I know, I know," and Hamish turned his head and screamed, "FERGUS!"

An extremely old dwarf, bent nearly double with age and with a long white beard that touched the floor, emerged from the shadows along the wall and tottered forward . . . slowly.

Hamish groaned. "Oh, for the love of—would you 'urry up there, Fergus? You're gonna die before you get to the bleedin' table!"

And, in fact, Kate could see dwarves exchanging money, presumably making bets whether or not Fergus would die before he got to the table. But then Captain Robbie stepped up and supported him the rest of the way.

"So, Fergus," said Hamish, "you know this"—he snapped his fingers and a serving dwarf, bowing obsequiously, brought the transcript forward, and Hamish flattened it on the table and read—"this 'golden cavern' below the Dead City that Mr. I'm-Such-a-Bloody-Smart-Wizard was talking about."

The old dwarf's voice came out in a quiet, shaky rasp. "Oh yes, yes . . . golden cavern. Dead City . . . secret passage below the . . . the . . . the . . ." Kate thought he was going to be stuck on the word indefinitely, but then he managed to get it out: ". . . the throne room."

"That's right, Fergus, that's right. In the Dead City. A secret passage below the throne room. You said you knew a way to that cavern, ain't that right?"

Fergus didn't respond.

"Fergus?"

For a second, Kate thought he might actually have expired.

Clearly, a few of the dwarves agreed, for there was more exchanging of money.

"FERGUS!"

"Hmm? Wha . . ." The old dwarf had fallen asleep.

"You told me you know a way into this 'ere golden cavern?"

"Ah yes, there's a way. Dangerous, though. Dark passage . . ."

"Right, then," Hamish said, looking satisfied. "That's settled. Now, you"—he looked at Dr. Pym—"are gonna hand over the key to this 'ere vault, and maybe, just maybe, I won't chop off all your 'eads when I come back with me magic book. How's that sound, then?"

"I'm afraid that's not possible, Your Highness," Dr. Pym said mildly. "You see, I am the key."

"What?"

"Neither the main entrance to the vault nor the back door has a lock in the traditional sense. The door was sealed by an enchantment. It can only be opened by a designated few."

As Kate and Michael watched, Hamish's face went from his normal unhealthy pallor to red to deep red to purple to finally almost an indigo color, like a bad bruise. Then he started screaming—

"You think I'm an idjit?! You think because you say that, I'm gonna take you along so you can do some hoinky-doinky magic and escape with me book?! You think—" Hamish stopped himself. "Wait, you said a few—it can only be opened by a few. Who else can open it?"

Dr. Pym opened his mouth, then paused.

"Ha! I caught you, didn't I? Who else?"

"I'd rather not say," Dr. Pym replied.

"You'd rather not say, you'd rather not say!" Hamish pointed at Michael. "Chop off that one's 'ead!"

"Wait!" Dr. Pym said, sighing. "Very well. The vault will open under my hand or . . . the hands of these children."

Both children whipped their heads around and looked up at Dr. Pym. He, however, was staring at Hamish.

Michael whispered, "What's he talking about?"

"I don't know." Kate had no idea if Dr. Pym was lying, if this was some plan he hadn't told them about, or if he was, in fact, telling the truth. And if so, how was it they could open the vault? What did that mean?

For his part, Hamish seemed to accept Dr. Pym's statement as being perfectly reasonable. He scratched his chin (or he scratched his beard; his chin was under there somewhere) and wrinkled his brow thoughtfully. "Aye, I figured there was something to do with them brats. Wandering through the maze and they come bang up to the secret door. Fishy, that was. Right! Someone lock up the wizard, and collect them runts! We're going on a field trip."

Kate heard the words before she was aware of having spoken. "I won't help you."

The hall fell silent. Hamish leaned forward onto the table so that he rested on his knuckles like a gorilla. His voice was slow and full of menace. "What did you say?"

"I won't help you open the vault." Kate wasn't entirely sure why she was standing up to Hamish. Obviously, she didn't want him to have the book. But mostly, she reflected, she just thought he was gross. She let go of Michael's hand so that she could cross her arms, thinking it made her appear more resolved.

"Un-bloody-believable." Hamish looked to the dwarves on either side of him. "You hear the cheek on this one? Whose bloody throne room is this anyway? Who's the bloody king of the bloody dwarves? Oh, you'll help me, my girl! Trust me, you will help me. What is this? Stand Up to the King Day? I don't think so. 'Cause if it was . . ." He paused, unsure how to continue, then said, "Well, there ain't no such day!"

"Whatever," Kate said, turning her head imperiously to the side. "I'm not helping you."

Hamish stood there, snorting in anger and glaring at her. "You've got spirit, lass, I'll give you that. 'Owever, unfortunately for you, I don't need your help, since according to this silly prat of a magician, all's I need is your pretty little hand." He threw a fork at one of his soldiers to get his attention. "Oi! You there! Bring me that little tart's hand. But leave the rest of her! I'll teach her who's king round 'ere!"

"You're no dwarf!"

The entire hall, Hamish included, turned and looked at Michael. The King raised his hand to stop the dwarf who'd taken a step toward Kate.

"What did you say, boy?"

Michael was red-faced and furious and his hands were clenched into fists at his sides. "I said you're not a dwarf! And it's true!"

Kate immediately understood what Michael meant; she knew

how gravely Hamish, a real, actual dwarf king, must have disappointed him.

"I know more about dwarves than almost anyone," Michael continued hotly. "All my life I've read anything I could find. They were the bravest soldiers, the most loyal friends. People were always underestimating them, but they always won because they were the smartest and worked the hardest."

The dwarves who'd been slouching at the table had perked up as Michael spoke. Kate saw Captain Robbie staring at her brother, a stunned expression having broken through his soldier's mask.

"But, you," Michael said, "you're a disgrace."

"Is that right, then?" Hamish said coldly.

"Michael," Kate whispered, reaching for his sleeve to pull him back. But all Michael's focus was on the dwarf king, and he took a step forward, out of her reach.

"That's right. And if you knew half the things my sister has done, it'd be you kneeling to her and not the other way around. She's twice as brave as you could ever be. We only want the book so we can get home. You just want it because you're greedy. You want to cut off someone's hand—cut off mine." And he stepped up and laid his thin wrist on the table.

For a long moment no one moved or spoke. All the hundreds of dwarves in the hall, those sitting at the table and the ones standing at attention, were as still as statues. Kate was both terrified for and unbelievably proud of her brother. Michael, the little boy who'd gotten picked on at orphanage after orphanage, who'd frequently had to have his younger sister bail him out of fights, whose glasses were routinely stolen and thrown into toilets, was now standing up to an ax-wielding (and clearly unstable) dwarf king. He looked so small and thin. Yet his hand was perfectly still upon the table and he was staring boldly at Hamish. Kate had always known Emma was brave, but she had never thought of Michael that way. She vowed she would never do him that disservice again.

Hamish shrugged and gave a casual wave. "Fair enough. Chop off 'is hand . . . then the girl's too."

Kate looked desperately at the wizard. "Dr. Pym, do something!"

"Now!" Hamish cried, slamming his fist on the table. "Make with the choppity-chop!"

A soldier stepped forward, pulling his ax free from his belt. He didn't get more than two steps before he was sent sprawling, his ax clattering away across the floor. Captain Robbie had struck him across the chest.

"What—" Hamish began. But Captain Robbie turned on him, and the righteous fury in his voice overrode the King's.

"No, brother. I won't let you do this."

If it was possible, the tension in the hall became even greater.

Hamish rose up to his full height, which being a dwarf was not that considerable. His small eyes burned with anger, but he kept his voice low. "I think maybe you're forgetting who's king here, eh, brother?"

"I am no traitor," Captain Robbie said. "And perhaps we should retrieve this book just to keep it from the witch. But we should be helping these children. Not seeking our own gain.

"This boy is right. You dishonor our people, and I do you good service by stopping you. You have lost yourself, brother. This corruption and laxity has gone on too long. It must be stemmed. Think what our mother would say if she could witness what you have become." He gestured to include the entire hall, the overturned tankards, the drunken dwarves. . . .

For a brief instant, Hamish seemed to waver and Kate allowed herself to hope. Then he raised his hand, jabbing a short finger at Captain Robbie. "Hold that traitor." Three dwarves rushed forward. Captain Robbie made no attempt to resist.

"Your Highness," Dr. Pym said, "if I may speak. It's true, I would rather I controlled the book myself, but forced to choose between having it in your possession or in the Countess's, I choose you. But I warn you, a severed hand will not open the vault. A living child must perform the duty. Ensure their safety, and I promise, the children will help you."

For a moment, Hamish looked as if he might argue, then he grunted and, picking up a slice of chocolate cake, waved it toward the wizard and Captain Robbie. "Fine. Lock the two a' them together. I'll deal with 'em when I get back. We leave immediately."

The two lines of armored dwarves turned and marched out of the hall.

Dr. Pym knelt beside Kate and Michael. "I'm sorry for this. You will have to manage on your own."

"Wait!" Kate said. "You were telling the truth? About the vault?"

"Oh yes, it will open for you."

"But how do you—"

"My dear, the moment you stepped into my cell, I saw that

the book had touched you. That could only have happened if you and your brother and sister are the children I have been waiting for." Then he smiled, and in the way he looked at her, it was as if her face held confirmation of something he had long suspected. "And that it should be you, of all children. I was not mistaken in the signs. . . ."

"What do you mean?! I don't—"

"There is no time to explain. However"—he lowered his voice to a whisper—"you must be the one to pick up the book. Not Hamish. You understand? I can't tell you how to do it, but you must make sure you are the one. It is essential." Then he put his hand on Kate's head and mumbled a few words. She felt an odd tingling.

"What did you do?"

"The book has chosen you, Katherine. You alone can access its full power. But it will not do your bidding until your heart is healed. I hope I have given you the means."

Before Kate could ask what he meant, the dwarf guards were dragging him away.

"Someone bring them brats," growled Hamish. "And wake up Fergus."

CHAPTER FOURTEEN
Granny Peet

"Come now, wake up, wake up! No good pretending you're still asleep . . ."

Emma groaned and burrowed under the stiff, heavy blankets. She lay there in a state of half sleep while the woman's voice kept chiding her to get up. Her first thought was that the voice belonged to Miss Sallow, the ornery, House of Bourbon–hating housekeeper at the orphanage. That would mean that everything that had happened—finding the book, going into the past, the Countess, Gabriel—had been a dream. But it had all been so real! Everything had seemed so . . . What was that smell?

She opened her eyes and found that she was lying in a bed in a dimly lit wooden cabin. The air was smoky and close, the floor made of packed earth, and what she'd taken for blankets were actually piles of old animal hides. She turned her head. In the center of the room, a thin boy crouched at a fire, his back to her, stirring something in an iron pot and filling the cabin with the smell of cooking meat and vegetables.

Okay, Emma thought, so it wasn't a dream.

"There you are. Sit up now. You're not dead. Not yet anyway."

The person speaking shambled into view from behind the bed. She was a very fat, very old woman, and she had a great deal of tangled gray hair and a face with more wrinkles than Emma had ever seen. Her hands were gnarled with arthritis, and dirt was caked under her yellowed, claw-like nails. She wore an old black dress and a black shawl and at least a dozen long, dangling necklaces that were decorated with charms, feathers, beads, tiny jars and vials, bits of root and bark, dried flower petals, the tooth of some enormous animal, and several small, beautifully carved wooden boxes. She shuffled forward in a pair of extremely worn deerskin moccasins, her necklaces jangling softly. If Emma had seen her on the street, she would've thought she was a crazy lady. She pretty much thought the same thing now.

She drew back as the woman reached toward her.

"Who are you?! Where am I?! Where's Gabriel?! Don't come near me!"

"Touchy one, aren't you?"

"You'd better get away, or when Gabriel gets here, he'll kill you!"

"Gabriel, Gabriel. He warned me you'd be a fighter; yes, he did." The old woman had a mumbly, singsongy way of speaking.

"Gabriel brought me here?" Emma said, relaxing her guard a little.

"If he hadn't, think you'd be alive and talking to me? No's the answer. Ah, but do you not remember? Think now."

And in a flash, it came back to Emma. . . . Standing on the edge of the chasm, feeling that sudden hot jolt . . . looking down and seeing the feathered end of the arrow sticking out of her side . . . her fever as Gabriel carried her through the maze. Instinctively, her hand went to her stomach.

"Now, now," the old woman said, "let Granny do that."

She pulled up Emma's shirt (Emma noticing only then that she'd been changed into a fresh, unfamiliar set of clothes). There was a patch of hardened mud a few inches to the side of her belly button. The old woman's yellow nails picked at its edge, and the mud began to flake off. Emma stared, half horrified, half fascinated, expecting to see a great hole going straight through her side. But when the last of the mud had flaked away, there was only a small pink scar.

"Hmph," the old woman said, "not bad work."

Emma was dumbfounded. "But how . . ."

"I know a thing or two, yes, yes, old Granny Peet knows a thing or two." She shuffled away, cackling softly to herself.

"I want . . . oh." A wave of dizziness swept over Emma and she had to lie back down.

"Food, what you need now. Granny's own stew. Make you strong."

"I need to talk to Gabriel. My brother and sister are lost."

"Not lost, no, not lost." The old lady was mixing and pounding something in a bowl, moving about with practiced assurance, adding a sprig of this, a dash of that, opening various vials and jars attached to her necklaces to tap in a bit of this silver powder or shake out a few drops of that green liquid, mixing and grinding all the while. "Found."

"What do you mean? You mean they're here? Where are they?"

"Not here, no. Still under the mountain. Found a friend. Always where you least expect it." She glanced toward the boy at the fire. "Hurry with that stew."

"What're you talking about? What friend? Where?"

The old woman scraped what she'd been mashing into a wooden cup, added water, swirled it about, then held it toward Emma. "Drink."

At first, Emma tasted only dirt, but when she got past that, there was mint and rosemary and honey and what she could only call sunlight and, if it were possible, birdsong. She lowered the cup. She could feel a soft golden wave traveling through her blood, spreading down to the tips of her fingers and toes, to the ends of her hair, warming her from within. "Wow."

The old woman smiled, multiplying the wrinkles in her face. "Maybe Granny knows something, hmm?"

"Who'd they find, Kate and Michael?"

"The wizard."

"Wait—you mean Dr. Pym?! They found Dr. Pym?! How do you know?"

"Saw it, how else? Silly question."

"Well, we have to go find them! Dr. Pym has to kill that stupid witch! She's awful! Where are they? We should go right now!"

The old woman shook her head, picking up a basket from the

floor. Emma could hear jars rattling inside. "You have a different path." She pulled back the leather flap hanging over the doorway, briefly letting in the full morning light. She turned to the boy at the fire. "Make her eat. I'm going to Gabriel."

"Wait!" Emma called. "I want to—" But as she stepped out of bed, her strength failed her and she crumpled to the floor.

The boy left the fire and helped Emma back to bed. It was then Emma saw that he was not a boy at all, but a girl, maybe a year younger than Kate, but thin and wiry with close-cropped hair.

She was rough, more or less shoving Emma into bed; then she went to the fire, ladled stew into a wooden bowl, and carried it over, wiping a spoon on her shirt as she came. "You can feed yourself, can't you? You're not a baby?"

"Course I can," Emma said stubbornly, though truth was, even after drinking the old woman's potion, she was weaker than she had ever felt in her life. She took the bowl and spoon from the girl. The stew was a yellowish broth with hunks of meat, vegetables, and potatoes. It smelled like heaven.

The girl sat on a stool, crossed her arms, and stared at Emma as if to make sure she finished it all.

Emma wanted to stare back, but she was also ferociously hungry, so she alternated between glaring at the girl and slurping up greedy spoonfuls of stew.

"I thought you were dead. Gabriel brought you in last night. Another five minutes, Granny said, it'd have been too late."

"She's your grandmother?"

"Nah. Everyone just calls her Granny. Granny Peet. She's a wisewoman. Does magic. That's how she cured you. Course she owns your soul now."

Emma stopped eating.

The girl gave a lopsided smile. "I'm kidding. She's not like that. You believed me, though."

"Did not."

"Sure you did. You thought Granny Peet had your soul in a jar or something."

Emma decided she didn't like this girl and was going to ignore her.

"Gabriel said the witch had you locked up but you escaped; that true?"

Emma shrugged as if it was no big deal.

"She's got them men digging in the Dead City, down under the mountain. I snuck in there. Seen 'em."

Emma stopped eating, her curiosity piqued. "What's the Dead City?"

"Place the dwarves used to live. See, long time ago, they had a city under the mountain. Then one day there comes this big earthquake, right?" The girl seemed to get excited telling the story. "Half the city just got swallowed up. Killed lots and lots a' dwarves. That's when they left and built that other city. Nowdays, people think it's haunted. Won't even go there. But I ain't afraid." She looked at Emma. "You know what the witch's got 'em digging for?"

Emma stared down at her food. "No."

"I won't tell anyone."

"I said I don't know. How come the Countess doesn't have you locked up?"

The girl laughed. "She don't mess with us. Only the towns-people. You ask me, they deserve what's happened to 'em. Lettin' themselves get caught like that. I'd have fought her. I don't care if she killed me. Them townspeople're a bunch of cowards."

Emma spooned up a last carrot, then lifted the bowl and drank the broth. She was thinking of the children trapped in the mansion and how if they tried to escape, the Countess would hurt their mothers or fathers. "What's your name?"

"Dena."

"Well, Dena, you don't know what you're talking about. So why don't you just shut your stupid mouth."

The girl jumped up, her hands balled into fists. "If you weren't sick and smaller than me, I'd make you take that back."

Emma threw away the bowl and leapt out of bed. The old woman's stew must've had something in it besides meat and veg-etables because Emma suddenly felt as strong as she ever had.

"Go on and try it!"

A second later and the two would've been rolling on the ground, fighting and punching like wildcats, but just then the flap over the door opened and a man stepped in. He had the same long dark hair as Gabriel, but he was smaller, more slender, and his face was young and unscarred. Whether he understood what had been about to happen or even cared was impossible to tell, for his ex-pression did not change. Glancing at Emma, he said to the girl, "She needs shoes." Dena hesitated for a moment; then, huffing in annoyance, she bent and pulled a pair of worn mocs from under the bed and shoved them in Emma's hands.

"Come with me," the man said, turning and raising the flap.

"I want to see Gabriel."

The man looked back over his shoulder. "Gabriel sent me." And he stepped outside. Emma slipped on the moccasins and ran after him, throwing one last defiant glance at Dena.

The village was nestled in the shoulder of the mountain between a pair of pine-studded ridges. Stepping out of the hot, close cabin, Emma paused to take a breath. The air was cool and fresh and filled with the smells of a summer morning. Emma saw that there were maybe two dozen wooden cabins, some set back among the thick-waisted trees, others crowding in to form the borders of a central thoroughfare that stretched up the slope (if "thoroughfare" can be used to describe a twenty-foot-wide strip of dirt). Emma walked behind the young man, wondering where all the people were; then they rounded a curve, and she saw. The entire village, or what she assumed was the entire village, was gathered in front of a single cabin. The people were listening to a group of six or seven old men. Emma was too far away to hear, but it seemed like a council of sorts. As Emma and the young man approached, the old men fell silent, their eyes trained on her. Emma's guide nodded respectfully, then held back the flap of the door so she could enter the cabin.

The room was dark, and darker still once the flap fell to. The young man hadn't followed her in. Emma stood there, letting her eyes adjust. There was a foul, poisonous smell in the air. A large dark shape came toward her. Emma blinked and recognized

Granny Peet. The wisewoman took Emma by the arm and drew her into the cabin.

"Where's Ga . . ."

The question died in her throat. The old woman had led her to a bed at the back of the room, where Gabriel lay, eyes closed, naked to the waist. Half a dozen deep cuts crisscrossed his arms and there was a vicious gash in his side. But it was not the wounds that made Emma suck in her breath and bite down on her lip. Blossoming outward from each of the cuts, visible under the surface of the skin, were thick black tendrils.

"Poison," Granny Peet said. "It reaches his heart, he's finished."

"So do something!" Emma pleaded. "Save him! Do something! You gotta!"

"Not so easy, child. The ingredients in the antidote are very difficult to find. Used all I had saving your life. Gabriel insisted." She picked up a bowl half filled with a chunky yellowish paste and began stirring. "I don't know, I don't know. . . ."

Emma looked down at the giant man. He'd saved her, and now he was dying. It wasn't fair. There had to be something—

Emma yanked her head back. Granny Peet had suddenly snatched at her face.

"What're you . . ."

But the old woman wasn't looking at Emma. She was staring at the end of her thick yellow fingernail, from which hung suspended a single one of Emma's tears. Granny Peet gave a thoughtful sort of mumble, then shook the tear into her bowl, told Emma to hold still, and collected half a dozen more tears, adding them all to the yellowish mixture.

"Hmm," she murmured, shuffling around the bed, stirring, "maybe . . ."

"You . . ." Gabriel's eyes were open. ". . . Wanted to see you . . ."

Emma forced herself to smile and put as much cheerfulness and confidence into her voice as she could manage. "I'm okay. All because a' you. And you're gonna be okay too. Granny's gonna fix you like she did me. She says she can for sure. Good as new." Across the bed, the old woman began smearing the concoction on his wounds. Emma could hear it beginning to bubble and hiss.

"I am . . . glad to see you well," Gabriel said, and closed his eyes.

Please, Emma thought, please let him be okay. . . .

She placed her small hands in one of his. The medicine must've burned terribly, for he clenched his hand into a fist, crushing both of Emma's. But she didn't let go. She would not let go.

CHAPTER FIFTEEN
To the Dead City

Kate and Michael walked in the center of the group, directly behind the dwarf assigned to carry the ancient, white-bearded, and
loudly snoring Fergus on his back. Hamish marched up front.
There were seven in their party.

There had been no fanfare when they departed the dwarf city.
Hamish said if his people knew he was leaving, they'd insist on
throwing a parade and he'd be kissing babies for days on end. Kate
caught the other dwarves trading glances, and Fergus even
snorted, then tried to disguise it as a cough, then ended up actually coughing horribly for nearly a minute.

They'd left through a small, out-of-the-way gate and proceeded along a series of well-maintained, torch-lined tunnels. All
the while Hamish kept up a constant chatter about the history of

the Dead City, various legends associated with it, how many bicep curls he did every morning. . . .

Kate moved close to Michael.

"You shouldn't have stood up to Hamish like that," she whispered, then squeezed his hand. "But it was really, really brave."

Michael looked embarrassed. "It was no big deal."

"Yes, it was. Emma would've thought so too."

Their conversation was muffled by the rattling of the dwarves' armor, the clank of iron heels on stone, Fergus's snores, Hamish's droning commentary, and when Michael spoke again, Kate had to ask him to repeat himself.

"Do you think she's okay?"

"I do," Kate said, with more confidence than she felt. "And like Dr. Pym told us, Gabriel is with her. He won't let anything happen."

"I wonder if we'll ever see her again."

"Of course we will. Don't even think that."

Michael nodded, and then quickly changed the subject, saying he didn't understand why Hamish wasn't bringing more dwarves. The Countess couldn't have that many Screechers. Why not just order his army to drive them away?

"It's the *salmac-tar.*"

The dwarf who'd spoken was walking behind them. He had black hair, a black beard, and a thick, heavy brow. He looked younger than the other dwarves. He made a point, Kate noticed, of keeping his voice low. "Like a year ago, right, King found out that ever since the witch got 'ere, she's been talking to them slimy, dwarf-murderin' fiends. You know about them, right?"

Kate nodded, remembering her dream in the dungeon . . . the pale, sightless creature advancing on Gabriel, its claws tapping on the stone floor of the maze. . . .

"Well, she's been promising 'em stuff. Baths're what they need, ask me. Point is, she's protectin' 'erself. Building alliances. So now if Hamish—the King, I mean—tried to attack 'er Screechers, she'd have 'ordes and 'ordes a' *salmac-tar* to 'elp 'er out. Be open war, wouldn' it? King don't want that."

"What's your name?" Kate asked.

"Wallace," he said, then added, for no obvious reason, "the dwarf."

The party had been walking for nearly an hour, and they came out of the tunnel to the edge of a large crevasse. Kate and Michael could hear, but not see, water flowing in the darkness far below.

"The Cambridge River," Hamish proclaimed, kicking a rock over the edge. "Runs down through the mountains, past the town, and right up to the dam. Used to be how we traded with them idjit townspeople. Till the witch came. Woman has no respect for the forces a' commerce. Come on now. The bridge is close. We can cross over into the old kingdom."

"Hamish would make a good tour guide," Michael said as they walked along the edge of the crevasse. "He's really well informed."

" 'E used to be one," Wallace said. " 'Fore the Queen died, when visiting dignitaries would come, 'e'd show 'em around. Always did a right fine job. When 'e was sober, I mean."

As they neared their destination, Kate found herself thinking about the things Dr. Pym had said. Why should a vault sealed more than a thousand years ago, a magic vault that would only open for a few special people, open for her and Michael and, she assumed, Emma? How was that possible? And what had the wizard meant, "that it should be you, of all children . . ."? Her of all children what? And what about him saying the book had chosen her, but to access its full power, she first had to heal her heart? The more Kate thought about everything, the more confused and troubled she became.

They arrived at an arched stone bridge guarded by a single dwarf. Seeing the King, he went down on one knee.

Hamish asked for news from the Dead City.

"Nothing, Your Highness. Though whatever that witch is looking for, she'd better find it in a hurry. Them townsmen ain't gonna last much longer. Not with how them Screechers whip 'em and starve 'em and work 'em night and day. You ask me, we should drive them out a' our mountains and—"

"Right, but who asked you, eh? You just stand there and hold your bloody spear, you nit!" Hamish shook his head and started over the bridge, muttering, "Everybody's got a bloody opinion."

On the other side of the bridge, Hamish ordered his dwarves to take off their armor. He didn't want them making more noise than they had to. Then he poked Fergus awake.

"Come on, you old coot; time to sing for your supper."

Fergus opened his eyes. They were rheumy and unfocused. "Hmm?"

"We crossed the stone bridge. How do we get to this golden cavern, then?"

"The golden cavern . . ." He seemed to have no idea what Hamish was talking about.

"Aye, the golden cavern, the golden cavern! If you were lying and don't know—" He seized the old dwarf's beard.

"Through the gate," Fergus murmured. "West along the ridge. There's a doorway marked with crossed hammers, and then stairs, many stairs. . . ."

"Right," Hamish said, turning to the group, "you lot 'ad better be like mice."

They crept down a dark, poorly maintained tunnel, which ended abruptly at a large iron door. Hamish dug beneath his beard and pulled out a heavy key. He fit it into the lock, took a breath, and turned it. The bolt shot back loudly, the sound echoing down the corridor. Kate felt the dwarves cringe.

Hamish looked back, sheepish. "Sorry 'bout that."

The tunnel ended some twenty yards past the door, giving out onto what looked like a huge, brightly lit cavern. Hamish silently ordered them onto their bellies, and the five dwarves and two children got down and crawled forward. Kate could hear the sounds of hammering and smashing, shouted orders, the crack and slap of whips. Then she and Michael were at the lip of the cavern, looking over.

They were several hundred feet above the floor of the city, which—as far as Kate and Michael could tell for its borders stretched away to darkness—entirely filled the hollowed-out heart of the mountain. Kate thought it resembled nothing so much as a vast snow-globe metropolis, one that had been shaken and shaken until towers collapsed, buildings crumbled, and fissures tore open the streets. It was the corpse of a city, left to rot for centuries.

Until now.

Directly below them, dozens of hissing gas-powered lamps poured down light onto the ruins. Most of the work was taking place in a giant roofless building. Kate could just make out men-sized shapes moving about, but they were too far away and there was too much dust in the air to see clearly what was happening. Not that it mattered. She knew the building had to be the old throne room, and the shouting and the snap of whips told the rest of the story.

"Calmartia," Hamish said quietly. "The Dead City."

"I can't believe it," Michael whispered, pushing back his glasses, which were threatening to slip off his nose, "an ancient dwarf city. I wish I had my camera."

Kate did not mention that she had seen this city once before. In a dream two nights before, she had seen it being destroyed.

Hamish motioned them back from the edge.

"Keep low and silent," he hissed, "or we are all dead."

Granny Peet eventually shooed Emma out of the cabin.

"But—but—but—" she stuttered as the old woman hustled her to the door. The black tendrils of poison under Gabriel's skin had faded, but he had yet to reopen his eyes. Emma wanted to be there when he did.

"I need him alone," the wisewoman said. "I'll call you soon enough."

Outside, the morning was nearly gone and the crowd in front of the cabin had disappeared. Emma stood there, looking up and down the dirt street. The only signs of life were a few dogs nosing through the remains of breakfast.

"Is he gonna die?"

Emma turned. The girl Dena stood at the side of the cabin. Emma guessed she had been trying to peer in the windows.

"Course not," Emma scoffed. "Take more than a bunch a' Screechers to kill Gabriel."

Dena didn't say anything. She just stood there, looking at her.

"What?" Emma demanded. "He's gonna be fine!"

Dena neither spoke nor moved.

Emma turned away and sat down on a log. She scooped up a handful of pebbles and began pitching them one by one at an iron pot. After a few moments, Dena came and sat beside her. She gathered up her own handful of pebbles but instead of throwing them just moved them from hand to hand, sifting out the dirt.

"My parents got killed last year."

Emma looked at her, but Dena was focused on the pebbles going from hand to hand.

"They were up near Cambridge Falls. Some of the witch's Screechers caught 'em. Probably thought they were from the town. Trying to escape or something."

". . . Really?"

The girl nodded.

Then Emma said, "My parents disappeared. Ten years ago."

"Are they dead?"

"No. I mean . . . I don't know."

They were both silent for a moment.

"I'm sorry," Emma said, "about what happened to yours."

"Gabriel tried to get everyone to go fight the witch then, but they wouldn't do it. Same like they won't do it now. Bunch a' cowards." And the girl hurled the entire handful of pebbles so they clattered dully off the pot.

"What do you mean?" Emma asked.

"That's what they're in there talking about," Dena said, nodding up the hill to a large two-story rectangular cabin. "Last night, Gabriel woke up the whole village, yelling that they all had to go fight. He was almost falling over 'cause of the poison. Now they'll just talk about it and talk about it and won't do nothing. They're all— Hey, where you going?"

Emma was striding up the dirt lane. She could feel the blood in her cheeks, and the edges of her vision were clouded with anger. Gabriel had told them they had to fight. Emma was going to make sure they did.

She pushed through the flap and into the warm, smoky air. It was a single large room. The old men Emma had seen earlier were gathered around a fire in the center, while the rest of the village ringed them on benches, stood against the walls, or looked down from the tiered balconies above.

One of the old men was speaking:

"We've no way of knowing how powerful the witch truly is! We have a responsibility, yes. But not to the people of Cambridge Falls. We have a responsibility to our blood! To our history!" He was beating his cane against the ground, raising small clouds of dust. "What if we fight her and lose? What revenge would she take? We don't know. We don't know what she could do. We can't risk it!"

He sat down to much murmuring. In a flash, Emma had leapt up onto a bench—

"You're all gonna die!"

The entire meeting hall—the old men in the center, the people on the benches and against the walls, the ones in the balconies overhead—all turned from whomever they were talking to and looked at her.

"You think you don't do nothing, she's just gonna let you go?! Is that how stupid you are?!" A voice inside Emma's head said she should probably not call these people stupid, but she ignored it. " 'Cause that's the stupidest thing I ever heard in my life!"

The old man who'd spoken raised his cane and pointed it at Emma.

"Remove that child!"

Emma saw a woman move toward her. She wished Kate were here. People listened to Kate. "It's true! I've seen it! Everything's dead! The trees! The animals! They're all dead! I've seen it! This place is gonna be cursed!"

"Remove her!" the old man croaked, stamping his cane on the ground.

"No."

Everyone stopped and turned, including Emma. Granny Peet's large, somewhat shabby form stood silhouetted in the doorway. She dropped the flap and shuffled forward to stand beside Emma.

"She has come to us from the future. If she says these mountains will become a wasteland, then I believe her."

"But, Granny," the old man said, a new tone of respect in his voice, "if what this child says is true—"

"It is true! Are you deaf or—" Emma began, until a look from the wisewoman silenced her.

"How are we to know what caused this devastation?" the old man continued. "Perhaps in the future this child comes from, we did fight the witch. And failed. Perhaps what the child describes was her revenge."

"Call him an old chicken," Emma hissed.

Granny Peet ignored her. "Then we must make sure we do not fail."

She took Emma's hand and led her forward till they stood beside the fire, in the center of the old men.

"I have been wisewoman of this village longer than most of you have been alive, and yes, if we confront the witch and fail, we are doomed. All we are, all our history, all our stories, will be wiped from the memory of the world. And yet"—she turned slowly, looking across the congregation—"we have no choice but to fight."

Emma noticed a strange thing begin to happen. The wrinkles were fading from the old woman's face, her eyes grew brighter, the curve in her back straightened. The old Granny Peet, wrinkled and hunched, was still there, but as she spoke, this other woman, tall and proud and beautiful, appeared as well. It was as if one were laid on top of the other.

"We all know the stories that tell of an object of great power buried in these mountains. Many of us believe these stories are what drew the witch. But what is this object she seeks? What is it capable of? The stories do not say."

Granny Peet paused. Emma could see men and women leaning forward. Overhead, balconies creaked as those above shifted to better hear.

"It is a book.

"There were once three great books of magic, the most powerful books of magic ever written. But they were lost, thousands of years ago. Even so, all wizards and wise people know of them, know of their power. Each one has the ability to reshape our world.

"Long ago, I came to believe that one of these books was buried here. But which one, I did not know. Now, thanks to this child, I do."

She laid her hand on the back of Emma's neck. Emma could feel the twisted, callused hand of the old woman and the smooth, strong hand of the young one.

"The book hidden in these mountains, the one the witch seeks with all her might, is the one that holds the secrets of time and space. It is called the *Atlas*."

A murmur swept the room, and even though she was standing beside the fire, Emma felt a chill run through her. Granny Peet raised her hand. The murmuring stopped.

"The *Atlas* allows the user to step through time. To move across the map of history. That alone should seed fear in all our hearts. But there is more." Emma felt the crowd of listeners press in even further, each of them hanging upon the old woman's words. "If a person can truly harness the book's power, he will be able not only to move through time and space, but to control it. The very fabric of our world will be subject to his whim. On that day, all our lives, the lives of all those we love, the lives of every person on this planet, will be at his mercy. The *Atlas* cannot be allowed to pass into the hands of the witch."

She stopped speaking. From the corner of her vision, Emma saw the beautiful ghost woman crumple and fade till once again only ancient, elephant-skinned Granny Peet stood beside her. For a few long moments, there was nothing but silence. Then a tall, muscular man stood at the back of the room.

"I will fight."

And one by one, they rose from their places on the benches or stepped forward from the walls until every man between sixteen and sixty was standing, declared and ready to fight.

The old man sighed. "Very well, if we must, we must. But who shall lead?"

"I shall."

Gabriel was standing in the doorway, a blanket draped around his shoulders. In a moment Emma was hugging him, burying her face in his side to hide her tears.

CHAPTER SIXTEEN
The Black Lake

Keeping close to the rock wall and moving as silently as possible, Kate, Michael, and the small band of dwarves made their way along the ridge above the old city until they arrived at a doorway into whose arch was carved a pair of crossed hammers. They passed through and found themselves in a dark chamber. Hamish rummaged under his beard and pulled out a fist-sized crystal, which he tapped against the wall. Immediately, white light filled the space, revealing a nearly vertical staircase corkscrewing away into darkness. Hamish jabbed the old dwarf, Fergus, awake.

"Oi! You'll get plenty a' sleep when you're dead, which'll be soon enough, trust me. This 'ere's the right way to go, yeah?"

Fergus blinked his rheumy eyes and peered down the stairs.

"Aye, that's the way. Down, down, all the way down. Left, right, another right, third left, sixth right, eighth left and on down, follow your nose is all. . . ." And he fell asleep again.

"Oi! Keep 'im awake; we're gonna need him. Bloody 'ell."

The staircase was narrow and steep and full of sharp, unexpected turns ("Like whoever made it wanted you to break your neck," Michael whispered, then added, "I bet it wasn't a dwarf; they probably used an outside contractor"). Fortunately, the other dwarves had produced crystals similar to Hamish's, so Kate and Michael could at least see where to put their feet. What bothered Kate more than anything was that each time they reached a place where the stairs split, Fergus would be prodded awake and forced to tell them which way to go. She pleaded with Hamish to write down what the old dwarf said so they wouldn't always be waking him, but Hamish scoffed at the idea.

"You'd love that, wouldn't you? Writing things down! There'll be no writing as long as I'm around! You can bet on that! Ha!"

The further down they went, the colder it grew; soon icicles were hanging from the ceiling and Kate and Michael could see their breath before them. Kate noticed that the dwarves had begun looking about nervously.

"Supposed to be haunted," Wallace whispered. In his right hand, he held the glowing crystal; his left gripped the haft of his ax. "It's why few dwarves ever come here. Too many died bad in this place. There're stories of dwarves who've gotten lost in the dark and felt icy hands—"

"Maybe you could tell us later," Kate suggested.

Wallace glanced at Michael, whose eyes were nearly as wide as the lenses of his glasses. "Aye," he grunted. "I can do that."

"Stop!"

The cry had come from Fergus, who Kate had supposed was still sleeping against the back of his porter. His shout caused the children to look up (they had been staring at their feet, fearful of missing a step and tumbling down the stairs), and it was then they noticed that the staircase was ending and they had arrived in a cavern. Fifteen feet away was another doorway, and the stairs resumed their downward spiral.

"This is it," said the old dwarf.

"Here?" Hamish said. "This can't be it."

Kate had to agree. The cavern was a raw room of earth and rock. The only notable points were the two entrances and a small dark lake at one end.

"Nope," Fergus said, climbing to the ground and settling himself against the wall. "This is it."

"Is that right?" Hamish sneered. "This is the golden cavern you were soooooooo certain you could find?" He grabbed Fergus's beard and gave it a vicious tug. "If you've led us wrong, you old pile of bones, I'll make you eat your beard!"

Fergus chuckled. "Course this ain't the golden cavern. That's through there, it is." He pointed at the black lake. "Down to the bottom of the water, you find a tunnel, swim through, through, through, come up, bang there you are, golden cavern neat as you please. Careful, though." Fergus pulled out a long clay pipe and began to pack the bowl. "Something lives down there. Dark and wiggly it is."

He lit a match and gave the pipe three short pulls, his cheeks caving inward. Then he leaned back and blew a large, lazy smoke ring. None of the other dwarves had spoken or moved.

"This," whispered Wallace, leaning close to Kate and Michael, "is not good."

"What do you mean something lives down there?" Hamish demanded. "What lives down there?"

The old dwarf shrugged. "Dunno. Never gone in there meself. Not daft, ye know."

"THEN 'OW THE BLOODY 'ELL DO YOU KNOW IT GOES TO THE BLOODY GOLDEN CAVERN?!"

As far below the city as they were, Kate wondered how the Countess's Screechers couldn't hear Hamish's ranting.

Fergus calmly blew another smoke ring. "Me brother went through. Told me all about it."

"So why am I not talking to your brother instead a' you, you worthless old cod?!"

"Suspect 'cause 'e's dead. Remember it clear as day. I was sitting 'ere, right where I am now, enjoying me pipe. I do like a good pipe. Dennis—that's me brother—he disappears into the pool there, I wait, wait, wait, awful long time, finally 'e comes back out, 'ead bobbing up yonder, saying, 'Fergus, old boy, there's a tunnel and it leads to a beautiful golden cavern!' 'A golden cavern?' I says. 'Aye,' 'e says. 'And is it real gold?' I says. 'Not real gold,' 'e says, 'it's—*urp!*' "

"Urp?!" Hamish sputtered. "What the bloody 'ell does 'urp' mean?"

"Nothing. That's the sound he made when the monster ate 'im. Grabbed 'im around 'is neck and down 'e went. *Urp*."

For a long moment, no one said anything.

Then Hamish exploded. He jumped around, screaming and spitting and smashing anything he could with his ax. For a second, Kate thought he was going to attack Fergus, who was sitting there smoking his pipe and not bothering to hide the amused grin on his face.

"Traditionally," Michael whispered, "dwarves aren't big swimmers."

"I'm not sure the swimming is the problem," Kate replied.

Huffing noisily through his beard, Hamish stuck his face into the old dwarf's. "So this is your secret bloody way, sending us traipsing through some underwater monster's living room?"

Fergus shrugged. "Not my way. The way. The only way."

Hamish glowered, and Kate saw his knuckles tighten on his ax as if he were considering lopping off the old dwarf's head, but then he turned. "Right! Into the drink, you lot!" He sneered at Kate and Michael. "And yeah, that means you brats too."

Fergus sent out another smoke ring and chuckled quietly. "*Urp*."

The party gathered around the black pool. The dwarves had to take off their heavy boots and leave behind all but their lightest knives. Kate and Michael removed their jackets and shoes. Kate transferred the two photos she was carrying, the one of herself in the bedroom and the photo Abraham had given her, the one he'd said was the last picture he'd ever taken, into her pants pocket. Seeing Abraham's photo brought back the morning she'd spent in his room with Emma. It seemed to Kate that, though only a few days had passed, the memory belonged to another life.

"Are you going to be okay?" Michael asked.

"Of course. I'll be fine." Of the three siblings, Kate was far and away the weakest swimmer. The first few orphanages they'd lived at hadn't bothered giving the children lessons. When Kate finally did learn, she was nearly nine, and she had never overcome her fear and unease in the water, her sense that she was always struggling not to drown. And now, as she stuffed her balled-up socks into her shoes, her hands were trembling.

A couple of the dwarves gingerly dipped their toes in the water, only to pull them out quickly. "Maybe it's dead, whatever it was," Kate heard one mutter. Fergus was still chuckling and smoking at the back of the cave. Black-bearded Wallace approached with two glowing crystals.

"You'll be needin' these. Dark as pitch down there, looks like."

"Thank you," Kate said. Despite the light it gave off, Kate found the crystal was cool in her hand.

"Right, then." Hamish stepped to the edge of the pool. "No time like the present," and he seized a dwarf and threw him in.

There was a large splash, and the dwarf's head reappeared as he thrashed about, struggling to stay above the surface. "Under the water, you!" Hamish shouted, snatching up a large rock. Seeing he had no choice, the dwarf took a breath and dove. Kate watched the glow of his crystal slowly fade and disappear. There was another splash as Hamish pushed a second dwarf into the pool.

One of the dwarf guards began to back away. "I can't swim, Your Highness."

"Then it's 'igh time to learn!"

A splash, and he disappeared as well.

Hamish turned on Kate and Michael. "You goin' in yourselves, or you rather I toss you? Either way, you're getting wet!"

"Come on," Kate said.

She and Michael waded into the dark water. It was so cold that Kate's feet and ankles began to ache almost immediately. They came to a ledge; the water barely reached to Kate's knees. The next step would take them into the abyss.

"Michael, your glasses."

"Oh, thanks." He fumbled them into his pocket, trying not to drop his glowing crystal.

"You'd better go first. You're a faster swimmer. I don't want to hold you back."

"Kate—"

"It'll be okay."

Even as he nodded, she wondered just how unconvincing she must sound. And for a brief moment, she realized the insanity of their situation. They were inside a mountain, under the remains of an ancient dwarf city, about to dive into a black pool where a monster might or might not still be living, all so they could retrieve a lost magic book. What was she thinking? She had started to take a step back, pulling Michael with her, when a rough hand shoved her from behind.

"In ya go!"

They were swallowed by icy black water. Almost immediately, Kate saw Michael's crystal begin to move away. He was swimming downward. She followed, terrified at the thought of losing him. After a few strokes, Michael leveled off. That's when Kate saw another light, off in the darkness, and another, faint and fuzzy, past that. She realized how far they had to go.

Don't panic, she told herself, don't panic.

They had entered a kind of narrow trench, walls on either side, the rocky ceiling directly above, and below them . . . well, Kate didn't look below them. She concentrated on the light from Michael's crystal and her own jerky, weak stroke. It was impossible to say how much time passed. Her arms grew heavy. Her heart hammered in her chest. Worst was the pressure in her lungs; it felt as if they were collapsing upon themselves, squeezing out every last ounce of air. She tried to tell herself that she wasn't falling behind, even as the glow from Michael's crystal grew more and more faint.

Then something struck her foot.

Panic shot through her, and she whirled about. She saw a mass of flailing limbs and thought for a moment it was the monster. Then she recognized one of Hamish's dwarves. He was making wild gestures, urging her to move aside. She did and he swam past, with strokes even more crazed and unschooled than hers. He was perhaps five feet further on when three long fingers slid up out of the darkness and seized him by the leg. The fingers were a cancerous yellow-green, each one nearly a yard long and as thick around as a man's arm. The dwarf hacked at them with his knife, bubbles exploding around him, but he was already being pulled down. Kate tried to scream and her lungs filled with water. Choking, she swam to the top of the trench, pounding at the rock, searching for air, for escape. The crystal fell from her hands. She grabbed at it, fumbling, but it slipped into darkness, and then there was nothing but darkness, all around her, enveloping her. . . .

"Kate! Kate!"

Her eyes opened. A second later, she was coughing and hacking, the foul-tasting water spewing from her nose and mouth. Michael pounded her on the back.

"Come on! Come on!"

"Michael . . . I'm okay. . . ."

"I thought . . . I thought . . ." He hugged her tightly.

"Hey there now, let the lass breathe."

Kate felt Michael being pulled away. Wallace stood over them. Water was dripping from his long black beard, and his matted hair was plastered to his face. All about them, dwarves were wringing out their beards, shaking water from their clothes, and meanwhile everything was suffused with a soft golden light emanating from thousands of points on the walls and ceiling.

"What happened?"

"Wallace found you floating in the tunnel. He pulled you out. He told us"—Michael lowered his voice—"he told us what happened."

The dwarf was helping her to sit up. "Thank you," Kate said. "You saved my life."

Wallace reddened, then, glancing about, he said quietly,

"Captain Robbie told me to look out for you two. But keep that between us, then, eh?" He gave a very unsubtle wink.

"Are you really okay?" Michael asked.

"Yes," Kate said, though even as she said it, she noticed that her whole body was shaking and the tips of her fingers were blue.

"Right, then!" Hamish was a few feet away, coiling his beard into a rope to squeeze out the water. "Spread out, lads! There's a door hidden here somewhere." He looked at Kate and Michael. "You two brats can help."

"No!" Michael said fiercely. "My sister's cold and wet. She needs to get warm."

Hamish looked about to argue, but then he saw how Kate was trembling and waved his hand. Wallace pulled out flint and a piece of black wood and somehow, in moments, had a fire going. Michael had Kate move close to the flames.

"Drink this." Wallace held out a leather flask.

Kate took a sip and nearly gagged, but immediately a warmth spread through her body. The shaking stopped. Her fingers returned to their normal color.

"You too," Wallace said to Michael.

"What is it?"

"Whiskey. Me ma's own special mash. She always said it could bring back the dead."

It did not take Hamish's dwarves long to find the hidden doorway. There was a cry, and Kate saw the dwarves clustered at a spot along the golden wall, staring down a tunnel that had not been there moments before.

"Now that's more like it." The dwarf king was beaming. He snapped his fingers at Kate and Michael, who were still huddled around the small fire. "Right. This ain't a picnic. Let's go get me book."

Fifty yards down the passage, the band came to a door. Kate's first thought was that they'd made a mistake. This was not the door to a secret vault. It was more like the door to someone's bedroom. Painted white wood with a brass handle. There was even a small plaque in the center that read PRIVATE.

Kate thought the plaque had to be someone's idea of a joke.

Hamish grasped the handle and pulled.

The door didn't budge.

He braced his foot against the rock wall and pulled again.

Nothing.

"Dr. Pym said it would only open—" Michael began.

"Shut it, you!" Hamish snapped. He ordered a pair of his dwarf guards to take hold of him, and together the three of them strained against the door till Hamish's hands slipped off the knob and they fell to the ground in a grunting pile. Hamish leapt up, searching for anyone who might be laughing.

The dwarves were stone-faced.

"You there"—Hamish pointed at the one dwarf who'd carried his ax through the tunnel—" 'ave a chop at it."

"I doubt it's actually wood," Michael said. "An ax won't—"

"Oi! You want a great bloody sock in the mouth? Then shut your bleedin' piehole! Now 'ave at it!"

Kate and Michael stepped back as the dwarf raised his ax, took two running steps, and swung with all his might. There was a clang, the sound of shattering metal, and something flew backward. The something was the dwarf; he lay stunned upon the ground, his ax in pieces beside him. The door did not have a mark on it.

"Right," Hamish said, "had to try. Guess here's where we see if it was worth bringing you kiddies along. Come on, we're not getting any younger."

"I'll do it," Kate said. She was thinking the door might be booby-trapped, and if so, she didn't want Michael getting hurt.

But as she stepped forward, Kate found herself wishing more than anything that the door would not open. If it didn't open, she and Michael and Emma were not special. They were just three ordinary children and everyone would see that and let them go.

She reached out and took hold of the brass knob. Please, she thought.

There was a soft click, and the door swung open.

CHAPTER SEVENTEEN
Inside the Vault

The first thing Kate felt—as the door opened, revealing a high-ceilinged room lit by crystals in the walls, and there in the center, sitting on a stone pedestal as if it had been waiting for her, the book, their book—the very first thing she felt was that after everything that had happened in the last few days, this—the fact the vault door had opened for her and no one else—was the worst turn yet.

We're in deep trouble, she thought.

Hamish knocked her to the ground as he rushed past.

"No!"

Hamish's fingers paused inches from the book's leather cover. He turned to Kate, who was being helped to her feet by Michael and the black-bearded Wallace.

"No?!"

"You can't touch it."

"Oh, I can't, can't I? Well, just you watch, missy—"

"You'll die."

Kate saw Michael glance at her. She had no idea what she was saying. All she knew was that Hamish couldn't touch the book first. Dr. Pym had said so.

"You're lying," the dwarf king sneered.

"Michael and I are the only ones who can pick it up. Dr. Pym told me. But go on if you don't believe me. See what happens. Except you won't, 'cause, you know, you'll be dead. But go ahead." She crossed her arms and tried to look unconcerned.

Hamish turned from Kate to the book, back to Kate, then back to the book. It was obvious he wanted it very badly. But finally he muttered something under his breath, spat, and then snapped his fingers angrily. A dwarf grabbed Kate by the arm and dragged her forward. Hamish leaned in, his breath warm and rotten in her face. "If you're playing with me, girl, you and your brother are dead, understand? I'll cut your throats and feed you to that monster in the pool. Now—bring me that book!"

Propelled by Hamish's shove, Kate stumbled to a halt a foot from the pedestal. The book appeared to be glowing, the light in the vault enhancing its natural emerald hue. It was then—standing above the book with nothing and no one between it and her—that she finally heard it.

The book was speaking to her. It told her it had been waiting for her for a thousand years. It told her to claim it as her own.

She reached out and lifted it off the pedestal.

Now what? she thought.

She felt a tug in her stomach, and the floor disappeared beneath her feet.

"Hello."

Kate blinked. She was in a study, books and manuscripts in piles everywhere, a small fire crackling in the grate. Outside the window, she could see the tops of cars passing in the street below. Snow was falling, muffling the sounds of the city. But what truly caught her attention was the man sitting three feet away: he was swiveled toward her in his chair, a paper- and book-strewn desk behind him, dressed in his habitual and habitually rumpled tweed suit, pipe in one hand and a teacup halfway to his mouth as if he had been in the act of taking a sip when Kate had stepped out of thin air. Naturally, he was smiling.

"Can I help you?" Dr. Pym said.

For a moment, Kate could only stand and stare, trying and failing to grasp what had happened.

"Dr. Pym—" she began, then stopped, remembering her mistake in the dungeon the night before, when it turned out he hadn't the foggiest notion who she was. "Do you—do you know who I am?"

"Of course," he replied amiably. "You're the young lady who just appeared in my study."

Her heart sank. She had traveled even further into the past, back to a time before their meeting in the prison. And not just into the past—to another place. As she looked out the window, seeing the cars, a lamppost, everything that suggested a normal human city, it was obvious she was somewhere very far from

Cambridge Falls. How was any of this possible? She hadn't placed a photograph in the book. She hadn't even opened it!

"My dear," the old man said, interrupting her thoughts and pointing with the end of his pipe at the book, "is that what I think it is?"

"Yes—but why did it bring me here? All I did was touch it!"

"Did you now? Fascinating."

"I picked it up before Hamish could! Just like you told me to!" She knew he wouldn't understand what she was saying, but she couldn't help herself. It was all pouring out.

"Hamish? Is that oaf involved in this?"

"Wait! You must've known what was going to happen! That's why you told me to touch the book first!"

"I did? Can't say as I remember—"

"No, not now! In the future! But how would you know the book would take me here? Unless . . ." Kate could feel the answer tugging at her, that she just had to keep talking. "You must've done something! Back in the dwarf throne room! When you told me to make sure I touched the book first! You put your hand on my head and I felt this tingling. You must've done some spell to make the book bring me here!"

Dr. Pym leaned back in his chair, placed his teacup on a messy stack of papers, stuck his pipe in his mouth, and proceeded to pat himself down for matches. "I think you had best tell me everything. But first"—his pipe lit, he shook out the match, then reached forward—"why don't you give me that? I suspect the type of magic that brought you here is somewhat unstable, and I don't want you popping off."

"But what if the book disappears and I can't get back? It must already exist, right? In this time?"

"Ah. I take it the book has disappeared once before?"

"Yes."

"And this other instance, how much time passed before it vanished?"

Kate thought back. She and Emma had gone into the past, found Michael, been captured by the Secretary and dragged to that strange fantasy ball, then had been forced to sit on the patio talking to the Countess. . . .

"Half an hour. About."

"So we have a bit of a window. Come, come."

He held out his hands, and Kate relinquished the book. Dr. Pym placed it on the desk behind him.

"Now," he said, "from the beginning."

Kate stamped her foot in anger. "No! I've already told you twice; you just don't remember because it hasn't happened yet!"

"Well, that hardly seems my fault."

"But there's no time! Hamish is going to have his dwarves kill us if we—"

"My dear, why do you keep mentioning Hamish? That scoundrel would never have the authority to kill anyone."

"But he's king of the dwarves!"

Dr. Pym chuckled. "No, no. I'm afraid that simply couldn't be. I am close friends with the present queen. Esmerelda, lovely woman. And she agrees with me that Hamish would make a disastrous king. Robbie is to assume the throne."

"But she died without a will!" Kate could hear herself shouting. "And because Hamish was older, he got to be king! And he wants the book! He's in the vault right now with Michael! Well, not now-now, future-now!" She knew she wasn't making much sense. She wanted to pick up something and throw it at the wizard to make him understand. "And you can't do anything because you're still locked in the dungeon back in the dwarf city!"

"Oh, that is bad," Dr. Pym said, exhaling a cloud of smoke. "Very bad indeed. But I'm afraid I still don't understand. How could Hamish get into the vault? It's quite impossible without . . ." He stopped and gazed at Kate. His voice became very soft. "You. You opened the vault."

Kate nodded.

He leaned forward. "You say you have a brother?"

"And a sister! Michael and Emma! And they're both in trouble! You have to do something." Kate could feel her eyes welling with tears.

"Oh dear," Dr. Pym said quietly. "I'm afraid now I must insist you do tell me everything. From the beginning."

"Stanislaus?" It was a woman's voice. Kate turned, listening to footsteps approaching down a hall, the voice getting closer. "Richard's stuck at the college. I think we should just go ahead and have lunch, don't you? And who are you talking to?"

The door opened and a young woman entered. She was wearing jeans and a gray sweater. She had dark blond hair, hazel eyes, and a kind face. She was casually beautiful. The moment Kate saw her, two things happened. First, she realized the woman she was looking at was her mother. Second, the floor disappeared beneath her feet.

"WHERE IS IT?!"

Kate stood at the pedestal, bathed in greenish light, gasping, her heart hammering in her chest. Before she could begin to process what had happened, she was seized by the arm and yanked around.

"Where is it?"

Her face was sprayed with spittle. She was dimly aware of being shaken violently. The book. That's what he was yelling about. The book was gone. But so what? She had seen her mother.

"You tricked me! You and that wizard!"

. . . Her mother. She had seen her mother.

"I'll kill you!"

Kate saw something flash in Hamish's hand, then heard footsteps behind her, and she was wrenched out of his grip and thrown to the ground. She could hear Wallace arguing with the King that they might need Kate to get the book back; they had to bring her to the wizard. She knew he was saving her life.

"Are you okay?" Michael was kneeling beside her. "You disappeared, then you came back, but the book was gone. What happened?"

Kate gripped her brother's hand. "I saw—"

There was the sound of a blow, and Wallace staggered back. Hamish was breathing loudly through his beard, one hand grasping his knife, the other curled into a meaty fist. For a moment, the dwarf king glared at Kate, then he sheathed his knife and barked, "Bring 'em! But if that wizard don't get me book back, they all die! The old man and the brats!" And he turned and stalked out of the chamber.

A dwarf grabbed Michael by the collar and dragged him into the tunnel. She hadn't been able to tell him. Another dwarf approached Kate, but Wallace waved him off. He placed a gentle hand on her shoulder and guided her toward the door.

"You all right, then?" he asked quietly.

"Yes," Kate replied, her mouth dry. "Thank you."

Walking down the dark tunnel, Kate replayed the memory of her mother entering the room. She wanted to lock in the details before they had a chance to fade. She saw her mother's blond hair and hazel eyes, her face, intelligent, gentle, surprised at finding this girl standing before her. Richard! That was the name her mother had said. That had to be their father. Kate marveled at how seemingly so little—a voice in a hall, a name, a woman walking through a door—could mean so much.

But (and here Kate felt herself growing angry) why hadn't Dr. Pym told them he knew their parents? Why would he keep that secret? Could he find them now? And how was it that simply touching the book had sent her into the past? For that matter, how had she come back with no book at all? Her head spun with questions. Kate forced herself to stay calm. She had seen her mother. For now, that was enough.

The party arrived in the golden cavern and clustered around the pool. The dwarves stared at the dark water nervously. Kate could tell Michael was burning to talk to her, but the guard held him back.

Hamish was ranting about the things he was going to do to Dr. Pym. "I'll rip 'is bleeding spine out! I'll make 'im eat his own foot!" And, still ranting, he pushed the first dwarf into the pool.

The monster did not reappear, and the journey back through the trench was uneventful. As she swam, Kate could see the twin lights of Michael and his guard ahead, and the few times she looked back, Wallace was there, knife gripped in his hand, staring into the darkness below, ready to protect her in case of attack. But nothing happened.

Then her head broke the surface of the pool, and she sucked in the stale cave air and heard a voice that froze her heart.

"Ah, there she is."

Cold hands lifted her up. As the water cleared her eyes, she saw that all the dwarves, including old white-bearded Fergus, were on their knees, hands bound behind their backs. A dozen black-clad figures, brandishing swords and crossbows, stood guard over them. One of the Screechers held Michael by the shoulders. He looked frightened but unharmed.

Kate's eyes went to the speaker, who was moving toward her, giggling and rubbing his hands.

"My dear, my dear," cooed the Secretary, smiling his gray-toothed smile, "how very nice to see you again."

CHAPTER EIGHTEEN
The Raven

Emma and Gabriel, along with the girl Dena and the rest of the band, climbed the mountain along no trail that Emma could see, but that Gabriel and the others seemed to know by heart. Gabriel explained they would circle the peak to a secret tunnel that the village scouts used to spy on the Dead City. The way was steep and rocky, and they had been climbing for less than half an hour when Gabriel abruptly picked Emma up and swung her onto his back.

"We must move more quickly."

Gabriel had not wanted to take Emma. But Granny Peet had insisted.

"She is tied to the *Atlas*. If you find it, you will need her."

"That's right," Emma had said. "And you gotta take Dena too. Or I'm not coming."

And so Emma had been outfitted with new clothes and boots and a knife and, an hour after the meeting, she and Dena and the small band of men had been given a blessing from Granny Peet and had set off up the mountain.

Gabriel called for them to stop in a stand of pines just below the summit while he sent a scout to the tunnel entrance. The men squatted and checked their weapons in silence. Gabriel was conferring quietly with two of his men, so Emma wandered off through the trees. Ten yards in, the mountain gave way to a sharp cliff. Emma found a boulder jutting out past the trees and scrambled up the side.

Lying on her stomach, she had a view out across the valley, and for the first time in two days, she saw Cambridge Falls. The blue expanse of lake shone jewel-like in the midday sun, and on its far side, Emma could make out a dark clustering she guessed was the houses of the town.

Seeing Cambridge Falls again, the place where everything had begun, made her think of her brother and sister. Granny Peet had said Dr. Pym was with them. That gave her hope. Perhaps Kate and Michael would even be waiting in the village when she and Gabriel returned. Wouldn't that be something? Arriving in the village having defeated the Countess's Screechers, leading all those poor, grateful men. Michael would no doubt want to hear the details of the battle, but she'd just wave her hand and say, "Oh, you know how battles are. You've seen one, you've seen them all." And if Kate scolded her for abandoning them back in the tunnels, Emma would apologize and tell Kate she was absolutely right. "Though," she would add after a moment's pause, "if I hadn't gone back, I couldn't have saved Gabriel's life, but you know best, Kate dear." Emma smiled, and for a moment she actually relaxed, allowing herself to savor the warmth of the rock beneath her, the cool of the wind against her face, and what was, in many respects, a beautiful summer's day.

"You oughta get down from there."

Emma lifted herself up and looked back over her shoulder. Dena stood just inside the trees.

"Someone could see you."

Emma laughed. "Who's gonna see me up here?"

"You don't know. The witch, she's got ways. You shouldn't take the chance."

Emma sensed the girl was right; unfortunately, whenever someone told Emma she "should" do this or "shouldn't" do that, her lifelong habit had been immediately to do the exact opposite.

"Let her see me. I'm not afraid of her."

Just then a *caaawww* echoed across the valley. Emma looked up to see a large black raven soaring high above their heads. She felt a sudden queasiness in the pit of her stomach as she remembered what Abraham had said the night they escaped from the mansion, that the Countess used birds as spies. Emma was trying to make up her mind what to do when she heard feet pounding down through the trees, and Gabriel was there, calling to her in a fast, angry hiss:

"Get down! Now!"

She scrambled off the rock, skinning the heels of her hands.

Gabriel unslung his long rifle and put it to his shoulder. The bird was flying away from them, and though it grew smaller and smaller with each wingbeat, Gabriel didn't fire. He merely followed it, as if there were an invisible string stretching from the bird to the tip of his rifle. With each passing second Emma's panic rose, and she prayed for him to shoot, as if by killing the bird he could erase her fault. Finally, he did, when the bird was no more than a black speck against the blue. For a moment, nothing happened, and Emma was sure he'd missed. Then the bird torqued sideways and fell in a twisting spiral into the trees.

The other men were beside him now, gathered at the edge of the cliff.

"One of her messengers. She knows."

"Perhaps." Gabriel slung the rifle back across his shoulder. "Our only hope is speed. We leave immediately."

As one, the men disappeared into the trees up the hill.

Emma seized Gabriel's hand. She was on the verge of tears. "Gabriel, I'm . . . It's my fault. Dena told me to get down, but I was stupid. . . . I . . ."

Gabriel knelt beside her. She expected him to be angry. The mission was already dangerous; now it was only more so. But when he looked at her, he seemed simply disappointed. Somehow, it made her feel even worse.

"If the raven was tracking us, it has been tracking us since the village. Seeing you made no difference. Come."

He turned and allowed her to clamber onto his back. She locked her arms around his neck, burying her head against his shoulder as he rose and started up the mountain. Hot, silent tears streamed down her face, her fantasies of a minute before, of acting haughty when she saw Kate and Michael, returning to haunt her. She promised herself she would be smarter. She would do whatever Gabriel said, sacrifice whatever was asked, if only it meant seeing her brother and sister again. She would be better.

Emma closed her eyes and let herself be borne, effortlessly, up the mountain.

CHAPTER NINETEEN
The Battle of the Dead City

Hamish had refused to get out of the pool. He stood there, waist-deep in the black water, knife in one hand, roaring at the Secretary and his Screechers to come get him. But something must've brushed his leg, for he gave a yelp and, with one remarkably nimble leap, flew out of the pool. He was fallen upon and bound immediately. Even then, with a Screecher's boot on his neck, he kept up a string of curses.

The Secretary ignored him. Grinning victoriously at Kate, he jerked his football-shaped head toward the stairs, and the *morum cadi* yanked the dwarves to their feet and began marching them up toward the Dead City.

Kate and Michael, the only two whose hands weren't tied, were allowed to walk together, in the middle of the group. Wallace and the white-bearded Fergus were at the head, while Hamish, who sounded like he was being dragged protesting up each step, brought up the rear.

"Kate . . ."

"I know. It'll be okay."

"You always say that. How is it going to be okay?"

Kate had to admit Michael had a point. "I don't know. But it will be. I'll think of something."

She took his hand and for a moment they walked in silence, listening to Hamish cursing the Screechers behind them.

"So what did you see?" Michael asked, even more quietly than before. "What were you going to tell me?"

Kate opened her mouth to tell him about their mother, but the words that came out were, "I saw . . . Dr. Pym."

"You saw Dr. Pym? In the past?"

Kate had to shush him, and he continued in an excited hiss:

"Oh, Kate, that's not a coincidence. Absolutely not! The odds would be . . . Well, I'd need a calculator, but it would be highly, highly unlikely that the book would happen to take you to Dr. Pym. You'd better tell me everything."

So as they climbed the steep corkscrew of stairs, she told Michael about Dr. Pym, the study, the snowy city outside the window. But though she commanded herself—Tell him who you saw, he deserves to know—each time she started to, she was seized by an inexplicable fear. In the end, she said nothing, and the memory of seeing their mother stayed locked inside her.

"Amazing," Michael said. "He's up to something. Some wizardy plot; I can feel it. But how were you able to come back without the book? You need it to move through time. Then again, the book took you to Dr. Pym and you didn't need a photo. It's all very curious."

"I kno—"

Suddenly, Kate heard something and looked over her shoulder. The Secretary, wheezing from the climb, had come up behind them. "What are you two birdies talking about?"

"Nothing."

"Oh, I'm sure, I'm sure. Just so happy to see you again. Very bad losing you in the tunnels. Couldn't tell the Countess that. Thought to myself, Where will they go? Clever little birdies like them. To the book, of course. So off I hurried to the Dead City. And came you did. Saw you and the little dwarvsies, sneak-sneak-sneaking around." He coughed violently and hacked something gray against the wall. "But where is little sister? Separated? Lost? Dead, perhaps? Such a shame." He clucked his tongue in exaggerated sympathy, and Kate had to fight the urge to knock him backward down the stairs.

She gripped Michael's hand fiercely. "Don't listen to him."

They climbed on in silence and, half an hour later, entered the Dead City.

The Screechers led Michael and Kate and the dwarves down rutted, debris-littered streets between the shells of ancient buildings. Overhead, dozens of lamps hissed gassily, casting everything in a yellow-green hue. Everywhere they passed Screechers. There seemed to be no end to the black-clad ghouls. Finally, the party stopped at the edge of what Kate guessed had once been the main square. Four enormous open-air cages had been erected, and the children watched as a line of thin, hollow-eyed men were driven into one by a crew of Screechers. More men—perhaps fifty total—huddled in the other cages. They sat or stood about listlessly, like ghosts, but as awareness of the dwarves and even more—or so it seemed to Kate—of her and Michael spread among them, the men began to gather at the bars of their cages, staring at the children with wide, sunken eyes.

The Secretary hissed an order, and she and Michael were wrenched apart—Michael and the dwarves herded toward the cages, while the Secretary, with a clammy hand locked about her wrist, dragged her toward one of the shattered buildings that ringed the square.

He brought her to a room on the second floor and shut the door.

"Have a seat, my dear."

The room was empty save for two chairs, a desk, and a gas lamp that hung on a chain from the ceiling. The setup of the furniture, along with the air of displeased authority, reminded Kate of Miss Crumley's office at the orphanage. How long ago had that been? A month? A year? Had it even happened yet? Of course, Miss Crumley's office wasn't missing a wall the way this one was. Kate stepped toward the edge, hoping to see Michael in the square below.

The Secretary slammed his hand on the desk, startling Kate.

"Little birdies should do what they're told. Now pleeeeaaasssse, have a seat!"

Reluctantly, Kate came and sat across from him. The man folded his hands and attempted something like a smile. It was then Kate saw the tiny yellow bird peeking out of his jacket. The head and beak were visible for only a moment, then disappeared. The man seemed not to have noticed. He was staring at Kate with a hungry expression.

"So, my dear, you opened the vault?"

Kate shrugged.

"Don't know what that means, do you? But I do. Didn't I see it, hmm? Yes, moment you arrived. Before even the Countess, I saw." As he spoke, his fingers twisted themselves into knots. "The first dwarfie we caught told me how you opened the vault when no one else could. How you touched the book and, poof, disappeared. Then came back, but no book. Just you. Dim-dumb Hamish couldn't have been happy about that, could he?" He clucked his tongue. "Not happy at all. But"—he gave Kate another of his hideous smiles—"to business—once you touched the book, exactly what happened? And please, be as precise as possible."

Kate said nothing.

"Not talking? Of course, so brave. Such a heart. But . . ." He turned his head and whistled. A few moments later, the door opened and a Screecher entered, carrying a brutal-looking crossbow. He took up a position behind Kate, where the open wall looked out over the square. Kate watched in horror as he fitted a bolt into the instrument and cranked it back.

"What's he doing?!"

"Why, he's going to kill someone. Now, I'll not pretend I'm going to harm your brother. You both are far too valuable. However, for every one of my questions you don't answer, he will kill a man from Cambridge Falls, no doubt the beloved father to one of those dear children you met back with the Countess. Understand?"

Kate nodded numbly.

"Excellent. So you touched the book and . . ."

"I . . . went into the past."

"See, that wasn't difficult. When in the past?"

"I'm not sure. A few years, I think."

"And?"

"And then I came back."

The Secretary barked at the Screecher, shocking Kate with the abrupt harshness of his voice. "Kill one!"

"Wait! Wait! Okay . . . Dr. Pym was there."

"Ah! So the old wizard has his hand in this. I suspected as much. A powerful adversary. Very powerful indeed. And perhaps this wasn't the birdie's first time meeting the good doctor, hmm? You had a previous acquaintance?"

"Yes," Kate said quietly.

"The picture becomes clear. And did anyone else attend this pleasant reunion?"

Kate hesitated. The Secretary raised his hand.

"Yes! There was . . . a woman."

"A woman. Any guesses who?"

Kate shook her head.

"So just a random woman. Of no importance. Hmm." He scratched the side of his head with a jagged nail, then looked at the Screecher. "I changed my mind. Kill the brother."

Instantly, the Screecher brought the crossbow to his shoulder.

"No! I'll tell you! Please!"

The Secretary held up a finger. The black-garbed creature paused, waiting.

"It was . . . my mother."

"Your mother? That's very odd. Very odd indeed . . ." As Kate watched, he took the yellow bird from inside his jacket and began to caress its head, cooing, "What's he doing, my love? Why the child's mother? How could . . ." The Secretary began to giggle. "Yes, yes, of course, ingenious. And elegant. Clever old man." He stowed the bird in his jacket and gave Kate his widest, most revolting grin yet. "Well, if the book is in the past, you'll just have to go back and get it, won't you, my dear?"

"What're you talking about? That's impossible! I can't!"

"Ah yes, for how can you go into the past to retrieve the book if you need the book to go into the past? Doesn't make a great deal of sense, does it? A conundrum. A puzzle. Indeed. Shall I tell you?" He jumped up, scuttling around the desk till he was in front of Kate, pinning her shoulders back and staring into her eyes. "You've been having visions, haven't you? Things you can't explain. That is because part of the book has passed into you. You and your little brother and sister are the chosen three. And the *Atlas* has already marked you as its own!"

Kate's mind was spinning. The *Atlas*. It was the first time she had heard the name.

"What do you . . . what do you mean, marked me?" Kate couldn't stop her voice from trembling.

"The *Atlas* is an ocean of power. A few drops of it now run through your veins. Can't the little birdie feel it?"

As much as Kate wanted to tell the stringy-haired man she didn't believe him, the fact was, she did. Ever since that night in the orphanage in Cambridge Falls when the blackness had crept off the page and into her fingers, she had known something in her had been changed.

"You mean, I can travel through time?"

The Secretary let out a rough laugh and released her. Kate felt the blood returning to her shoulders. The man began pacing back and forth, yanking on his fingers as he spoke.

"No no no no no! By yourself, not possible, not possible! But with the help of a powerful witch or wizard? Oh yes. You see what the old man did? He wanted to hide the *Atlas* from the Countess and her master. Where safer than in the past? So he puts a spell on the little birdie, makes her travel back in time. Then he has the birdie leave the book with him, thinking the two of them can retrieve it anytime they like."

"But it'll disappear!" Kate cried. "It's already disappeared!"

"True," the Secretary said, mock-thoughtfully. "The book's no more! E-vap-o-rated years ago!" He smiled at Kate and then did something truly repellent—he winked. "But what if old man Pym sends the birdie back to the second just after she brought him the book? Hmm? What about that?"

Finally, Kate understood. Yes, the book was gone. It had disappeared a half hour after she left it in the past. But for that half hour, however many years ago, the book had existed. Dr. Pym would simply have her return to that window in time.

"But how can he send me into the past?! I still don't—"

The Secretary's patience was ebbing.

"Is the birdie deaf? The power is in her now! The wizard can call upon it!" Leaning close, he ran a filthy finger along Kate's cheek. "Must've anchored her here with the same spell that gave the memory, hmm? Made it easy to reel her back. Kept his birdie on a short string, didn't he?"

Kate was trying her best to put it all together. In the throne room, Dr. Pym had done something to her, cast some spell that had made the book (or *Atlas*, as the Secretary was calling it) take her to a moment in the past. And somehow that same spell had kept her tied to this time, so once she'd given Dr. Pym the book, she was yanked back to the moment she'd left.

The Secretary was pacing again, rubbing his hands together. "Ingenious, ingenious! To hide it in the past! Thinks he's foiled the Countess. She can look all she wants, but no book, no *Atlas*, hmm? Doesn't exist! Gone gone gone! Only too bad for him, the Countess also has the power to send the birdie back in time. And she will, my dear. Oh, she will."

"But"—Kate hated asking the wretched man anything, especially this, but couldn't stop herself—"why was my mother there?"

"Why? Why? That is everything!" he shrieked gleefully. "Yes, a brilliant detail. You see, the sly old fox knew that one day he would have you retrieve the prize, and even with the power in you, it is no simple thing to send someone across time. Before, his spell could borrow on the power of the *Atlas*. Now, there's just the little birdie. Much more difficult. Requires a strong connection to the moment you wish to reach. A bond, yes? So what did the wise doctor do? He gave you a memory that would outshine all others. One that would burn like fire in your heart. He gave you your mother."

Kate didn't dare move. She had been holding herself together through force of will, but in that moment, she felt as if she were suddenly about to break apart.

Just then there was a squawking and something large and black tumbled through the open wall and crashed onto the floor. The Screecher swung around his crossbow, but the Secretary screamed, "No!"

It was an enormous black bird. The creature was wounded and flopped about in a circle, making desperate cawing noises.

"Something is wrong," the Secretary said. "Gather the host. Fortify the entrances—"

His command was cut off by a hard *thuck,* and the dark end of an arrow suddenly protruded from the Screecher's chest. The creature fell to its knees; a foul-smelling smoke rose, hissing, from the wound.

"ATTACK!" the Secretary shrieked. "We are under attack!"

Gabriel's band had entered through the dark northern end of the city. Two Screechers standing sentry had been felled by arrows, another by Gabriel's falchion. Emma was amazed at how silently the large, heavily weaponed men moved. They were like deadly shadows, sliding among the ruined buildings, and it thrilled her to be with them.

Gabriel stopped everyone along a half-destroyed wall a block from the center of the city. They were close enough to the gas lamps to see clearly, and Emma could hear, out in the square, shouting and the sounds of blows. Glancing down the wall, Emma saw the men spreading out, disappearing down alleys and into buildings to take up closer positions around the square.

Dena was beside her. Gabriel had placed them in the charge of a young warrior only a few years their senior, giving the boy strict orders to keep the girls back once the action started.

Dena poked Emma in the side and the two of them, the boy, Gabriel, and half a dozen others passed through a gap in the wall and into the ground floor of a building that bordered the square.

A memory came back to Emma. It was from one night a few months earlier. She, Kate, Michael, and the other orphans at the Edgar Allan Poe Home had been taken to a baseball game in Baltimore. Emma couldn't remember anything about the game itself, but she remembered the long tunnel they'd walked down, the muffled sounds of the crowd, the darkness, and then the sudden explosion of light as they'd entered the stadium. It was like that now, crouching with Dena at the hollowed-out window, staring at the harsh, bright scene before them.

There were at least three dozen *morum cadi* in the square, most of them gathered near four large cages. Inside the cages, Emma could see fifty or so sickly-looking men huddled about. Immediately, her heart filled with pity. She thought of the Countess, dressed up in her finery, having pretend balls in the Cambridge Falls mansion. Someone should lock her in a cage and see how she liked it! In her mind, Emma went ahead and put Miss Crumley in the cage as well. She knew the orphanage head wasn't the same kind of evil as the Countess, but as long as Emma was locking people up, she figured why not.

Emma's gaze stopped on a group of figures in the farthest cage. They were half the size of the men and, for a brief moment, she thought they were children. Then she noticed their beards and the stockiness of their arms and legs and realized she was looking at a group of dwarves. Emma reflected that if Michael were here, he would be having like nineteen heart attacks. Personally, she couldn't see what the big deal was. They were short, okay, and their beards were kind of funny, but she wasn't going to go out and start a fan club. As she was thinking this, the largest of the dwarves, the one with the filthy blond beard who'd been hurling abuse at the Screechers, moved, and Emma let out a gasp.

Ignoring the hiss from the young warrior, Emma scampered past Dena to the break in the wall where Gabriel knelt. He was fitting a thick black arrow on the string of his bow. Emma seized him by the arm and pointed. It was all she could do not to cry out. In the farthest cage, standing among the dwarves, wearing clothes she had seen him wear a thousand times before and an expression that even from this distance told of bewilderment and fear, was her brother, Michael. A black-bearded dwarf stood beside him, his hand on Michael's shoulder.

Gabriel nodded, indicating that he'd seen Michael already, and gestured to a building across the square.

The whole front of the building was missing, allowing Emma to see directly into the rooms. There, on the second floor, sitting between a Screecher and a short figure in a suit whom she immediately recognized as the Countess's secretary, was Kate.

Questions swirled through Emma's mind. How had her brother and sister come to be here? Were they all right? How had the Secretary found them?

A pained cawing cut the air, and a black shape fell out of the darkness and into the room where Kate was being held. There was a soft twang beside her as Gabriel released his arrow. The Screecher with Kate staggered and fell. Then—it was all happening so quickly now—the Secretary gave a strangled shout, there was a volley of rifle fire, the thick *swoof* of a dozen arrows taking flight, the broken thudding as they found their targets, and all was chaos and shouting. Dropping his bow, Gabriel pulled the falchion off his back, gave a great, bellowing cry, and leapt through the gap in the wall. The battle had begun.

Kate lay on her stomach beside the motionless body of the Screecher. A dark, foul-smelling ooze was leaking from its wound.

"Birdie!"

The Secretary was behind the desk. He'd scurried for cover in the first moments after the attack.

"Come here!"

She ignored him. Propping herself on her elbows, she inched forward till she had a clear view into the square. It was a mass of dark, struggling figures; there were shouts and cries, sickening crunches, the clang of metal on metal, and, above everything, the inhuman shrieks of the Screechers. Kate felt the familiar sweeping weakness, the inability to draw breath, and, to her surprise, she found she was furious. No, she told herself, it's not real! Her anger must've given her thoughts force, for while the screams were still awful, the invisible hands crushing her lungs vanished almost at once.

Breathing deeply, Kate sent Gabriel a silent thank-you.

She stared down into the square, trying to make sense of what she was seeing. Who was fighting who? How did they not all hit each other accidentally? Then, just as she was noticing the bare heads of the attackers and feeling relief that they were men and not some strange underground race of mole people—she didn't actually know if there were such a thing; she would have to ask Michael—she saw Gabriel himself.

He was in the thickest knot of the fighting, carving his way through the Screechers with long, vicious swings of his falchion. He looked unstoppable, and the sight of him gave her hope. But only for a moment. For as Kate watched Gabriel hack his way through the Screechers, she noticed that more and more of the Countess's black-clad horde were pouring into the square. At the start of the battle, Gabriel's men and the *morum cadi* had been fairly evenly matched, but with each passing second, the balance was shifting to the Screechers. Gabriel's men would soon be completely surrounded, and that would be that, the end.

"Kate!"

Michael's voice penetrated the din, and she looked left, toward the cages. Michael and Wallace stood apart from the pack of dwarves and men massing at the bars. Michael jumped, pointed toward the fighting, and shouted something. It was lost in the clamor, but Kate understood. He'd seen Gabriel and thought they were going to be rescued. He couldn't see that Gabriel and his men were doomed. They needed help. They needed two, three times the men.

An idea seemed almost to explode in Kate's mind. She turned to the dead Screecher, reaching beneath its tunic. The corpse had an unnatural, cold hardness; just touching it made Kate nauseous, but she forced her hand between its body and the floor, feeling along the creature's belt. Earlier, when it had entered the room, she'd heard a soft jangling. Come on, she thought, come on. . . . Her hand closed on a bundle of keys.

A weight slammed down on her.

"No, no! Bad birdie! Bad-bad-bad!"

The Secretary had thrown himself on top of her. Clammy hands scrambled for her wrists. He was panting, his breath warm and sour against her cheek. Kate struggled, but the man was much stronger.

"Must be punished, yes. Disobedient. The Countess has ways. Ways to make you obey. Bad birdies must learn—"

He was still hissing threats when Kate turned her head and bit down on his ear. It tasted foul and sweaty and the man shrieked, but she kept biting, harder and harder, till she tasted blood and he let go of her wrists. Then, using all her strength, she pushed against him. She'd only planned on getting him off her back, but she heard his shriek change and looked in time to see him disappearing out the open wall. She crawled to the edge. The Secretary lay without moving on the ground. Well, Kate thought, serves you right, and she spat to clear her mouth. Turning back, she reached under the Screecher, took hold of the keys, and yanked them free. Then it was down the stairs, out the building, and across the square.

Michael had squeezed through the crowd of men and dwarves, and they embraced awkwardly through the bars. She wanted to ask if he was okay, but there was no time.

"Gabriel's here!" Michael began. "He—"

"I know. He needs help."

She was looking at the ring of keys. There were a half dozen. She would have to try them all.

"The silver key! With the hole in the center! Hurry!"

It was a man who'd spoken. He was as thin and filthy as the others, but there was still fire in his hollow eyes. Something about him struck Kate as familiar.

"Hurry, girl!"

With nervous fingers, Kate started to fit the silver key in the lock.

"Oi, now! That ain't the way!"

A hairy-knuckled hand reached through the bars and grabbed at the keys.

"I'm the king, right? Only fittin' I'm the one opens the door! Protocol and such!"

"Stop it!" Kate yelled. "There isn't time!"

"Stop it?" Hamish snorted, still yanking at the keys. "Who're you to tell me to stop anything, eh? Who's the bloody king here?"

"Watch out!" Michael cried.

Kate looked over her shoulder. A Screecher was running at her, sword raised to strike. Suddenly, the creature jerked about and collapsed. Two arrows were buried in its back.

"See there? Now quit actin' the brat and let go or—woof!"

The keys were released. Wallace had stepped up and calmly punched his king in the gut.

"Go on," Wallace said. "Open the door."

Kate fit the key in the lock, turned it, and a flood of men came pouring out. The man who'd told her which key to use was among the first.

"Free the others," he commanded. "Do it quickly!" And he picked up the sword from the fallen Screecher, shouted, "Follow me!" and charged toward the battle. Weak and sickly as the men had seemed minutes before, they ran after him, grabbing what weapons they could—swords, shovels, axes—along the way.

Hamish lumbered out, still gasping, and pointed a sausagey finger at Wallace. "You'll get yours one day, laddie. Don't you worry." Then he snatched up an ax, marshaled the other dwarves, and charged into battle. Kate had to admit, whatever else Hamish was, he was no coward.

Michael nearly knocked her over with his hug.

"I know," Kate whispered as she hugged him back, "I know; it's okay."

Wallace stood a few feet off. He'd picked up a short pickax. Kate could see he wasn't going to leave them. She kissed the top of Michael's head. His hair was unwashed and greasy, but she couldn't have cared less.

"Come on. We need to free the others."

"Lemme go!"

"Gabriel said—"

"My brother and sister need me!"

The moment Gabriel and the other men had charged into the square, Emma had set off. Kate and Michael were nearby and in trouble. She wasn't going to wait around with her hands in her pockets. She would free Michael from his cage (she wasn't quite sure how yet), the two of them would get Kate away from the Secretary (she wasn't sure how she'd accomplish that either, but it would probably involve her being incredibly brave while Michael scribbled some nonsense in his notebook), and then they would all three finally be together (of that she was absolutely sure). There was just one problem. The young warrior, her and Dena's appointed guardian, had intercepted Emma as she made her break and now held her, struggling, a foot off the ground.

"You gotta let me go!"

"Gabriel wants you to—stop!"

He grabbed Dena by the ankle just as she was climbing out the window, knife in hand, clearly intent on joining the battle.

"Let go a' me! I'm gonna kill a Screecher!"

"And I gotta help my brother and sister!"

They continued like this for several minutes, the two girls struggling, pleading, threatening, Emma warning the boy (he really was just a boy) that if he didn't let her go by the time she counted to five, he was going to be really, really sorry, then counting to five and announcing she would give him to ten, but then that was it (Emma knew the boy was only doing what Gabriel had told him, so she didn't think it really fair to bite and kick her way free, which made her threats finally somewhat empty), and Dena doing much the same on her side of the young warrior, prying at his fingers, digging her nails into his hand, and the boy wondering what he had done to make Gabriel punish him like this, when they heard a low, raspy hiss.

They turned as one. The Screecher stood there, sword drawn and watching them.

Immediately, the young warrior dropped Dena and Emma and reached for his falchion. But the girls had sent him off balance and he stumbled backward, tripping over a pile of rubble and falling just as the Screecher's sword cut the air in front of him. Without thinking, Emma grabbed a stone. The Screecher was moving in for the kill when the stone bounced off its head, drawing the creature's attention. At the same moment, Dena attacked from the other side, burying her knife in the Screecher's leg. The creature let out one of its terrible, breath-crushing shrieks and sent Dena spinning with a backhand blow. It pulled the knife free and—

There was a thick, crunching *chunk*. Everything stopped. The creature looked down. The young warrior had buried his falchion halfway through its body. The boy stood, yanked the blade free, and then brought it down, driving the monster to the ground. The creature's body lay there, smoking. The whole thing had only taken a few seconds.

The young warrior wiped his falchion on the back of the Screecher, then faced Emma and Dena.

"All right, we'll find your brother and sister." He looked at Dena. "And you can help kill any Screechers we meet on the way."

Together, the three of them moved out of the house and along the edge of the square. Groups of *morum cadi* continued to spring from the shadows of the city, and the young warrior had to force Emma and Dena to take cover as the creatures ran by. At one point there was an explosion when a gas lamp ignited. It collapsed into a building, and soon a fire was raging on the far side of the square. Their views of the battle were fragmented and confusing, but even so, it soon became clear that Gabriel's fighters were badly outnumbered.

And then something unexpected happened.

Emma and Dena and the boy had paused in an alley between two ruined buildings and were watching the fighting with sinking hearts when a group of men rushed past from the direction of the cages. It took Emma a moment to realize that the men were prisoners and must've somehow gotten free. Her next thought was of Michael. Had he been freed as well? Was he safe? From the alley where she and her companions crouched, they couldn't see to the cages themselves, but more and more men were running past. They were a sight to behold: thin and ragged and wielding such weapons as they could scavenge, they fought with a ferocity that even Gabriel's men couldn't match. They had been prisoners for nearly two years. This was their moment.

And they weren't alone. Emma saw the stout blond dwarf, flanked by several other, smaller dwarves, chug past, huffing and puffing through his thick beard. He literally bulldozed into a pack of Screechers, knocking them to the ground, and then, without stopping, he set about chopping his way through the Countess's

303

army. Rather than surrounding Gabriel's band, the *morum cadi* were now being forced to fight enemies in front and behind. The tide of the battle was turning.

After they had opened the last of the cages and the last of the men had half stumbled, half charged toward the battle, Wallace made Kate and Michael climb to the third floor of one of the buildings overlooking the square.

"Look!" Kate cried when the three of them had gathered at a blown-out window and could take in the scene in its entirety. "They're winning!"

The two groups of men—Gabriel's band and the newly freed prisoners—had surrounded the amoeba of dark figures and were steadily carving it into smaller and smaller pieces. A yellowish haze hung over the battle, which puzzled Kate until she recalled the rancid vapor that escaped the bodies of expired Screechers.

"They aren't screaming as much," Michael said.

It was true. The air was being rent less frequently by the creatures' inhuman shrieks, mostly, it seemed—and this was the encouraging fact—because there were fewer of the monsters. Just then, one of their cries was cut short. The sound echoed away across the cavern before finally fading into the darkness. Kate held her breath. The next cry came a few seconds later. It was followed by another, then another, but these were not the dead shrieks of the *morum cadi*; the shouts came from the men, yelling because the battle was over and they had won.

"They did it," Kate marveled. "They really did it."

"You deserve credit too, girl." Wallace's eyes glowed warmly under his dark brows. "Hadn't been for your quick thinking, whole affair would a' gone very different. Aye, no doubt a' that."

Michael clucked his tongue. "It's just such a shame." He saw the other two looking at him like he'd lost his mind. "Not having my camera. It's a historic moment."

Footsteps pounded toward them. Wallace whirled about, raising his pickax. Kate just had time to glimpse the figure charging at her and think, No, it can't be, and then Emma was in her arms. And it was her! It really and truly was her! Kate and Emma hugged, cried, broke apart to look at each other, then hugged and cried some more. Even Michael, whose sense of personal dignity as the only boy in the family kept him from ever appearing too effusive, had to remove his glasses and rub at his eyes because he "got some dirt in them."

"Emma, it's you, it's really you; oh, Emma . . ." Kate kept repeating her sister's name over and over, pressing her close as if she would never let her go ever again.

"I'm so sorry." Emma had tears streaming down her face. "I know I shouldn't have disobeyed you. You said not to go back, but—"

"No, shhh. It's okay. You're here now."

"Yes, but she did disobey you," Michael pointed out.

"Michael—" Kate gave him a warning look.

"Oh, who cares," he said generously. "All's well that ends well, right?" And he gave Emma a manly pat on the shoulder.

"Are you sure you're okay?" Kate asked. "Really, truly okay?"

"Yes, I'm fine. I was with Gabriel. I saw you both before the battle, then I spotted you in the window here. Oh, this is Dena and I-Don't-Know-His-Name." Emma gestured to the two figures who'd followed her up the stairs and who Kate was only now noticing. One was a dark-haired, serious-faced girl not much older than Emma herself; the other was a teenage boy who held a fearsome-looking weapon similar to the one Gabriel carried. "Gabriel told him to watch out for us, though we kinda saved him—"

"Hey!"

"This is Wallace!" Michael blurted, pointing at their companion.

"Hi," Emma said. She turned to Kate. "You wouldn't believe all that's happened—"

"Wallace is a dwarf!" Michael was grinning broadly.

"Yeah," Emma said, a little annoyed at being interrupted. "I figured that out."

"Dwarves are real!"

Emma rolled her eyes and groaned. "I knew he was going to do this."

"Just tell your story," Kate said. "I want to know everything. What happened after you left us?"

"Right! So I got to the bridge, the rope one, remember, and Gabriel was fighting these Screechers, and I saved his life! But then I got shot in the stomach!"

"Oh! I had a dream, I saw you hurt—"

"I'm okay now. Gabriel took me to his village—on the way he had to kill this monster; I was asleep for that part so I couldn't help—and there was this wisewoman named Granny Peet, and she fixed me! She said you found Dr. Pym! Is that true? I wish you could meet Granny Peet, she's one of the good ones, she—"

Kate wanted to tell her to slow down. But before she could, there was a high-pitched shriek from the square.

"FOOLS!"

They turned. The Secretary had climbed onto a massive mound of rubble. Kate was shocked he was alive, much less moving around, and she watched as the men—who with the battle over had begun seeing to their wounded—stopped and faced him. The Secretary's head was bleeding, his suit was ripped, and there was something wrong with his right arm, which he cradled against his body. The man was shaking with hatred and rage; Kate could see spittle flying from his mouth.

"You are all fools! You think you can fight the Countess? Defeat the Countess? You have no idea of her power! You will all die! All of you will die!"

"Is he crazy?" Emma said. "He lost. Why doesn't someone conk him on the head?"

"What's that noise?" Michael asked.

Kate listened, and at first heard nothing. What was Michael talking . . . She stopped; there was a soft pattering in the far, dark reaches of the city. It grew louder, and Kate realized it was moving toward them. Glancing down, she saw the men in the square had heard it too.

"You will all die! All of you!"

The sound quickly became a thrumming, a pounding. She felt it through her feet. The windowsill vibrated under her hands.

And then Kate saw the blackness beyond the lights become liquid and surge toward them.

"No," Wallace whispered. "Can't be . . ."

"What?" Kate grabbed at his arm. "What is it?"

"There!" Michael shouted.

The dark tide had reached the perimeter of the gas lamps.

Kate stared, and all hope inside her died.

The Secretary was giggling hysterically, hopping up and
down. "Yes! Yes! Yes!"

There were hundreds of them, a gray-green mass of hunch-
backed figures, scurrying along the streets, scrambling over the
ruins, close enough now the children could hear the snarling and
growling, the scrape of their claws on stone, and still, under and
above it all, the pounding of their feet, like the onrush of a storm.

"What are those?" Emma cried.

"The *salmac-tar*," Wallace said. "The witch has summoned
them."

Kate, of course, had seen such creatures before. In her dream,
she had watched Gabriel fight one as Emma lay unconscious on
the floor of the maze. They were the sightless, razor-clawed monsters that lived in the deepest bowels of the mountains. She remembered Wallace telling them how the Countess had made
alliances with the creatures. This was her doing. The witch had
called up this evil to destroy them.

"TO ME!" Gabriel roared. "TO ME!"

No! Kate thought. No! They had to run. There were too few
of them. They were tired. Wounded. The Secretary was right.
They were all going to die.

But already a line was forming with Gabriel at its center, and she watched as men and dwarves alike raised their weapons, and then Gabriel, tall, fearsome, bleeding from a dozen different wounds, stepped forward so that he stood in front of the line, alone, waiting for the wave to crash.

"What's he doing?!" Michael said. "He's crazy!"

"Shut up!" Emma cried; her voice was desperate, breaking, betraying all her fear. "He's showing them how to be brave! He's—he's—"

She threw herself against Kate, burying her face in her sister's chest and sobbing. Below them, the creatures poured into the square, snarling, hissing; Gabriel raised his falchion; Kate pressed Emma to her breast even more tightly—

Brrruuuuaaaawwwhhhh!

Instinctively, Kate's head whipped toward the sound. It had come from somewhere off in the darkness. A horn, she thought. That was a horn.

"They stopped!" Emma cried.

Kate looked back. The *salmac-tar* were only yards from Gabriel; their numbers filled the square. But the entire gasping, drooling mass had indeed stopped and was turned toward the sound.

" 'Ells bells," Wallace said, and Kate saw that the dwarf was grinning. "It's about time."

BRRRRUUUUAAAAAHHHH!

Michael suddenly let out a yelp (it sounded sort of like "Wah-ha-hoo!") and jumped, jabbing his finger in excitement. "Look look look look look! Look who it is!"

A short figure was racing up one of the half-lit streets toward the square. He was encased head to toe in dark armor so only his face and beard were visible (the plaits of his beard slapping against his breastplate as he ran); he held a great, shining ax in one hand and a bone-colored horn in the other. Despite the darkness and the distance, Kate recognized him immediately.

"It's Captain Robbie!"

"Who?" Emma asked.

"He's our friend!" Michael said. "Well, he did lock us in jail, but that was just following procedure. You can't fault him for following—"

"Why'd he come alone?" Emma interrupted. "He's gonna get murdered. Dwarves are so stupid."

Before Michael could argue, Captain Robbie reached the edge of the square, planted his feet, and blew once more into the horn.

BRRRRUUUUAAAAWWWWWWWHHHH!

The sound echoed across the cavern, fading, fading, and then silence. No one stirred. Not the *salmac-tar*, not Gabriel or the men, not Wallace or Dena or the young warrior, not the children. Then they heard it—a rhythmic, metallic pounding, growing louder and louder, and then legions of dwarves were charging out of the darkness, filling the streets, their axes reflecting the glow from the lamps, their armor clanking and jangling, their collective breathing an even, reassuring *huph . . . huph . . . huph*. When they reached the square, Captain Robbie stepped forward and barked a command. The army stopped.

"What's he doing?" Emma demanded. "He needs to attack. He should be killing those things! Dwarves are so stu— Whoa!"

Kate reached for her sister. The entire building had begun to sway and rock. Dena fell into the young warrior, knocking them both to the floor. Looking out the window, Kate saw that everything, the whole ruined city, was in motion.

"What's going on?" Emma yelled over the tumult. "What's happening?"

"Damn my soul!" Wallace shouted. "It's a bloody earthquake! Hold on! Hold on!"

"No!" Michael was gripping the windowsill as you would a ship's railing during a storm. "It's Dr. Pym!" He pointed, and Kate and Emma saw the white-haired wizard, standing atop a building, his arms raised out over the city. "He's doing it!"

"What the bloody 'ell for?" Wallace shouted. "He'll kill us all!"

"Kate!"

Emma tugged at her arm, and Kate looked toward the square. At first, she didn't understand; the main body of the monsters seemed to be sinking. Then she realized—the earth was opening up under them. The thought barely had time to register before fully half the horde was swallowed up in a screeching, tumbling mass, disappearing into darkness. Just as quickly, the fissure closed, the shaking and rolling stopped, and the children's own building came to rest. Kate turned back to Dr. Pym. The old man had lowered his arms and was calmly taking out his pipe. She made a mental note never to doubt the wizard's power again.

"Dwarves"—Captain Robbie raised his ax—"ATTTTT-AAAAACCCK!"

The remaining *salmac-tar* turned and fled.

"No! No!" The Secretary was jumping up and down, tearing at his meager strands of hair. "Fight! You must fight!"

But his cries were useless. The *salmac-tar* were clambering over each other in a panicked attempt to escape. Gabriel and the men had stepped back to let the charging dwarves pass through, and above it all, above the clashing of the armor, the thunderous stamp of boots, the frenzied terror of the monsters, Kate could hear the voice of the dwarf captain, filling the cavern:

"Drive them, brothers! Drive them to the pits! Drive them! Drive them!"

And she knew then, finally, the battle was over.

"You see, when Katherine touched the book and traveled into the past—four years from this point, which for you three is not the present at all but already fifteen years into the past—she told me everything that was going to transpire with the missing will and Hamish becoming king, et cetera and et cetera . . . I, armed with this terrible knowledge, went immediately to Queen Esmerelda (Robbie and Hamish's mother and a very dear friend of mine). Then and there, she wrote out her will proclaiming Robbie the next king and had the document notarized and sealed, and together we secreted it away. . . ."

Dr. Pym was explaining to the children how it was that he and Robbie had escaped Hamish's dungeon and come to arrive in the Dead City with a brigade of armored dwarves. They were all of them—the children, Dr. Pym, Robbie, and Gabriel—crammed into the room where, before the battle, the Secretary had interrogated Kate. It was now being used as a sort of informal headquarters as messengers pushed past one another on their way in and out, and Robbie and Gabriel huddled around the desk with a group of hotly arguing men and dwarves.

The children had been summoned there without being told why—following the battle, they had been in the building across the square, bringing each other up to date on their respective adventures. Upon entering the room, Emma had literally launched herself into Gabriel's arms, crying, "You did it!" For her part, Kate wished that whoever was in charge would've chosen a different meeting place. The memory of biting into the Secretary's ear, and the sour sweat-and-blood taste that accompanied it, had returned the moment she crossed the threshold. She wondered when she would get to brush her teeth again.

"You might well ask," Dr. Pym continued (he had led the children a few feet away), "why I waited as long as I did to produce the queen's will. But here is the crucial point—I needed Kate to enter the vault, touch the book, and bring it to me in the past. Only by hiding the book in the past could I protect it from the Countess. And I knew if I merely bided my time, this was exactly what would happen. Therefore, I waited. When I finally deemed the moment was right, I had Robbie summon his lawyer. . . ." Dr. Pym then revealed the location of the will; it was recovered and examined by a panel of judges, as well as by handwriting and fingerprint experts, dwarves being sticklers for protocol (this received an approving nod from Michael), and the will being verified genuine, Captain (now King) Robbie mustered his army and marched to the Dead City.

"So you see," Dr. Pym concluded, "it is as clear as a summer's day."

"I don't get it," Emma said.

"Which part, my dear?"

"The whole part."

"Dr. Pym planned it all," Kate said. "He knew Hamish would be listening to us in the dungeon. He tricked him into taking me and Michael to the vault. He made sure I touched the book first. He planned everything."

"But"—Michael had been taking notes; now he paused, addressing the wizard—"did you only know to do all that because Kate had gone into the past and told you what was going to happen? Were you just pretending not to recognize us in the dungeon?"

"That requires a bit of a complicated answer," Dr. Pym said, scratching his chin thoughtfully, "as there are now two versions of the past. In the original past, I knew nothing of future events and no doubt based my actions upon the connection I saw between your sister and the book. However, in the rewritten past, which occurred after your sister retrieved the book and went back in time . . ."

Kate was watching the wizard. Her feelings toward him had changed. He had outsmarted Hamish and the Secretary, made Robbie king, saved Gabriel and the men; Kate now truly believed he was on their side. But he was still not telling them everything he knew: about their parents, obviously, but also about her and her siblings' role in all that was happening. In the throne room, he'd said they were the children he'd been waiting for. And the Secretary had said almost the exact same thing, that she and Michael and Emma were the chosen three. What did that mean? What was the wizard hiding?

". . . I knew how events had played out in the other, now-alternate past," Dr. Pym said, "and wishing things to proceed in exactly the same way, I attempted to behave as I might have done had I been ignorant of the future. This is the version of the past, Michael, that you and I remember. Katherine, being the time traveler, is the only one who remembers the original past. So, to answer your question, as far as your memory is concerned, yes, I did pretend not to recognize you in the dungeon; as far as your sister's memory is concerned, no, I had absolutely no idea who she was."

Michael looked at him. "Now I don't get it."

"Then just understand this," Dr. Pym sighed, "if Katherine had not shown the resourcefulness she did, King Robbie and I would still be in the dungeon, and all of Gabriel's men, all the men of Cambridge Falls, would be dead."

" 'E's right"—Robbie had stepped over from the group at the desk—"and should you ever need my strength or my people's, you've only to ask." With that, the new dwarf king bowed so low before Kate that the braided tips of his beard brushed the floor.

"Oh please," Kate said, blushing deeply. "Don't do that. It's really kind of embarrassing. Anyway, Michael did as much as I did."

Robbie straightened up. "Aye, true enough." He coughed into his fist and assumed a formal tone. "Michael Whatever-Your-Last-Name-Is, it was you telling off Hamish for the prat he was that reminded me what it means to be a dwarf. In recognition of that, I do hereby appoint you Royal Guardian of All Dwarfish Traditions and History." He snapped his fingers, and a dwarf stepped forward and handed the King a small badge, which he pinned to Michael's sweater.

"Your H-Highness . . . ," Michael stammered, "I—I wish I'd had a chance to prepare some remarks."

Robbie clapped him on the shoulder. "Ah, lad, you'd have made a grand dwarf, a grand dwarf."

Emma looked less than thrilled to see Michael getting so much attention, and as Robbie gave Michael a furry kiss on each cheek, Kate heard her mutter, "I'm the one that got shot with an arrow." Emma had been, of course, impressed to hear about Michael standing up to Hamish and placing his own hand upon the chopping block, or perhaps not so much impressed, Kate reflected, as dumbfounded, since she'd kept repeating, "Really? Michael did that? Really? Michael?" In any case, Kate was about to tell her to quit muttering and let Michael enjoy his moment when he turned toward them, grinning and puffing out his chest, a look of pure joy upon his face, and before Kate knew it, she and Emma were both hugging him, saying how proud they were of him, Emma punching him in the arm only a little too hard. It wasn't till Michael cleared his throat and offered that he might say a few words after all that Kate jumped in and suggested that later might be better.

"Yeah," Emma said, looking immensely relieved, "we always love to hear you talk about dwarves and stuff, but we got other things to talk about first. Like the *Atlas*! We should probably talk about that!"

"My dear," Dr. Pym said, "how did you learn that name? I'm quite amazed."

Kate saw Emma glance at Michael and give a pleased little shrug. "Oh, I know lots of things. Did you know that's what it's called, Michael?"

Michael shook his head.

"Well, that's what it is, all right. The *Atlas*. You should write it down so you don't forget."

Kate did not mention that she had heard this from the Secretary.

"Your sister is indeed correct," Dr. Pym said. "Each of the Books of Beginning has a unique name. Technically, the book we are searching for is the *Atlas of Time*—"

"That's right," Emma said, nodding seriously. "Technically."

"—but it is usually just referred to as the *Atlas*, an appropriate name, as the book contains maps of all possible pasts, presents, and futures and allows one to move through both time and space. But now is not the moment to get into all the whys and wherefores."

"Sure," Emma said, "we can get into those later. All the whys and stuff."

In listening to Dr. Pym, it had occurred to Kate that ever since hearing the book's true name, she had begun to think of it as the *Atlas*. The name simply felt right.

"What about Hamish?" Michael asked. "Is he really not king anymore?"

"That 'e is not," Robbie said. "I sent 'im back to the palace, said I wanted it scrubbed top to bottom by 'im personally. And to shave off that beard a' 'is. Disgusting it was."

"Hamish used to be the king," Emma informed Gabriel; he also had left the group around the desk and entered their circle. "He tried to cut off Kate's hand. Then Michael stopped him. At least, that's the story—"

"Hey!"

"Fine, you're a hero." Emma rolled her eyes. "Go polish your medal."

Robbie told them that upon hearing he was no longer king, Hamish had tried to commit suicide by chopping off his own head. However, all he succeeded in doing was knocking himself unconscious, and it required several buckets of cold water to bring him around. This was, Robbie added, the closest Hamish had come to a bath in months.

As the others continued talking, Kate stepped over to the blown-out wall and looked down into the square. The battle won, the dwarves had erected a field kitchen and set about boiling huge vats of carrots, onions, tomatoes, and beef, the smell of which had quickly overwhelmed the rancid stench of expired Screechers. Now men who hadn't had a decent meal in two years gobbled down bowls of stew as fast as the dwarf servers could bring them to the tables.

Kate turned to look at the cages.

The Secretary was the sole prisoner. He was in the nearest

cage, cradling his hurt arm and rocking back and forth. Was it true what he'd said? Did Dr. Pym intend to send her back in time to retrieve the *Atlas*? Her heart quickened at the thought that she might see her mother again. At the same time, she felt a stab of guilt. Twice now—first with Michael, then with Emma after the battle—she'd told her story of touching the book and going into the past. Neither time had she mentioned seeing their mother. Why? What was her reason for keeping it secret?

Kate became aware that the Secretary was staring directly at her.

"Enough! We must act!"

Tearing herself from the man's gaze, Kate turned back to the room. The speaker was the gaunt, fierce-eyed man who'd told her which key opened the cage doors. He was leaning forward on the desk, and Kate suddenly noticed his tangled mass of red-brown hair and realized why he'd looked so familiar.

"We know your son! Stephen McClattery! We met him!"

She added quickly:

"He's fine! We saw him a couple days ago, and he was totally fine."

The effect of Kate's words was instant and dramatic. It was as if the man had been straining against a rope, and the rope was abruptly cut. His head dropped, and his whole body seemed to sag forward. Kate knew this must be the first he'd heard of his son in two years. He probably hadn't even known if the boy was alive or dead. Finally, the man wiped at his face and looked up. There were smeared tear tracks on his grimy cheeks.

"Thank you," he said thickly. "But every moment we spend talking gives the witch more time to take revenge on our children."

"Right you are," Robbie said. "Doctor, you want to tell the young 'uns what we need from 'em?"

"Here is the situation." Dr. Pym adjusted his tortoiseshell glasses, a process that made them no less crooked. "Our next task is to march to Cambridge Falls and liberate the imprisoned children, including your friend Stephen McClattery."

"He's not my friend," Emma muttered. "He's actually pretty annoy—oww!" She glared at Kate. "Why'd you poke me?"

"The issue," Dr. Pym continued, "is that as long as the Countess holds the children hostage, we can't risk a direct assault on her house."

"But you're a wizard," Michael said. "You made an earthquake. Can't you do something?"

"Unfortunately, the Countess has set up certain barriers around the house and town that limit my capabilities. We must resort to more conventional means. Which again brings us to you three. You were able to escape the house. I wonder—"

"Oh! Oh!" Emma's hand shot into the air.

"Yes, my dear."

"There's a secret passage! It goes from the room where the kids are and comes out the side of the house. Abraham took us through. But we could find it again! Easy!"

"We already told him about that," Michael said. "Back in the dungeon."

"True," Dr. Pym said. "But I was going to ask you to tell everyone else. Wonderful foresight, my dear."

"You're welcome," Emma said, and smiled triumphantly at Michael.

"Right, then!" King Robbie clapped. " 'Ere's what we do: a few of us creep up to the house, slip the nippers out through this secret passage all sneaky-Pete; once that's done, 'ello-'ello, the rest of us make our attack! Aye, that's a brilliant plan, that is!"

There was general nodding and murmuring.

Michael was nervously fingering his new badge. "What if the Countess already knows she's lost the battle? Won't she be expecting us?"

"Perhaps," Dr. Pym said, "but we have little choice except to proceed and hope for the best. As Mr. McClattery pointed out, many young lives hang in the balance. Now, Gabriel and I and the children will—"

Just then there was a large thud, and everyone looked to see Kate lying unconscious on the floor.

"Feeling better, my dear?"

Kate blinked. A trio of concerned faces stared down at her. She forced herself to sit up. She had been laid on a very hard, very lumpy couch in a room she didn't recognize. Emma, Michael, and Dr. Pym moved back to give her space.

"What happened?" Emma asked. "You were standing there and then you, like . . . fell over."

Kate pressed her fingers to her temples. Sitting up had made her light-headed. She could hear, outside the door, many footsteps moving quickly past.

"I think I'm just tired. And hungry."

"Well," Dr. Pym said, "you have all had a very trying day. We'll get you something to eat."

"And drink," Michael said. "I bet we're dehydrated and don't even know it."

"Your brain's dehydrated," Emma said.

"Very likely," Michael replied. "The brain's the most sensitive organ in your body."

Emma muttered something inaudible.

Kate looked around. There was a single gas lamp on the floor, and stacked against one wall were baskets of turnips, onions, carrots, sacks of potatoes. The cooks were clearly using this room for storage.

"You're certain that's all it was, my dear? Hunger?" The wizard was staring at her intently.

Kate closed her eyes. She could still see it happening. . . .

"Katherine?"

She wished he would stop pressuring her. She knew why she'd fainted, and she had no intention whatsoever of talking about it.

"Perhaps I could help if—"

"Why didn't you tell us you knew our parents!"

Instantly, Kate realized what she'd done. She'd only meant to distract everyone, to get them talking about something besides her fainting. But she'd spoken in haste, and now . . .

She glanced at Michael and Emma and saw their confusion. How long did she have before they put it together?

"When should I have told you, Katherine?" Dr. Pym had taken off his glasses and was cleaning them on his tie. "In the dungeon? I've already explained why it was important to pretend I had no idea who you were. And in the original past, well, then I truly had no idea who you were."

"But you gave me that memory!" Now that it was out, Kate wanted an answer. "You sent me to that moment! You had to have known!"

"Well, I suspected, yes. Partly from your story. But also because one cannot look at you and fail to see your mother."

This silenced Kate. She looked like her mother? Against her will, she felt a thrill of joy.

"Wait!" Emma cried, finding her voice. "What're you talking about? How's Dr. Pym know our parents?"

"Your parents"—Dr. Pym replaced his glasses—"are very close friends of mine. Richard and Clare. Those are their names."

"But—no! That's not—you would've told us! You—why didn't you tell us?"

"Again, my dear, when could I possibly—"

"When we met you!" Emma was almost shouting now. "When we got to that stupid orphanage in the first place!"

"My dear Emma, that is more than fifteen years in the future. I can't very well explain why I did something that I haven't done yet."

"But how . . ." Michael was looking at Kate.

Here it comes, she thought.

". . . did you find out Dr. Pym knew our parents?"

Kate swallowed. Her throat was like paper.

"Our mom . . . was there. In the past. When I saw Dr. Pym. I . . . didn't tell you."

For a long moment, Michael and Emma simply stared at her. On their faces were expressions of utter disbelief. Not that Kate had seen their mother. But that she hadn't told them. Emma began crying, and the sight of it almost broke Kate's heart.

"Emma—"

"Where are they?!" Emma wrenched her head toward Dr. Pym. "Take us to them! Take us there now!"

"Emma—"

"Now! I want to see them now!"

"My dear," Dr. Pym said, "don't you know I would like nothing better than to do just that? But I'm afraid it's not that simple."

"Why not?!" Tears were streaming down Emma's face.

"He can't take us now," Michael said quietly. "He has to stop the Countess first."

"Shut up!" Emma snatched off the badge Robbie had given him and threw it into the corner. "And that's what I think of your stupid medal!"

"Emma, stop it!"

Emma jerked away from Kate's hand.

"Don't touch me! You lied to us! You should've told us and you lied to us!"

"I know, I'm sorry." Again Kate reached for her sister and again Emma pushed her away.

"I said don't touch me!"

Kate had to stand because Emma was also standing, and this time when she reached for her, Emma didn't fight but let her sister hold her, and Kate felt how tight and angry she was, but she kept holding her and whispering, and slowly Emma's sobs eased and her body relaxed.

Finally, she asked, "Are you okay?"

Emma nodded, sniffling, and wiped her sleeve across her face. She went to the corner of the room and retrieved Michael's badge.

"I'm sorry. I hope it's not dented."

Michael forced a laugh. "*You* dent a piece of dwarf craftsmanship? Not likely." But then he looked at her and offered a real smile. "It's okay."

"Now," Dr. Pym continued when they were settled and Michael was once again wearing his badge, "believe me, I do understand how confusing all this is and how badly you three want to see your parents. And I promise that once the Countess is defeated and the children are safe, I will answer any questions you have. But today, we have a great task before us and many whose lives depend on our success. That must be the focus of our efforts."

"But can't you tell us anything?" Kate said. "Where they live? What their jobs are? Anything?"

Dr. Pym sighed. "Very well. Your parents are academics. Professors."

"Our parents were teachers?" Emma's tone was decidedly unexcited.

"What was their field of study?" Michael asked.

Emma let out a moan. "This is like the greatest day of your life, isn't it?"

"They are magical historians. It is not, I should say, a discipline treated very seriously in the academic world. But your parents believe in the importance of what they are doing. And they are both interested in the Books of Beginning. In fact, that was

326

how they met. At a conference in Edinburgh. Your mother was delivering a paper dispelling a theory that a ninth-century Japanese shogun, called Rosho-Guzi, the Eater of Lives, had been in possession of one of the Books. Your father came up to her afterward, and, six months later, they were married. You see, children, the Books are in your blood."

"How did you meet them?" Kate asked.

"In my own personal search for the missing two Books, I made a practice of following the current academic research. I read your parents' articles and felt they were people I could trust. We began to work together. Of course, I hardly imagined who their children would turn out to be. In hindsight, yes, there were signs. . . ." He shrugged and let his hands fall. "But then, four years ago, just after Christmas, Katherine appeared in my study and that was that."

At the mention of Christmas, a memory shook loose in Kate's mind, and she saw a tall, thin man standing in the doorway to her bedroom. The memory was from that last night with their parents. The pieces suddenly fell together, the feeling she'd had—in the library in Cambridge Falls, in the dwarfish dungeon—that she'd met Dr. Pym before. . . .

"It was you! You took us from our parents!"

"Perhaps. But again, what you're talking about has yet to happen."

"Fine," Kate said. "What did you mean, 'who their children would turn out to be'? Who are we?"

"You three are very special. And one day, when we have the time, I will explain it all."

Kate started to argue. They deserved to know—

"And you will. When the moment is right. Katherine, you must learn to trust me." He stood. "Now, I want to see how Robbie and Gabriel are coming along."

"Wait," Michael said. "What's our name?"

"Your name. Yes, I suppose I can tell you that. Your real last name . . . is Wibberly."

The children looked at each other.

"Wibberly?" Kate said. "You're sure?"

"Oh yes. It's Wibberly, all right."

"At the orphanage, they said our name started with *P*!"

"Did they? That's odd."

"But you must've told them to call us that!" Kate protested. "You're the one who took us there! Why would you tell them to call us P when our name was Wibberly?!"

"I imagine I was trying to keep you hidden. The children W would've been too much of a tip-off."

"So why not just give us a different name?!" Michael said. "Smith! Or Jones! Anything! Do you know how much we got picked on having a letter for a last name?"

"Hmm, I suppose I didn't think that through. Apologies there. Now I must go. We will talk more later."

For a long time after the wizard left, none of the children spoke. Outside the door, they could hear the army beginning to move.

"Wibberly," Kate said. "It does . . . feel right."

"Yeah," Michael agreed. "It does."

"I still like Penguin," Emma said. "But I guess Wibberly's okay."

"I'm sorry," Kate said. "I should've told you right away about seeing Mom. I guess I just . . . I was afraid if I talked about it, I might lose it. Lose her. Again."

"I understand," Michael said. "That's why I write stuff down. It's too easy to forget things. You write something down, you know it's there."

He ran his hand over his notebook, and Kate suddenly saw him, a boy who'd had a whole life taken away, clinging to what he could.

"Will you tell us now?" Emma asked. "Please?"

Kate looked at the two of them, saw the trust they still had in her, that they would always have in her, and wondered how she could've kept something like this to herself. It belonged to all of them or none of them. As she reached for the memory, she found that already some of the details had grown distant and fuzzy. She didn't panic. She forced herself to focus on what she knew, the clothes their mother had been wearing, the color of her hair, the words she'd spoken, and the more she talked, the more she found she remembered; she described the warmth of her tone, a small mole on her cheek, the way her hand had rested on the doorknob; she talked about the room, describing the fire in the grate, the swirling reds and browns on the rug, Dr. Pym's impossibly cluttered desk, the snow falling gently outside, and soon it was as if she was there again, standing before her mother, only this time Michael and Emma were with her and it was their memory as well. Kate knew that as time went on, Emma and Michael would change details to suit themselves, what their mother had been wearing, the things she'd said, the snow would become a rainstorm, but it made her feel better knowing that the memory now belonged to all of them, and together they would hold on to it, and hold on to their mother, more tightly than she ever could alone.

Afterward, they were all silent. The air seemed to have gotten cooler, and through the walls came the reassuring sound of barked orders and of men and dwarves at work.

Then Kate said, "I had a vision. That's why I fainted. Not because I was hungry or anything."

She told them she had seen the battle in the Dead City. Only it had been different. There were fewer Screechers. And no dwarves or hordes of monsters rushing up from the deep. Just Gabriel's small band of men. And they had won. They had beaten the Screechers. And then Gabriel's men and the freed prisoners had joined forces and marched on the town.

"But that's not how it happened," Emma said. "You must've seen it wrong."

Kate shrugged. "It's what I saw."

"Was that the whole thing?" Michael asked.

"No."

Kate said that in her vision, the Countess knew Gabriel and the others were coming and she moved herself and all the children to the boat in the center of the lake.

"But why would you see something that didn't happen?" Emma insisted. "It doesn't make sense."

"Maybe it did happen," Kate said. "Maybe it still does. Right before the vision, Robbie and Dr. Pym were talking about marching on the town. I think my vision was a warning."

"Warning about what?" Emma said. "Gabriel saved those kids, right? You must've seen that too?"

Kate reached into her pocket and pulled out the two photographs she'd been carrying. They were still damp from her swim through the underground lake. There was the one of her in their bedroom in the house in Cambridge Falls, which Kate had thought of as their ticket home, and there was the other one, the last picture Abraham had ever taken. She studied Abraham's photo, the dark figures emerging from the forest, the flare of their torches. She turned it over.

"No. The dam broke, the boat went over the falls, and the children died. With her last breath, the Countess cursed the land." She handed Michael the photo. "Abraham took this when it happened. Look at the back."

Written in a tiny scrawl were dozens of names. Kate pointed to one.

Michael read, "Stephen McClattery."

"They're all going to die."

"No!" Emma jumped to her feet. "It's not gonna be like that! That was the other past! That's what you saw! Before we ever got here! You said yourself Dr. Pym wasn't there! And the dwarves! They gotta be good for something! They'll stop her! It'll be different this time! We weren't there to help! It's gotta be different! We'll save the kids and then Dr. Pym will take us to see our parents! You heard him! He promised! You heard him, Kate!"

The door banged open; Wallace stomped in.

"Right, then. It's chow time for you lot. Hup-hup-hup! Left foot. Right foot. Come on; army'll be leaving soon!"

"Go ahead," Kate said. "I'll be along in a second."

Michael slid Abraham's photo into his notebook, then he and Emma headed out with the dwarf. At the last moment, Kate called her sister back. She held out the other photo, the one of her in their bedroom. "I think you should hold this."

"Really? Why?"

Because I want you to have a picture of me, she almost said.

"I just . . . think you should. Go on now."

And then she was alone.

Kate knew with absolute certainty that if she did nothing, if she merely allowed Gabriel and Robbie and Dr. Pym to proceed with their plan, the children would die. Despite everything they'd done, nothing would be different. Time, Kate was learning, was like a river. You might put up obstacles, even divert it briefly, but the river had a will of its own. It wanted to flow a certain way. You had to force it to change. You had to be willing to sacrifice. Kate thought of her promise to Annie and the other children that she would come back for them.

She reached into her pocket and pulled out the key she'd used to open the cage. She would've liked to have seen her parents.

Ten minutes later, a man passing the Secretary's cage noticed the door was open and the prisoner was missing. At the same moment, Emma, running to fetch her sister, found that she too was gone.

CHAPTER TWENTY-ONE
Devil's Bargain

The air told Kate when they were getting close. It was no longer the damp, stale air she'd been breathing since the previous morning; this was clean, fresh. The Secretary must've sensed it as well.

"Almost there," he gasped, tightening his grip on Kate's arm, which he seemed to be holding more for support than control, "almost there . . ."

No guards had been posted outside his cage, and Kate had been able to sneak up unnoticed and whisper her proposal through the bars.

If the Countess would free the children and leave without harming anyone else, Kate would deliver the *Atlas*. But the Secretary had to get her to Cambridge Falls before Robbie and Gabriel's army. Could he do that?

Yes, the man had sneered, there was a way.

Now, as the pair stumbled along the tunnel, Kate holding aloft their pilfered lantern, she thought about Emma and Michael. Given the chance, she would've told them that her visions weren't like movies. She didn't watch them happen; she lived them. She had been on the boat as it went over the falls. She had felt what the children felt as it plunged toward the rocks. Their terror had been hers, and she would do anything to spare them that pain.

She and the Secretary rounded a bend, and for the first time in two days, Kate was in the open air.

They were high over the valley, on a path cutting down the side of the mountain. The moon was full, and it bathed the entire world in a calming, silvery glow. The sheer sense of space took her breath away. Kate thought it was the most beautiful sight she'd ever beheld.

The Secretary fell to his knees at the edge of the cliff and started drawing in the dirt with his finger.

"What're you doing? The others will be after me! We have to—"

"Quiet! I need to concentrate!"

Kate looked back toward the tunnel. She expected at any moment to hear her name being called, to see the light of approaching torches.

"There." The Secretary straightened up, wiping his hands on his jacket. "Done."

"Done what? All you've done is draw a line in the dirt!"

"Ah, but it's a special line."

"Dr. Pym and Gabriel are going to be here any second! You said you knew a way to town!"

"I do; this way. Step over the line."

Kate looked at the not entirely straight yard-long scratch in the dirt. Stepping over it would mean stepping off the cliff and into thin air.

"You're joking."

"It will take you to the Countess. It is magic she granted me."

"Uh-huh. Well, there has to be another way. If we run—"

The Secretary lurched at her, shoving his sweating face into hers.

"There is no other way! Your friends will be here soon! Does the little birdie want to save the children? Then birdie has to fly! Fly, fly, fly . . ."

He stepped back, gesturing to the line like a gruesome maitre d'. Kate noticed he was clutching something in his hand. It was the tiny yellow bird she'd seen earlier, but its body was motionless and limp.

"What about you?"

"Very kind of you to ask, very kind. But only room for one birdie. Griddley Cavendish will find another way."

"How do I know you're not trying to kill me?"

He smiled his filthy, cracked-toothed grin. "You don't. Now—fly."

Her insides felt like they had turned to ice. She took a trembling step to the edge of the line. A breeze blew in off the valley, pushing back her hair. She looked down. Far below, she could make out the rocky base of the mountain. Then she heard it—the faint echo of a shout. And again. It'd come from the tunnel; someone was calling her name.

Kate closed her eyes and stepped off the cliff.

Her foot struck something solid. She heard a sound like water slapping against metal, the low rumble of an engine. She opened her eyes. She was on the deck of a boat; the moon reflected off the surface of the lake. The Secretary's magic had worked.

"Katrina . . ."

Kate spun around. The Countess stood there, flanked by two *morum cadi*. She clapped gleefully.

"You're here! I'm so happy!"

After failing to find her sister, Emma had run to tell Michael and discovered everyone in an uproar over the fact the Secretary had disappeared from his cage. She pulled her brother aside.

"You gotta help me find Kate. She wasn't in the room."

Dr. Pym overheard this and lunged toward them, grasping Emma by the arm.

"What did you say?"

Emma told him, and Dr. Pym let out a long sigh. "Oh, this is very bad."

Just then, a man was brought forward. He had seen two figures running toward the eastern end of the city.

Dr. Pym told Gabriel, "Go. We will catch up," and the giant man turned and like that was gone. Dr. Pym instructed Robbie to put together a larger group and follow as quickly as he could.

"Come, children. I fear your sister is about to make a grave mistake." And the three of them set off after Gabriel.

As they hurried along the dark tunnel, Dr. Pym pressed Michael and Emma to tell him what they knew. There was no mistaking his seriousness, and Michael and Emma held nothing back. They told him about Kate's vision, about the Countess gathering the children onto the boat, about the dam being destroyed, how all the children had died. They told him that Kate believed the vision was a warning.

"I should have been more careful," Dr. Pym muttered, striding faster and faster. "I only pray we are in time."

When they emerged from the tunnel onto the side of the mountain, Gabriel was kneeling, studying the earth in the moonlight.

"I do not understand. The tracks show the man ran off alone down the path. But the girl"—he paused, glancing at Emma and Michael—"her tracks say she stepped off the cliff. I do not think she was pushed. But nor do I see a body on the rocks below."

"What?!" Emma's voice spiked with panic. "No! You gotta be wrong! I'm sorry, Gabriel, but it's dark and all; you probably just didn't see it right! Read those tracks or whatever again!"

Dr. Pym was looking at the line the Secretary had drawn in the dirt.

"There is no body," he said, "because Katherine is with the Countess."

He explained that the line was a portal.

"So can't we use it too?" Michael asked.

"No. It was designed to transport one person. Stepping across it now would mean stepping to your death." He wiped it out with the toe of his shoe. There was the sound of footsteps, and Robbie and several other dwarves, along with a few men, came sprinting out of the tunnel. "We are too late," Dr. Pym said. "The Countess has her. Gabriel and I and the children will go immediately to Cambridge Falls. When your forces are mustered, lead them down this path. It will take you to the town."

"You're mad," the dwarf gasped. "If the girl's with the witch, our goose is cooked. Anyway, take you bloody hours to get to town on foot."

"Then we mustn't dawdle. Just follow the path." Nodding to Gabriel and the children, he started down the trail, moving with his brisk, long-legged stride.

"Dr. Pym!" Michael and his sister hurried after him, struggling not to trip as the rocky path snaked down the mountain, Gabriel following close behind. "King Robbie's right. It'll take us hours to get there like this."

"Yeah," Emma said, "why don't you make one of those portal things?"

"Unnecessary. I know a shortcut. Stay close now."

As he said this, the children noticed that they were walking into some kind of mist or cloud, which was strange since moments before the sky had been perfectly clear. Soon the mist became so thick that Dr. Pym ordered Michael and Emma to hold hands so that neither wandered off the edge of the cliff. They followed the wizard by the dim outline of his back, and, when that had been swallowed up, by his voice, calling to them through the fog,

"Careful now, there's a tricky bit here. Careful . . ." Then, as if not being able to see wasn't bad enough, their other senses began playing tricks on them. They smelled trees they knew weren't there, heard nonexistent water slapping against a bank; even the rocky slope of the mountain seemed to level out and become soft. Michael was just making a mental note to do more research on the disorientating effects of fog when Dr. Pym announced:

"And here we are."

Michael gasped.

"How . . . ," Emma began.

"I told you," Dr. Pym said, "I knew a shortcut."

They had stepped out of the fog and were standing at the edge of the lake in Cambridge Falls, looking out across the moonlit water. Michael glanced back to see Gabriel emerge from a misty tunnel in the trees. Once he'd joined them, Dr. Pym went on:

"My friends, we have reached the most difficult part of our task. I needn't remind you of the lives at stake. Katherine and the children are on the boat with the Countess. I will see to them. Gabriel, you'd best hurry to the dam. I fear the Countess may have sabotaged it. Do what you can."

"I'll go with Gabriel," Emma said. "He might need me." She looked up at the giant man. "You might."

"Very well," Dr. Pym said. "Michael, my boy, you're with me. Quickly now, and good luck to us all."

Kate closed her eyes and called up the image of the book-lined room: she pictured the fire in the grate, the snow falling outside, Dr. Pym at his desk with his pipe and cup of tea; she saw her mother enter, heard her say that Richard was still at the college; every detail was vivid and clear. . . .

Kate opened her eyes and saw the red satin curtains, the armchairs upholstered in deep velvet, the mahogany-and-gold table; from the corner, a Victrola played a high, haunting melody as gas lamps flickered on the walls, the light refracting through an ornate crystal chandelier. She sighed. She was still on the boat. Still in the Countess's cabin.

"Katrina, you are testing my patience."

The Countess was wearing a black gown that made her white skin almost luminescent, and in the wavering light, her eyes changed from violet to indigo to lavender in the space of moments. She poured herself a glass of wine and looked at Kate with a bored expression.

Since she had arrived on the boat, nothing had gone as Kate had planned. Starting with her demand to see the children . . .

"My dear, that's quite impossible. But I admire how you're always thinking of others. We're very alike in that way."

"If you've hurt any of them, I won't help you get the *Atlas*."

"Oh, oh, oh, look who's learned the name of her magic book! Brava, *ma chérie!*"

"I mean it!" Kate had shouted, trying, unsuccessfully, to keep the quaver out of her voice. "I'll let you kill me first. I know about the monster you keep here."

"Aren't you clever! As it happens, I released that nasty thing before I came aboard. I thought it could greet the townsmen when they arrive."

"What? You can't! You—"

"Now now, did you come to save the children or a mob of loutish townsmen? I'm afraid you can't do both."

"Fine," Kate had snapped, telling herself that Dr. Pym and Gabriel were more than a match for any of the witch's creatures. "Let the children go, and I'll get you the book."

The Countess had clucked her tongue. "I think you're confused about the order of things. First, you bring me the *Atlas*. Then, my charges go free."

"That's not—"

"Darling, be reasonable. You must know the children are my only protection! Not that I need protection from you; you're an angel! But I suspect you've been consorting with some less than savory characters, dwarves and wizards and the like? I forgive you, of course. We all make mistakes when we're young. I could tell you about a certain Italian dancing instructor. No, no, book first, children second!"

"But—"

"The instant I have it, I'll release them! I give you my word!"

The Countess had looked at her with a taunting expression, and in that moment, Kate realized how fully she had placed herself in the witch's power. Gripping the arms of her chair, she'd thought of the children locked somewhere in the belly of the ship and asked what it was she had to do.

"My love, it is the easiest thing in the world!"

Apparently, Kate had only to imagine the desired moment; then, once she held it firmly in her mind, she would, with the Countess's assistance, be transported to that time and place. Did Kate remember when she and her brother and sister had first traveled into the past? How they had placed a photo upon the blank page?

"What's that got to do with it?"

"Well, you can't imagine that the *Atlas* was designed, all those thousands of years ago, for use with photos! The photo merely provided a clear image. Given a specific destination, whether through a photo, a drawing, an image in your mind, or even—if you had enough control, which, sadly, you do not—the statement, 'Take me here,' the *Atlas* would obey. We do not have the *Atlas*. However, some of its power now resides in you, and the same principle applies."

So again and again, Kate had closed her eyes and pictured herself in Dr. Pym's study, and again and again, she opened them to find herself still in the cabin.

Her frustration boiled over.

"It's not working! You said you'd help me!"

"I am helping you," the Countess sighed. "In ways you cannot understand. But are you truly imagining yourself in the past? Envisioning the exact moment in time in which you left our precious book?"

"Yes! I'm doing everything! Maybe I just can't—"

"Shhh." The Countess came and placed a hand on the back of Kate's neck. The cabin was uncomfortably warm, and the young woman's hand was cool. "You must relax or the magic will never come. How far into the past are we speaking of?"

Kate exhaled, wanting to knock away the Countess's hand and at the same time loving how good it felt.

". . . Four years."

"Four years. And where are you? Describe it."

"It's a room. Like a study. There's a fire. It's snowing outside. Dr. Pym is there."

"Anyone else?"

Kate thought of lying, but what was the point? She needed the Countess's help.

"My . . . mother. She comes in."

The Countess let out a small "Ah," as if Kate had just shown her something beautiful. "And how do you feel about your mother?"

"I love her."

"Of course you do. But is that all? She did abandon you and your brother and sister."

"She had to. They were protecting us."

"Really? How do you know that?"

Kate had no answer.

"I see." The Countess was caressing Kate's hair. "And when she went away, who did she leave to take care of your brother and sister?"

"She told me to."

"But you were just a child!"

Kate knew the outrage was an act, but part of her couldn't help responding, the same part that was worn out with the strain of caring for Michael and Emma, the part that for so long had prayed for someone to come and say, "It's okay. You can stop now. I'm here. I'll take care of you."

"Perhaps removing this will help."

Kate saw the Countess's hand pass before her; there was a

flash of gold; and when she looked up, she had to stifle a cry. The Countess had somehow unclasped her mother's locket.

"A gift from her, I'm guessing. You were touching it as we spoke."

"That's mine—"

"Oh hush. This memory is about your mother. That's why the wizard chose it. Your feelings are the gateway. You feel love, yes, and loss. But that's not all." Her fist closed over the locket. "Magic such as this demands you lay yourself bare. Your parents deserted you. Tell me you don't feel anger, frustration, even rage. If you want to save the children, you can't shut anything out."

"I'm not!"

"Continue to lie, and their deaths will be on your head."

Kate tore away from the woman's gaze. She found she was trembling.

"I know you're afraid. But this is the only way."

Kate could see the end of the chain, dangling; she could just reach out and grab it.

"Katrina."

A long moment passed. Kate listened to the eerie melody from the Victrola, watched the gaslight wavering against the walls. She nodded.

"Good. Now close your eyes."

Kate obeyed. Once more, she put herself in the study, imagining the falling snow, the smell of Dr. Pym's tobacco, the fire. She pictured her mother coming in. And then, because nothing was happening, she finally let go, and all the anger and fear and doubt she'd held at bay for so long flooded her heart. Why had their parents abandoned them? What possible reason could they have had for leaving them on their own? For ten years, Kate had held their family together all by herself and the strain had almost broken her. She wondered if their parents had ever tried to find them. Or had they just walked away? Started a new life with—

There was a yank in her gut, and Kate knew it had happened.

She opened her eyes, and there was her mother, exactly as she'd left her, hand on the doorknob, mouth frozen in surprise. Kate glanced at Dr. Pym. He sat at his desk, smiling.

"Oh my." Her mother took a step back. "You were just here, and then you . . . Oh my . . ."

Emma and Gabriel were crouched behind a fallen tree at the edge of the wood, forty yards from the dam. Three *morum cadi* with torches stood guard. Gabriel had unslung his bow and fitted an arrow to the string. Two arrows more were stuck into the ground. He was waiting for a cloud to cover the moon.

Emma looked up past the mouth of the gorge to the wide black expanse of the lake. She tried to imagine the dam breaking and all that dark water rushing down and over the falls, carrying along the boat, the children, her sister, everything. They couldn't let that happen.

"Gabriel . . ."

"Shhh."

He'd turned and was staring into the trees behind them.

"What is it?"

"I don't know. Something . . ."

A shadow swept over them, and Emma looked up to see the last glowing sliver of moon disappear from view. There was a soft *swooft* beside her, then another, and two of the torches fell burning to the ground and Gabriel was pulling back a third arrow; then it too was gone and Emma watched as the last remaining torch stumbled and vanished into the gorge.

"Quietly now," Gabriel whispered. "There may be others inside."

They ran across the open ground, Emma stepping around the smoking bodies of the Screechers as Gabriel paused to retrieve a torch. The top of the dam loomed over them, rising seven or eight feet above the lip of the gorge. Up close, the structure was massive, and Emma realized that she'd thought of the dam as a single solid block of wood. It wasn't; there was a door, and Gabriel opened it, exposing a set of stairs going down. He went first, waving Emma forward when the way proved clear; then it was down two flights through the dank air, Gabriel's torch lighting the steps, and out onto a kind of balcony.

"Whoa." Emma stopped dead, staring.

Faint orangish lights were strung up throughout the dam, outlining a network of wooden beams that stretched from wall to wall like the ribs of some enormous beast. It felt strange to be standing there, with a dozen flights of stairs still below them and the body of the dam curving away; the impression was one of great space. At the same time, the front and back walls were only twenty feet apart, so everything seemed narrow and compressed. Emma gripped the railing to steady herself.

"Weird how it's all hollow, huh?"

Gabriel didn't respond.

"What's that noise?" Emma asked.

An eerie, unmoored groaning rose and fell all around them.

"The pressure of the water causes the wood to rub against itself."

Emma tried to picture the water massing against the curved face of the dam. It seemed to her she was in the belly of a giant wooden whale.

"There."

She looked to where Gabriel was pointing. Far below, through the dim orange haze, she could make out a handful of green lights, spaced across the front of the dam.

"Gas mines. We have little time. When the light goes red, they will explode."

Questions sprang to Emma's mind: Exactly how long did they have? How did you turn a gas mine off? What was a gas mine? Before she could ask any of them, Gabriel shoved her to the floor and something flew past with a terrifying shriek.

Gabriel was on his feet instantly, whipping off his bow. Still flat on her stomach, Emma craned her neck upward. A dark shape was weaving between the beams of the dam, circling back in their direction. She watched as Gabriel's arrow ricocheted harmlessly off the creature's hide. Two more arrows fared no better, and the creature landed vulture-like on a crossbeam a few yards above.

Nothing Emma had encountered, not the Countess's Screechers, not the sightless, shadow-dwelling *salmac-tar*, nothing had prepared her for this. The thing had the body of a man—the same arms, legs, shoulders—but Emma's first thought was of an enormous bat. It had leathery wings, long talons that gripped the wood, and a gray-black hide bristling with dark hairs. Its skull was oddly narrow, with eyes that were little more than black slits, and its lower jaw jutted out horribly, displaying dozens of needle-like teeth. Emma could almost feel them tearing through her flesh.

Gabriel dropped his bow as he lifted Emma to her feet.

"What . . . what is it?"

Gabriel unsheathed his falchion. The creature was watching them, hissing. "It is what the witch was keeping on the boat. I thought I sensed it in the woods." He turned Emma so that she met his eyes. "You must defuse the mines. Everything depends on you. You understand?"

"What about—"

"Do not worry about me. And whatever happens, do not look up. Go!"

He gave her a shove toward the stairs. She paused to look back and saw the creature rise up, its wings spreading wide, jaws gaping, all those teeth gleaming in the darkness. She saw Gabriel raise his falchion.

Then she ran, the creature's shriek following her down the stairs.

Michael and the old wizard were skimming across the lake toward the Countess's boat. They'd found their own boat ("dinghy" was the word that occurred to Michael) abandoned on the shore.

"Ah, Providence!" Dr. Pym had exclaimed.

The boat's oars proved unnecessary; Dr. Pym had merely

whispered a few words, and the craft shot off, skipping over the surface of the water.

"But won't they see us coming?" Michael was gripping the sides for support.

"Not to worry," the wizard called back, the wind whipping away his words, "to the unfriendly eye, we will appear as no more than a patch of mist. Quiet now. We draw close."

Their boat began to slow, and Michael could discern a pair of dark figures on the deck of the Countess's ship. Dr. Pym said something under his breath, and to Michael's surprise, the two black-clad forms suddenly grasped the railing and leapt into the water. He waited for them to emerge, but after a few moments the water settled and he knew they were gone.

Dr. Pym was tying their boat to a ladder bolted down the side of the ship.

"Quickly, my boy. The noise may bring others."

Their feet were scarcely on the deck when Michael heard pounding boot heels and four *morum cadi* charged out of the darkness, two from either side. Dr. Pym took Michael's arm and whispered, "Don't move," and the creatures were pulling their swords, close enough now that Michael could see the unearthly pallor of their skin, and he braced himself as blades flashed all around him, the clanging crashing against his ears, and just as Michael realized the Screechers were fighting each other and paying not the slightest attention to either him or Dr. Pym, all four fell, smoking and lifeless, to the deck.

He gaped at the wizard. "How did you do that?"

"Confusion and misdirection. The mainstay of any parlor magician. Come along now." And he strode off down the deck.

They met two more of the Countess's guards; the first they nearly collided with while rounding a corner. Before it could attack, Dr. Pym waved his hand, and the creature dropped its sword, sat down, and proceeded to stare off into space.

"Much better," Dr. Pym said. "This way, I believe."

He led Michael through a doorway and down two flights of narrow metal stairs to a hallway deep inside the ship where a single *morum cadi* stood guard over half a dozen doors. Dr. Pym muttered something inaudible, and the Screecher lowered his sword and his face broke into what Michael considered a fairly gruesome grin. Dr. Pym reached out and touched the creature's lips.

The thing that used to be a man swallowed twice, flexed its jaw, and spoke.

"How can I help you, sir?"

The voice was stiff and croaking, as if it had not been used in a hundred years.

"How many of you are there on the boat?"

"Ten."

"So there's one more. No doubt on the bridge. And the Countess is in her cabin with the young lady?"

"Yes, sir."

"Very good. I take it you have the key to the children's cells?"

It was then Michael finally heard the scared, muffled voices of the children. They echoed forth from either side of the hall. The children were calling out, crying, banging on the walls with their fists. The banging was so constant and steady he'd been mistaking it for the thrum and whine of the engine.

The creature drew a key out of its ragged tunic.

"I want you to open the doors, lead the children out in an orderly fashion, and help them into this young man's boat. Is that clear?"

"Yes, sir."

Dr. Pym turned to Michael. "I'm going to deal with the last of the *morum cadi*. Then I will find your sister. Ferry as many children as you can to the shore. You will have to make a few trips."

"Okay."

"I'm very proud of you, my boy." He gave Michael's shoulder a squeeze. Then, to the guard, "This young man is in charge. Do whatever he says," and he was gone, disappearing up the metal stairs.

Michael looked up at the mottled green face of the Screecher. He took a deep breath, adjusted the badge Robbie had given him, and tried to sound confident.

"All right, let's get them out. But stop smiling. It's creepy."

"Clare, allow me to introduce Katherine. . . ."

Even as he said their names, the wizard's eyes were traveling between Kate's face and her mother's. She could see him making the connection, realizing who she was.

". . . Katherine, this is Clare. . . ."

It seemed to Kate that time had slowed. It wasn't magic. It was the fact of standing here as the wizard introduced her to her own mother.

Her mother was smiling now and saying something, but Kate could make no sense of the words.

Her mother put out her hand.

Kate looked down. Her own hand was stained with dirt and grime, and there was dried blood from where she'd cut herself on a rock. She suddenly realized how she must look; after all, she had not changed clothes in days, she'd run through a rainstorm, slept in a dungeon, swum across an underground channel, had a floor-rolling, ear-biting wrestling match with the Secretary; she felt the dirt and grease in her hair, the rips in her clothes, the fatigue that was no doubt showing in her eyes; she understood that her mother's smile was one of pity for the poor creature before her.

"My hand's dirty."

"Oh please." She clasped Kate's filthy hand in both of hers. "It's so nice to meet you, Katherine. You look as if you've had a very long journey. Can I get you anything? Water? Tea? I could heat up some hot chocolate. And 'Katherine' is so formal. Do you think I could call you Kate?"

Kate felt an enormous sob welling inside her. She'd waited for this moment for years; so why was it that all she wanted was to get the book and leave? She pulled her hand out of her mother's and shook her head stiffly.

"No, I'm fine."

Dr. Pym coughed. "I think the young lady came for this." He reached onto the desk and lifted the *Atlas*.

"What is . . ." Her mother stopped herself, staring at the emerald-green tome. ". . . Is that . . . It can't be."

"Yet it is."

"But, Stanislaus, you told us it was locked away! You said it was safe!"

"For the moment, that remains true. But apparently things are going to change. You see, this copy is from the future. And Katherine here, at great personal cost, brought it to me for safe-keeping. Now, I can only assume, she has come to take her copy back." He added, "Before it vanishes into thin air."

"Yes, but—she's just a child—"

"Clare—"

"Tell me you haven't actually involved this poor girl!"

"These are desperate times. And it wasn't me per se. Though future-me—"

"She's a child, Stanislaus! Look at her! She can barely stand! Lord knows what she's been through!"

"It's okay," Kate broke in. "I can do it. It's okay. Really."

"My dear"—Dr. Pym leaned forward in his chair—"I have to ask, is it safe?"

It was a logical question; of course Dr. Pym would want to know that the danger had passed before he gave her the book. But it caught Kate unawares, and in that moment, she felt his gaze sharpen. Luckily, she recovered quickly, sighing and letting the tension melt from her shoulders. "Everything's fine. At last." She even offered him a little smile.

"Very good," said the wizard, and he handed over the *Atlas*.

She expected to feel the yank in her gut, to blink and find herself in the Countess's cabin, but she held the book, heavy and familiar in her hands, and nothing happened.

"Now"—Dr. Pym stood—"I will leave you two alone." And

without giving Kate any indication of what she was supposed to do—tell her mother who she was, not tell—he was gone.

"I'm sorry," her mother said the moment the door was closed, "but I am very, very upset. Not at you, of course. I'm angry at whoever pulled you into this. You're much too young."

Kate said nothing. She just stood there, the book clasped to her chest.

"I know I shouldn't question Stanislaus. If he thinks you're up to it, I have to believe him. He's a great man, you know. Besides being a wizard and all that. Richard and I—Richard's my husband—we'd both trust him with our lives."

It was so peaceful in the room, with the fire beside them, the snow falling gently outside, Kate felt she could just lie down on the rug and go to sleep for years.

"Are you sure I can't get you something?"

Kate shook her head.

"Where did Stanislaus go? Is he supposed to be sending you back to where . . . or whenever you're from?"

"Last time it just sort of happened. I don't know why it's not now."

"You know, Richard and I have been involved in the search for the Books of Beginning for quite a while now. With Stanislaus, of course. Is that really the *Atlas*?"

She leaned in, and Kate smelled her perfume. She knew it immediately. The years seemed to slip away, and Kate could hear her mother's voice, asking her to protect her brother and sister, promising that one day they would meet again. Kate felt something inside her break open.

"My . . . brother and sister and I found it."

"You have a brother and sister? What are their names?"

Kate looked down, unable to meet her mother's gaze.

"You're in trouble, aren't you? Is Dr. Pym helping you? In the future, I mean. Oh dear, does that even make sense? What about your parents? You really are so young."

Kate felt her eyes welling with tears, and she bit her lower lip to keep from crying.

"Oh, you poor thing . . ."

And before Kate realized what was happening, her mother had stepped forward and was holding her. There was no stopping the sobs. They quaked through her body as if all the tears dammed up over a decade had suddenly broken free. Kate found herself crying for the times she'd held a sobbing Emma or Michael and promised them that yes, their parents were coming back; she cried for the missed Christmases and birthdays, for the childhood she'd never had; she collapsed into her mother's body, letting herself be held, crying, finally, because this was her own mother, stroking her hair and murmuring, "It's okay, everything's going to be okay. . . ."

Then, abruptly, her mother's hand stopped. Kate didn't move; she could tell something had happened. Her mother took a step back, holding Kate by the arms while staring deep into her eyes.

"Oh my . . . Are you . . . You're—"

Kate felt the tug in her stomach, and the scene vanished. She was never to hear those next words. But even so, Kate knew that in that last moment, her mother had recognized her own daughter.

"You see, my dear," said the Countess, lifting the book from Kate's hands, "I knew you could do it."

CHAPTER TWENTY-TWO
The Dire Magnus

"Have you been crying? I must say you look dreadful. There's a mirror if you'd like to freshen up. Oh, and this is yours."

Kate felt the locket dropped into her hand. Numbly, she fastened it around her neck. Her vision was blurred, and she could taste the salt from her tears. With an effort, she pushed the thought of her mother, the memory of being held in her arms, from her mind. She was back on the boat, and the children needed her.

"Let them . . . let them go."

"Hmm?"

"Let them go."

"Let who go?" The Countess had carried the book to a table across the cabin and was turning the pages, a greedy, almost ugly look on her face.

"The children! You promised! You—"

The Countess flicked her hand, and Kate's entire body went rigid. She tried to open her mouth, but it was clamped shut.

"To think, I now possess the *Atlas of Time*! And that it came to me when I had finally given up hope, when I was prepared to ride to oblivion with these miserable brats! My master is not one to tolerate failure lightly. There would have been no returning to tell him that the men of the town had revolted! But now I have the book, and all is changed." She caressed the blank page, and her voice fell to a whisper. "Nor will I relinquish this power. Even to him. I see that now. The *Atlas* is intended for me alone. It found me." She smiled at Kate. "Of course, the dam will still be destroyed and the children will die. But it really is no more than they deserve. Tiresome place, Cambridge Falls."

She lied, Kate thought. She was always going to kill the children, and now she has the book too. Sick at heart, Kate cursed herself. Why hadn't she told Dr. Pym about her vision? Why did she always think she was the one responsible?

Please, she thought, please . . .

And then, as if her wishing had summoned him:

"Loyalty is certainly not what it used to be."

The old wizard stood in the doorway, tweed suit, glasses askew, his face a mask of quiet fury. He glanced her way, and, for a moment, their eyes met. Kate saw that he understood why she'd done what she had and he forgave her everything. The relief she felt was so profound that, had it been possible, she would have burst into tears.

The Countess laughed. It was a hard, bright, joyless sound.

"I didn't know we were expecting visitors. Am I correct in guessing that you are the great Dr. Pym?"

"I am Stanislaus Pym."

"May I say, sir, it is an honor to meet you." She curtsied, a mocking smile playing on her face. "To what do we owe the pleasure?"

"I am here to free the children and reclaim the book you stole."

"Oh. Oh, oh, oh. I'm afraid that's going to be difficult. You see, the children will all be dead in a few minutes; afterward you're certainly welcome to their corpses, I won't stop you there. As for the *Atlas* . . . No, this is simply not going to work. May I offer you a glass of wine instead?"

"I did not come to play games. I will give you one last chance."

The Countess giggled and gave a little hop. "Or what? Or what? Tell me! What will you do?"

"I will be forced to destroy you."

The Countess made a shocked *oooooooohhhh* face and clapped her hands over her mouth.

"Katrina, did you hear? Did you hear what the awful man said? Well, you drive a hard bargain, Doctor. I guess I have no choice." The Countess picked up the book, proffering it in her small white hands. "Here. Take it, you beast."

Dr. Pym raised his hand, and the book inched toward him. Just then shadowy claws leapt out of the dark corners of the room, clamping on to his arms and legs and pinning him to the wall. Instinctively, Kate tried to run to him, but the invisible force held her where she was. She watched as Dr. Pym struggled but was also held fast.

"Oh, poo! Is it over? After all the stories one hears about the great wizard, mysterious powers, tra-la-la, I confess I feel cheated. But I guess everything in life is a bit disappointing, isn't it?"

Kate stared in disbelief. Was that it? Had Dr. Pym really lost?

The Countess turned to the table, setting down the book and pouring herself a glass of wine. She was humming. She clearly meant to savor her triumph.

"I know what you're thinking, Doctor dear. How will my master react when he learns I plan to steal his prize? Well, he won't be happy, I'll tell you that. But never you worry; once I've wriggled free the secrets in these pages, I will be as powerful as he."

"Hag, you are a fool."

She pouted. "Not nice."

"You have no idea of the depths of his power. Or, may I say, mine."

"Grandfather, if you're trying to anger me so I kill you more quickly, I promise it will work."

To Kate's amazement, Dr. Pym smiled. "You truly believe it possible he doesn't know what you're planning? That you could have one single thought he hasn't anticipated? You were doomed from the first moment."

Something like fear flashed across the Countess's face. But she shook it off.

"You are funny! Isn't he funny? But I think you forget, Mr. Funny-Man-with-Your-Funny-Eyebrows—which you should really consider trimming, *quelle horreur*—I have more than the *Atlas*: I have the girl. Soon, I will have her brother and sister. With them will come the other Books, and then even my master will bow before me. The prophecy is coming true, *mon oncle*, and there is nothing you or he can do to stop it."

She raised her glass in a toast and drained off her wine.

Kate's mind was racing. A prophecy? What prophecy? And what had the Countess meant, "Soon, I will have her brother and sister. With them will come the other Books"? She felt dizzy, as if, despite the Countess's spell, she might suddenly tumble over onto the floor.

"Oh, lambkins, I see confusion in your young eyes. Has the mean old wizard not explained what fate has in store for you?" She wagged her finger at Dr. Pym. "Shame on you, keeping the poor girl in the dark."

"Witch, I forbid you—"

"You forbid me? What a laugh! No, no, it is high time Katrina found out why she and her siblings are children of destiny. I wager you haven't even told her what the Books are capable of! Well, my dove"—she skipped across the room and leaned her head close to Kate's, as if they were two schoolgirls exchanging secrets—"do you remember the night you arrived, how I explained the history of the Books of Beginning? How there were three Books into which an ancient council of wizards wrote down the secret magics that brought this whole world of ours into being? No need to nod—you couldn't anyway—I see you do remember.

"Well, *mon ange*, let us think for a moment: if this magic was used to create the world once, a person might reasonably ask, why couldn't that same magic be used again? The answer is, it could! That is what is so tantalizing! With the power in the Books of Beginning—one of which, the *Atlas of Time*, you so graciously brought to me, I thank you for that, the other two are still out there somewhere, waiting—with the Books' power a person could simply wad up all of existence like a poorly done sketch and begin afresh with a new sheet of paper!"

"And only a mad person would even imagine doing such a thing," Dr. Pym said.

The Countess groaned. "Has he always been so tedious? Of course you wouldn't destroy the world on a whim! Though you certainly could. For instance, say you wanted a world where everyone wore red hats? Using the power of the Books, you would simply get rid of this world and create a new one where red-hat-wearing was de rigueur. Or green hats or blue hats or really whatever-colored hats you wished!"

"Totally and completely mad," Dr. Pym said.

"Or you could create a world where every creature lives and breathes solely to serve you. I think you begin to see, my sweet Kat, why the search for the Books of Beginning has consumed so many lives. It is the promise of ultimate power. Which leads us"— she brought her face even closer—"to the reason you and your brother and sister are so dreadfully important."

In the corner of her vision, Kate saw that Dr. Pym's eyes were half closed and his lips moving.

"Long ago," the Countess whispered, "at a time when the Books had not been seen for a thousand years, it was foretold that three children would one day find the Books and bring them to-gether. Yes, three children! One for each volume! You see, my dear, you and Michael and little Emma are the key." She touched a soft hand to Kate's cheek. "I'm afraid your journey is far from over."

Kate didn't have to glance at Dr. Pym for confirmation. She knew, on some deep, instinctual level, that the Countess was telling the truth. It explained so much. Like how she'd been able to open the vault under the Dead City. A dwarf-made door locked with enchantments and yet she, a normal human girl, had been able to open it easily? How was that possible unless the person who'd sealed the door—that is, Dr. Pym—knew she was coming? And how would he have known she was coming unless there'd been a prophecy? A prophecy also explained why they'd been sent away from their parents. Someone looking for the Books—perhaps even the Countess's master—must've figured out who she and Michael and Emma were! Kate could imagine the danger, the terror her parents must've felt. Of course they let Dr. Pym take their children. Kate could almost hear the wizard promising, "I'll hide them. They'll be safe." It suddenly all made sense.

"But enough of this," the Countess said. "It's time to kill this silly old wizard—"

She turned and raised her hand.

Just then, an icy wind blew through the cabin. It rattled the china and set the chandelier swinging. It seemed to Kate to cut her to her very bones.

"What're you doing?" The Countess advanced on Dr. Pym. "Stop it! I command you!"

"My dear, it isn't me." And as he spoke, the lights flickered again and went out. For a moment, everything was still. Silent. Then, in the darkness, Kate heard the far-off sound of a violin. The song it played was beautiful, ancient, chilling, and it was growing louder.

"He is coming," the wizard said. "The Dire Magnus is coming."

Emma would not look up. Gabriel had given her a job, and that was all that mattered. Everything else, the shrieks, the grunts, the thuds of blows, of bodies hitting wood, she shut out, along with the knowledge of how much Gabriel had already fought that day and how tired he must be. Gabriel had given her a job, and she would not fail.

The stairs had been built directly into the side of the gorge, and she ran down them, flight after flight, till she was even with the six green orbs that formed a glowing dotted line along the front wall of the dam. There were tiers of narrow catwalks built into the wooden face, and Emma leapt onto one and raced across, feeling the emptiness all around her, the mountain of water pressing to get in, trying desperately to ignore the sounds of the battle that was raging above. She stopped in the dead center of the dam.

Up close, she saw that the mines were composed of two parts. There was a glass egg the size of a grapefruit, in which the green-yellow gas swirled and flowered ominously, and this was nestled in a circular metal base, which was itself stuck to the wall of the dam by a grayish putty. Emma stared at the first mine, wondering what she was supposed to do. Couldn't Gabriel have given her a hint?

How was she supposed to know how to defuse a mine? No one had ever taught her that in school. Her classes had all been about useless things like math or geography. As she stood there, it seemed to her that the gas was changing colors, taking on a dark, orangish hue. That, she decided, was probably not good. She briefly contemplated just smashing the egg, but considering that whatever this thing was, it was supposed to explode, she thought that might not be the greatest plan. It occurred to her that Michael would know what to do. He'd probably read all about defusing mines and could make you a diagram in his stupid little notebook. She wasted a few moments being angry as she imagined Michael parading around with another medal given to him by that annoying dwarf king, till finally, no other ideas presenting themselves, she reached out and placed her hands on the egg.

It was warm to the touch, and she could feel the thinness of the glass. Too much pressure and it would certainly crack. Closing her eyes, Emma gave a gentle tug. The egg didn't budge. She pulled harder. The egg remained firmly attached to the metal base and the base to the wall. Emma took a deep breath and prepared to pull with all her strength. Before she could, something happened. Searching for a better grip, her left hand dropped an inch, and the egg moved.

Carefully, Emma turned the entire egg counterclockwise. There was a dull scraping as glass rubbed against metal, but soon Emma saw that there were grooves etched into the lower part of the egg, and she turned it more quickly. Moments later, she was holding the egg in her hands. Free of the metal base, the glass began to cool, and the vapor lost its threatening hue, shifting from orange to yellow to green and, finally, becoming clear and disappearing entirely.

The metal part's heating it up, Emma thought.

She looked at the other mines, which were now throbbing orange-red. Gabriel had said that when they turned completely red, they would explode. Time was running out. She set the glass egg on the catwalk and sprinted to the next mine.

Meanwhile, high above her, Gabriel was in the fight of his life. After sending Emma away, he had leapt onto one of the six-inch-wide beams that arced between the walls of the dam and, with both hands, swung his falchion into the side of the creature. It was a blow that would have cleaved a man in two. But the blade glanced off the creature's hide, and a moment later, Gabriel was flying backward, struck with dizzying force. He ricocheted off a beam, fell ten feet, careened off another beam, and finally caught himself on a third. Looking up, Gabriel saw the creature had not followed its attack. It stayed perched above, grinning down at him. Gabriel understood: it was saying it could kill him whenever it liked. Gabriel knew then that this would be the last battle of his life. So be it, he thought. He only needed to survive long enough for Emma to defuse the mines.

The creature flew at him, and Gabriel tried to roll away, but its talons ripped deep gashes in his side. The monster turned and came back with terrifying swiftness, sweeping him off the beam and into the air. Gabriel hammered at its back and head with the butt of his falchion, then felt himself raised high overheard. He scrambled for a hold, but the beast flung him down. His body crashed through beams as if they were matchsticks, and he thought he would plummet all the way to the bottom, till with a bone-cracking thud, he hit a beam and stopped. He pulled himself up. He could feel his broken ribs scraping against each other. His falchion was gone. Looking down, he saw Emma. She had defused three of the mines. Just a little longer.

There was the sound of wingbeats, and he moved just as the creature flew past, its claws tearing through the wooden beam. As it pivoted in the air below him, Gabriel leapt, landing full on the creature's back. They dropped fifteen feet before the beast adjusted to the weight. It shrieked and tried to claw at him, but Gabriel pulled his knife and began sawing into the soft tissue of the wings. For the first time, the creature's cry became one of pain. It flew crazily through the web of girders, frantic to dislodge the man on its back. Gabriel's head slammed into a beam, and he fought to remain conscious as he continued ripping through the muscle of the wing. Unbalanced, the creature swerved, and Gabriel struck his head again; this time, everything went black.

On the catwalk, Emma was just getting to the last mine when she heard something crashing down through the beams and had to look up. She saw a dark shape plummeting toward her. A moment later, a body smashed onto the catwalk.

"Gabriel!"

He was covered in blood, his left arm was bent at a strange angle, and there was a large bruise on his forehead. But he was alive. She could see his chest rise and fall.

She heard a shriek and looked up to see the creature coming toward them, leaping from girder to girder.

"Gabriel! You gotta wake up! Gabriel!"

The giant man did not stir.

Spotting another catwalk twenty feet below theirs, Emma set her shoulder against Gabriel's side and pushed. It was as if he were made of stone. But she kept pushing, straining, trying not to listen to the sounds of the creature getting closer. Ever so slowly, Gabriel began to move. He rolled off the edge and landed with a crash twenty feet below.

A thud shook the catwalk, and Emma spun about to see the monster standing there, jaws open in a grotesque grin, its wounded wing dangling from a strip of sinew and muscle. She knew she should be terrified; it was really the only natural response. But instead of fear, she felt a pure, blazing anger.

"Look at you! You know how stupid you look?! You shouldn't a' messed with Gabriel! You're lucky he didn't kill you! What're you gonna do with that wing now, huh?"

As if in response, the creature reached back, ripped off the wounded wing, and hurled it into the void. Then, without pausing, it seized its healthy wing, twisted it around and around, and, with an awful ripping and shrieking, tore it free as well. Holding the bloody wing in one taloned fist, the beast took a step toward Emma and screamed.

Emma's mouth fell open in horror, and now, finally, the fear came. This creature was going to kill them. She commanded herself to be brave or, at least, to pretend. Gabriel deserved that much.

"You're . . . you're . . ."

But try as she might, no more words would come. The creature took another step, close enough that Emma could feel the warmth of its breath on her face.

Don't cry, she ordered herself, don't you dare cry.

Then she saw the mine, just to the creature's left, turn blood-red, and without thinking, Emma leapt off the catwalk. The fall felt like forever. When she landed beside Gabriel, pain shot through her ankle, but her scream was drowned out as the mine exploded.

The gunwales of the boat rode just a few inches above the water. Michael had crammed aboard as many children as he dared, mostly the younger ones, though he'd also brought three boys his own age to help work the oars. He'd left at least thirty children on the Countess's ship, promising he'd be back. There had been no sign of Dr. Pym or Kate, and Michael had been tempted to send the boat on without him and search for his sister.

But he couldn't leave the children.

Now, as the overloaded boat pulled across the dark lake, he thought back to when the Screecher had opened the cell doors and fifty terrified children streamed into the hall. For a few moments, they teetered on the edge of riot as Michael struggled to make himself heard over the din.

"Please, you have to be quiet, please. . . ."

Had it not been for the Screecher, he might've lost control completely. But the creature shouted for silence, and the children, shocked to hear actual words coming out of its mouth, complied instantly.

"Good," Michael said, "now—"

"You!"

He was spun around to face Stephen McClattery.

"What're you doing here?! And how's that thing talking all a' sudden?"

For a moment, Michael just stared. Only recently, this same boy had tried to hang him. Michael could almost feel the cord around his neck.

"Well?!"

Shaking off the memory, Michael explained as quickly as he could how he and Dr. Pym had come to rescue them, how Dr. Pym was a wizard and had put a spell on the Screecher, how Kate was being held by the Countess, how they had to get the children off the boat as fast as possible. . . .

"You have to believe me. We don't have time to—"

"Right," Stephen McClattery said, "let's get moving, then."

The red-haired boy herded the silent, still-terrified mob of children up onto the deck and, once there, helped Michael cull the twenty youngest. Stephen McClattery and the Screecher then worked together to pass the children down the ladder and across to Michael in the boat. Michael kept hoping he would see Kate and Dr. Pym appear at the railing, Kate safe and smiling, Dr. Pym announcing that the Countess was defeated and all was well, but soon the boat was full and it was time to go and his sister was still nowhere to be seen. Stephen said he'd stay behind and keep the others organized till Michael returned for the next boatload.

"I know you'll come back. I shoulda believed you before. You and your sisters are all right."

"There's something else," Michael said. "Your dad's on his way."

Stephen McClattery was perched on the ladder, one foot resting on the bow of Michael's boat. His mouth opened, then closed.

"Me and my sisters met him in the Dead City," Michael went on. "We told him you're alive. He's on his way here with the other men."

A long moment passed. Their boat rocked gently on the water.

"I'm sorry," Michael said finally, "I've gotta go."

The boy swallowed and nodded, but still said nothing. Even so, the look in his eyes was one that Michael would never forget. Stephen McClattery pushed them off, and as the boat drifted away, Michael saw the boy draw a hand across his face, then turn and climb up the ladder.

Annie, the girl the Countess had dangled off the dam that first day, was in the boat beside Michael.

"Don't worry," he told her. "We'll get everyone."

She'd nodded up at him from the bottom of the boat, her hands clutched around her doll.

It took a few minutes to coordinate the rowing. At first, the oars slapped at the water randomly, the boat making little or no progress, once even going in a full circle. But Michael got the rowers into a rhythm, calling out, "Row . . . row . . . row," and soon they were pulling steadily across the lake.

Then, halfway to shore, when Michael's back was aching and he was wondering what earthly reason Dr. Pym could've had for not keeping their boat bewitched, there was an enormous *PHOOM*, and a giant plume of water shot into the air near the dam. He grabbed at Annie, yelling for everyone to hold on; a moment later, the shock wave nearly swamped them.

Then Michael was seizing the oars, shouting, "Row! Row! Row!"

"He is coming, he will be here. . . . How did this happen?! What am I to do?!"

"I should think you might have prepared for this eventuality before you betrayed your master."

"Silence!"

The lamps were back on, but the violin was growing louder by the second. The Countess paced the cabin, the book clutched to her chest. Seeing her scared made Kate even more afraid. How terrible must this Dire Magnus be if the Countess, who had an army of undead soldiers at her command, who upset as she was still managed to keep Kate frozen and Dr. Pym pinned to the wall, trembled at the mere thought of him?

"It just seems to me," Dr. Pym said mildly, "that you might have put more thought into all this."

"I said silence, you fool!" The Countess was a cornered beast, dangerous and terrified.

"Well, I don't really see how I'm the fool. I didn't betray a being ten times more powerful than myself and expect simply to get away with it."

The Countess whirled on him. "It was you, wasn't it? You told him! Sent him some sort of message!"

A knife gleamed in the Countess's hand where none had been before. Kate strained to move, but it was no use. The music was growing ever louder, its pitch climbing as the tempo spun faster and faster. The Countess advanced on Dr. Pym.

"If I'm to die," she hissed, "it will not be alone."

Kate wanted to scream at Dr. Pym to do something, say some spell, spit on her if he had to.

Then, quite abruptly, the music stopped.

So did the Countess, knife poised above the wizard, her face a mask of rage and fear.

"My dear," Dr. Pym said, "I'm afraid your time has come."

And like that, the Countess crumpled to the floor.

Kate felt the grip on her relax; she almost collapsed herself, so great and immediate was the sense of liberation. Dr. Pym was free as well, but he signaled Kate to stay where she was. He was staring at the motionless body of the Countess. The *Atlas* lay beside her on the floor. What was he waiting for? This was their chance. They had to grab the book and run. Escape before—

The body on the floor moved.

Slowly, the Countess got to her feet. But something was different. Her blond hair had turned a deep shade of green, and her eyes glittered as if set with diamonds. If anything, she was even more beautiful and magical than before. For one brief moment, the shining eyes rested on Kate, then she turned to Dr. Pym and smiled.

"Stanislaus, it has been far too long."

And Kate understood: she was not looking at the Countess.

"So my sweet Countess was going to betray me and keep the

Atlas for herself. My, my, when did loyalty become such a rare commodity?"

The creature stretched out the Countess's arms as if admiring how long and slender they were. It was a strange sight, watching someone appraise their own body.

"Perhaps the fault," Dr. Pym said, "lies not in the follower, but in the leader's inability to inspire."

The green-haired being laughed; it took Kate by surprise, for it was a real laugh, easy, mirthful, nothing like the bright, empty laughter of the Countess.

"Touché, Stanislaus! You are no doubt right! As always, my old friend! And this young woman, I wager, is unfailingly loyal to you."

Kate stiffened as she (he?) approached. Up close, Kate saw that the green of her hair was not the emerald of an open field but the deep green-black of a jungle, the color seeming to move and shift as if alive, and there was a hunger in those glittering eyes that terrified Kate. Once again, she heard the violin. Faint at first, it was calling to her, inviting her to dance; it told her the day was ending, the world was on fire; it told her to dance while there was time to dance; it told her of burning cities, of people running in fear, of darkness, destruction, chaos, and ruin; come, the music called, join the dance, join the dance. It reached deep, deep inside her, and to her horror, Kate felt part of her respond; she wanted to spin away, to live if only for a moment, before it all ended, no cares, no thoughts, and then she was staring at a skeleton with glittering eyes, and she yanked back as if she'd been teetering on the edge of a cliff. The music stopped.

The Countess stood before her, green-haired, diamond-eyed, not the Countess, but not a skeleton either.

"Stanislaus, it seems your protégée doesn't wish to join my dance. It's only a matter of time, my dear. We all dance in the end."

Her chest heaving, Kate did her best to put on a fearless, defiant glare.

"Such bravery. That's good. You'll need every bit. You are one of them, aren't you? The children of the prophecy. I see it in your eyes." The creature reached out and stroked Kate's hair. She could hear the eagerness in his voice and feel how his hand trembled with excitement. "Do you know how long I've waited for this moment? I watched mountains climb out of oceans. I've seen empires rise and fall. Entire races have died forgotten, and through it all, I have waited. Your Dr. Pym talks of loyalty; I have been loyal, my dear, such loyalty as has never been seen, for I always knew that one day we would find each other."

Kate stared into the ancient, glittering eyes and saw it all. She saw the centuries he'd waited. She saw how the world had changed about him and yet he'd never lost purpose. How could she fight such resolve? This was her fate. There was no escape.

From across the room, Dr. Pym said, "You cannot stay here."

"Hmm?"

"Look at your hand."

The creature called the Dire Magnus held up the Countess's hand: to Kate's shock, the knuckles were growing thick and knobby; veins were beginning to push against the pearl-white skin. The Dire Magnus seemed neither surprised nor particularly worried.

"Clever Stanislaus. You invite me here to defeat my own servant, knowing full well I cannot linger. You've lost none of your wit, my friend. No matter"—he looked at Kate—"I have seen what I needed to see."

He turned then and picked up the book. He was aging quickly now, middle age, old age, and it was a bent-backed crone who shuffled across the cabin and offered the *Atlas* to Kate. The once-beautiful face was lost in wrinkles, the green hair was dry and patchy; smiling at Kate, he showed two rows of broken yellow teeth. His words were a hollow croak.

"The end is near, child. I will be coming for you. Our destinies are one. I will be coming, and when I find you, all the world will dance. . . ."

At these words, the creature departed; Kate felt his presence leave the room, and the Countess's body dropped to the floor and didn't move.

Dr. Pym staggered.

"Dr. Pym!"

"I'm fine, my dear. Simply the strain . . . He was pushing so hard. . . ."

"What happened to him?"

"The Dire Magnus cannot take form here. He must possess another, and the Countess . . . was too frail a host. . . . I will explain later. . . . We must hurry. . . . There is little time. . . . We . . ."

He collapsed. Kate ran to his side, and she was still shaking him and calling his name when she heard the explosion.

CHAPTER TWENTY-THREE
The Children of Cambridge Falls

Emma's ears were ringing. Her ankle throbbed, and she was drenched, head to toe. All around her, huge jets of water streamed through cracks in the face of the dam. The sound was deafening. She looked but didn't see the monster. Was it possible the explosion had killed it?

The dam groaned; more boards cracked and splintered.

"Gabriel! You gotta wake up! Gabriel!"

His eyes opened; he wasn't dead.

Thank you, Emma thought, though it was unclear exactly who she was addressing, thank you thank you thank you.

Gabriel sat up, cradling his injured arm. "How did I get here?"

"You were fighting that monster; only he must've been fighting dirty or tricked you 'cause you fell on that." She pointed to the catwalk above them. She thought for a moment and added, "But

you bounced real hard and landed down here." If he didn't remember her pushing him off the catwalk, she saw no need to offer
that information.

"The mines . . ."

"Yeah, one of them exploded! That monster was standing
right beside it. We gotta get out a' here! Come on!"

Limping, they set off down the catwalk. The river was pouring in, filling up the hollow center of the dam. By the time they
reached the stairs, water was already splashing about their ankles.
Emma knew that once the dam filled with water, the pressure
would be too much: the whole thing would simply snap and wash
away. Then anyone still on the Countess's boat would die.

But Dr. Pym had to have rescued Kate and the others by now!
What good was him being a wizard if he couldn't do something as
simple as get a bunch of kids off a boat!

She let her annoyance at Dr. Pym distract her from the pain
in her ankle. It helped as she climbed the stairs. They were
halfway to the door when Gabriel suddenly stopped.

"Gabriel, what're you doing?! We—"

Then she saw it. The creature was climbing up through the
ribs of the dam, jumping from one beam to another. Her heart
sank. What did it take to kill that stupid thing?

"Your brother was right. It fears water."

It took Emma a moment to understand what he meant and
recall how, back in Gabriel's cabin, two days and what felt like a
lifetime ago, Michael had suggested the Countess was keeping the
monster on the boat because it was afraid of water. And now, as
a new crack opened in the front wall and a fresh jet blasted

through, Emma watched the creature howl and spring clear of the water's path.

But still, it continued to climb.

"We gotta hurry!" Emma shouted. "It's gonna beat us to the door!"

Gabriel nodded and, with his good arm, hoisted Emma onto his shoulder. He took the stairs three at a time. The higher they went, the more the dam swayed and shuddered. Up they raced, amid the cracking and groaning, the thunderous pounding of the water, the sounds of timbers snapping, and as fast as Gabriel climbed, the monster kept pace. Again and again, it tried to move closer, but each time the dam splintered and a new jet of water forced it back.

Emma silently urged Gabriel to go faster.

Finally, they reached the top of the stairs, and Emma could see the door. Gabriel set her down. He was panting, and his clothes were soaked with fresh blood.

"Come on!" Emma cried. "We gotta hurry!"

"I am not going."

"What're you talking about? This thing's gonna fall apart!"

"The creature cannot be allowed to escape. When the dam breaks, it must be inside. That is the only way to kill it."

"So we'll lock the door! We won't let it out!"

Gabriel shook his head. "I must make sure."

Emma was growing frantic, trembling on the verge of tears. There was another massive crack! The landing they stood on dropped two feet.

"No! You— That's crazy! I won't let you!"

Gabriel knelt so their faces were close together. "I must do this. Or every person this creature kills will be my responsibility. Life gives each of us tasks. This is mine."

"But you . . . you . . ." She was crying freely now, but didn't care. She had to make him see why what he was saying was so stupid, why he had to come with her, but for some reason, all she could manage was, "You can't. . . . You can't. . . ."

Gabriel placed his hand on her shoulder and looked into her eyes.

"I do not know what happened with your parents or why they did what they did. But in all the world, I could have wished for no daughter but you."

Sobbing, Emma threw herself around Gabriel's neck. She told him she loved him, she would never let him go, she didn't care what he said, she loved him.

"And I you. But you must go." And he pulled her arms from around his neck and pushed her toward the stairs. "Go! Now!"

Shaking, hating herself with every step, Emma obeyed. Reaching the door, she looked back. Gabriel had turned to face the monster. He had no knife, no weapons, and as it sprang toward him, he leapt to meet it, grappling with the creature. Together, they plummeted into darkness.

Moments later, Emma was stumbling along the edge of the gorge, tears streaming down her face, repeating, over and over, "He's Gabriel, he'll be okay, he's Gabriel, he's Gabriel. . . ."

• • •

When Michael and the children reached the shore, they were met by a group of men and dwarves who'd come through the passage Dr. Pym had created.

" 'Ere, pull that boat up!" called a familiar voice. "Look sharp now! Ah, blast ya, I'll do it meself!"

King Robbie grabbed the stern of the boat and, with half a dozen men and dwarves leaping to help, hauled it onto land. As the men began lifting out the children, Michael finally released the oars. He'd never been so exhausted; pain arced across his back and shoulders, and he could scarcely raise his arms. He started out of the boat and promptly crashed face-first into the gravel shore.

"Come now, boy, you're all done in!"

It was Wallace. He set Michael on his feet but continued to support him, clearly fearful he might topple over a second time. Robbie and Stephen McClattery's father hurried up.

"There're . . . more kids."

"How many more, lad?" Robbie demanded. "Quick now."

"Thirty . . . at least. And Dr. Pym and Kate. Dr. Pym took care of the Screechers. I don't know about the Countess."

More men and dwarves had gathered round.

"We've gotta go back for them!"

"Get the boat in the water!"

"Hold now!" Robbie shouted. "We all 'eard that explosion. And you can 'ear the dam creakin' and groanin' from 'ere. You won't get 'alfway 'fore she bursts!"

"What're we to do, then? Let our children die?"

"Course not. But we gotta use our 'eads! 'Ow we gonna get

there and not get dragged down the gorge when the dam goes? There's the question, blast it!"

Most of the men and a few of the dwarves began shouting at once, some offering ideas, some cursing the Countess, some saying they didn't care if they were swept down the gorge, that those were their children on that boat; the arguing went on and on, with Robbie and Stephen McClattery's father calling again and again for order.

Michael looked at the Countess's boat, sitting there so still upon the dark lake. The dam gave off another mournful groan, like some great beast in pain.

And then it came to him. He saw how the whole thing would play out and that he was the only one who could save the children. He took off running down the shore.

"Oi! Lad!" Wallace yelled. "Where you going?"

But Michael just kept running.

Outside the Countess's cabin, there were children screaming. Inside, Dr. Pym would not wake up. No matter how many times Kate shook him and called his name, he just lay there. Finally, throwing one last glance at the unmoving body of the Countess, she placed the book on Dr. Pym's chest, grabbed him under the arms, and dragged him through the doorway, down a hall, and out onto the deck, apologizing each time she bumped his head.

The deck was pandemonium.

Terrified children were running and screaming in all directions. Twice, Kate was knocked to the ground, and the child who'd collided with her got up, screamed, and ran off in the direction he had come. There were torches visible on both sides of the lake, and many of the children were standing on the railings, calling into the darkness for their mothers and fathers.

Kate stared about in confusion. How had the children gotten free? Where were the Countess's Screechers? Had Dr. Pym done this? Even as she asked the questions, she realized that none of them mattered. The only thing that mattered was how she was going to get all these children off the boat.

"Hey!" Stephen McClattery was coming toward her. "That the wizard?"

The question surprised her. "How did you know—"

"Your brother told me."

"Michael? He's here?" She felt her panic rising. She'd assumed he was safe. If he'd come to rescue her and was now in danger himself—

"No, he already took a boatload a' kids to shore. Said he's coming back. Better hurry, though. You hear that explosion?"

"Yes." Kate prayed, guiltily, that Michael would not return.

"Dam's been groaning and creaking ever since. Got all the kids scared." He nodded to Dr. Pym. "So, he dead or something?"

"No. He just won't wake up."

"What about the witch?"

"She's in there. Dead, I think."

The boy's face broke into a broad grin. "Really? So we're gonna be okay, huh?"

Kate hesitated. Did she tell him the truth about the explosion? Tell him what all that groaning and creaking really meant? Could she trust him or would it cause even greater panic?

She never got the chance to decide.

Emma had a plan. It boiled down to this: find Dr. Pym and demand he fix everything. With that in mind, she'd run along the top of the gorge in a sort of staggering, hob-legged lunge—her ankle was really hurting her—doing her best to ignore the wailing of the dam and push back thoughts of Gabriel, wounded and weak, fighting the Countess's monster. In her heart, she knew he was still alive. And if she could just get to Dr. Pym, everything would be fine.

There was only one problem. As she neared the mouth of the gorge, she became aware of a cluster of scared-sounding voices rippling out from the center of the lake. With horror, Emma realized that the children were still on the boat. That meant Kate was still on the boat. Maybe Michael too. And certainly Dr. Pym.

Therefore, she had to be there.

She knew the village would have boats, and so she started over the narrow bridge that spanned the gorge, head down, running full tilt, not looking where she was going.

Suddenly, with a *whoof*, she was on her back, her head ringing. She scrambled to get to her feet, imagining she'd crashed into a Screecher; then a voice spoke:

"Are you all right? Didn't see you coming." A hand helped her up. "I heard the explosion, so I hurried down to take some pictures. 'Fraid I was looking the other way."

It was Abraham, and he had a camera hanging from his neck. He stared at her.

"You're one of them children I helped escape. What're you doing here?!"

The words spilled out. "Gabriel's in the dam fighting a monster! The whole thing's gonna break apart any minute! I gotta get to Dr. Pym! The kids are still on the boat—"

"Slow down, slow down. Who's Gabriel? Who's Dr. Pym? What monster?"

"No, listen! Those kids are still on the boat! We gotta—"

"Wait, the children are on the witch's boat?"

"Yeah! That's what I been saying! Are you deaf or something?!"

"We gotta get 'em off! If the dam goes—"

"Duh! That's what I was doing when you got in my way! That's why I gotta get to Dr. Pym!"

"Well, I don't know this Dr. Pym, but we gotta organize rescue boats. We need to get those children to safety!"

Fine, Emma thought, you do that, but I need a boat now! And she started to say that when there was a rending and scraping unlike any that had come before.

Emma turned.

Abraham gasped, "Oh dear Lord."

The dam was folding outward, split down the middle, and as the dark water rushed through, one entire half dislodged and was carried away. Emma threw herself against the railing, crying out her friend's name. To Abraham, who hadn't truly understood what she'd meant about Gabriel or Dr. Pym or the monster in the dam but who knew suffering well enough, it sounded as if the young girl's heart was breaking.

They were moving. Scarcely a minute had passed since Kate and Stephen McClattery had heard the unmistakable sound of the dam ripping free, and now, with each passing second, the boat was picking up speed.

Kate thought the gorge was like a giant mouth, intent on swallowing the lake and everything in it, including them.

She continued to shake Dr. Pym and call his name, but it was no use. And as she looked at Stephen McClattery running about, yelling at the children to grab hold of whatever they could find, she marveled that she'd come here to prevent this exact thing. How could she have failed so miserably?

Even so, Kate was strangely calm. After all, she had been here before. In her vision, she had stood on the deck of the boat as it hurtled toward the falls. That had felt real. This, by contrast, seemed almost like a dream.

"Hold on!" Stephen McClattery yelled.

Kate looked up to see the jaws of the gorge rushing toward them. She was unprepared for the impact, and it sent her flying, slamming her hard into a wooden chest. The shock jarred her out of her reverie. She saw Dr. Pym's body sliding toward the edge of the deck, his arm still draped limply over the book. Kate dove at the wizard, pinning him down as the boat spun clockwise. She braced herself as the opposite wall came flying at them.

They were in the gorge. There was no escaping now.

• • •

She couldn't think about Gabriel. Kate and Michael. Kate and Michael. Think about them. They were still alive.

But for how long? From where she and Abraham stood on the bridge, they'd seen the boat crash into the mouth of the gorge, get sucked into the narrow chute, and then be battered from one rocky wall to another, all the time going faster and faster. If that wasn't bad enough, the other half of the dam had finally broken free, which meant nothing now remained to stop the boat as it hurtled toward the falls. And all she could do was watch. Emma had never felt so helpless, so hopeless.

"Emma!"

Michael ran panting up the bridge. She threw her arms around him, sobbing.

"Michael, you're alive! I thought you were on the boat!"

Michael was so out of breath he couldn't speak, and it allowed Emma to say a few more times, "You're alive! You're alive!"

"Kate and . . . Dr. Pym. They're on the boat. With the kids."

"I know! What're we gonna do? Oh, Michael, Gabriel . . . he's . . ." But she found she couldn't say the words to pronounce her friend dead. Not yet.

"That's Abraham!" Michael was staring at the man beside her. "That's good."

"I know that's Abraham! So what? Kate's on the boat! Why doesn't Dr. Pym do something?! He should be—"

A sickening crunch made them turn. The boat had slammed into the wall of the gorge just fifty yards away, close enough that they could see the panicked children swarming the deck. Another moment and the boat would pass beneath the bridge.

"Make sure he takes the picture!" Michael was climbing onto the railing.

"What? What're you doing? Michael!"

"Make sure you take the picture!" Michael yelled at Abraham.

"Here now, lad . . ."

"Michael, get down!"

Standing on the railing of the bridge, Michael glanced once over the edge, then turned and looked at his sister. Something in his manner made Emma pause. She couldn't have said why it was, but it occurred to her suddenly that Michael was her older brother and how she never thought of him that way.

"I love you," Michael said, and jumped.

"MICHAEL!"

Emma flung herself against the railing in time to see her brother falling through darkness as the boat appeared below them, huge, spinning, doomed; she saw him land on the deck and roll, and then he was gone, the boat wheeling away toward the mouth of the falls and there was nothing, anywhere, to stop it.

"MICHAEL! MICHAEL!"

She screamed so hard that her voice cracked, and she would've kept on screaming, but she heard other cries; dark-clad women from the town, their shawls trailing, their hair loose, were emerging from the trees along the ridge; they ran with torches and lanterns and called to the children on the boat, and there was something so familiar and haunting about the scene that Emma kept staring; then Abraham's camera flashed—he'd been holding it down by his chest and seemed surprised it had gone off—and Emma understood what Michael had said.

Make sure he takes the picture. . . .

He'd meant the picture Abraham had given her and Kate that day in his room, the one Abraham had said was the last photo he'd ever taken, the one with the names of the children written on the back. But why had Michael wanted him to take it?

A wailing rose along the ridge, and Emma turned to see the boat spinning about and teetering, backward, on the lip of the falls; for one excruciating moment it hung there, and Emma gripped the railing of the bridge and said her brother's name once more, almost a whisper, "Michael"; then the bow rose, the stern went down, and the entire boat, and all its passengers, disappeared over the falls.

Michael had landed on a pile of tarps. It took him a few seconds to get his bearings, for the boat was spinning faster and faster down the gorge, slamming first into one wall, then the other. All around him, children were clinging to railings, to ropes, to each other, screaming and crying. He glanced back and saw the silhouetted arc of the bridge. He prayed Abraham would take the picture, that Emma had understood. Then he put it out of his mind.

He was running down the side of the boat in a drunken stagger, calling Kate's name, when someone grabbed his arm. It was

Stephen McClattery. He was holding a young child and had an astonished look on his face.

"You came back! Again! How'd you even—"

"Where's my sister?"

Stephen McClattery pointed to the front of the boat.

Michael shouted, "We need all the kids together!"

"You crazy?! They can't move!"

"They have to! It's our only chance!"

"But—"

"Just do it! Bring them to my sister! Go! We don't have much time!"

For a brief instant, the boys stared at each other; Michael was younger than Stephen McClattery, scrawnier, but there was no question who was now in charge. Stephen McClattery nodded, turned to two boys standing nearby, and began yelling orders. Michael took off running.

When he got to the forward deck, he found two dozen wailing, terrified children and Kate, up against a wall, her arms in a sort of hug around Dr. Pym and the book. Dr. Pym was unconscious.

"Michael? What're you . . ."

He knelt beside her. "Kate, look—"

"No! You shouldn't have come back!" She began crying and hitting him. "Who's going to take care of Emma? You shouldn't have come back!" Then she wasn't hitting him anymore, just leaning against him, sobbing, "You shouldn't have come back. . . ."

"No! Look! I brought this!"

He dug into his jacket and pulled out his notebook. Opening it carefully, for the wind was whipping all about them, he showed her the photograph. Kate immediately recognized the dark figures running out of a wood, carrying torches and lanterns. It was the picture Abraham had given her and Emma.

"We can use it! We can put it in the book!"

But Kate was already shaking her head. "What about the others?"

"I got 'em!" It was Stephen McClattery, and he was dragging half a dozen children with him. "Part of 'em anyway! They got the rest!"

He waved to the far side of the deck where the two older boys had just appeared, herding a group of children. By Michael's count, there were now more than thirty panicked children packed into the front of the boat.

"Make them hold hands!" Michael shouted. "Hold hands!"

Stephen McClattery and his lieutenants took up the cry and ran about, pushing kids together, yelling in their ears, but whether the children didn't understand or were simply too terrified to obey, either way, it was hopeless.

"We need Dr. Pym!" Kate was shaking the old wizard fiercely.

Michael thought for a moment, then told Kate to stop, and he dug into Dr. Pym's pockets till he found the tobacco. He shoved a wad of it under the wizard's nose, and almost immediately, Dr. Pym snorted and his eyes blinked open.

"Hmm," he said groggily. "What's that?"

"Dr. Pym," Kate cried, "we're on the boat! We're about to go over the falls! We have a photo, but we need the children to hold hands!"

Dr. Pym nodded, appeared to think, then said, "What's that?" again, as if he'd not understood a single word.

As Kate repeated what she'd said, Michael looked up and saw that they had run out of water. There was nothing but air before them.

"Kate—"

That was as far as he got. Just then they struck a rock with such force that the entire boat spun around so the front was now the back.

And still they were rushing forward.

"It's too late!" Stephen McClattery shouted. "We're going over!"

The deck of the boat started to rise, and for the first time, Michael heard the roar of the falls.

"Kate," Michael said, "I'm sorry, I thought . . ."

"It's okay," she said, and squeezed his hand. "It's okay. We're together."

"Take the photo, Katherine. Be ready."

It was Dr. Pym. His voice was sharp; it snapped them back.

Kate took the photo from Michael and opened the book; Dr. Pym was whispering something, and Michael suddenly found Stephen McClattery grasping his hand; he in turn grabbed his sister's arm, and then, as the boat dipped forward and the deck continued to rise, a strange calmness came over the children, and each one reached out and in the darkness found the hand of another child, forming one long chain snaking around the deck, and Dr. Pym was still whispering as the chain grew longer and longer till the last child was joined in, and the deck was so steep now that Michael had to brace himself to keep from sliding, and he looked down and saw past the boat to the nothingness below, and they were falling, all of them, falling, and Dr. Pym shouted:

"Now!"

And the boat plunged forward.

"It'll be okay," Emma repeated, for the fourth or fifth or ninth time. "It'll be okay."

For a few seconds after the boat had gone over the falls, there had been a terrible, drawn-out silence. Then they heard the crash, far below, and the women on the ridge fell to their knees and wailed. Amid the shrieking, Emma heard other voices, men's voices, coming along the gorge behind her. But she didn't turn. Just as she didn't run to the cliff to look over, or stare at the spot on the falls where the boat had disappeared. She kept her eyes fixed on the woods behind the women. And waited.

Please, she thought, her hands clenched around the railing of the bridge, please . . .

And then there was a different cry. One that stopped the women on the cliff and made them turn. It was a young girl's voice. She was calling her mother.

The girl was no more than seven or eight, and as she came running out of the trees, one of the women cried out and ran to meet her, folding the girl in her arms, and then there were more cries, and children streaming out of the woods in twos and threes, and tearful reunions began happening all along the ridge, and Emma felt the tight knot of fear that was binding her dissolve, and she was running down the bridge toward the trees, the pain in her ankle forgotten, knowing they would be there, knowing they would never desert her, running into the waiting arms of her brother and sister.

CHAPTER TWENTY-FOUR
Rhakotis

"Remember," Dr. Pym said, "by going into the past, you children changed history. We must therefore imagine what would have transpired had you not traveled through time."

Kate, Michael, and Dr. Pym were sitting on the side of a fallen tree. Ten minutes had passed since the boat had gone over the falls and they had appeared in the woods, and still, all around them, families reunited for the first time in two years, mothers and fathers who minutes before had thought their children lost for good, were clasping each other in disbelief.

Dr. Pym was in the process of answering one of Michael's questions. Michael had wanted to know how the *Atlas* could've gotten from the vault in the Dead City to the study underneath the house. It was the sort of academic, essentially pointless question that he found fascinating. Kate was only half listening. She

394

was watching Emma, who had wandered off to the edge of the gorge. For now, Kate thought it best to give her sister space.

"So," the wizard continued, "in what I will call the original past, prior to all your time-jumping, the Countess would have searched for, but not discovered, the *Atlas* under the Dead City. Led by Gabriel, the men of Cambridge Falls would have shaken off their captors and rebelled. The Countess, knowing her master would not accept failure, would have destroyed herself and the children, and, in the process, cursed the town.

"Now, in any version of events, I would have found myself in Hamish's dungeon. Let us assume I eventually freed myself, though not in time to thwart the Countess. Fearful that the witch's master would send another emissary to pick up where the Countess left off, I would have removed the *Atlas* from the vault. From there, I can easily imagine how I might have taken over the Countess's house and constructed an underground room to serve as a new repository. It would have appealed to my sense of irony, as if I were placing the book under her very nose. Then I would simply have woven a new enchantment so that if one of the three of you showed up, the door would reveal itself. Is that more or less what happened?"

Michael said it was.

"Well, there's your answer."

They all fell silent. Michael seemed to have run out of questions. It was Kate who finally spoke:

"It's time, isn't it?"

"Yes," Dr. Pym replied. "You have done what you came to do. It is time."

Kate rose and crossed to her sister. The wind was whipping up over the lip of the gorge, carrying spray from the falls.

"Are you cold?" Kate asked.

"No."

"Emma, we did a really good thing."

Emma said nothing.

"I'm so sorry about Gabriel."

"He's down there somewhere."

Kate didn't reply, but she put her arm around her sister, and together they gazed at the dark water rushing over the falls.

"Dr. Pym wants us to go, doesn't he?"

"Yes."

"Okay."

They walked over to Michael and Dr. Pym. From her jacket pocket, Emma pulled the photo she'd taken of Kate in their bedroom, the one she'd snapped just before they'd gone back in time to rescue Michael. She gave it to her sister. Around them, families were beginning to drift toward the town.

"Will you be there?" Kate asked. "When we get back?"

"Believe me, it is my firmest intention."

"Dr. Pym—" Emma began.

"My dear, Robbie and his dwarves are already looking for Gabriel. He will be well taken care of."

"Dwarves are excellent trackers," Michael said. "G. G. Greenleaf—"

"Michael," Kate said.

"Yes?"

"Be quiet."

"Okay."

Emma and Michael joined hands, and Michael took hold of Kate's arm. Kate opened the book. She stopped.

"Dr. Pym . . ."

Kate picked up something from between two pages. It was Abraham's photo showing the women running along the top of the gorge, the one Michael had given her as the boat was hurtling toward the falls. Kate didn't understand. She'd used this picture to move them through time. It should've disappeared!

"Ah," Dr. Pym said quietly, "so it's happened."

"What do you mean?" Kate demanded. "What's happened? Why's it still here?"

"Katherine, do you recall what I told you in Hamish's throne room?"

"No, but—"

"Try and remember. It will make things clear. Either way, I will explain in the future. For now, put the other photograph in the book. See if it disappears. My guess is that it will not.

"Please," he said when he saw her hesitate, "trust me."

"I do," Kate said. And she meant it.

Kate handed Abraham's photo to Michael, who slid it in his notebook, and then she made one last check to ensure that she and her brother and sister were touching. She noticed something sliding along the shadows of the trees. She looked closer, but whatever it was had faded into the darkness. Just get on with it, Kate thought, and with that, she placed the photo of herself on the blank page. There was the familiar tug, the scene before them disappeared, and then they were in their bedroom in the mansion, and once again there was the feeling of being held in place as they watched the other Kate and the other Emma prepare to travel into the past to rescue their brother, then Kate watched her other self place the photo in the *Atlas*, vanish, and they were released.

"Boy," Emma muttered, "are they in for it."

"Did the photo disappear?" Michael asked.

"No," Kate said, showing it to them. "It's still here."

Just then they heard the door open behind them.

"So Your Majesties are here after all!"

The children turned; the old housekeeper was standing in the doorway.

"Miss Sallow," Kate said, "we didn't—"

"Hear me knocking the last ten minutes? Thought you'd play a joke on old Sallow? What a laugh you must've had! I wasn't aware I was employed at the Comédie-Française."

"Miss Sallow—"

"Dr. Pym is below and wishing the pleasure of your company. Will you be making an appearance or should I say their royal highnesses wish to stay in their chamber making bon mots and fa-la-la-ing at an old woman's expense?"

Kate whispered to Michael and Emma, "Go on. I'll catch up. I want to hide the book."

As soon as her brother and sister disappeared with the old lady, Kate turned and stuffed the book under the mattress. Her hands were shaking. She knew that the photos not disappearing was important. But how? What was it Dr. Pym had told her in Hamish's throne room? If only she could focus; if she could just clear her head for a moment. But there was so much else to think about: the prophecy and all that entailed; the other two Books of Beginning; the Dire Magnus, he was still out there; her mother. . . . Her mother had known who she was; her mother had recognized her. Kate was still thinking of that, or not thinking of it so much as reveling in the warmth of the memory, when she drew back the blanket and stood. That's when it came to her. Dr. Pym had told her that she was the only one who could access the book's full power. *He means I can move through time*, Kate thought, *that I don't need a photograph*.

But he'd said something else as well. What was it?

She had to find the wizard.

"Katrina . . ."

Kate spun around. An ancient woman, a crone, bent-backed and wrapped in a ragged, filthy shawl, shuffled forth from a panel that had opened beside the fireplace. Her arms were little more than bones; the skin that clung to them was slack and spotted with sores. Lank strands of hair hung from her skull. Her blackened, swollen feet poked through the cracks in her shoes. She smiled, showing a mouthful of brown teeth. Kate's eyes shot to the door; Emma, Michael, and Miss Sallow were long gone.

"Fifteen years," the Countess croaked. "Fifteen years I've waited. For you it's been a matter of moments. You stepped across time as you would over a crack in the floor. But I've waited, *mon ange*, every day, every hour, for fifteen years; waiting for when we would meet again."

She moved between Kate and the door, blocking her escape.

Not that it mattered; Kate couldn't move. Fear held her in place. The Countess was alive. But how was that possible? Kate didn't have to ask what the woman wanted. She had come for the *Atlas*.

"You can't believe your old friend the Countess is still creaking along, can you? You thought my old master killed me, yes? No, no! He merely took back his power! Left me empty and weak! A wretched sack of skin and bones. You didn't know that I woke up on the floor of that cursed boat, that I dragged my broken body onto the deck and saw you and that wizard and the rest of the brats. I knew what you were doing. Oh yes, and I joined your little chain at the last moment. When you saved the children, my sweet Kat, you also saved my life."

She began laughing; it turned into a coughing fit, and she hacked something into her fist, which she wiped on the edge of her shawl.

"Afterward, I stayed hidden in the trees and watched the children reunite with their pathetic mothers and fathers. I couldn't risk facing your wizard. But I saw you and your brother and sister with the book, and I knew then that I would wait. Everyone would believe I was dead. Even my master would think I had perished when the boat went over the falls. I saw how the *Atlas* could still be mine!"

She seized Kate's arm. Her nails were black and splintered.

"Year after year, I waited. The townspeople didn't recognize me. The same children I had once imprisoned brought me food and water. I was patient. Then, one day, I heard of the three children who had come to the house across the river. I had long ago discovered the hidden passages in the walls; unnoticed, I slipped in, I crept along, I watched, and there I saw you, my beautiful Katrina, not a day, not a moment, older. . . ."

She was close now, her sour breath washing over Kate's face.

"Give me the *Atlas*."

Kate hesitated. Should she scream? Would anyone hear her?

"I know what you're thinking, my dove. But your Dr. Pym won't hear you. He's too far away. You know who will hear you? Little Michael and Emma. They'll come running. And I will make you watch as I kill them both! I've waited too long—give me the *Atlas*!"

From the folds of her shawl, the crone drew a long, rusty-toothed knife. Kate let her eyes go to the knife's edge, then back to the hag's eyes.

"Promise you won't hurt Michael or Emma."

"Please"—she smiled horribly—"I'm not a monster."

"And you'll leave right after."

"Like I was never here."

"Okay, then."

Kate turned and reached under the mattress. She had no intention of handing over the book. She merely wanted the witch to think she'd won so that her guard would relax. Gripping the book's cover, Kate stood up suddenly, spinning around, swinging the leather-bound tome with all her might at the Countess's head—

The old woman's hand shot up and caught the book. They stood like that, Kate holding one end, the Countess the other, her nails digging into the emerald cover.

The witch began cackling. "Tricky little girl. Not so trusting anymore, are we? Fortunately, the Countess is stronger than she looks. Now—LET! GO!"

The Countess gave a terrific yank, and Kate's hands slipped. But it was too much; the crone lost her balance, and the book fell, landing open upon the floor. Kate and the witch both dove for it—

Then the Countess was clawing at the book, hissing, jabbing her knife at Kate's face, and Kate was leaning back, her fingers locked over an open page, refusing to let go, refusing to let this woman win, and as the blade came toward her, Kate did the only thing she could think of. Closing her eyes, she reached for the magic in the book with every fiber of her being, and prayed that Dr. Pym was right.

She felt the tug immediately. Strange as it seemed, Kate had the sense that the *Atlas*, and the power inside it, had been waiting for her all this time. But the thrill only lasted a second; then it was as if she was cast in the middle of a great ocean, far from the sight of land. The Countess was still with her, but only as a presence. Kate started to feel herself sinking, and she realized that she could just disappear, vanish into time itself. Maybe that was okay, maybe that's what was meant to happen. But then, as she had in the bedroom, she found herself remembering being held by her mother, remembering how her mother had recognized her, and a flame of pure love sparked in her breast. In that moment, the rest of what Dr. Pym had said came back to her.

Before she could access the book's power, her heart needed to heal.

Okay, she thought, imagine you have a photograph. Tell the book where to go.

The next moment, she was blinking in the sunlight, standing on the roof of a building in a brown, sun-baked city. Red dust hung in the air while shouts rose from the street below. The Countess had fallen to her knees, gasping for breath. Her knife lay on the ground, and Kate kicked it away.

"How did you . . . how did you do that?"

"I don't need a photograph anymore. The *Atlas* just does what I want."

"No, it's not possible. . . ."

"Really? Look around. Seems pretty possible to me."

"But you can't—"

"Actually, I think I always could. I just wasn't ready. Dr. Pym knew that. He told me the book wouldn't listen to me till my heart was healed." Kate was speaking more to herself than to the Countess. She needed to say aloud what she now knew. "Imagine having one question at the center of your life, and until you answer that question, you'll always be lost. For me, it was wondering if our parents had really loved us. How could they, when they'd abandoned us? But when you helped me go back in time, my mother knew who I was. She recognized me as her daughter. I'll never question her love again. It's like knowing where north is. Whatever happens, I'll have that to guide me."

The Countess had struggled to her feet. Her once-violet eyes were black with hatred. Kate wasn't scared anymore. In fact, she felt a remarkable sense of calm.

"It's funny, if you hadn't sent me back in time, I never would've figured that out. Though then again, I'm pretty sure Dr. Pym planned it all from the moment he gave me the memory of my mother. I'll have to ask him when I see him."

"Child, I am going to rip—"

Her threat was cut short by an explosion in a nearby street. The Countess whirled about.

"Where are we? Where have you brought us?"

Kate shrugged. "I forget the name of the city. It's the one you told me about, where the council of magicians first wrote the Books. You said it was destroyed by Alexander the Great. I told the *Atlas* to take us there."

"You brought us to Rhakotis?"

"I guess."

"You foolish girl! Look!"

The Countess pointed one long, crooked finger, and Kate turned. Behind her stretched an endless blue sea, shining in the sun, and upon it were thousands and thousands of ships. Kate could hear drums sounding across the water, and as she watched, balls of flame shot up from the decks of the closest ships. The missiles crashed about the city; in the space of a few seconds, a dozen fires were raging all about them. Kate could hear people screaming as they ran for safety.

"We must go! Help me, and I will help you! You have power. I see that now. The *Atlas* has claimed you! But you have no idea what lies ahead! Help me, and I will help you!"

"Why would I need your help?"

"Because I know my master. He is always searching. For you

and your brother and sister! For the Books! The Dire Magnus will find you!"

At the mention of his name, Kate imagined she heard the violin. She knew it was only in her head, but even so, the memory of the music chilled her. The Countess lunged closer.

"You have seen him! You know he will break your magician like a twig and then you will all become his slaves! I can help! Help you get the other two Books! Don't you see that is your only hope? He will never stop searching! You must get the Books first!"

"We'll hide—"

The old woman hissed and waved her gnarled hand dismissively. "Hide? For how long? Your entire lives? He'll find you! He'll find you, and through you he'll find the Books, and then he will ravage this world! I have told you what the Books can do! And"—she paused, leering—"I would have thought you cared more for your parents."

Kate's heart lurched in her chest; she suddenly found it hard to breathe.

"What . . . what do you mean?"

The Countess smiled, sensing she had gained the upper hand. "So, the wizard hasn't told you yet? Too bad, too bad. But I still have my old ear to the ground, don't I? Especially when it comes to *mon petit oiseau*. Ten years ago, the Dire Magnus finally tracked you and little Michael and Emma down."

"But how . . ."

"The prophecy, of course! There were signs. But the wizard was too fast. Spirited you away. Your sweet parents, not so lucky! No, no, not so lucky at all." She came closer. "Ten years now, ten years your loving parents have been the prisoners of the Dire Magnus!"

"You're lying."

"Oh, be nice to think so, wouldn't it? But you know I'm not! The Dire Magnus has your parents, and the only way you'll get them back is to find the other two Books first! For that, you need the Countess's help!"

Her parents were prisoners. That was why they'd never come for them. Terrible as it was, Kate felt a strange sense of relief; her own history finally made sense.

There was a ripping in the air, and Kate and the Countess both looked and saw another fiery salvo, even larger than the last, erupting from the ships. The city was doomed. The Countess seized Kate's arm.

"Now! Take me back! I am your only hope!"

But Kate shook her head and said, simply, "No. You stay."

She wrenched her arm free at the same time as she reached for the magic. The last thing she saw was the Countess flying at her as the sky around them filled with fire.

A second later, Kate was standing in the bedroom, alone, holding the emerald-green book.

"Hey! What're you doing? I thought you were hiding that." Emma was at the door. "Are you okay?"

Kate realized she was holding her breath. She exhaled.

"I'm fine. I just—Emma, what's wrong? What's happened?"

Her sister had tears in her eyes.

"You gotta come, Kate! You gotta see!"

CHAPTER TWENTY-FIVE
Ghosts of Christmas Past

As Kate hurried with Emma through the dark hallways of the house, she couldn't help noticing that everything was in a state of extreme disrepair: mirrors were crusted with grime, cobwebs clung to the corners, mouse-eaten rugs covered creaking, dusty floors. In short, the house looked exactly as it had before they'd gone into the past. Emma wouldn't tell her what had happened, which was fine, actually, as Kate was still thinking about all the Countess had said, how the Dire Magnus was holding their parents prisoner, how their only hope of rescuing them was to get the other two Books. She knew she had to tell Michael and Emma. But first she wanted to talk to Dr. Pym.

They stopped at the door to the ballroom. Emma faced her.

"Are you ready?"

Without waiting for an answer, Emma turned the handles. As

407

the doors swung open, Kate was assaulted by a blast of light and music. The ballroom was filled with people, eating, drinking, talking, and for a moment, Kate thought they had stumbled into the Countess's ghostly St. Petersburg gala. Only this wasn't the Countess's gala. The music was festive. There was a huge tree in the center of the room. The walls were hung with garlands and holly. The guests, while dressed in their seasonal best, were very clearly not the cream of St. Petersburg society. And then there were the children. They ran about, weaving between the adults, chasing one another and yelping with high spirits.

"What is this?" Kate said.

Emma didn't reply, and Kate saw that she was being noticed. One partygoer would look over, whisper to another, who would whisper to another, who would whisper to another; in just a few seconds, the entire ballroom had fallen silent and turned to stare.

"Emma, what's going—"

She was drowned out as every person there began to cheer and clap.

"Okay," Kate said, "this is creepy."

"There you are! Welcome! Welcome!"

Dr. Pym, wearing the same tweed suit she'd seen him in fifteen years and not five minutes before, emerged from the applauding crowd. He was beaming. "A Merry Christmas, my dear! A Merry Merry Merry Merry Christmas!"

He bowed, folding himself nearly in half.

"Dr. Pym," Kate said, ". . . who are . . . What's going on?"

"Why, it's a party!" Then he lowered his voice so only Kate

could hear. "Have no fear. The Dire Magnus cannot harm you tonight. I have seen to it."

Kate nodded dumbly. She was staring at the crush of party-goers closing in on them.

"Uh-huh, but—"

Michael stepped up behind the wizard. "It's okay, Kate. Everything's all right."

And indeed, all the people seemed to want to do was shake Kate's hand, say thank you, and wish her a Merry Christmas. They were men and women of all ages, and Kate saw that many had tears in their eyes, and they held on to her hand as if they'd been waiting for this moment for many years and were unwilling to let it pass too quickly.

"Dr. Pym," she said as she emerged from the embrace of a round woman who'd blubbered all over her shoulder, "who are these people?"

"These are the fine people of Cambridge Falls. We host an annual Christmas party here at the house. I find it a good way to dispel bad spirits. Though I still can't persuade Miss Sallow to clean the place properly. She really is a dismal housekeeper."

"Don't you see?" Emma cried. "They're the kids! The ones we saved! All grown up!"

Just then a young couple with a baby walked up. Both the man and the child had curly red hair.

"It's really you," the man said. "We hardly believed it when Dr. Pym said you'd be here tonight. You don't look at all different. Smaller, I guess, but that's to be expected."

Kate had the feeling she knew this man, but she couldn't say from where or how.

The woman smiled. "They don't recognize you, dear."

"Right, of course. I'm Stephen McClattery. I grew up a little. And this is Annie, my wife. Do you remember her?"

". . . Oh . . . ," Kate said, ". . . OH!"

"I had glasses," Annie said.

"I remember." Kate was thinking of how she had once held this girl, now a woman, in her arms.

"We'd like you to meet our daughter," Annie said. "We named her Katherine. We owe everything to you. We all do. Everyone here."

Kate looked at the baby and felt her eyes welling with tears. Choking, she was able to murmur, "She's beautiful."

" 'Ere now!" cried a hearty voice. "Lemme through! I want a crack at 'em!"

The dwarf king Robbie McLaur was pushing his way good-naturedly through the crowd. He wore a red-and-green-checked vest, and his beard was neatly plaited into four braids, each tied with an emerald ribbon. With his vest, his braided, beribboned beard, and his general air of smartness, Kate thought he looked like nothing so much as the most prancing of all prancing ponies—that is to say, she thought he looked marvelous.

Michael exclaimed, "Your Highness! No one told me you were here!" and immediately dropped to a knee.

Emma groaned. "You are so embarrassing."

" 'Ere now, none a' that from you!" Robbie dragged Michael

to his feet and clasped him in a ferocious hug. "A sight for sore eyes, lad! All three a' you! A sight for sore eyes!"

Then Kate saw the other dwarf standing a few paces back. He wore a red-and-gold vest and was grinning broadly through his black beard.

"Wallace!" she cried, and ran forward.

Laughing, he wrapped her in his short, muscular arms, then stepped back to better take her in. "Last I saw you was in the Dead City near fifteen year ago. In fact, you mighta been wearing them exact clothes."

"Wallace, I'm so sorry about what I did—"

"Now, now, no apologies. Things turned out right in the end."

"Aye, that they did," Robbie cut in. "Not least, we've reestablished ties with the Cambridge Falls–ians. Not a bad egg among 'em! Oh, before I forget, Hamish sends his apologies he couldn't make it."

"Really?" Kate said.

"Really?" Michael said.

Robbie roared with laughter and slapped Michael's back so hard that Michael nearly toppled over.

"Course not! I've got that degenerate back at the palace 'anding out presents. I make 'im dress up like Santa every year. Bounce 'em young dwarfies on 'is knee. Lord but 'e hates it!"

Kate saw that her sister was standing on her toes, straining to peer out over the crowd. Kate's heart sank, realizing what, or who, Emma was searching for. Kate knew that now was the time to go to her. But just then she was waylaid by another pair of grown-up children who wanted to meet her, thank her, have her kiss their child. When she turned back around, Emma was gone.

She found her sister outside, on the back patio, the same one where, fifteen years earlier, the three of them had sat with the Countess while the witch had explained the history of the Books of Beginning. That night had been warm, filled with the end of summer. It was winter now; a hard crust of snow covered the stone-flagged patio, and Kate could see her breath. She closed the doors behind her, shutting out the noise of the party, and crossed to her sister. Emma was staring at the dark line of trees, her arms wrapped tightly around herself. Kate wondered if she even felt the cold.

"I thought he'd be here," Emma said. "I thought . . . I mean, everyone else is here. Those dwarves and . . . I just thought he'd be here too. Stupid, I guess."

Kate put her hand on her sister's back.

"I'm sorry."

They stood like that for perhaps half a minute, neither moving nor speaking. Kate wondered if she should make Emma come inside. It was too cold to be out without a coat, and she wanted to tell her and Michael what she'd learned about their parents. She was about to speak when Emma let out a gasp and bolted down the stone steps and out into the snow.

"Emma! Wait! What're you . . ."

Then she saw the dark shape that had separated itself from the trees and was moving toward them.

No, Kate thought. It can't be. . . .

Emma was running through the knee-high drifts, shouting

the name, and when she reached the figure, she threw herself into its outstretched arms.

Kate heard Emma's muffled voice. "I knew it! I knew it. . . ."

Moments later, the man, still holding Emma, stepped up onto the patio. He was wearing a long bearskin coat, and snow had gathered on his shoulders and hair. The face was more lined than Kate remembered, and there were gray streaks at his temples. Emma's face was buried in his collar.

"Hello," Gabriel said.

Kate nodded, still dumbstruck.

"You're cold. We should go inside." And he stepped forward and opened the door.

"Ah," Dr. Pym said as Gabriel approached with the two girls, Emma walking beside him now, clutching his hand, "you made it. I heard there was quite a bit of snow your side of the mountain."

Michael stared, his expression, Kate suspected, much as hers had been a few moments earlier. "I thought he was . . . Wait . . . How . . ."

The wizard was smiling, enjoying the confusion and saying nothing.

"It is good to see you," Gabriel said in his deep, serious voice.

"I'm sorry," Kate said. "But Michael's right. How . . ."

"Am I not dead?"

"Well . . . yes."

"Because Gabriel's too tough for some stupid monster!" Emma blurted. "Ain't that right?" She wiped at her face, and Kate saw that she was crying with happiness.

"I have you to thank," Gabriel said to Michael.

"Me?"

"Him!" Emma said. "He didn't do anything! I'm the one who took apart those mine thingies! I'm the one who pushed you off the catwalk!"

Gabriel looked at her.

"I mean," Emma said quickly, "found you on the catwalk. After you fell there, when you'd bounced off the first one."

"Had it not been for your brother," Gabriel continued, "it might not have occurred to me that the monster feared water. But that was how I finally defeated it. As the water rose, I was able to drown the hellish creature."

"And you still escaped," Kate marveled.

"The last thing I remember is running up the stairs as the dam fell to pieces around me. King Robbie and his dwarves found me unconscious at the edge of the gorge."

"That we did." The dwarf king tucked his thumbs in his vest pockets and swayed back and forth. " 'Ad a devil of a time trying to move 'im. Lad weighs more'n a draft 'orse."

"Wow, I guess dwarves are good for stuff after all," Emma said generously.

Then she pulled Gabriel down, and Kate saw her whisper something in his ear, and she heard Gabriel reply, "I know, me too. . . ."

Kate looked at Dr. Pym. "So it's all right, then. Everyone's okay?"

"Much more than okay. Look about you; this is all thanks to you."

And Kate looked at the families arrayed before them and thought, We did this, whatever else happens, we did this.

"Now," Dr. Pym said, "if you will excuse me, I've been eyeing that cider—"

"No! I have to tell you something—"

"Yes, my dear?"

"I . . ."

The old wizard was waiting. So, in fact, were Michael and Emma, Emma holding Gabriel's hand, Michael standing with King Robbie and Wallace. Both looked happier than Kate had ever seen them.

"Yes, Katherine?"

Kate knew that the moment she told them what the Countess had said, that it was up to them to rescue their parents from the Dire Magnus, the night was over. She thought of what a long journey they'd had to get here, how far they still had to go. Michael and Emma would need tonight.

"I . . . just wanted to say Merry Christmas, everyone."

And so the evening went on, and there was singing and dancing, caroling around the fire; Stephen McClattery apologized for having tried to have Michael hanged, and they told him not to worry about it; the children saw Abraham, hobbling about with a camera, and they hugged him and thanked him for everything; Wallace and King Robbie taught the children dwarf Christmas carols that seemed to have only passing mentions of Christmas and be much more about the benefits and drawbacks of various mining techniques (Michael took notes); there was a long table with the best kinds of food imaginable: roast pig with maple glaze, lamb and mint jelly, crispy golden potatoes, garlic-and-cheese mashed potatoes, steaming bowls of chowder; the desserts alone took up two tables, one of which was devoted entirely to different varieties of donuts: chocolate donuts, cinnamon donuts, chocolate-and-cinnamon donuts, powdered donuts with raspberry filling, with blackberry filling, with strawberry or blueberry filling; Michael pressed Emma to try what he promised was a delicious mushroom donut, but she told him not to be disgusting; there were apple and pear and honey ciders, steaming vats of mulled wine, great frothy mugs of hot chocolate, a keg of dwarf ale that King Robbie had brought and that seemed to be extremely popular; and adults who'd already come up and thanked the children came up a second and a third time, dragging along Abraham to take their picture; and they met children named Kate and children named Michael and children named Emma, so many that Kate wondered how when a mother called her son or daughter home in the evening, she didn't get half the town's children stomping through her door; and the children ate too much and drank too much, and the only person who was grumpy in the least was Miss Sallow, and that was simply the way she was.

Kate tried her best to join in, but the thoughts of all that had happened and all the Countess had said wouldn't go away. Who was the Dire Magnus? What did it mean that she could use the *Atlas* without a photograph? Was there more to the prophecy than what the Countess had mentioned? And what about the other two Books? What powers and secrets did they contain? There was so much she didn't understand.

And then there were the questions about their parents.

Thinking of what they must have gone through, what they must still be going through, made Kate dizzy with fear and sadness.

But even so, there was one thing she did know for certain.

If their parents were alive, then she and Michael and Emma were going to find them. She didn't care how powerful the Dire Magnus was, or that to rescue their parents they would have to find a pair of magical books that had been missing for thousands of years; she and Michael and Emma were going to put their family back together and nothing was going to stop them.

"Kate!" Emma ran up, Michael just behind her, their faces bright with joy. "King Robbie's gonna whistle 'Deck the Halls' through his nose! Dwarves, right? This should be hilarious!"

"Nose-whistling is an ancient dwarf tradition!" Michael protested, then added, "But it should be pretty funny."

"Come on, Kate! You gotta come!"

"You really shouldn't miss it."

"Robbie's gonna whistle Christmas carols through his nose?" Kate laughed. "What're we waiting for?" And, smiling, she let herself be led away by her brother and sister.

COMING SOON

Book II

IN

The Books of Beginning
Trilogy

BY

John Stephens

John Stephens spent ten years working in television and was executive producer of *Gossip Girl* and a writer for *Gilmore Girls* and *The O.C.* He holds an MFA from the University of Virginia.

John and his wife have a dog named Bug and sometimes live in Los Angeles. Visit EmeraldAtlas.com to find out more about *The Emerald Atlas*, the Books of Beginning and John.